PARALLEL HEAT

Deidre Knight

A SIGNET ECLIPSE BOOK

SIGNET ECLIPSE
Published by New American Library, a division of
Penguin Group (USA) Inc., 375 Hudson Street,
New York, New York 10014, USA
Penguin Group (Canada), 90 Eglinton Avenue East, Suite 700, Toronto,
Ontario M4P 2Y3, Canada (a division of Pearson Penguin Canada Inc.)
Penguin Books Ltd., 80 Strand, London WC2R 0RL, England
Penguin Ireland, 25 St. Stephen's Green, Dublin 2,
Ireland (a division of Penguin Books Ltd.)
Penguin Group (Australia), 250 Camberwell Road, Camberwell, Victoria 3124,
Australia (a division of Pearson Australia Group Pty. Ltd.)
Penguin Books India Pvt. Ltd., 11 Community Centre, Panchsheel Park,
New Delhi - 110 017, India
Penguin Group (NZ), cnr Airborne and Rosedale Roads, Albany,
Auckland 1310, New Zealand (a division of Pearson New Zealand Ltd.)
Penguin Books (South Africa) (Pty.) Ltd., 24 Sturdee Avenue,
Rosebank, Johannesburg 2196, South Africa

Penguin Books Ltd., Registered Offices:
80 Strand, London WC2R 0RL, England

First published by Signet Eclipse, an imprint of New American Library,
a division of Penguin Group (USA) Inc.

First Printing, October 2006
10 9 8 7 6 5 4 3 2 1

Printed in the United States of America

To my three angels—Samantha Jenkins, Julie Ramsey, and Elaine Spencer. You make every workday a blast, and you always have my back. This one's dedicated to you!

Love,
Charlie

ACKNOWLEDGMENTS

There are many wonderful people who helped as I wrote this book. First and foremost I want to thank my amazing and talented literary agent, Pamela Harty of the Knight Agency. Her skill, expertise, and support contributed greatly to making this book truly shine.

Also, megathanks to my support staff within the Knight Agency office. You're all angels and keep me together day after day: All my gratitude to Samantha Jenkins, Julie Ramsey, and Elaine Spencer. You've done a fabulous job learning the intricate workings of agency life! And to my fellow agent and friend, Nephele Tempest: You rock the West Coast!

And heartfelt thanks go especially to my husband, Judson Knight, for listening to my endless speculations on story lines and for making it possible for me to pursue all my dreams. My daughters, Tyler Knight and Riley Knight, make every day sparkle and are my truest inspiration. Mommy loves you both very, very much!

To the fabulous NAL publishing staff—Kara Welsh, Claire Zion, and Anne Bohner—thank you for your faith in me and in this series, and for publishing it so well.

My gratitude goes out to fellow authors Susan Grant and Merline Lovelace for assisting with the daunting problem of writing about F. E. Warren Air Force Base. Merline's gracious sharing of her photographs proved invaluable!

Angela Zoltners, as always, is my touchstone. I love

you, girlfriend! Thanks for always listening, reading, and helping me stay on track.

Kathy Baker, as always, you're a gem, and thank you for all your support. I appreciate you very much.

Vickie Denny helped tremendously with my online presence. Big warm hug and thanks to you!

To Whitney Lee: Not only are you a special friend, but your belief in me has meant the world. Thanks for all your hard work on foreign rights for this series.

Nancy Berland and her team have put all their muscle behind this series and behind me as an author, and I will never forget all that you've done! Big warm hugs and thanks to Nancy Berland, Elizabeth Middaugh, Deanne York, Kim Miller, Carol Smith, Linda Leonard, and Susan Avary.

Research was a bedrock of writing this book because I had to tackle many subjects that I was unfamiliar with. For contributing their knowledge and expertise, I'd like to thank a number of people. First, FBI special agent Norman Scott and FBI special agent Monique Kelso, who met with me in Wyoming (Monique drove a long way for that dinner!). Without your insights, this book would be far less authentic. FBI language specialist Monica Alvarez, your willingness to discuss the language specialist profession contributed directly to the character of Hope Harper—huge thanks!

To Rick and Janice Ramsey, thank you for supporting me so wholeheartedly—whether in research or signings or sharing your multitalented daughter. Big thanks!

To everyone at Lockheed who assisted me by showing me the ins and outs of high-tech and furturistic aviation, my heartfelt gratitude. So far, not all that much of that powerful research has made it into the series, but stay tuned until next week! My thanks to Bret Luedke (F22 Chief Test Pilot), Keith Bilyeu (F22 Business Development), J. R. Reynolds (Senior Manager for Security and Emergency Services), Rick Ramsey (Senior Manager of Marietta Facilities), and Janet McBride (Facilities Site Lead Administrative Assistant).

To Joe and Lourdes Knight: The gracious offer of your lake house allowed me to finish this book. Thank you.

And last, but certainly not least, once again a giant smooch and hug to my longstanding e-group of writing women: Kath, Tas, Mel, Nephele, Micha, Blanca, Anne, Tara, Bennie, Crystal, Stacey, and Angela. You guys helped me find the way through to living my dream!

What happens now has happened in the past, and what will happen in the future has happened before. God makes the same things happen again and again.

—Ecclesiastes 3:15

Bl'alastraka
A Refarian Book of Intimate Love
Author Unknown; English Translator Unknown

VERSE TEN, LATENT TEXT: Mating cycles shall be AVOIDED, not embraced, as to engage in the heat is considered a debasing of all that is lovely and pure in the Refarian mating rituals. This principle aside, should the mating fever be requisite for CONCEPTION—if the male is only fertile, or at his RICHEST fertility during a cycle—then the heated mates shall find no shame at their predicament. Our ancients cycled for centuries, enduring the untenable seasons as a means of siring offspring. Let us not be shamed by the NEEDS of procreation; however, let us embrace a higher state of mind unless we are given no alternative.

Certain rumors exist in regards to the D'Aravni and D'Ashani and D'Alari houses, that these high-blooded Refarian royals are given to deep, torturous mating calls. VERSE TEN shall be a noted exception for these lines (or any lifebound to them) who, because of breeding or temperament of blood, find their cycles UNAVOIDABLE.

SIDE TEXT ADDENDUM: A word about INTERSPECIES cycling: when Refarian emissaries first explored Outer Worlds in hundreds of years past, it was discovered that non-heated species reacted with particular VERVE to our race's mating calls. Should an INTERSPECIES UNION be contemplated in such circumstances, take heed and proceed with utmost caution—consider this, our love rites advisory!

Prologue

First Timeline—The Future

There weren't many places a dead man could go if he hoped to survive; at least that's how Marco had always regarded the matter. Back on Refaria as a boy, in the midst of warfare and revolution, he'd learned that soldiers who embraced the afterlife had an uncanny way of finding it. Right now, he wished he could lock in on some eternal, mystic wormhole that would shoot him straight out on the other side of his current hell.

He was literally in the middle of nowhere, hunkered down in the back corner of some dive on Highway 189, the perfect geographic location for him after everything tonight. *He* was nowhere; nameless; lost. He didn't even know which bar he'd landed in, only that there were a half-dozen pool tables and a haze of cigarette smoke shrouding the place. And beer . . . racks and racks of beer, and Marco didn't give a damn about his protector's vows, not now, not tonight. He was going to get drunk and free-fall into a painless state of oblivion if it was the last thing that he did.

His waitress returned, her low halter top revealing a small butterfly on her right breast, and slid yet another bottle of Heineken across the scuffed wooden table toward him. He nodded mutely at the woman before staring down at his swarthy hands. He'd already lost count of how many bottles he'd tossed back since his arrival, and the cut on his forehead still hurt like hell, but that hardly mattered. Taking another heavy swig of beer, he felt the world around him grow even hazier—

the dark bar was so cloaked in cigarette smoke that he could hardly tell if it was the effect of the alcohol on his system or just the cloud hanging over the place. His eyes burned, and for a moment he closed them, feeling the world swim woozily all about him.

Yes, let me forget, he thought. *In All's name, just let me forget tonight.*

Throughout the barroom, rough wooden picnic tables were positioned, little more than graceless constructions of two-by-fours slapped together at haphazard angles—as if the working-class regulars who populated the place required nothing more than basic stalls for their drinking pleasure. In fact, Marco had been lucky, managing to land one of the only real booths in the joint, and even then, the garish red leather beneath him was ripped and cracked, at least ten years past its prime.

Through the din of loud honky-tonk music, he could hear the phone at the bar ring, jarring him from his dazed state. The bartender—a burly guy with tattoos up and down each arm—grabbed it off the receiver. After listening a moment, he cupped his meaty palm over it. "Eh! Jordo!" he called out. "Your old lady wants you home!"

Around the nearest table, a group of men erupted in bawdy laughter, slapping the guy who was obviously Jordo on the back while making crude comments.

Even he has someone who cares about him, Marco thought miserably, sinking down into the booth. *But not me.* Not that he'd ever had a woman of his own. No, he had always led a solitary existence when it came to matters of the heart. Still, people had cared for him, important people. But not now. He was utterly alone—without his Circle, without his king and queen, without his homeland. He was, quite simply, a protector without a protected. And maybe he did deserve to die as payment for his crimes. At least that would end the torment that had hounded him for the past year as he had secretly loved his best friend's wife.

Marco leaned his head back heavily against the wooden booth, and glanced around the bar through slanted, half-opened eyes. Jordo and his pals were gone—most everyone was gone, as a matter of fact—he'd probably been here sopping up his sins with booze for at least three hours. He'd have to ride his Harley somewhere before the night was done, but where? He had no home anymore, not after tonight.

Alone, alone. The only way for someone so vile to be.

After a sluggish, dizzying moment, he raised his eyes at last and saw someone who looked vaguely familiar. A golden-haired angel stepping out of the haze and walking straight toward him. Why couldn't he place the woman, moving so easily his way? And then, within a heart's beat, she was standing just in front of him, smiling faintly. She was blond, beautiful, and seductive as hell. But someone else's lover, not his.

"Hi, Marco." Her high-timbred voice was raspy, and she clasped his shoulder as if they were old friends. "We meet at last." She trailed her fingertips down his arm familiarly, and a shower of electricity shot through his arm and chest. No way was she human.

He lolled his head forward again, narrowing his eyes. "Do I know you?"

"Well, let's just say you know of me." She slid uninvited into the booth beside him. "You've certainly seen me before, though not up close. Never like this."

He inventoried her features: waving golden hair, blue eyes—*lots* of hair, he amended. Long and shimmering. Small frame. . . . "Thea," he said finally, taking another sip of beer. "Thea Haven."

She smiled in satisfaction. "You have been watching, haven't you?" Her voice seemed to trill in victory.

"It was my job," he answered dully, refusing to rise to his enemy's bait.

What was Thea Haven after? And why was she suddenly here, tonight of all nights? It made no sense at all. His thoughts were clouded and dim from the alcohol—that had to be it.

"Right," she replied slowly, drawing the word out for effect. "Yes, I hear Jared really respects your hard work on his behalf." Her voice was tinged with bitter irony.

He raised his eyes again and found her staring at him meaningfully—flame darting in her pale eyes. She knew. Somehow the woman knew everything that had happened tonight! Or maybe it was only his drunken mind playing tricks on him. Suddenly the dozen or so beers seemed like a really bad idea. He leaned his elbows forward on the table, burying his face in his hands for a moment. Anything to stop the bar from spinning tortuously around him.

"Why are you here?" he groaned quietly. "What do you want, Thea? Really?"

"Well, that's simple enough," she replied seductively. "I want you."

Marco slowly lifted his head and met her eyes—and swore he heard her call his name somewhere within his mind; he couldn't fight, not like this. Not tonight.

Jared's enemies had planned their attack extremely well, and all he could do was surrender.

He lay back on the bed naked, the frayed hotel bedspread on the floor in a red tangle. Thea peeled off her underwear, sliding in after him. Her eyes took in the length of his body, the sinewy bulk of it and his solidly muscled torso. She had never seen a more beautiful man in all her days, not even her cousin, Jared Bennett. No, Marco possessed something even more alluring, perhaps because his beauty was of the reckless, dangerous variety. His dark skin was incredibly rich beneath her fingertips as she traced her hands across the silky black hairs that dusted his inner thighs, then between his legs. He shifted his hips in reaction, causing the cheap mattress springs beneath them to creak and groan.

His eyes were shut tightly, an expression of painful ecstasy dancing across his features. She began trailing kisses down his firm abdomen, lower . . . then even lower still, taking him into her mouth. He cried out, and she drew him in deeper, then eased him out again. He gasped her name, cupping her shoulders hungrily within his large hands.

Thea liked the feeling that she was pulling this Refarian soldier toward the brink, a man trained for every potentiality—except this one, apparently. A man sworn to resist all his king's enemies. For the briefest moment, she simply liked being with Marco McKinley, period.

But she quickly buried that thought. She couldn't afford to feel anything for this man, and yet the emotions radiating off of him were so strong, so intense, it was hard to resist, especially since his gift of intuition left him wide open to her. If Thea chose to, she could feel everything happening within him. *Maybe just for a moment,* she thought breathlessly. *What harm can one moment bring?*

As she opened herself ever so slightly to him, she had a strong flash—and it was something she found nearly impossible to believe: This was Marco's first time with a woman. Any woman. *That* was certainly something she could use to her advantage. She pulled away, gasping, and he opened his nearly black eyes. She could read the undisguised pleasure in his lazy gaze. *Yes,* she thought with a wicked smile, *this plan is working to perfection.*

She rubbed her thumb over the swollen tip of his erection. "You're a virgin," she breathed huskily, and tightened her grip.

His dark eyes flashed—with what she wasn't sure. He almost seemed to panic for a moment, then just as quickly the emotion passed, replaced with something much harder. *Colder.*

"Who would I have ever made love to, Thea?" he asked wearily, letting his hands drop away from her shoulders. His face became guarded, and she couldn't read his expression.

He was pulling away from her—and that simply would not do.

She climbed on top of him, straddling his waist as she drew her face within a breath of his own. "A beautiful man like you could have his pick. Any woman would thrill to pleasure Marco McKinley, sovereign protector."

At those words, he closed his eyes tightly shut again. "No," he groaned, "they would not."

"You're stunning." She pressed her lips against his ear, even as she squeezed her thighs around him and felt the sensation of her toes against the hairless place behind his knees. "Anyone would be a fool not to love a man such as you."

Oh, Marco, she thought, I *could love a man such as*

you. Quickly, she pushed that thought from her mind. *Never!* She had a mission here, nothing more. *Don't buy into your own words, Haven.*

Slipping one hand between his legs, she trailed her fingertips over his hardened length, teasing him. Seducing him. Controlling him. A virgin who'd never lain with a woman in his life? Well, this had certainly played to her advantage!

She'd seen the look of pleasure flare in his eyes when she called him beautiful. Good. Then that same quiet voice whispered in her mind again. *He is beautiful . . . unbelievably beautiful.* He'd taken her breath away when she'd first seen him tonight, his black hair windblown from the motorcycle, and his smoldering good looks perfectly offset by his black leather jacket and faded blue jeans. She'd been keeping him under surveillance from afar for months, but tonight had been her first really good look at him. For a fleeting moment, she'd found herself disconcerted by his dark Refarian features: the rich, black eyes; the olive skin brushed with a touch of gold; the formidable size of his body. And then she realized why his appearance unsettled her so badly—Marco reminded her of someone else, someone she had strong feelings for.

Their kiss continued and so did her swirling emotions, spiraling crazily inside her mind and body. *Someone familiar. Someone important. Gods, of course!* she realized with a shocking jolt, and for a moment she pulled apart from him, gazing into his black, slightly slanted eyes. He blinked back at her, his face ruddy with emotion. His full lips parted, waiting for another of her kisses.

Of all the men in the universe, why did Marco have to look like her cousin, Jared Bennett, the only man she'd ever loved? But before she had time to react to that association, Marco cupped her face roughly, pulling her close for a much hungrier kiss, his tongue heatedly exploring her mouth. She could feel his heart racing wildly against her chest while her own hammered out a twin crescendo. *These feelings—this attachment—will not do,* she reminded herself. *You are here for one purpose only.*

And with that, she silenced the unexpected, quiet

voice of desire this man had spoken within her . . . once and for all.

She'd laughed at him, at his virginity and inexperience. That had been the final humiliation of this cursed day. He had felt so damn powerless against her as her hands had kneaded his thighs, as she'd rubbed and teased his rock-hard erection until he ached beyond expression. As their kisses grew rougher and fuller as she cradled her hips so perfectly against his, teasing him into a thrusting motion—letting him know what would come next beyond any question or doubt. As he met every gyration of her hips, he knew one fact for certain—he was totally losing control in the arms of his enemy, going over the edge, and there would be no coming back. Never again, not after tonight.

This woman didn't just have him in the palm of her hand—she had all of him, his very soul even. No one had ever taken his body and simply pleasured it. He'd been a servant, a warrior, for so long, he'd always thought of himself as the property of others. Yet tonight she was worshipping his body, and it felt achingly, powerfully, disastrously good.

The gash on his forehead throbbed painfully, and as he became aware of it, her finger traced it lightly. Had she felt his pain? Their kisses stilled, and he stared up into those blue eyes as she touched his wound. Everything about her was the opposite of him. She was all lightness, golden hair, blue eyes—where everything about *him* was so dark. Even in the half-light of his room, he could see how olive his skin looked next to her fair complexion. She traced the throbbing place on his forehead with the tip of her finger.

"Let me fix this," she breathed. She lifted her hand to help him, and he captured her wrist roughly. He knew Thea Haven had been gifted with healing abilities, but he didn't want to be healed.

"No," he growled.

She raised her eyebrows in surprise. "Why not?"

He released her hand slowly, and she resumed tracing her fingers lightly across the wound until he flinched slightly in pain. The cut was physical proof of his crime—he'd kissed his queen tonight, even when he realized the advance was unwelcome. In return, Kelsey had sent him sprawling, headfirst, against her bookshelf.

"I want the scar," he breathed. "I want to remember tonight from now on."

"They really got to you, Marco, didn't they?" She began trailing hot kisses across his jawline.

He groaned softly. "Yes, but now you're getting to me in whole new ways."

"You've been lonely." Her tongue flicked softly against his earlobe, then she tugged on it between her teeth.

How could he stand up against this? He didn't care what she really wanted with him: This was all he needed tonight.

"Yes," he moaned quietly into her hair, taking her full breasts in both of his hands.

She nuzzled his cheek. "You need this. Me."

"Yes," he agreed softly, raking his hands through her luxurious blond hair. There was so much of it, and it was all over his face.

"What will you do to have me?" she teased, straddling his naked body with her own. God, she was so close to him, he could just slide inside her easily; he let his hand find the warm place between her legs. Earlier he'd caught a brief glimpse of a soft tuft of dark blond hair there. She was incredibly wet for him. Could she want this as much as he did?

"What . . . ever," he gasped, "I need to do." He thrust upward clumsily, trying to push himself toward her, but she lifted, holding herself away. He had no idea how to get what he wanted, not without seeming as inexperienced as he was. His face burned with shame, and he tried to work his way into her again—she raised her hips coquettishly, lifting just out of reach.

"No, no, Marco. Tell me," she urged with a wicked smile. She was hovering over him now, straddling him. If he weren't careful, he might lose control before he ever came inside of her. "Tell me what you will do."

"I'll make love to you," he gasped unsteadily.

She ran her fingers through his hair and laughed, a quiet, seductive sound—the sound of a devil temptress—

and said, "That's not what I want, Marco. You know what I want."

He didn't understand what was happening at all. Not what she wanted? She was so wet for him, so seemingly full of desire. But in his heart, he did know what she was after—had known since she'd first appeared in the bar tonight.

"Then what?" he asked, sucking his breath in quickly. He felt like he was begging her now. He let his hands wander roughly across her backside, cupping her bottom, pulling her closer to him.

"I want you to make love to me, yes. But that's not all." She hesitated, sitting up on top of him until she gazed down at him seriously. "I want you to come to our camp. I want you on our side. Jared will never take you back—you do know that, don't you?"

He felt something turn over in his chest, and for a moment thought he might be sick. She had put voice to the words that he hadn't yet allowed to fully form in his mind. Damn her.

She did know—everything about tonight; he was certain of it now. That he'd kissed his queen, and then afterward Jared—his protected and king—had banished him from camp forever. Did their enemies have the compound bugged? How else could they have known what transpired in the king's chambers, in private?

"Raedus is the true king," she continued, softly stroking his hair away from his forehead. "Jared is only the leader of a tiny little rebellion; it's not his destiny to rule anymore. Someone with your"—she paused, brushing her fingertips over his lips to emphasize her point—"exceptional talents belongs with a real king, Marco."

Suddenly, she captured his hand in her own—so quickly he couldn't stop her—and a small beam of light emitted from the palm of her hand, falling upon his wrist. Immediately his royal seal appeared in the air between them, the one true proof that he was part of the most elite circle of royal protectors. He was among the last of the Madjin protectors, one of a dying breed.

"This is who you are, Marco," she said, gesturing at the undulating royal emblem where it swirled in the darkness between them. "Jared never respected it, never appreciated it. But Raedus will—he needs you. Our alliance needs you," she whispered and began trailing hot kisses across his forehead, along the edges of his painful cut. Her kisses ended on his eyebrow. "And I need you. Badly."

He closed his eyes as he felt her stinging kisses along his forehead. They seemed to electrify his pain, intensify it. He tried to pull away from her, and she raised her head slightly, meeting his gaze. Those blue depths were so bleak, but somehow shot full of passion, just like the ocean at Mareshtakes could be—shining, tempting, and treacherous.

She touched his forehead once again. "Why would you want this scar?" Her voice was surprisingly gentle and sympathetic.

He steadied her face within his open palms, studying her thoughtfully; when he did finally answer, his voice was an electrified hush: "Because it's who I am now, Thea."

In the near darkness, she smiled faintly. "Good," she breathed, tracing her finger along his eyebrow. "So you know then."

He could only nod. He wanted inside of her . . . now. No more toying with it. *Mine,* he thought. *She can be mine . . .*

She can never be yours, the voice disagreed, *but now she owns you—all of you, from your body to the depths of your soul, they all do. For eternity.*

And the worst part was . . . he no longer cared.

Chapter One

Present Day—New Timeline

The entire camp smelled of sex—the musky, unmistakable scent of mating. The aroma perfumed the air, wafted throughout the main cabin and even outside onto the deck where Thea Haven stood. And as if that wasn't annoying enough to an unattached, unmated Refarian female, Thea knew exactly who was having said sex: the one man she'd loved for her entire life. The one man she'd waited for, even when other available males within their rebel faction had come forward, suggesting a coupling with her. The one man she'd always been told she would one day marry—her cousin, the exiled king of Refaria.

Thea blew out a heavy sigh, fighting back the tears that welled in her eyes anew; Jared wasn't just having sex with any other woman. No, he was completing his mating rites with his new wife. His human wife. And the scent of that mating burned Thea's nostrils like hot sulfur. Gods above, sometimes she absolutely hated being an intuitive.

Perhaps if she took a snowmobile over to Base Ten, she could get some reprieve from all the swirling hormones and heat at work here in the main compound. Besides, if she took up residence in the barracks at the base, that would decrease the likelihood of bumping into the newly joined couple on a regular basis. At least for a while. Seeing Jared's mating glow had been like a slap in the face, and she could only imagine what she'd glimpse now that their rites had been completed. As of tonight, Jared and Kelsey were forever lifemated, bonded, and married. Completely soulbound, and there was no going back from that.

Thea stepped back inside the main cabin, ignoring the soldiers whose faces turned curiously in her direction. She knew the gossip that was flying about their rebel forces; that the commander had finally taken a wife, after so many years, and that it wasn't Thea Haven, the council's formal choice. She also detected some of the less kind gossip about her: That if she'd been the sort of woman who could capture a mate, then perhaps the king would have claimed her as such, not gone wandering among the aliens on this godsforsaken planet to find his bride.

The gossip burned her ears and broke her heart because Jared's soldiers would never speak ill of their king and commander. He was beloved and followed, never questioned, and he held the unerring loyalty and respect of every last soldier in his ranks. So there could only be one person to blame for such a disastrous interbreeding mistake as had occurred between Jared and Kelsey. And that one person was none other than herself, Thea Haven, the king's cousin and once-intended bride. Her shoulders alone bore the blame, and she felt the weight of that unspoken accusation in every gaze that turned upon her as she strode through the cabin toward her quarters, even from all her own subordinate officers. Her rank in the Refarian army no longer mattered, however, for as of today she had been unofficially reclassed and reassigned.

Quite simply, she was now the woman who had failed to win the king's heart.

"You can't stay over there on a permanent basis." Scott Dillon scowled at her. Thea was central intelligence advisor over Jared's entire army, and Scott was military commander, Jared's second in command.

"Look, it's just for a while." She pitched her uniform, other casual clothes, and some underwear into her bag. Scott watched the belongings accumulate, never commenting on the intimate articles. She continued: "I can't deal with being around the two of them, not yet. Seeing them all the time, breakfast, lunch, dinner . . . it's too much."

"You can't deal with it?" Scott's tone was sharp, corrective. He was her superior officer in every way, and his arch reply underscored that fact. "They are your king and queen and you serve them. I suggest you remember that fact."

She sank onto the side of her small bed, and the tears she'd been fighting all day finally flowed freely. "Scott, please. I know my place. No one can accuse me otherwise." She wiped at the tears. "It's just . . ."

Scott dropped onto his haunches, his large, dark eyes becoming even with hers, his momentary irritation quickly replaced by compassion. Scott was, in many ways, like a brother to her. They'd fought side by side for a long time now, from the time Thea entered the military at the age of sixteen, and they'd been outposted together here on Earth for the past six years. "Go on," he encouraged with a nod. "What were you going to say?"

"He was going to be my husband, not hers," she blurted, the tears starting in earnest. "From the time I was an infant we were always promised to one another. Always. Scott, you of all people know how it was supposed to be."

"That was before the war escalated, Thea," he reminded her gently. "Everything changed after that . . . for all of us."

Oh, and it had changed all right. Jared's parents had been murdered when he was still only a boy, placing him on the throne at barely ten years of age. He had been exiled at seventeen; become a fierce rebel leader by eighteen. Somewhere in all that fighting and bloodshed and loss, they'd all lost their innocence too, but more than that, they'd lost who they were truly meant to be.

"So we blame yet one more thing on this war!" She brushed at the tears angrily.

"It isn't blame, Thea." Scott shook his head, gazing hard into her eyes. "It's the facts."

She rubbed her eyes. "Jared deserves to be happy. I

told him so. I *want* him to be happy! But he's forsaken his throne in marrying that, that . . ." She shook her head in disbelief. "Th-that *human*!"

"A human who is now our queen," he rebuked gently.

"So you've already pointed out."

"And Jared's throne, well, I don't think the old ways should apply while he's in exile," he continued.

She threw up her hands in anger. "All the more reason that he should have married me and not her!"

"But he didn't, Thea," Scott pressed carefully. "He chose Kelsey Wells, who is now his bonded lifemate and wife. And she is, therefore, your queen. Your queen, Thea . . . think about that. You've got to stay here, in the main compound, and work past these emotions."

Thea leapt to her feet and spun from him, pacing the length of her small quarters in agitation. "Have you not heard the rumors?" she blurted, feeling angry and hurt that Scott wasn't more on her side.

"The rumors will settle in time," he answered simply. So he, too, had caught the gossip that she'd sensed buzzing all about them like agitated bees.

She paused before her small closet mirror, staring at her reflection. Pale blue eyes stared back, eyes she'd once heard described as "holding no emotion." Maybe all her fellow soldiers thought she was cold and without feeling. Maybe that's why they could be so cruel in their gossip. "They're all blaming me," she whispered heavily.

"Of course they are," he said. "We always bear the brunt of his choices; the people love Jared too much to ever condemn him."

For a moment she gathered her thoughts. "I need to know, Scott. Do you genuinely support this royal union? Is that what you're telling me?"

Scott rose slowly to his feet and turned away, putting his strong back to her. He braced his hands on the door frame of her bathroom, clearly considering his answer. As Jared's best friend, she knew he often found it difficult to take a disloyal stance, but he was also a bitterly truthful man. It was one of the things she trusted most in him.

"I am not sure how I feel." He sighed. "She is a good

woman, a true ally to us and to our commander, and I believe they love one another very deeply. But . . ."

"Say it, Scott," she urged, closing the distance between them.

"But"—he drew in a somber, heavy breath—"I believe that Jared should have secured the succession. I believe he should have mated with you and produced an heir."

She couldn't help feeling a smug sense of satisfaction. "Thank you."

He turned toward her again, his black eyebrows hitching upward. "But that does not mean I oppose their union now."

She nodded, dropping her gaze to the floor. "Of course not."

"It is done. They are joined, and you will stay here, in this compound, and work things out with them."

"Scott!" She'd been so sure he understood her pain.

"I won't back down on this point. You stay here and you smooth out the situation—with Jared and with Kelsey."

"I don't know that I can," she admitted, feeling her throat constrict painfully.

"Time has a way of healing many things, Lieutenant," he promised her with a faint smile.

"And time has healed your own heart?" she shot back, knowing all the secret, heavy pain that Scott bore on his shoulders.

His expression darkened, and for a moment he said nothing, then at last admitted, "I'm a lost cause; we all know it. You, on the other hand, will find a mate in time."

"But no one who is like me, Scott. There's only one other person on this planet who understands what I am—who is like me at all. And now he's joined to another."

"You may be surprised what the gods have in store for you yet."

No, she thought, *I will die a virgin, without love, without a soulmate. And without my soul's completion.*

Scott must have read the hopeless expression on her

face because after a moment he patted the front of his jacket pocket, his car keys jangling in answer. "You know what you need, Lieutenant?" he asked, his eyes gleaming mischievously. "Shore leave."

She gave a bitter snort. "This despicable planet *is* our shore leave."

"I mean you need to go off-base. You should come to town with me and let your hair down a little." Thea knew precisely how Lieutenant Dillon let his own hair down: By bedding as many human women as he could possibly take, night after night, week after week, year after year.

She shook her head. "That's your escape, Scott," she said. "Not mine."

His black eyebrows quirked upward. "Never know until you try it. These humans are . . . surprisingly enjoyable."

"Quite obviously." She frowned.

"Come out with me, and let's get your mind off things here. You'll gain a little perspective," he promised. "And this situation might not seem quite so hopeless if you do."

Thea stared down at her boots, taking in her military-issue slacks, her decidedly unappealing uniform that was the furthest thing from sexy. She had a few civilian outfits, but nothing stunning, not if she hoped to actually hook up with someone in a human bar. "I-I don't know, Scott. It feels really strange to me."

"Have you ever gone out in town?" he pressed. "Ever done more than a military maneuver or mission off base?"

"Never."

"My point exactly. Perhaps getting to know these humans might help you understand Jared's position a bit more."

"You dislike humans as much as I do," she scoffed. "You just like to sleep with them."

He flashed a dark grin. "They're fabulous in bed, it's true. And I have little respect for their species, but still"—he hesitated, his expression growing strangely guarded—"there's something about them. Something worth understanding, at least. If for no other reason, because we love our king."

Almost as if an observer, she heard herself saying, "Yes, Scott. I'll go with you," and wondered why she felt a sudden shiver of precognition, as if her entire destiny would hinge on this momentary decision.

Jared Bennett stared at the ceiling over his bed, marveling that his new wife lay sleeping in his arms. Not just any wife, either: Kelsey was his soulmate, the one he'd first met as a young man on the verge of his awakening, and then lost for more years than he cared to count. How long had it been since that time of their initial meeting? Fourteen years? Fourteen years of aching separation—all without even realizing it. The elders had stolen their memories of one another in an effort to protect their king, and only by a miracle had they ever come together again.

Kelsey stirred beside him, the thick tumble of auburn hair winding about her bare shoulders. Jared's breath literally hitched in his throat, and his entire body tightened in awareness of his mate.

"Hello, your sleepiness," he purred in her ear.

She blinked back sleep, rolling onto her side toward him. "What time is it?" she asked with a yawn.

"Not quite midnight."

"You're not getting up, are you?" One auburn eyebrow shot upward in a question. The incompatibility of their sleep cycles had already proved annoying, especially for Jared, who wished to be bedding his new mate as many hours a day as humanly—*and* Refarianly—possible.

"I'm expected down at Base Ten," he said, glancing at his watch. "I've been occupied with"—he buried his head against her chest, nuzzling her—"better things the past few days. And perhaps I may stay occupied a bit longer." He laughed, drawing her right nipple within his mouth, suckling and nibbling it until she groaned in delight.

"Ah, yes, I believe I may indeed stay occupied for quite a bit longer. At least until two A.M.," he teased, then closed his lips around her nipple again.

She groaned, tugging his head upward. "Jared, I just gotta have more than four hours of sleep a night."

"You may nap later," he suggested, cupping her other generous breast within his palm. Immediately both nipples grew puckered and alert; perhaps that meant he could rouse her as well. His groin tightened in sharp pleasure and his breathing grew much more rapid. Aching to see her better in the darkness, he allowed his vision to heighten, taking in every dip and curve of her very feminine body. He growled his pleasure at the sight of her again, and this, well, his wife seemed to like it a great deal, just as she always did.

Almost as if reading his thoughts, she whispered, "I love your noises."

His face instantly burned. "It . . . is not human, though, is it?" he asked uncertainly. "Human men do not make such sounds during mating?"

"Well"—she leaned on one elbow, assessing him in the darkness—"not exactly. But that's part of what turns me on about it." She brushed her fingertips through his short hair, regarding him.

Inside, he felt a yelping cry of hunger, but wrestled to suppress it—this time. He swallowed hard. "My alienness arouses you?"

"Duh, Jared!" She laughed, cupping his face within the palm of her hand, feeling the prickling hairs of his new beard growth. "Don't you think that's obvious by now?"

"Yes, obvious. Perhaps."

They had discussed the most intimate aspects of his biological nature: His mating cycles, his impending infertility, and although the conversations had caused him a great deal of shame and discomfort, she did seem at ease with their natural differences.

"I love you, Jared," she assured him. "I think I loved you from the first, all those years ago. And, frankly, your mating cycles . . . the idea of them, well, it really turns me on."

"It does?" he asked breathlessly, his heart hammering hard. Between his legs, he felt a rigid tightening, one that she seemed to sense as well, sliding one hand between his thighs, inching it upward until she made contact with his erection. Her hand was cool against the smooth, warm skin, and he quivered in pleasure at the unexpected contrast.

He reached for her, ready to roll her beneath him, but she stopped him with her other palm, pushing him onto his back again. "No, Jareshk," she whispered, using his intimate name, the one she'd called him by when they were much younger, "let me pleasure you. I wish to pleasure my king."

With a rumbling sigh of arousal, he let her know how that plan thrilled him. As she took him firmly within her palm, he arched his back, rising into the motion. He felt no inhibition with his mate; every aspect of self-consciousness faded from his mind whenever they made love. Again and again he bucked his hips upward to meet her, aware that she knelt over him, watching, studying the uninhibited reaction that her stroking elicited from him.

His chest rose and fell with unrestrained, panting breaths. Kelsey, meanwhile, increased her friction, rubbing her thumb harshly over his swollen tip. Shaking all over, he swam into the world she created for him, lost himself, felt the tremors begin anew—the same ones he'd felt after the first sealing of their union. Shuddering, trembling, lost, lost, lost. Oh, so lost with his human mate.

Fever. That one word sounded in his mind like a pulse flare. *Fever. Blood fever.*

"Oh, gods!" he cried, aching for a release that he couldn't seem to find. *"Mlshka strk!"* he yelled, and didn't bother to interpret for his new wife. *Can't interpret, not now, not now.* With the speed of a mountain lion, he suddenly spun her, had her beneath him. And with even faster speed, he sheathed himself inside her, hard and fast.

This fever, this heat, he thought, tumbling headfirst, thoughtlessly into sensations he had never experienced in all his thirty years. He knew he wasn't gentle, but he couldn't possibly hold back as he drove into her over and over again, flexing his hips, taking her with the unspent need of a Refarian changeling. *"Mlshka strk,"* he murmured again, unable to stop his most primal mating urge. "Ah, ah, Kelsha, *mlshka strk.*"

"What does that mean?" she asked breathlessly, arching beneath his raging thrusts. "Tell me."

Gasping, he buried his face in her hair. It was impossible to translate, impossible, even, to speak English. He could only moan his need, slipping both hands beneath her full bottom. *Mlshka strk . . . mlshka strk . . . mlshka strk.*

Beneath him, she ground her hips upward, urging him onward. "Tell me . . . what . . . it means," she begged, and for a moment he stilled inside of her, just gazing into her pale eyes. All facility with human language escaped him, and literally no words came to mind that she would understand.

"Ah, K-kelsha," he finally managed to stammer, pressing his eyes shut. "N-no translation. No English." How could he possibly explain something as primal as what he felt in her arms at this moment? Impossible, utterly so!

Kelsey wrapped her arms around her husband, aching for him every bit as much as he obviously longed for her. But she also felt a secret euphoria. Already, in such a short period of time, something about their lovemaking had begun to change. And in a very significant way. Perhaps the very act of their bonding had accomplished it; she wasn't sure, but it hardly mattered if her hunch was correct because whatever he kept murmuring in his own language could only mean one thing.

She wondered if he knew. If her husband possibly understood that what was happening here in their wedding chamber was far more than simple lovemaking. He groaned against her cheek, working both palms beneath her so he could pull her up under him as tightly as possible. She wrapped her thighs around his waist, allowing him to drive in even deeper; such a large man, he filled her to the hilt, choking the very breath from her lungs.

She held him closer than a heartbeat, raising her hips to meet each of his hammering thrusts. "Jareshk! Jareshk, love!" she whispered huskily, stroking her hands over his warm back, damp with the sheen of their sweat. Beneath her fingertips, she traced the outline of his spine, digging her fingers into his flesh.

Again, he cried something in Refarian, something she couldn't possibly understand, and then he stopped. Completely, and for just a slight moment he pulled back and stared down into her eyes, his face flushed hot and his eyes wide and unblinking. His whole body shook with tremors, and for a moment she wondered what more would happen within the man as his season took him fully by the throat and demanded its due.

"I-I don't be-believe it," he stammered breathlessly, still staring at her with wild eyes. She gave him a wicked, wifely grin in return, but said nothing.

He buried his face against her shoulder and, with one last powerful thrust, came inside of her, his glorious, burning warmth filling her completely. Nuzzling her, he murmured, "Love, oh gods, you know what this means?"

"Yes, sweetheart, I do." She brushed a thrilling kiss against her lifemate's cheek in return. "You're in your season."

And Kelsey had no doubt that everything they'd already known in their brief time together was about to spin on its very axis.

Chapter Two

Thea watched Scott peruse the barroom. He knew his way here, extremely well. She'd heard plenty of rumors about her commanding officer, heard tell of his late-night visits to Jackson and Teton Village, how he'd come prowling for human female companionship in the local bars. And he'd owned up to those rumors a while ago, just before dragging her off-base to come out with him. Not that Thea could blame the lieutenant: Their mutual life of soldiering was a lonely one, and as second in command over their whole army, it was difficult for Scott to find a Refarian who would consider him as a potential partner. He was under the mistaken impression that the women in their camp found him unattractive. Truth was, the respect they held for him, as well as his ability to intimidate them all, was simply too much for most of the females in their ranks to deal with, so they avoided him on a social level.

He ducked through the barroom doors, nodding familiarly toward the bouncers and confirming the long-standing rumors: Scott Dillon was very familiar with this aspect of the human realm. Thea, for her part, stayed as distant from the species as she possibly could. She made just one exception, and that was for the only human-Antousian hybrid in her life—the very man leading the way into the bar.

"Over there." Scott nodded toward an open table. She followed him dutifully, trying hard to ignore the scent of so many humans gathered in one place. The overpowering aroma was enough to make her feel nauseated, and certainly reminded her of the reason she'd fled the compound in the first place: One human woman had just ruined her life.

Scott waved at a waitress who approached their table, and Thea could hardly conceal her discomfort at this kind of proximity with the alien species. She preferred the seclusion and shelter of their military ranks as much as possible. She'd had assignments and missions among the humans, of course, but never found a reason to come and, gods forbid, socialize among the species.

"What'll you have?" the waitress asked, and Thea blinked back at her, unsure of the proper response. Scott answered confidently for them both, ordering a pair of Heinekens, a drink that Thea had never tasted before.

Scott's keen black eyes scanned the room, searching, hunting. She saw his nostrils flare almost imperceptibly, and as she studied him she observed such undisguised hunger in his intense gaze that she found herself wishing she could share his passion for pursuit. If only she believed a desirable human—or a desirable man of any species, for that matter—might appear in this bar tonight. She sighed, sinking hopelessly into her chair, and glanced around the place.

"Give it time," Scott coached knowingly.

"I have all the time in the world," she shot back, studying her hands where she'd spread them on the table. It was just too humiliating, realizing that she'd sunk quite so low.

"Since you're here, you might as well look," he told her. "Wouldn't hurt you."

"I don't know why I came," she admitted in a miserable voice. "This is your scene, Scott, not mine."

"You'll never know until you try."

She didn't reply, but did dare to lift her eyes, feeling her face flush hot at just the knowledge of the reason she'd come tonight. It was shameful, that someone of her royal lineage had been reduced to cruising for a lover in a public venue like this one. Common, really, and not the way her mother had raised her to be, a daughter of nobility who was impeccably bred. Still, so long as she was here, she might as well look, she thought, daring to glance around.

There were men all around the bar: rangy men, short

men, fat men. Old and young, grizzled and baby-faced. If only she knew how to go about it, perhaps she could have her choice among them just like Scott apparently did with the women around this town. *Scott has found great satisfaction among the female of this species,* she thought. *Maybe I could find some comfort here too.* She felt a weird kind of hopefulness spring to life in her heart, and again swept her gaze about the smoke-filled barroom.

At first she found no man who even appealed to her, but something caused her to quake deep inside, something that urged her to press forward. A quiet voice of intuition that coiled about her body, wooing her, singing to her. In her lap, she wrung her hands in sudden agitation, feeling heat build in her abdomen. It was the heat of her core self—her other, true nature, the one of swirling flame and power. *What am I feeling?* she wondered, trembling in expectation. *Why is my fire escalating?* Panicked, she glanced at Scott, but he'd propped his hands behind his head and cocked back in his chair with a smug look on his face. He was oblivious to her sudden onslaught of aroused emotion.

"Wh-what's happening to me?" she wondered, not even meaning to voice the feeling aloud.

"Told you, Haven." Scott's cynical, sideways smile spread wide. "It's a really good bar."

Her eyes watered and the fire inside her belly twisted tighter. She wondered if she should leave, her Change had begun to feel that imminent. There wasn't a rational explanation for the sensations quivering throughout her body. Scott didn't understand—he couldn't possibly, not without being Refarian Argante. She had a dual nature, something that only she and Jared possessed because of their rare and royal bloodlines. Only one man had ever brought out this excited compulsion to Change: Jared Bennett.

"No, Scott," she hissed, leaning toward him, "there's someone here. Something that's . . . affecting me. Very powerfully."

His black eyebrows lifted toward his hairline, his expression growing more serious. "What do you think it is?"

She glanced about them in a heated rush, feeling even her lips quiver in anticipation. "I . . . don't know. I don't. Gods, this is crazy."

"Is it a premonition?" he asked, tilting his chair back to the floor and leaning close. "Are you picking up on something?"

She shook her head. That wasn't it; it was a person, someone who was both arousing and confounding her without so much as revealing himself. She sniffed at the air, but the rank smell of human was too overpowering, clouding her senses.

"Keep looking," he urged seriously as the waitress returned, bearing their two bottles of beer. Once he paid the woman, he slid hers toward her, cautioning, "Maybe you shouldn't drink this. Better keep your senses open."

"Or maybe it would help me calm down," she suggested, placing a palm over her lower abdomen. Such fire! Such intensity! Every cell in her body begged her to Change, right here, in full view of her enemies, and it was all she could do to tamp down that painful need.

Scott waved his hand, urging her to take a drink, and tilted his own bottle back for a long chug of the liquid. She did likewise, and coughed at the unfamiliar, bitter taste. She had drunk champagne and wine at various celebrations in their compound—and had consumed alcohol back home—but never anything like this strange beverage. Still, it instantly caused a soothing effect, so she took another quick swig, then, gripping the bottle with both trembling hands, she searched the bar again. Someone—or something—had been inciting her Change in the most powerful way she had ever experienced. Not even in her mating cycle had she ever yearned like this. Never in her life had she experienced such pure craving.

When she'd almost thought her intuition wouldn't solve the riddle, her eyes took in a sight of unbelievable, rugged beauty. There by the pool table stood one of the most breathtaking human creatures she had ever seen. Pool cue gripped in both hands like a battle stick, he watched the game unfold, reminding her of an ancient Refarian warrior. Upon seeing him, the heat coursing through her body took another spiraling turn upward. *He was the source! The one calling out to her somehow.*

Yet he never so much as looked in her direction; instead, his alert gaze was riveted on the action of the pool game.

The human was at least as tall as Jared, and wore black jeans that clung to what were obviously extremely powerful and well-muscled thighs. For a moment, her mind supplied an abrupt image of her own thighs locked around those large, sturdy ones. She felt his breath panting against her cheek, heard him murmuring her name over and over. She closed her eyes, shivering, and tried to shake such lurid imagery from her mind. When she opened her eyes again a moment later, he had shifted position, sidling around the edge of the pool table languidly.

She now had a much better view of the human stranger. His skin was dark, olive-toned, and his body, all range and height and shadow. Sleepy, hooded eyes studied the play of his companion. They were such dark, sensual eyes that they riveted Thea's full attention, forcing the very breath from her lungs. No longer aware of Scott or the furnace inside her body, it seemed the entire world around them receded completely, leaving only the two of them. She couldn't possibly look away, not if she tried. She could only stare at the man and wish. Wish that she weren't a soldier, in a war, here on an alien planet. Wish that he were a man she might find common cause with, and not only for one night. Wish that he might turn and notice her, catching her eye across the smoke-filled barroom.

It's because he reminds me of Jared, she told herself. *He's tall and beautiful and rugged—of course this man makes my heart ache.* A wave of despair welled anew. But then the unexpected happened; he did turn and notice her, pinning her with his penetrating, fathomless gaze for at least ten full seconds before finally glancing away. The languid look was gone from his dark eyes then, just for that moment, replaced by something sharp and fierce and hungry; separated by distance, separated by species, nevertheless Thea Haven swore she heard him speak within her mind.

Marek Shaekai.

And somehow, some way she knew that name.

*   *   *

Jared padded across the bedroom, and reached for his robe where it lay across the back of his desk chair. He had to shower and get down to Base Ten before third shift began. Staring over his shoulder one last time, he marveled at the sight of his sweet human wife, already asleep again in his bed. Slipping into his bathrobe, he settled at his small corner desk for a quick overview of the coming day. Stretching his back, he leaned into his chair and smiled. All these years and he'd been alone. Fought alone, lived alone. For the first morning in his life, he was beginning a day's leadership with his soulmate by his side. It was a deeply pleasing thought.

And he was dwelling on that deeply pleasing thought when something unexpected caught his eye. Propped there on his desk, right beyond his open laptop, where it had been blocked from his view until now, was a plain white envelope. Scowling, he stared at the crisp envelope for a full twenty seconds before reaching for it. First, he gave the vellum a sniff and utilized his somewhat limited intuitive abilities to ascertain if the item was dangerous in any way. *Probably from one of our people,* he thought. *A note congratulating us upon our wedding day, nothing more. Harmless.* Still, years fighting in this war had taught Jared that nothing should be accepted at face value, and he proceeded with caution.

That was when he noticed how the envelope was addressed: *My dearest Jared and Kelsey . . .*

Thea swore the black-haired man had spun a web about her, somehow magnetizing her to this very spot. "I know him," she whispered to Scott, nodding in the man's direction. "Maybe not precisely, but . . . I heard his name."

Scott frowned. "What do you mean?"

"In my mind, using my intuition," she explained, and her commanding officer nodded briskly. "It's not a name I've ever heard before, but it doesn't sound human."

"You think he's one of us?" Scott asked, gazing intently at the stranger.

Thea felt her body quake anew as she watched Marek Shaekai bend low over the table, positioning his cue. Rippling, powerful shoulders hunched over the stick, his eyes narrowing with a steely expression. *Dangerous! He's terribly dangerous.* She knew it in the marrow of her being, just as she knew he was someone vitally important in her life. His dark hands closed around the pool stick, and for a brief moment a quicksilver set of images shot through Thea's mind, dizzying her.

She pressed her eyes closed and the scene in the bar dissolved. The moment itself dissolved, too, catapulting her into the future . . . or the past . . . or somewhere else entirely, she couldn't be sure. The images felt like memories, as certain as if they had always existed. In a dark room Marek Shaekai held her hard within his arms, fastening her furiously against his solid body. The muscled bands of his chest pressed against her cheek, and she wanted to move, but couldn't, no matter how hard she tried to pull away. Between their two souls a cascade of emotions battled for dominance. Uncontained rage. Pain. Betrayal. *You aren't capable of love,* he spat in her ear. She wanted to deny it, wanted to tell him that of course she could love. But then he pressed his mouth against her cheek, blowing out hot, arousing breaths and murmured, *Thea, you can't ever love me because you're damaged.*

Blinking her eyes, she discovered Scott's hand on her forearm. "You all right?" he asked, his gaze flicking about the bar, studying the exits, the entrance. She knew he intended to make his move toward Marek, but she reached out a stilling hand.

"You can't go talk to him," she warned in a thick voice. "It's not safe."

"How do you know?"

She watched as Marek stood again, a gleam of triumph in his sultry gaze when he scored in his game. For a dangerous enemy, he seemed awfully preoccupied with a simple barroom activity, and unaware of any potential threats. Against the nape of her neck, she felt prescience whisper in a deep, husky voice: *I could love you, Thea, if I were still capable of it, but you took that from me.*

"We n-need to go," she barely managed to stammer. "Right now."

"No way," he gritted. "You're telling me this guy may be an enemy, possibly Refarian or Antousian or gods-only-know what. We aren't leaving, not now. We have to check him out."

She tugged on his arm, panting, feeling heat sweep downward from her cheeks into her neck. "He's not dangerous to us, Scott," she blurted, needing to get out of the bar as quickly as possible. Needing to be anywhere but here, near this threatening man.

"Of course he is, and that's what you're sensing."

She shook her head adamantly. "Not to us, Scott. He's dangerous to *me*. Only to me—"

"All the more reason I'm staying to find out who he is," he insisted, cutting her off.

"It's not physical." A dubious look came into Scott's eyes, and she blew out an anguished sigh. "You won't understand, but I've got to go. Please, let's just go."

Her friend and commander did not budge from his seat, but instead locked his own brightly penetrating gaze on her. "Tell me why," he said, and she instantly knew he was beginning to soul-gaze her; he would discover the truth whether she told him or not. She had no choice, not when the man staring into her eyes was an Antousian hybrid who possessed the ability to see deeply into anyone's soul.

So she drew in a strengthening breath, her eyes searching out Marek as she might an addictive poison, and prepared to whisper the truth to Scott, the thing she had slowly come to intuit from the very first moment her gaze had locked with Marek's across the smoky barroom.

"Thea? You going to tell me who he is or not?" Scott persisted.

"I think he's my lover," she said, unable to wrench her gaze away from the man. Already, he had her in the palm of his very hand.

Chapter Three

Jared had been staring at the letter for at least five minutes, perhaps more, and still its contents were no more palatable than when he'd first opened it. The handwriting was almost indecipherable, consisting of a tight, loopy scrawl that proved very difficult to read. Jared glanced over his shoulder to where Kelsey slept, safely tucked beneath his thick bedspread. If the letter was to be believed, it meant she was in terrible danger. *Why must those I love most always be unsafe?* he wondered with a painful spasm of melancholy and regret. Unsure how best to proceed, Jared set about reading the document once again, determined to understand its contents before waking Kelsey. Spreading the sheet of paper beneath his palm, he began to read:

My Dearest Jared and Kelsey,

This is the most difficult letter I've ever had to write. There's so much I need to tell you, but time is running out. I'm not even sure I can make you understand. Still, I'm going to try. That's the least I can do after everything tonight.

I have come back to your time from ten years in the future. You've known what the mitres can do, that it gives us power over multidimensional space. Easy enough, you're thinking, anyone could claim that knowledge. Well, try this: Kelsey contains the mitres codes within her mind, and none of your enemies could possibly know that fact. But I know it, which is what proves that I'm exactly who I claim to be—someone who has come to warn you. To protect you, his true king and queen, with his dying breaths.

My name is Marco McKinley and I will come to you in two years, my king and queen, to serve as your protector. I'm of the Madjin Circle, and have served the royal family for as long as I can remember.

Kelsey, trust me when I tell you: You are the Beloved of Refaria. Ask Jared, and he'll explain what that means. The codes can't be removed from your mind; because of your human DNA, the data fused with you, altering you in a significant way. You're part Refarian now, with your own unique powers and abilities. Over time, you will develop them, and over time, you'll teach us how to use the mitres weapon.

Jared, if we do meet again in the future like I believe we will—if I should do something that seems completely unforgivable . . . traitorous even . . . I beg you not to turn me away. I beg your forgiveness in advance; plead for your trust and friendship no matter what may come in the future.

You see, I arrived today as your enemy, ready to see you both die. But I'm ending this day—for reasons far too complicated to explain—ready to die for you instead. Because the two of you have always been, and will forever be, my beloved king and queen.

Yours,

M.

It had to be authentic; there was nothing else the letter could possibly be. Who was Marco McKinley? Jared rose from his desk and began to pace the bedroom in agitation. There were too many revelations, too many facets of the document that cast his wife in a dangerous light. The data in her mind . . . the future betrayals. He had to send Kelsey away, back to Laramie. Having her resume her "normal life" was the only way he could possibly protect her, at least until he could sort out a better strategy.

From his dresser, he scooped up her neatly folded

clothes, the ones she'd worn here several days ago. "Love," he said gruffly, settling on the side of their bed, "you must wake." Slowly she stirred, rolling away from him, instantly settling into sleep again. "Kelsey," he persisted, "wake up. *Now.*"

Her clear blue eyes fluttered open, taking him in through a sleepy haze. "What's happened?" She squinted at the soft lighting coming from his desk.

"You need to get dressed." He pressed the clothes against her chest. "Quickly, please."

She frowned at his formality. "Why?"

"Because you must." Perhaps if he spoke simply, invoking his authority, things would go more smoothly between them.

She bolted upright in bed, both auburn eyebrows knitting together in confusion. "Has something happened? What's wrong?"

He rose from the bedside, putting his back to her. "You have to leave." He kept his voice as even and emotionless as possible. Never mind that it was a farce of what he truly felt; he busied himself with methodically donning his uniform. "There is a situation, and it will be best for you to return to Laramie now."

"What kind of situation?"

"That does not matter," he answered evenly. "You must go."

"Like hell!"

"Kelsey." He sighed, pausing as he tugged a simple black T-shirt over his head. "This will be so much easier if we don't fight about it."

Behind him, he heard her feet spring lightly to the floor, and before he could catch his breath, she grabbed his arm. "Jared, this isn't happening. No way in the world are you trying to send me away, not now. Not like this—it's the middle of the night! We just got married." His spine stiffened, and he stood still as a statue, his hand on the waistband of his uniform pants. "Tell me you aren't serious!" she cried. "You can't possibly be."

Slowly, with infinite composure, he turned to face her, schooling his face into an impassive mask of stone. "Mate, there has been an incident," he said, not quite meeting her pained gaze. "I've had to make decisions in the past hour, ones that will affect you and me both. I must send you as far from me as possible. Laramie can't be"—his throat tightened painfully, a solid knot lodging in it—"far enough away, love. I would send you to Refaria if I could, I swear it."

The anger dissolved from her expression, her familiar blue eyes filling again with love. "But what *happened*, Jared? Tell me what's going on here. I won't go if you don't tell me why."

"Isn't it enough that I ask it?"

"No," she answered quietly, "it's not."

He closed his eyes, feeling his jaw flex and tense. Gods, the woman had a way of penetrating his most careful composure; she always had. "Kelsey, please," he begged, shaking his head. "I'm sending Thea and Anika with you, but you've got to get out of this camp."

"Did I do something wrong?" she asked, her soft voice wavering uncertainly. "If I did, just tell me."

Without thinking, he cupped her face within his palms, and crushed his lips against hers, needing to taste her. Within his deepest self, he felt his Change threaten to overtake him, just that quickly. His love for this human was beyond elemental, it consumed everything within his soul. How could he send her away like this?

Her lips parted hungrily, her tongue exploring the warmth of his mouth as both of her hands closed around his neck. For long, endless moments they communicated that way, just feeling one another. Flickering beneath the surface, their connection begged to open wide—he sensed her trying to release it, felt her reaching, plumbing the depths of his soul. But he refused, breaking the kiss, pushing their bond aside.

Angrily, she wiped her mouth. "Why did you do that?"

"Because you're only making it harder."

"You're way into this unilateral stuff, Jared, but I'm an equal partner in this relationship. I may not be the king," she said, "but I'm sure as hell your wife—and that makes me the queen, doesn't it?" He bowed his head in shame, but said nothing. "*Doesn't* it, J'Areshkadau?"

"Yes," he answered simply, "you know that it does."

She clasped him by both shoulders. "Then tell me

what has you so freaking upset! You're scaring me." He couldn't shut her out, not as bonded as they already were. He'd thought himself able, and yet staring into her searching eyes, seeing such strong love reflected there, he couldn't possibly keep any secrets from his wife.

Finally, for want of a better strategy, he slipped from her grasp and walked across the room, claiming the letter. "Here," he said, handing it to her. "This is what has changed everything."

Thea watched as Marek unexpectedly made for the door, quickly vanishing between a throng of new arrivals to the bar. "He's leaving," Scott announced, rising from his seat. "We have to follow him."

Everything within Thea wanted to object, wanted to put as much distance as possible between the stranger and herself. But she was a leader, and she knew better. "Come on, let's go." She leaped to her feet. "I'll go after him, you bring up the rear." Her heart hammered out a loud crescendo, causing a deafening roar within her ears. Marek was absolutely the most dangerous man she'd ever encountered; every instinct within herself told her as much. Still, she couldn't resist her desire to understand why precisely he was affecting her so strongly. More than that, they had to learn his identity.

Following in his wake, she shoved her way through the bar patrons, nearly sending a waitress's tray careening to the floor. "Hey! Watch it!" the woman called after her, but Thea didn't waste time looking back. She was out the front door and onto the ice-covered sidewalk like a flash of lightning.

Outside, the wintry air assaulted her, burning her lungs. With a quick glance down the sidewalk she spotted Marek moving at a brisk pace. He was already at least twenty paces ahead of her, his long legs allowing him to cover large distances much faster than she could. He had to be more than a foot taller than her; she had always been far too small for a Refarian, and at moments like this one she especially despised her petite size. Picking up her pace to a near run, she closed some of the distance, but then her boot slipped on a section of black ice, sending her sprawling onto the sidewalk.

By the time she'd recovered, Marek Shaekai was nowhere to be seen.

In exasperation, she broke into a full-fledged run, rounding the corner that he'd undoubtedly taken. Vaguely she registered that a heavy, clotting snow had begun to fall, flakes of which kept stinging her eyes. She blinked, quickening her pace, but something unexpected stopped her in her tracks, choking the very air from her lungs as powerful arms took hold of her, lifting her off of the ground and pulling her into a dark, hidden doorway. Before she could cry out, or shout to Scott, one immense hand spun her against a hard, solid body while the other covered her mouth. Her eyes darted wildly, trying to locate Scott, but beyond the doorway all she saw was the empty nighttime street being covered in silent snow.

Behind her, she felt the solid bulk of Marek's frame, felt his heart beating quickly against her neck. He had her; he had her right where he wanted her, trapped within his implacable grasp. She struggled, but his iron grip prevented her from squirming at all, lodging her with incapacitating strength against his large chest. She couldn't see him—he had pinned her from behind—but she had no doubt as to her captor's identity.

"Let me go," she tried to shout, but because he clasped her mouth tightly shut, nothing more than unintelligible, guttural sounds came out.

Behind her, she heard him chuckle, his hot breath fanning against the top of her head. "A real wildcat, aren't you?" he breathed, bending low so that his mouth grazed her earlobe. "I like that in a woman."

She tried to elbow him in the ribs, but he had her completely captive, held by one large arm that might as well have been made of steel. So she made a screeching noise, and he responded with low, growling fury—the unmistakable sound of an irritated Refarian male.

"Be still or I'll have to really aggravate you," he cautioned silkily, his voice a husky rumble of sound. "Neither one of us wants that, now do we?"

He seemed to wait for her response, but she refused to rise to his bait. In the silence she became painfully aware of his breath against her nape, the huffing sound of it, so quick and urgent. His forearm tightened about her rib cage, his knuckles grazing the underside of her left breast, and instead of feeling frightened, gods forbid, she felt aroused. Electrified. On edge as if the man had just stripped her bare, ready to devour her. Slowly, the hand cupping her mouth slipped away. "You aren't going to scream," he said knowingly. "So I might as well let you talk."

She heaved air from her lungs, a cloud of breath instantly forming. "Let me go, you asshole," she snarled. "Or I will scream so loud every cop in Jackson will come after you."

"You wouldn't." A deep, rumbling laugh escaped his chest, but he made no move to release her; with his free hand he slowly scraped his knuckles against her cheek, outlining her jaw for a long, impossibly seductive moment. She shivered at his touch, cursing herself for the unstoppable attraction she felt toward him, her enemy. Rough fingertips traced down her nape, trailing around to the base of her throat; for a moment, he hesitated, lingering over the straining beat of her pulse. When she thought he would never stop, she began to quiver at his touch. Then, and only then, did he ask, "Why did you follow me?"

"I didn't."

He blew out a hot breath against her cheek. "Like hell."

"Why were you in that bar?" she shot back.

"I like that place," he whispered in her ear. "Got a problem with that?"

"I-I should know you—you're recognizable to me." She spoke in euphemisms rather than come straight out and admit that she knew he was a fellow Refarian.

"I'll take that"—he nuzzled her cheek significantly—"as a compliment."

She was about to argue with him, when suddenly the click of a weapon drew their attention to the street. Standing there, silver pistol trained on them both, stood Scott Dillon. She released a grateful breath. "Let her go," he commanded Marek in an even voice. "Or I'll finish this now."

Marek eased the tension of his forearm, allowing her to slip from his bracing grip. "No problem," he said in a voice like sleek gravel. He held out both palms in blameless surrender as she stumbled out of the darkened doorway toward Scott's side.

"You're coming with us," Scott ordered, using the barrel of his gun to indicate the direction he wanted Marek to walk. *He must be planning to take him to the Suburban,* Thea thought, feeling as if her heart had been permanently lodged in her throat.

Marek gave a slight nod and made a step to leave the darkened doorway. Scott's gaze never wavered from Marek, his stance that of a long-time soldier. Thea assumed a similar posture, her gaze sweeping in a full arc around them, but then, seemingly from nowhere, came a new voice: "Drop your weapons."

Thea whirled in the direction of the newcomer and discovered that Marek's companion from the bar stood behind them all. He was of medium build and had messy blond hair, looking much more a ski bum than an adversary.

Scott lowered his weapon, holstering it with a fluid movement. "Let's take this off the street," he ordered.

Good work, Dillon, she thought. *Keep command of the situation.*

"Where do you propose we go?" Marek asked with a smug grin. "It seems we've reached a stalemate."

"Back in the bar," Thea said. "That's a neutral enough meeting ground."

For a brief moment Marek and his companion exchanged a glance that obviously communicated a great deal, then both nodded in reluctant agreement, the other man holstering his weapon too.

"We have a lot of talking to do," Scott said. "Starting with who you are and what you're doing here in Jackson."

"The better question, Lieutenant Dillon"—Marek paused dramatically, smiling at Thea in devilish provocation—"and *Lieutenant Haven,* is what you hoped to accomplish by engaging us. That's the answer I want to hear."

Scott hunkered over an open bottle of beer; they'd all ordered drinks in order to avoid undue attention from anyone within the bar. "You have us at a disadvantage," Scott said, taking a long swig from his bottle. "Knowing our names when we're not sure who you really are."

Marek nodded seriously, his voice low. "It doesn't matter who we are. What matters is that we're your allies."

"An ally doesn't hold someone prisoner," Thea fired back angrily.

He stared at her for a full five seconds before answering, his almond-shaped eyes narrowing intensely. She felt almost as if she could lose herself in those depths, as if every time she made eye contact with him some secret language buzzed through her mind. His eyes were so dark they almost seemed black, rimmed by a thick fringe of inky lashes that gave them a moody, sensual quality. "I wasn't aware that holding you in my arms translated to holding you prisoner," he finally stated huskily.

You're just trying to be infuriating! she wanted to snap. Instead she opted for a more even-tempered response: "Marek Shaekai, you aren't the only one who knows the score here."

The velvet lashes lowered slightly, his expression becoming guarded, but otherwise he displayed no recognition of the name.

"It *is* who you are, isn't it?" she persisted.

"That's another man's name," he answered coolly, "so you don't know quite as much as you think you do, Haven."

"You're Refarian—both of you," Scott interjected with a glance between the two men. "We know that much."

Marek leaned forward in his chair, planting both elbows on the table. Dropping his head and speaking so softly they all had to lean closer, he whispered, "And you, Scott Dillon, are *not*."

"No, I'm not," Scott agreed in a subdued voice.

Marek indicated Thea with a slight movement of his hand. "Our business isn't with you, Dillon—it's with her."

Thea's heartbeat increased, a rushing noise filling her

ears. "What about me?" she heard herself ask breathlessly.

"We've always made the royal families our business," Marek answered with a nonchalant shrug. "And you are naturally part of that concern."

"All right, cut to the chase," Scott insisted with a scowl. "Who the hell are you people and what is your position?"

"We're Madjin," Marek answered with an obvious flash of pride. "For all our lives, it's the only thing we've ever been."

Thea felt her face burn hot. The Madjin no longer existed—couldn't possibly exist, not in any universe or on any planet. An elite, prestigious band of royal protectors, they had guarded the king and his family for thousands of years. When the revolution had begun, the Antousians decimated their small circles—or at least the pitiful remnant that had managed to survive so many years of war already. The last of them, Jared's personal protector Sabrina, had vanished two decades ago, and no one—despite Jared's tireless efforts to locate the woman—had ever heard from her again.

"Th-that's not possible," Thea stammered, glancing toward Scott, whose own face had seemingly drained of color. "The Madjin are dead."

This time it was Marek's companion who smiled, something bright sparking in his eyes. "You'd be surprised just how alive we are," he said with a quiet laugh. "And we can prove it to you—quite easily, as a matter of fact."

"How can you prove it?" Thea demanded. The ways of the Madjin were so secret, so sacrosanct, that no one had much reliable knowledge about them. "We know almost nothing about the Madjin," she continued, "which makes proving your claim more than a little problematic."

Marek glanced between them with an intent expression. "Simple," he said. "Take us to your base and allow us a meeting with the commander. That's how you'll know we're legitimate."

"Oh, I just bet you'd love that," Scott said, his voice cold and precise.

"It's the only way you'll ever really know," Marek persisted. "Because there's just one man who can authenticate our identities for you, and that's Jared Bennett."

Chapter Four

Marco lay wedged across the bench seat of the Suburban, both hands tied roughly behind his back. Thea Haven had done the honors with her very own belt, both she and Dillon insisting on the measure for security reasons. She'd wrangled them into prone positions—Riley on the floorboard, Marco sprawled face-first across the seat—all the maneuvering an effort to protect them from discovering the compound's position. Neither he nor Riley had bothered explaining that they already knew the location of Jared's compound; hell, they could have guided everyone there blindfolded.

Even now as Dillon took turns obviously intended to mislead them, Marco found himself wanting to explain the futility of their plan. But he didn't. He remained with his face pressing into the artificial leather seat, wishing that Lieutenant Haven would move much, much closer. As it was, she sat behind him, leaning over the bench so that her pistol pressed into his lower back—which, unsettling as it might have been, didn't feel nearly close enough.

The woman did things to him, strange, alien things that left his mind muddled and his body titillated. Thank All he was facedown so she couldn't see the very obvious bulge in the front of his jeans, an eager erection he'd gotten the instant she fastened his hands behind his back. He told himself it was something about the belt, something about her roping him up like her very own steer that had turned him on this wildly. *You always were into bondage, Thea baby,* some distant voice hummed in his mind. *That's you, my little wildcat—you need that control.*

Pressing his eyes shut, he felt a headache swell, causing bright spots to fill his darkened vision. He had never met Thea Haven before in his life; sure, he'd had her under surveillance on plenty of occasions, even followed her when duty required it. But until tonight he had never once gazed into those clear, vibrant blue eyes. Eyes that had spoken volumes to him, wooed him closer, promised lifetimes of seduction. His swollen, aching erection pushed harder into the seat as he remembered. As he allowed the sensations he'd experienced earlier in the bar to fan to life all over again.

The Suburban made a series of turns, and Thea—for reasons he wasn't even sure of—dug the barrel of her weapon into his lower back with even more force. All of a sudden it seemed he couldn't breathe, couldn't think. There were only the swimming memories of something he had never once experienced in all his almost thirty years, not with any woman, not on any planet: He was remembering making love. And with Thea Haven, of all people, one of his protected.

Gasping, he fought the rising tide of nausea that always accompanied these blinding headaches. *What in All's name is this?* he wondered, cursing his strange abilities that sometimes left him open to this kind of sensation. *What am I picking up on about her? She's D'Ashani, utterly out of my league.*

But he knew it wasn't imagination, or even foreknowledge; the impressions and emotions were far too brilliant, unlike anything he'd ever felt before in his life. It took all his resolve not to simply roll onto his back and grab the woman, pulling her atop him with enough force to knock the gun from her hand. Then, and only then, he would cover her mouth hungrily with his own. Tasting of her, taking her, knowing her. It hardly mattered that in this imagined scenario, the pulse pistol would have already destroyed his spinal column and obliterated his internal organs. Good thing it wasn't an actual plan. *Just a desire*, he thought, *and I've mastered plenty of them as a Madjin warrior.*

On the floorboard beneath him he heard Riley's steady breathing. His brother was nothing if not a cool customer. Damn it all, but the guy would probably fall fucking asleep during the drive back to the Refarian compound. Then again, Marco had no doubt that Riley was happily connected with his lifemate, rattling along in deep, soulful conversation with her across their shared bond. Lucky bastard. He never had to be alone, not like Marco did. Marco had long ago accepted the hand he'd been dealt. He would never mate or even take a lover. Which meant that this insane attraction to the D'Ashani woman was out of the question. The emotions and memories—for surely that's what they were—had the material air of something experienced. Not pre-known, not imagined. But the pulsing life force of real events. The question was . . . how was something like that even possible?

The blinding headache tightened hard behind his eyes, and with it, a wash of memories came over him.

How could you have slept with him? he demanded, rounding on her in a dark, abandoned warehouse. *How could you have betrayed me like that?*

She laughed, a cold, lost sound that caused something hard to lodge in his chest. *You don't think this is love, do you, Marco?* She released a slow, jeering laugh. *Not with you of all people.*

Of course not, he said. *You're not capable of it.*

Shaking his head, he tried to beat back the tide of half memories, determined to battle away the onslaught. Perhaps this was a trick of their enemy, a strategy meant to divide them before their full circle could form completely around their king and queen. And they did have a queen now; he knew it because of Riley's intel from within the camp.

Although Sabrina hadn't authorized this first contact between the Madjin and their protected tonight, they had always been taught to improvise on an ad hoc basis. What other recourse had they been given, based on the unexpected meeting in the bar? None. So what if the elders' timetable for initial contact was still a good two years out; the Madjin were needed, now more than ever with Jared having taken his human wife. So no matter what objections Sabrina might raise tomorrow, he stood by this plan.

Dillon took another series of wrong turns, a true waste of time in Marco's mind. So he muttered against the seat, citing the precise location of the secluded mountain cabin where their king made his earthly home.

"Holy hell," Scott cursed from the front seat. "What's even the point?"

Thea leapt over the seat that separated them, straddling Marco. "You tell us who you are," she shouted, digging the barrel of her weapon into his back. "Right now!"

"My name is Marco McKinley," he stated calmly, feeling her tight thighs flex around his body. "Personal protector and guardian to the king. J'Areshkadau Bnet D'Aravni is my sovereign, same as he is yours."

For a long moment silence hung heavy in the vehicle's interior, with only the sound of Thea's rapid breaths punctuating the quiet. At last she asked in a much quieter voice, "Then who is Marek Sheakai? Why did I hear that name in the bar?" Thea cocked her pistol, shoving it between his shoulder blades.

For a moment he concentrated on her, on the feel of her lithe, compact body atop his rangy one, on the awareness of her scent filling his nostrils, nearly intoxicating him. Gods, she was an amazing woman—but completely off-limits to someone like him.

When he failed to answer, she drew in an unsteady breath. "Tell. Me. Why," she demanded, accenting each word with a jab of her pistol.

Finally he answered her question, in a voice so low only she would hear. "I have no idea why you heard his name, Lieutenant," he said softly. "But trust me when I tell you that he's dead, and he hardly matters tonight."

"He matters to me," she breathed.

"A dead man," he repeated. "Let's leave it at that, but you may call *me* Marco. And I am your protector too, my lady. I serve all the royal families."

"You said you served Jared—that you're his personal protector."

"That's true," he murmured against the seat. "But if you know the Madjin, you know we serve you all."

"Prove it," she said, pressing her palm into the small of his back. Every cell within his body reacted, a cascade of heat showering to his extremities. "You prove it now, before we get to Jared."

He could think of nothing except the feel of her fingers splayed against his body. His simple flannel shirt seemed nothing more than a ridiculously thin membrane, a flimsy barrier between their two flushed bodies. He swallowed hard, his eyes drifting shut. He knew what she wanted to hear; it was a sort of first-level proof to any of the royals they served, something no one outside the Madjin Circle could possibly know.

He would give Thea Haven the proof she wanted. *"R'thasme siet falne,"* he murmured reverentially. He'd not uttered those words since the day they'd inducted him into the Circle, and the hair on the nape of his neck bristled at his own quiet pronouncement. For a moment, she said nothing at all, though he sensed a kind of tension release from her body.

"In All's name," she finally muttered. "You've been telling us the truth. You're exactly what you claim to be."

"Unless I'm lying," he teased in a low, growling voice. "And then we're all damned to hell."

"Marco McKinley, I still have a gun," she said, pushing the barrel into his shoulders again. "Madjin or not, you've got a lot of questions to answer."

"At your service, Lieutenant Haven. Completely at your service."

If only he didn't wish to *service* her in such wicked, impossible ways, he thought with a miserable sigh—and if only he could rid himself of his raging, painfully obvious hard-on before they arrived at the compound.

"Okay, Jared, I admit it," Kelsey said, pulling the sheet over her breasts. "I have no clue what this letter really means. What's this 'Beloved of Refaria' stuff? And how could this guy possibly be telling the truth? I mean, time travel . . . a letter from the future? It's insane."

He paced the room, stripping out of his bulletproof vest. "Hasn't everything between us always been slightly insane?"

"Don't even go there."

"But you get my point, love," he insisted, stepping closer. "There are many things about my life here on Earth—and what I've told you about life on Refaria—that defy logic as you've always understood it."

"This letter flies in the face of everything I know as a scientist," she said, waving the sheet of paper at him. "Time travel is possible—at least in theory—but nobody on *my* planet has come close to harnessing that kind of power."

He took the letter from her hands. "That you know of."

"That we know of, yes." She felt unsettled beyond description. Why was it that with every passing day her new husband managed to further unravel the fabric of her world?

Jared settled his hip on the bed beside her. "Naturally I'd like to dismiss the authenticity of the document," he said evenly. "But there are too many aspects that beg serious consideration. For one thing, the reference to that prophecy about the Beloved of Refaria, and another because the author knows about the mitres data within your mind—"

"Other people in your camp know about that."

"No," he said simply, "they do not. Only Thea, Scott, and Anika possess that knowledge."

She chose her next words carefully, tucking the bed-sheet beneath her chin as she thought. "Maybe it's all some kind of ploy to divide us or something. What makes you so sure Thea wouldn't have done this?"

"No, not Thea. Not ever." He shook his head in vehement denial. "She's unfailingly loyal, most particularly to me."

"But she loves you, Jared—and you did choose me. That could shake even the strongest relationship."

"It wasn't her," he barked, and Kelsey couldn't help but smart at his defensive tone.

She persisted, "Then what about Scott? Or Anika? You'll have to question people whose loyalty you've never doubted before. Some of your followers are dead set against me, Jared. We both know it—just think about the elders, and how they erased our memories of each other. There's no way you can be sure that someone—someone *loyal*—wouldn't try something just to separate us a second time."

"I must ask myself what logical purpose a letter like this would serve," he reflected aloud. "How would it divide us—how would it misdirect me? I cannot see any such outcome from taking the letter seriously."

"Except that you want to send me back to Laramie." She shoved him in the chest with her open palm. "Right when it's actually possible that we could conceive a child—the heir to your throne. That's one hell of an outcome."

He grabbed at her hand, wrestling it against his own chest. Her argument had merit, especially given his approaching infertility. If they were to part ways right now, it was quite likely that he might never cycle again, which could mean the end to his line after nearly a thousand years of unbroken succession. It could mean the end to their dreams of a family and children and a life together—apart from the war. Gods, it was unfair, being asked to make such impossible decisions!

Leaping to his feet, he paced the room again and gestured toward their bed. "Only *we* know what happens between these sheets, Kelse," he argued, feeling his pulse skitter wildly. "Only we know what's starting here, between us, this . . . this uncontrollable *need*." He halted beside his wife, gazing into her beautiful blue eyes, and the flecks of gold in them electrified his entire body. At once the letter seemed less important, as did the strategy of sending her far away; those thoughts were replaced by a far more significant compulsion: the urge to mate. Now!

Wildly, he tugged his T-shirt over his head, and stood before his wife wearing only his uniform pants. With a wicked grin, he noticed how she licked her lips at the sight of his bare chest, her gaze flicking up and down the length of him. They were newlyweds, in some ways barely known to each other; every time she got a good look at his muscular body, he saw how it pleased her—which always, without fail, satisfied him to the very core. He felt warm heat flood his cheeks.

"You like what you see, don't you, mate?" he purred

at her, unsnapping his pants with an easy flick of his wrist. He took another step toward her. "You like my body very much."

"Jared!" she cried, half laughing, half urgent. "We've got to deal with this." She gestured toward the letter in his hand.

He allowed his pants to slide to the floor, pooling at his ankles so that he stood before her in all his naked, proud glory. His prominent erection leaped at the knowledge that they would come together again in mere moments. She would be his, again. They would mate. Again. And again and yet again. He growled his pleasure at the simple thought of joining with her that way.

"Jared," she protested softly, appealing to his higher nature, but there was only one thing his D'Aravnian self could think of at the moment. Mating. And mating some more . . .

Good grief, Kelsey thought. *Now that the man is at the edge of his season, all his earlier shame about his mating urges has fallen away completely*. It was apparent that Jared was about to toss the letter aside and ravish her, a thought that caused her own body to quake with a fevered wash of desire.

His eyes narrowed hungrily and he blew out a hot breath, reaching a hand to stroke his proud, hardened length. For a moment he stood gazing at her, slowly touching himself, even as he devoured her with his black gaze.

"You were saying?" he whispered, sliding one knee onto the side of the bed, edging much closer toward her. "Something about"—he gasped slightly—"that damned letter?"

She gulped, steadying her thoughts. "Jared, they could know about this," she tried to answer evenly. "About your mating season. Somehow they could know that it's finally happening."

"Only we know, love," he murmured dangerously, climbing over her. "And I know that this need is becoming more intense with every passing hour."

"Then don't send me away!" She slammed both fists against the mattress, fully aware that she sounded more like a petulant child than the queen of any realm.

He responded by mounting her, so quickly she hardly had time to anticipate the motion. In the space of a moment he had her pinned beneath his large, bare body, allowing their warm skin to slide together. "Just once," he panted against her cheek, nipping at her flesh. "Before I call the meeting. Just one more time, wife—or I swear this fever will take me forever." His voice was alien then, strangled, containing a mixture of rough awe and genuine fear.

"Just once," she agreed thickly, feeling his swollen shaft already pressing against her opening. "Just one more time."

Kelsey flexed and bucked beneath him, digging her fingernails into his shoulders, scrabbling at his throat. Jared's core heat had begun to blaze like ten angry suns. *Must slow down,* he cautioned himself, fully aware that he might Change any moment if he wasn't careful. And his human wife would never survive that. It was one thing to reveal his true nature to her, to allow her to gaze upon him as she'd done once before, but not this. Not his Change, not in the middle of this kind of intimacy.

Gasping, he stilled inside of her, wrestling to master his whirlwind of sensations. He buried his head against her shoulder, sucking in burning, furious gulps of air, and she stilled beneath him, sensing his momentary confusion. The truth was his two halves were locked in a brutal battle for dominance. His Refarian side was solid and corporeal—but his D'Aravnian nature was far more mystical and prone to dominance. *That* man was one of fire, a being of heat and blazing fury and intensity. And that was the man who begged to make love to his mate right now. *Impossible!* he cautioned himself, but still the heat kept on expanding within his abdomen and chest, filtering down his back and shooting straight into his loins like an aggressive, scorching arrow. *Unstoppable! Utterly unstoppable!*

He pulled apart from her with an unsteady exhalation. "Kelsey! W-we must cease!"

"Not now, no, Jared." She blinked up at him as if in a daze. "Not now, please . . . not now."

He rolled off of her, shaking his head. Damn it all, but his whole body was quaking: his hands, his legs, his fingers. Burying his face in both hands, he was about to explain the Refarian facts of life, how dangerous his natural self was to her human body, but was interrupted when, across their bedroom, his comm began to beep. He'd discarded his uniform hours ago, but had never bothered removing the communication unit from his sleeve.

"In All's name!" he muttered, sliding over her and marching toward where he'd left the thing. Nobody ever bothered him this early in the morning, no matter how early he might wake.

"Bennett," he barked into the piece, ready to dress down whoever among his soldiers had interrupted such a crucial moment with his bondmate.

"Commander," came Scott Dillon's urgent voice, "we need to meet with you as soon as possible, sir. There's been an incident."

Chapter Five

Upon entering the meeting room, Jared was surprised to discover the cause for Lieutenant Dillon's urgent transmission: two strangers who were seated at the large meeting table. Flanked by Scott and Thea, the two men were under heavy military guard. Jared immediately assessed the scenario: This room was where he and his elite officers strategized, planned, and masterminded their attacks. It was not, however, a place where they ever—under any circumstances—brought outsiders.

Scott and Thea each gave him a crisp salute, which he returned, and they then assumed a parade rest stance. But he hadn't served by either soldier's side for so many years without being able to recognize the tension visibly apparent in their demeanors.

"Tell me of our visitors," Jared commanded coolly, striding to the center of the room. "Who comes to see us at this late hour?" His gaze never left the two strangers seated at the table.

Thea took a step in his direction. "They're Madjin, sir," she answered, then quickly added, "That's what they claim."

Jared folded both of his arms across his chest. "I see." He leveled the dark one with his hardest gaze, instinctively sensing that he was the leader of the two. "And what do you say now that you've come into my camp?"

The man inclined his head, never daring to look Jared in the eye. "That, just as the lieutenant says, we are your sworn servants from birth."

"I don't suppose you need me to point out that the Madjin vanished long ago."

"We've been"—the dark haired one turned slightly toward his companion, but the other man kept his eyes down—"waiting for this time, my lord. We've been training, honing our skills."

"You don't expect me to believe that the Madjin would ever run from battle?"

"No, my lord. Not running," the dark one said. "Preparing. Waiting. Biding our time until the right moment. Guarding you from . . . a distance."

Jared couldn't contain a snort of disbelieving laughter. "Were you watching from a distance when Veckus captured me? Were you there those three days when he beat me within an inch of my life?"

A brief spasm of pain contorted the dark one's face. "No, my lord," he whispered. "Even we can not protect you when you insist on participating in aerial combat."

Beside him, Scott Dillon chuckled low. "Well, now, these boys really do know you, Commander." Jared felt his face flush hot.

Jared leaned his palm on the table until he pulled his face close to them both. "For what possible purpose would you have gone into hiding?" he insisted. "Tell me that—make me believe you—and I'll accept that the Madjin have returned."

"We have but one purpose, my lord and king: to put you—once again—upon the throne of Refaria," the leader answered, inclining his head low and spreading both palms open on the table until his forehead nearly touched the polished wooden surface. The man couldn't bow, not in his seat, but Jared understood his posture nonetheless. It was that of a most loyal Refarian servant.

"I don't believe you," Jared countered evenly.

"That is your prerogative, of course, my lord," the man's companion interjected. "But we do serve you. Completely."

Jared's thoughts went to Sabrina, his beloved protector, who had been more a parent to him than his own mother had been; or his father, for that matter. She had raised him until he was ten years old, nurturing him, training him, teaching him. When she had vanished shortly after his parents' murders, a part of Jared's heart had died and grown cold. It had stayed that way for far too many years to count. *Sabrina, why aren't you here now, my teacher?*

What the strangers claimed was beyond the realm of possibility. So what purpose did their lies serve? And how did it, perhaps, relate to the mysterious arrival of the letter?

"Tell me your names," he demanded, something eerie chilling his body. "Each of you."

The leader of the two remained with his forehead pressed almost flat against the gleaming table, and in a confident voice proclaimed, "I am Marco McKinley, personal protector to J'Areshkadau Bnet D'Aravni. I am Madjin, forevermore."

"I am Riley McKinley," his companion began, but Jared could hardly hear a word he said, for it was Marco's name ringing in his ears, deafening him. He turned to one of his soldiers, demanding a pen and paper.

When they delivered the items, he slid the paper before Marco. "Here, write your names—both of you." But he was only asking for proof. The mysterious letter in his jacket pocket already heralded the truth like a bold shout from the mountaintops.

With his left hand, Marco took hold of the pen, tilting the page slightly as he began to scrawl his name. Even from where Jared stood, he could see that he had difficult, crude handwriting. Not as if he were an unlearned man, but rather that it was something to do with his left-handedness.

When he finished, Marco handed the slip of paper back to Jared, averting his eyes. The Madjin had always believed eye contact with their protected to be a serious transgression; he could easily recall how few times Sabrina had ever met his gaze straight-on. Jared stared down at the page in his hand, and heard Riley ask, "Mine as well, sir?"

But he shook his head; with one scrawling sentence, Marco McKinley had identified himself as the author of the letter. And Marco McKinley sat before him now. The question was, did this man serve him as he claimed—or had he come for a much more nefarious and sinister purpose?

* * *

"Tell me of Sabrina. What do you know of her fate?" Jared asked, pacing around the table with his hands behind his back. Sabrina had been everything to him; her disappearance so close in time to his own parents' murders had nearly destroyed him as a young man.

"She lives," Marco answered simply.

"She lives?" Jared snapped his fingers. "Just like that. She lives?" He felt anger and emotion swell inside of him, making his eyes burn.

"She is our . . . leader. The leader of our unit and the highest member of the Circle."

Jared's eyes slid shut. "Sabrina is dead." Even as he said it, another part of his heart leaped with a hope that time and warfare had nearly killed: that he might find her once again.

Marco glanced up at him, his dark face serious and unflinching. "Sabrina *lives*, my lord. I would never lie to you."

Jared whirled toward Marco, slamming his fists onto the table. "Enough is enough," he raged. "If you are who you claim to be—if you are indeed connected with my protector, then prove it to me now!"

Marco sucked in a steady, quiet breath. "You were in the palace vaults waiting for her; she told you she would return, would come for you—but she couldn't make it back, the fighting around the palace was too intense. She kept trying, all night long, but was unsuccessful. When mortar rounds were fired into the tower wing, she knew she had no choice but to leave you behind. If she'd tried to make it back to the palace to get you—down in those vaults—she would have led your enemies right to you. And so . . . she left you. She left you, there in the palace catacombs, knowing you thought she was abandoning you. That night was her greatest loss during the war, she told me that. Even worse than losing her own son and husband in battle. She said"—Marco paused, daring to meet Jared's gaze with a meaningful look—"that she always thought of you as her own son."

Jared slowly turned from Marco, gathering his thoughts. Also at the table, Scott and Thea sat, waiting. They were all waiting. "She hid me in a secret compartment of the vaults," he admitted solemnly. "I waited long into the night, while the mortars and cannons kept firing. I stayed under my father's jeweled throne, curled in a tight ball. Too afraid to move, too afraid to breathe . . . and yet she never came." The memory was fresh as newly fallen snow; tears stung his eyes and he blinked them back.

"But she wanted to, my lord," Marco assured him.

Jared tossed the Madjin a look. "If she'd wanted to, protector, then she'd have come." Something cold clutched at Jared's heart. It was easier believing Sabrina dead than that she had never returned to his side.

"You'll have much to discuss with her," the one named Riley interjected, "after we have returned to her and explained the situation."

"You're not going anywhere, neither one of you—not until we have time to gather more intel. And not until you offer better proof that you're Madjin."

Thea piped in. "He recited the vow, sir."

"We have more substantial proof than that," Marco said, rising from his seat. The moment he did, every gun in the room whirled in his direction, accompanied by the loud clicks of the safety locks disengaging.

"Stand down!" shouted one of the soldiers, the other swooping in on Marco who thrust both hands high in the air.

"I'm unarmed!" he shouted back at them. With one cautious hand he lifted his shirt, reminding them that he had surrendered his weaponry to Thea earlier.

Jared indicated that the soldiers should drop their weapons, and Marco bowed before him, pressing one fist over his heart. "I am your Madjin, my lord. Yours personally as well as the queen's."

So they knew he had married. They knew that, for the first time in many years, the Refarian people did have a queen. "What is your proof, Marco?"

"I will have to show it to you."

Jared waved for him to continue, the hairs on the back of his neck prickling. There *was* a visual proof of the Madjin warriors, a brand they bore on the inside of their wrists. He had a vivid memory of Sabrina showing him her own mark one day when he was small, letting him know that his own royal seal wasn't as exotic as he feared. But she'd taken hers willingly—whereas he'd been born with his own wildly gyrating tattoo, marking him from birth as D'Aravni.

Marco dropped to his knees with a soft thud, rolling his shirtsleeve up to the elbow. Jared's heart rate increased significantly. Bowing his head, Marco lifted his left hand, allowing a bluish silver beam of light to fall on the underside of his other wrist.

"This is my royal brand," he stated softly. "It's what identifies me as protector to my king and queen. I am your sworn servant," he continued, his eyes meeting Jared's with piercing vibrancy. "This is all that I am. Serving you is all that I know."

Then Marco dropped his hand, and the seal disappeared again as the beam of light vanished. Slowly the Madjin lowered his sleeve and rose to his feet.

"I have seen this seal before," Jared told him in a quiet voice. "I bear a similar mark myself."

"Yes, my lord."

"Where is Sabrina now? I need to see her . . . must see her."

"In Jackson. That's where we've been living."

"At first light, you will go for her and bring her here."

Marco inclined his head respectfully. "Yes, sir."

"There is another matter to address in the morning," Jared told them. "We will meet again after breakfast. Thea"—Jared gestured to her and the MPs—"see both men to their temporary quarters."

Marco was about to answer when, behind them, the door opened. Anika appeared, flushed and breathless. "My lord, I'm only now returning from the base . . ." Her words died on her lips as one hand flew to her mouth. She stood beside him, arrested, her gaze riveted on the one called Riley McKinley. Jared turned to her, curious, wondering why the Madjin returned her gaze with such a wild-eyed look.

"What's going on here?" Jared demanded hotly. Anika shook her head, swallowing visibly, but said nothing. Jared persisted: "Do you *know* this man, Lieutenant?"

Anika worked her jaw, her eyes welling with tears, but made no reply. With both hands outstretched she stepped toward him, a cornered expression on her face. Jared ignored her extended hand. "He's someone to you," he hissed, walking slowly toward the other side of the room where Riley sat at the table. "Shall you tell me who he is to you—*precisely* to you—Lieutenant?" White-hot fury urged him on. Too many secrets were unraveling tonight. If his blessed Anika was at the center or even on the periphery of this Madjin conspiracy, he would never forgive her.

"My lord, please." She begged him with her large, familiar eyes. Eyes that had always offered friendship and loyalty and kindness. But tonight that friendship had been revealed as nothing more than deception. Jared knew it in his leader's heart.

She dropped her head, her hands trembling. "How did they get here?" she asked in a shaky voice.

"We met them in town," Thea interjected, shooting Jared a corrective glance, one that told him to take it easy on their friend and fellow soldier. Thea could do that as his cousin, cross the boundaries at moments when he needed her to do so.

He softened his voice. "I will repeat, Anika Draeus—who is this man to you?"

"He's my lifemate," she answered softly. "Riley McKinley and I were bonded together sixteen years ago. As children. I have only seen him once since that day."

Thea gaped at Anika, watching hot tears stream down her friend's face; Anika couldn't stop crying, nor could she break eye contact with her lifemate—even as she couldn't seem to bring herself to look *at* their king. Jared, for his part, wore an expression of controlled rage. He felt betrayed; it didn't take an intuitive to figure that much out, not when his usually composed features were contorted into a mask of strained emotion. His almond-shaped eyes had narrowed to slits, the red-gold skin of his face deepening in flushed color.

Thea slipped between Anika and their commander, sliding one arm around the woman's shoulder. "I think, perhaps, it would aid in the proceedings if the lieutenant stepped outside," Thea suggested. Then with a quick glance at Jared she added, "Cousin, you as well."

"I have nothing to say to Lieutenant Draeus. Or perhaps I should address her as Madjin now that her military rank means nothing?"

Thea pulled the much taller woman toward the door, but Anika—in her trademark style of open honesty—stopped before Jared, dropping to her knees. "You are my king, my lord, my commander. I live for no man but you. To serve you is my highest service."

"You are Madjin, are you not?" he asked coolly, staring down at the top of her dark head.

She hesitated a moment, then murmured softly, "Yes, my lord. I am Madjin."

"But you never thought to tell me?"

"I could not," she cried, glancing up at him. "It was for your own protection."

"How many others are in our midst?" he asked, sweeping the room with his furious gaze. "*Are* there others?"

Anika spoke in a thick voice: "Only Anna, my lord." Anika's twin sister, Anna, had not been summoned to the meeting chambers.

Jared blew out a weary, heavy breath. "Rise, Madjin protector," he commanded. "Now."

She nodded, standing before him obediently. For a long moment he assessed her, assuming a commander's pose as he took in her features, her clothing, her military bearing. Anika seemed to hold her breath during the whole of his inspection, raw pain in her dark eyes.

At last Jared turned from her, shaking his head. "Dismissed, soldier," he said, and she saluted him sharply—but he did not return the gesture, and Anika's kind features crumpled as she left the room. Thea glanced back at Riley McKinley and witnessed a similar, stricken expression on his face. It was hard to imagine that they'd been bonded lifemates—able to communicate, share tender intimacies—for all these years without actually being able to touch. And now their first reunion in such a long time was in the presence of their king, a man who believed them his betrayers.

Chapter Six

"You don't expect me to sleep under armed guard, do you?" Marco asked, gesturing toward the two soldiers who had followed them into the small bedroom. "I'm not capable of walking through walls—clearly even you realize I'm not an Antousian."

Thea wrapped her arms around herself, shivering. It was a colder than average night; outside the cabin a heavy snow continued to fall, causing a windchill factor of negative thirteen degrees. But it wasn't the weather that froze her. It was the simple fact that she believed Marco; she believed every single claim he'd made tonight, which meant his arrival had changed all their destinies. It also meant that the man wasn't about to run.

She gestured toward both soldiers. "Step outside, please." With a salute, the MPs obeyed, exiting the room.

"They will be right outside that door. With instructions to shoot first, ask questions later, should you try anything."

He glanced at her, a half-cocked, proud grin on his face. "I won't try . . . anything," he told her, his nearly black eyes gleaming suggestively.

She immediately blushed, and gave a brisk nod. "Good. I'm glad we understand each other."

"Do we?" he asked, stepping near to her. He bent low until he stared into her eyes. "Tell me—just how well *do* we understand each other, my lady?"

She stumbled backward from him, reaching for the door, but he caught her hand in his calloused, much larger one. "I didn't give a damn about the armed guards. I've slept through much worse," he growled, spinning her to face him. "I just wanted to be alone with you."

Without blinking, he stared directly into her eyes, giving her the sudden sensation of being read by the man. Easily. Not in the way that Scott sometimes soul-gazed her, but as if Marco deeply understood the whole of her nature, right down to the very marrow of her being.

Carefully, she extricated her hand from his grasp, gazing at her boots. "Well, you're alone with me now," she whispered, refusing to stare into those seductive, long-lashed eyes of his. "So tell me, Marco McKinley, what exactly *do* you want?" Every warning system in her body screamed that he was lethally dangerous.

"What do I want?" he repeated, laughing. "What do I want, here in my room, alone with you, Thea Haven? I think you know exactly what I want."

"To say to me," she quickly amended, cursing herself for such a stupid choice of phrasing.

"It's not what I want to say. It's what I want to do," he said softly, pressing his full mouth against her cheek and breathing in her scent. Among their people, sniffing of someone's face or neck was a blatant mating gesture, and as he lingered with his lips against her skin, slowly inhaling, he might as well have slipped both palms beneath her uniform shirt and cupped her breasts. She felt electrified, on fire like she had been at the bar when she'd first seen him. It was all she could do to refrain from returning the gesture, taking Marco's own scent into her lungs and savoring it.

Closing both arms around her, he tugged her flush against him, his groin pressing hard against her body. With a soft growl, he cocked his head sideways, pressing his face against her neck. Thea didn't dare move; didn't twitch or flinch. She stood as still as the rigid statues in the palace garden back in Thearnsk, even though her legs felt unsteady beneath her. It was almost like a parade inspection—a very sensual, forbidden one. Around her back, she felt him gather the material of her shirt within his fists; her body tightened in reaction. Still, she made no move.

"I need to know you." He nuzzled in closer, and then

suddenly there was the rough, wet feel of his tongue, flicking there at the base of her throat. More tasting of her scent, she thought, the room swimming hazily about her.

At last he exhaled slowly, his breath warm against her cheek. "Your scent's like wildflowers touched by sunlight. I could spend all night like this."

Coming to her senses, she held both hands out, shoving him away from her. "Don't," she snapped. "Don't do that. *Please.*"

One black eyebrow shot upward. "You wanted it in the bar," he suggested in a seductive whisper. "And you wanted it just now. I know exactly what you wanted tonight."

She slapped at his chest with her open palm. "I did not *want it*!" she cried indignantly, lust morphing into instantaneous and humiliated anger. "You are so damn sure of yourself!"

"Not nearly so sure as you think." His black eyebrows drew together, his expression growing troubled. "Or as I'd like you to believe."

"Oh, so we're being honest now, are we?"

"I've been honest from the first."

She shook her head, very aware that her fire had begun to churn again just from these brief moments around Marco. What was it about him that set her ablaze, inciting her Change faster than she could possibly resist? She stumbled past him, toward the door. "I—I have to go," she managed thickly. "I will speak with you in a few hours."

In a husky voice he called after her, "Are you certain about this?"

She glanced back at him over her shoulder, one hand on the doorknob. "About what?"

"About leaving me."

She pressed her lips into a tight line. "Why must every phrase out of your mouth be so suggestive?"

She turned the knob, hearing his steps behind her on the hardwood floor. Suddenly, both of his forearms braced about her, his palms flat against the door. "You'd better be sure," he cautioned in a whisper, lowering his mouth to her ear once again. "Because if you leave,

Lieutenant, you may never know what I saw in the bar. Or if I saw anything at all. You'll always wonder if you were the only one."

"Good night," she gasped shakily, and opened the door.

The moment Thea entered her quarters, she allowed her Change. Felt the warm, familiar fire engulf her whole body, felt the tendrils of power fan out through her extremities, transforming the whole of her nature. And for the first time since walking into that bar earlier tonight, she could breathe. Her whole body filled with joy and freedom as she embraced her most natural self, a being of pure energy and fire—and one without a corporeal body.

Marco, she thought, feeling her energy gyrate dynamically throughout her form, *what about you made this so necessary?*

She went long periods of time without allowing her Change—without even thinking about it. Other seasons brought such frank restlessness that she could hardly slake her thirst for it. But those impulses usually accompanied her mating cycles.

Tonight was different, she thought, with a pirouette and shimmy of golden glory. This night, a man had made her yearn to Change—and for once it hadn't been Jared. *No good can come of these feelings—look what loving Jared did to me!* That thought instantly dulled her exultant freedom, and all the thrilling fire inside of her turned ice-cold. She felt adrift, marooned in her natural form, and with a sullen groan of power, changed back to her Refarian body. She collapsed in front of the hearth, staring at the charred remnants of last night's fire, and felt surprisingly frightened. Frightened that any man had the power to ignite her like Marco McKinley obviously could.

Correction, she thought, planting her elbows on her knees glumly, it wasn't Marco. It had been her visions of him. No wonder she was frightened. Her gift of intuition never operated that way, not with such concrete images and dialogue. All those impressions about Marco had been much more like memories—very specific and concrete memories.

The dizzying impressions came rushing to the fore again, as vividly as if Marco were standing right in front of her. She felt his angry grip on her, felt the heat of his body. "You aren't capable of love," he snarled coldly. *I want to tell you how I feel*, she thought, pressing her eyes closed. She could taste the feelings, the need for him that she'd suppressed every waking moment she had spent near the man. He'd thought her dead inside, but she'd only been lost. So very, very lost. *Wake me, Marco!* she had desperately wanted to cry. *Make me alive again!*

Blinking back the eerie, quick-firing images, she felt her heart squeeze tight. *I'm capable of loving* you, *Marco*, a soft voice supplied in her mind, and she gasped, her hand flying to her mouth.

"What in All's name is happening to me?" she whispered, burying her face in both trembling hands.

The fact was, something supernatural had begun to weave its web between the two of them tonight; he'd obviously felt it too. And there was only one possible course of action, at least if she wanted to make sense out of the strange memories in her mind: She had to go back to his room. Tonight. But first there was something she had to bring with her, something he needed to know all about.

A soft knock came on Marco's door, and he sat upright in bed, instantly alert. He hadn't been able to sleep anyway, not with his thoughts darting wildly from one urgent topic to another. That, and his body had been tighter than a drum after being so close to Thea in this same room.

Maybe she'd returned, he thought with a hopeful lurch out of bed. He didn't bother dressing, but strode to the door wearing only his boxer briefs. When he opened it, Thea stood on the other side, her mouth set in a tense line. She had gathered her composure since her visit an hour earlier, but her cheeks still bore the telltale flush that he'd given her the last time. That blush deepened as her gaze slid over his half-naked body in subtle appraisal. "Back so soon?" he asked, leaning lazily against the door frame.

She held a book in her hands, and pressed it protectively against her chest, avoiding eye contact. "I must speak with you, Mr. McKinley. Tonight. It's a matter of great urgency." The two soldiers flanking her stared at him hard, but neither made a move. Slowly Marco pushed the door open, maintaining his position until she had brushed past him. Only then did he turn and pull the door shut, leaving the soldiers on the other side of the threshold.

"I'm assuming you had a private meeting in mind?" He folded both arms over his chest.

"Th-there's something we must discuss," she said, and he noticed that her voice had a trembling sound to it. Instantly he was worried, all pretense of flirtation and provocation falling to the wayside.

"What's wrong, Thea?" he asked seriously. "Did something happen after you left here?"

"No, that's not it." She shook her head, staring down at the slim volume held within her hands. "But you're right—I do need to understand what happened tonight," she told him softly, licking her lips.

He sat down on the edge of his bed, and gestured toward a chair on the other side of the cramped room. "Of course." He gave an encouraging nod. "Talk to me, Lieutenant."

"At the bar? Tonight? I heard things—in my head. Saw things," she explained, gesturing nervously with the book. "I need to know if that's what you were talking about earlier."

"I heard things too," he answered simply, trying his best to behave in her presence. She was confused and upset enough; she didn't need him baiting her, no matter how much he wanted the woman.

But she gazed at him with such unabashed emotion it was all he could do to keep his reaction to her under control. "You heard . . . me? In your mind?" she asked softly.

"Sure enough," he answered laconically. "Heard all kinds of things in my head."

"They were like memories, what I heard. What I saw."

He dared to raise his eyes again; it seemed that her own were blazing with wild energy. "I think they *were* memories," he answered, suddenly convinced that they had been. Somehow, someway, he knew it was true.

With shaking hands, she flipped open the book, holding it in her lap as she smoothed her palm over the page. "This was written by my ancestor, Prince Arienn D'Aravni. He tells in here about something that happened after visiting Earth and overseeing the mitres installation. . . ." Her voice trailed off, and she slammed the book shut. "This is madness." She pressed a hand to her temple. "I shouldn't even be here, shouldn't be reading this to you."

"I'm your ally, Thea. I thought you believed me."

"I don't know what to believe!" she cried, beginning to quiver all over. He wondered if she were experiencing more of the visions that they'd shared earlier.

He stared at her for a long moment. Her blue eyes were intensely beautiful; full of emotion and longing and pain. It took every ounce of his soldier's discipline to keep from simply storming across the room and kissing her. But he didn't; he forced himself to finally drop his gaze. Only this time, he was the one shaking.

"Tell me more," he encouraged her softly.

She stared down at the volume in her lap, methodically flipping the pages. "It's not like this material is classified," she rationalized in a husky voice.

"Go on," he urged seriously.

She traced her fingertip over the page thoughtfully. "After powering up the mitres, Prince Arienn began to have strange visions. And he continued to have them for many years thereafter. Usually when he was tired or under duress, but sometimes at odd, waking moments." She tapped the open page for emphasis. "In here, he describes experiencing something like memories. He could never scientifically explain or prove them, but he had a theory—that those impressions and sensations were actually his own memories, from a parallel dimension. He believed that when he used the mitres, he caused some kind of space-time rift."

Shivering, Marco reached for his T-shirt where he'd discarded it on the floor with the rest of his clothes.

Tugging it over his head, he caught Thea staring at his body, but forced himself to focus on the conversation at hand.

"So, let me get this straight: Prince Arienn never used the mitres, he just powered it up?"

"He seeded"—she hesitated, struggling for words—"some of his essence into the device. Jared says his energy is still inside the coiling unit, even now."

"Our lord's been inside the mitres chamber?"

"Yes, the night he unlocked the codes—he entered the chamber briefly, and that's when he saw the prince's energy inside the unit. It had faded to a soft green, not the usual bright glow of our kind, but it was there."

Marco nodded thoughtfully, unable to stop thinking that the woman before him had another identity, one much more primal and powerful; it was a deeply unsettling thought. All the more because the notion of seeing her natural form caused a sharp tightening in his groin. He pushed his knees together, hoping she wouldn't see the way his boxers tented upward sharply as a result of their discussion. "He was a dual being," he finally said. "Like you." *In All's name, why should the thought of her true nature turn me on like this?* he wondered, lustful thoughts fogging his mind.

"Yes, I'm a dual being," she admitted, bowing her head. "I-I don't . . . well, it's not something most people understand."

"I'm trained to understand everything about you, Thea."

She nodded. "Arienn left some of his energy there, and he thought that—even without actually traveling through time—his act of doing so had somehow altered the future. Enough so that it created a universe parallel to the one he lived in."

"What did you see tonight, Thea? While we watched each other in the bar?"

"Me, in your arms." She grew pensive, troubled, deep blotches of color staining her fair cheeks. "You said I wasn't capable of love," she admitted softly. "And I guess that I wasn't—not in that timeline."

"*Are* you capable of love?" he whispered, his eyes riveted on her.

"Many in this camp don't think so." Nothing could

have contained his surprise when shining tears filled her eyes.

"I don't believe them."

She flinched visibly, dropping her head. Marco's intuition detected a great deal of pain in the woman. *Some bastard has broken her heart! What kind of fool would let her get away?*

"Thea," he commanded gently. "Come over here. Right now." He indicated the place on the bed beside him. "You're upset—tonight's been hard on all of us."

"I'm fine." But she didn't seem fine; she seemed anything but all right.

"There's something I can do to help you, but you need to come sit beside me."

She snorted ironically. "I've heard a lot of come-on lines in my time, but that's a new one: 'There's something I can do to help you.' " Again she laughed softly, wiping at the tears in her eyes.

"Just because another man hurt you doesn't mean I can't help you."

Her head jerked upright, her eyes widening. "That's none of your business," she told him coolly.

"Thea, you're safe with me." Again, he touched the place beside him on the edge of the bed. "Now come here." Even he knew he was dancing with fire, bringing this forbidden attraction between them to the fore, but he couldn't seem to stop himself. He wanted her, and badly. But more than that, he wanted to offer her some kind of solace. The thought that she loved another man—one who had broken her heart and spirit—galled him to the extreme. And he knew he could take at least a glimmer of that pain away. His awareness of his gifts, what he could offer her, was almost more than he could stand.

She rose to her feet, but didn't take a step closer. "No unmated woman is safe in a man's bed," she argued in a shaky voice, "especially not with someone as dangerously beautiful as you."

He flushed at the compliment, but was more concerned with gaining her trust. "I've managed to control myself for the past twenty-eight years—I can survive a little while with you beside me."

She gave him a suspicious look. "Controlling yourself how, precisely?"

"With women," he told her honestly. "All women."

"You actually expect me to believe that you're a virgin?" She laughed. "Please, I'm no fool."

He extended both hands in a placating gesture. "Believe it or not—that's up to you, Lieutenant."

"Then you're . . . what? You must be—"

"I'm Madjin," he finished uncomfortably. No woman had ever questioned his sexual orientation. "We aren't allowed to take lovers."

"None among you besides Sabrina is mated?" she asked, aghast. "What about Anika and Riley?"

"They were bonded—not mated—and for a purpose. So they could communicate intelligence and information."

"That's very romantic."

"Actually . . ." Trying to explain his adopted brother's mad, intense love affair with his lifemate would be a difficult task. "They were bonded to one another at age twelve. There was no choice about it, so you're right—that's not very romantic, I suppose."

"But they *are* lifemates?" she persisted.

"There are a few bonded among us, but it serves a greater good. We're told to remain pure, alone. Servants."

"So the Madjin keep you alone, too. Like a monk?"

He grinned at her. "I'm no choirboy, Thea. Trust me about that, but still, despite"—he paused, staring into her eyes meaningfully—"all that we've both felt tonight, you really are safe with me."

"Gods, I crave safety." She blew out a long, tortured sigh, carefully crossing the distance that separated them. "And for whatever reason, being with you does feel right. Not safe exactly, but . . . absolutely right."

"Good. That's good," he soothed as she settled beside him on the bed. "Just relax, okay?"

She nodded and he brushed her long hair away from her shoulders, rubbing his thumbs along her graceful neck. He let them travel slowly, and with each touch he opened himself to her a bit, allowing peace to flow to her. He wasn't a healer exactly, but this was something related to his intuition he could offer. His eyes drifted shut, and he formed an image of a meadow, long grass waving slowly in a warm summer breeze, something he'd seen years ago with Sabrina and fixed on as an image of peace. He willed the picture and its accompanying sensations to blanket Thea, and somehow he sensed her relax beneath his touch. Relax . . . *yet come alive.* A strange, heady mixture of emotions that awakened instantly within him, as well.

Green grass swaying . . . golden sunlight playing on the field . . . peace . . . comfort.

She sighed softly, her head bowing beneath his touch.

How was it possible to feel someone setting you on fire, and yet become drowsy and serene all at once? Somehow that was precisely what Marco's gentle touch was doing to Thea's body. She was awash with desire for him—it was spiraling crazily, but she didn't understand exactly what was happening to her, not at all. And she was so very tired . . . needed to sleep. *Had to.* So she decided to lie down, only for a moment, and curled up on her side.

"I'm just going to close my eyes a minute," she said, nestling her head into his soft pillow.

"Sure," he breathed in the darkness, and she felt him settle beside her in the small bed. Her back was to him, and yet she was keenly aware of his warm body only a few inches behind hers. She wished he'd touch her some more, hold her, but the urge to sleep was just too overpowering.

Marco exhaled heavily as Thea's breathing changed, becoming soft and even. He should never have touched her like this, and it was damn sure that he should never have used his intuition to ease her burdens. It had wiped her out completely, and now he was stuck in an agonizing—and potentially compromising—situation. She was asleep in his bed, and all he had on were his boxers and a T-shirt. And the evidence of how powerfully she'd aroused him was pressing urgently against his soft cotton underwear. If she were to move any closer, she'd feel his rock-hard erection. Carefully, he snaked his hips a bit farther back from her, and sighed as he collapsed heavily against their shared pillow.

This was sheer agony, lying beside Thea in his bed like this, her muscular legs nearly grazing against his. Her thick, luminous hair spilled across his pillow, tickling his nose, and her scent was unbelievable—dancing across all his senses, awakening something in him. Closing his eyes, he tried to still his body's reaction to her. He knew he couldn't act on this insane attraction. As one of her protectors, his behavior was completely inappropriate. But that did nothing to ease his body's awakened reaction to the woman.

You've got to separate yourself from her. You're Madjin; she's D'Ashani. Back off, you fool.

And yet he couldn't. He absolutely *couldn't* break away from what he'd begun.

It wasn't that the Madjin weren't allowed involvements, but rather that unions were discouraged, silently frowned upon, because the heart had a way of encumbering fast decisions. That's what made this attraction to Thea so potentially lethal.

Her hair spilled across his pillow like spun gold, and he ached to run his hands all through it, just to know what it would feel like beneath his fingertips. Marco deliberated for a long moment, then very gingerly took a silken lock within his hand. He closed his eyes, feeling it beneath his fingertips, wishing this attraction could actually lead somewhere. He drew the lock to his lips, kissing the end softly, and prayed to All that he could be strong enough to let her go.

Suddenly, Thea stirred a bit, and rolled to face him in her sleep until she lay only a breath away from him. Her lips were close enough to kiss, and her thigh was dangerously near his erection.

He closed his eyes because he could hardly breathe, and yet panted heavily at the same time. He'd never been this close to any woman—not like this, in his bed, wearing only his boxers. Sure, he'd kissed a few girls when he was younger, but he'd never let anyone very close for fear of exposure, the threat of their knowing he wasn't human. He'd certainly never invited any of them into his bed. He was everything he'd claimed to be—a virgin, unmated and untouched on a genuinely intimate level. But he knew it wasn't just having a woman in such intimate proximity; it was Thea, pure and simple. Somehow they were connected, and deeply.

Marco exhaled heavily, his eyes fluttering open, and found Thea staring at him. His heartbeat sped up—not just out of desire, but because she left him feeling horridly exposed. *Found out.* And yet she kept on staring at him wordlessly in the darkness, the only sound between them their own breathing. Moonlight spilled through the window beside the bed, playing across her features, and Marco glimpsed raw, unabashed desire reflected in her blue eyes. A throaty sigh escaped her lips as she licked them slowly—and that one gesture was his undoing.

He bent closer to her, kissing her very tentatively, waiting for her to shove him away. Instead, her lips parted softly, and she returned the kiss with surprising passion. She wrapped her arms around his neck, tugging his head closer, welcoming him into her arms. So, he deepened the kiss roughly, and their tongues began to slowly entwine. It was the sweetest taste he'd ever known, and he closed his eyes, savoring it. He slipped his hands around her small waist, drawing her closer up against him as he took her mouth with another hungry kiss. Their tongues began an erotic dance, flicking together uncontrollably, and in response his whole body grew warmer as he felt some kind of unusual energy building inside himself.

He'd never kissed a fellow Refarian before, only humans, and this was decidedly different. *Thea* was different, and she affected him unbelievably.

He had to stop. *Had to.* They were fellow soldiers fighting in the same war; she was of a royal bloodline, and he . . . wasn't. But instead, he deepened the kiss, brushing his fingers through her hair, wedging her more tightly against him. She pushed her small hips up against his, and he moaned softly at the intimate contact. There was no way she hadn't felt his arousal—and his cheeks flushed deeply at the knowledge. He grasped her hips hard within his palms, fitting her against him, no longer caring what she felt. Hell, he wanted her to feel his erection, to know how turned on she'd made him. As her compact body fit snugly against his much larger one, she gasped, squirming against him in a sudden effort to pull away. But he kept her fixed against him with both hands, wanting her more than he had ever wanted anyone or anything in all his damnable life.

"Marco," she panted, clutching at him, even as she tried to get away. "We have to stop. We've got to."

He groaned, burying his face against her neck. "I know. I know." So much for his long-held virginity, he thought ruefully. This one woman could strip him of every illusion he'd fought so hard to maintain; his orderly life, his Madjin's discipline. Never before had he realized how fragile and tentative his self-possession could truly be.

Slowly, finger by finger, he eased his grip on her waist, gasping for every breath he drew into his lungs. "Bad idea, this," he groaned, nuzzling her. "Terrible, awful, ill-thought-out plan."

She rubbed her fingertips through the curling hair at the base of his neck. "Not really," she whispered, then, laughing, added, "Well, at least we know those visions weren't crazy. Not after this."

He pulled back so he could stare into her blue, ethereal eyes. "I've never wanted anyone so damned bad in my life, Thea," he told her frankly. "Visions or no, you turn me fucking on."

She smiled, cupping his face. "Too bad you're a monk."

Drawing in ragged, panting breaths, he managed, "Already told you . . . I'm no saint, but you're my protected." He groaned, shaking his head. He had crossed the line in a way he'd never imagined—and on his first night coming under Jared Bennett's leadership. What the hell had he been thinking? He closed his eyes, saying, "It's an untenable situation. I want this—you, but I have a duty to perform."

She released her hold on him, slowly sitting up in bed. "And so do I," she agreed quietly. "We've got to work together in a few hours, so it's best we put all of this"—

she waved her hand between them significantly—"behind us from now on."

"Absolutely. Agreed." His voice sounded thick and emotion-filled, even to his own ears.

She stood, smoothing out the front of her uniform, all soldier now—the passionate woman of a moment ago quickly vanishing beneath her facade of order and precision. "I look forward to it," she told him with a brisk nod, and headed toward his bedroom door.

Only after she was gone did he collapse onto his back with a groan of such pent-up need and frustration that he felt his body might explode. *Holy hell, I'm the last Refarian virgin,* he thought with a growl. It was a fact that had bothered him over the years, but it had always been a necessity. Suddenly his responsibilities and vows seemed an unbearable sacrifice—now that he knew what it might be to hold Thea Haven in his arms once and for all.

Jared found Kelsey sound asleep, twined in his thick comforter and sheets. It was pushing five a.m., and on her body clock, still very early for a human. He dropped onto the side of their bed, watching her sleep. Many decisions had been made tonight; many revelations had occurred. Yet again, everything had changed for the two of them, just as it had changed for his people.

Drowsily she stirred, eyeing him. "You're back." She rubbed her eyes.

He bent to kiss her forehead. "Yes, love."

"You're not going to make me go back to Laramie now, are you?"

With a smile, he buried his face in her mass of curls. "No, sweet Kelsey—you aren't going anywhere."

"Good," she said wickedly, wrapping her arms about him. He lay there, drinking her in, wishing that his body were still rocked with desperate tremors. Wishing that he didn't possess such a strange, finicky bloodline that left him fertile for only a brief window of time.

Kelsey ran her hands through his hair, stroking his upper back, kissing his bristling cheek. She thought he was still mad with mating fever, and he did desire her desperately, that was true. His heart and soul and being longed for her, but with the heavy revelations and burdens that had come, something had stilled inside of him tonight. He'd snapped back into his harsh reality, been reminded of what he'd always known: that leaders' hearts came last in matters of love. The war and its concerns had to come first, even above family and mating and heirs. Jared closed his eyes, groaning softly in her arms at the excruciating realization of what had changed between them in just a few hours' time. She giggled, lifting her hips against him, interpreting his groans as lusty need, but what Kelsey couldn't possibly know—what *he* couldn't possibly explain—was that already, somehow, the heat in his body had begun to cool.

His first mating season was ending before it had even truly begun.

Chapter Seven

Marco mounted the interior steps to the Jackson apartment he'd shared with Sabrina and Riley for the past two years, in a three-story boardinghouse where anonymity reigned. It was the longest he'd ever lived in any one place after a near lifetime of nomadic movement. First from Refaria to Earth when he was eight years old, then zigzagging across the US for the past twenty years: Santa Fe, New Mexico, as a boy; Portland, Oregon, when he was twelve; Jacksonville, Florida, when he was nineteen; Moscow, Idaho, when he was twenty-one. It had been a roundabout, hardscrabble existence, and he could click off the towns like mile markers on a two-lane.

Arriving on the narrow landing outside the apartment, Marco wrangled his keys, but Sabrina yanked open the door before he'd even turned the lock. Her eyes scanned the exterior hallway as she ushered him inside and closed the door behind him.

"We gotta talk." Marco pushed past her and into the living room.

"Where have you been? Where's Riley?" She followed behind him. "When you didn't come home—"

"Riley's fine, Sabrina." Marco sank onto their threadbare sofa, the single piece of furniture in the living room; like everything else in their lives, the furnishings in the apartment were minimal.

She focused her intense gaze on him. "Then tell me what happened."

"He's with our lord." He drew in a breath, bracing for her reaction.

She gave him a blank look for a moment, the facts clearly not computing. "He's with Jared?" she finally whispered in disbelief.

"We spent the night at the compound after a run-in with Thea Haven and Scott Dillon. They identified us at the bar last night." He dug his hands into the pockets of his parka—the apartment was never warm enough. "Jared knows everything. Trust me, it was a long damn night."

Sabrina stood in the center of the living room staring at him, blinking rapidly as she absorbed his revelations. She never aged or turned gray, relying instead on the shape-shifter's prerogative—to maintain her youth. At the moment, however, her usually warm brown eyes were bloodshot and lined by dark circles and she seemed much older than she normally did.

"Does he know about me?" she asked in a quiet voice, unconsciously placing her hand over her heart. Jared meant everything to Sabrina, even after so many years apart from him—and that was on a personal level. He meant even more to her as the true Refarian king.

He nodded. "He sent me for you. We're both to head for camp right away. Riley stayed there"—he laughed in realization—"I suppose as collateral. But we'll gain Jared's trust soon enough."

Her eyes drifted shut. "It's too soon." She shook her head, putting her back to him. "This is all wrong. The timing . . . all of it's wrong."

"You don't think I'm ready."

"How can you possibly be?"

"Isn't a lifetime of training enough?" He sprang to his feet, following her across the room. "How long do you and the elders intend to hold me back? I am called to this—there's nothing else I'm meant to do. I have given everything to the Circle! Everything, Sabrina. It's time that you let me walk out my calling. I'm his protector—*their* protector—and I'm needed, now more than ever. You of all people understand that."

She faced him again, staring hard into his eyes. "If it's too soon," she answered, running her hand down her neat braid, "it can only lead to destruction."

"Is that *my* destruction or *yours*, Sabrina?"

"We have to follow the elders, and they've said to wait," she reminded him sternly, walking toward the kitchen.

"Thea and I have been talking about some things—important things—and I need to be there." An unexpected fire fanned to life inside of his chest and abdomen, unsettling him completely. Just like he'd felt each time in Thea's presence!

She snapped her head toward him; if she'd been a horse, her ears would have tilted forward alertly. "Lieutenant Haven and you had time to talk about important matters? Already, in such a short period of time?"

His face burned self-consciously, and the fever in his belly nearly exploded at Sabrina's mention of the woman. "I'm moving into their camp," he told her boldly. "I've already made my decision."

She busied herself with opening a cereal box, methodically measuring out enough for both of them. He braced his hands against the kitchen counter, saying: "They need training; they need to learn how to link intuitively for their protection. And for their true power. How can they learn if I'm all the way down here?"

"You want to be near her," she said knowingly, opening the refrigerator.

Without meaning to, he lifted a hand to his flushed face, a mixture of desire and embarrassment sending warmth to the very crown of his head. It was as if his entire body had reddened and caught fire with the mere utterance of Thea's name! No woman had ever had this kind of effect on him, and he didn't like losing his composure.

"I do not want to be 'near her,' " he barked. "This has nothing to do with anyone, except our commander and queen."

"You're not of the same class as Thea Haven. You're Madjin and she's D'Ashani—do you even recall what that means to our people? Or have you forgotten after so many years?"

"I haven't forgotten that I've got a job to do—one I'd best be doing. You know what the commander asked me last night? He asked where we were when he was taken captive by Veckus. I gave an answer, but it wasn't the right one. He's been in this damn thing on his own for too long, I'm telling you."

"We answer to the elders," she reminded him softly.

"They have an agenda, always have."

"So you plan to go about this without their support? Without seeking their guidance?"

"I'll do the job I was trained to do."

"Well, then. Your mind is obviously made up."

Kelsey sat with Jared in his upstairs study, a hard snow falling beyond the windows surrounding their tower turret. Holding her hand, he had led his wife up the stairs to the fourth floor of the cabin, feeling Marco's letter practically burn a hole in his jacket pocket.

Somehow Jared had known that the letter had to stay secret, even from those he trusted the most. Well, secret from everyone except Kelsey, which was why he'd shared it with her from the first. But now he had new revelations—that Marco McKinley, the letter's author, was here in their camp. She sat with him before the fire, cross-legged, one hand knotting through her loose, riotously curling hair. Marco's handwriting sample was spread open on her jean-clad knee.

He needed her advice. He needed her wisdom. Most of all, he needed her to tell him that he hadn't lost his mind, and that with all that had changed in the past ten days—their marriage, Marco, the letter—he was still the man she'd met all those years ago at Mirror Lake. He needed her assurance that reality still spun on its comfortable axis.

"Okay, so let me get this totally straight—from what you told me last night, you don't know this guy?" she asked at last, glancing up from the paper. "Never even known his name? Nothing?"

"Until last night, I'd never heard of him, not from any quarter."

"Then, I guess the biggest question is . . . do you believe him?"

"The letter chills me. It already did before the man's arrival last night," Jared told her, standing to pace about the room, unable to sit still. "Everything in me says the document is authentic. As for Marco himself . . . I believe him as well."

"But the letter says he will come in two years—he came on the same day."

"When they used the mitres, they must have altered things . . . the timeline."

"You really do trust Marco?" she asked semi-incredulously. "And this letter?"

"He displayed irrefutable proof that he is a royal protector."

"One of the"—she paused, stumbling over the Refarian word—*"Madjeen."*

He smiled at her adorable accent. Somehow, strangely, Kelsey speaking Refarian was a massive turn-on. "He bears the mark of the Madjin, just as I bear my own royal seal. It's not something that can be faked. He is authentic."

She sighed, her auburn eyebrows furrowing deeply. "Why would he have planted a letter like this?"

Jared stopped his pacing, standing behind Kelsey. He placed his open palm atop her head; he needed their physical connection. "I do not believe that the Marco I met last night knows about this letter."

"So you trust him?" she asked again, reaching for his hand. Their fingers threaded together.

"You seem to find that surprising," he observed softly.

"Well, like I said last night, to believe the letter, you'd have to accept time travel and lots of other things that fly in the face of common sense," she said with a glance over her shoulder at him.

Jared cleared his throat, his now-familiar black eyes intense and serious. "Time travel is possible, Kelsey. Just not for *your* people, not yet."

As much as it sounded like something right out of science fiction, the Caltech guys, and then, later, other physicists, had all thought time travel possible for a while now. "Go on," Kelsey said at last, swallowing hard.

"The mitres technology—the data I left inside you—is the key. The mitres is a vast, powerful, monumental weapon. We've spent years trying to unlock the chambers and decipher the codes. Years trying to fully harness its power."

"How do you know for sure that it works?" she asked, her mind racing with thoughts about the mysterious mitres and its data, the very technology that Jared had left in her mind the night of the crash.

Jared grew quiet and thoughtful. "It was placed here in the early eighteen hundreds—Earth time. My ancestor, a young prince of the D'Aravni line, was the one who oversaw its installation. Earth was chosen for many reasons, Kelsey. Because your people and your atmosphere were genetically compatible with our own. Our genetic codes are 99 percent similar. Some even theorize that our two species emanate from the same genetic source, though nobody can be sure. Anyway, Earth was chosen for its safety, for its proximity to the wormholes that we navigate for our interstellar travel—and because your environment supported us easily. It was a match."

Kelsey had a hard time digesting everything that Jared was rattling off. The mitres had been here for more than two hundred years, undetected by humans—the thought gave her an eerie shiver.

"Where is the mitres?" she asked, a thought beginning to gain life in her mind.

Her husband smiled at her, a sly, warm look in his eyes. "You won't believe me if I tell you."

"Oh, I probably will." She laughed. Did Jared really believe she would doubt anything that came out of his mouth at this point? "Lay it on me."

He drew in a breath, tilted his chin upward, and leveled her with his most kingly gaze. "By Mirror Lake. That's where it's always been."

Mirror Lake. Where they'd met years earlier; where they'd shared their first kiss; where their tender memories of falling in love were wiped from their minds by the elders.

And where she and Jared had miraculously found one another once again on the night of his crash. Jared had once told her that her planet was extremely important to his people, that a long-standing tie between their two worlds existed. Now, the reality of those statements hit with the force of a blizzard wind. Her world was critical, priceless to Jared Bennett and his people.

"This mitres," she asked carefully, "what does it do? Really? Just time travel or . . . other things too?"

Jared dropped his gaze to his lap. "The mitres enables us to harness time itself, to bend it to our will as we become its master. The mitres is capable of altering time, creating portals of entry and exit throughout eternity and space. It gives us superiority over all our enemies who seek to kill our people." He paused, drawing in a breath, and Kelsey felt a chill snake down her spine. When Jared stared at her this intently, it always meant something would turn her world upside down. "And," he continued, "it's the only weapon giving us the advantage over Earth's enemies too. Otherwise, the Antousians would have destroyed you by now. Earth as you know it would no longer exist."

Kelsey absorbed his comments for a long time. Everything seemed to rush to the surface at once, each thought demanding air, sustenance, but she couldn't lock in on the most important thought and voice it. If this mitres technology was literally the only thing safeguarding Earth, then that meant the data in her mind was more crucial than she could ever have imagined. And that begged a very serious question: Was it better inside her mind or . . . outside?

It also drove home Jared's firm belief in the letter's authenticity. The author claimed that because she had the codes in her mind, she became a leader. The one the rebel Refarians—and the humans—rose up to follow. The author had called her the "Beloved of Refaria."

Maybe the information shouldn't be removed—and maybe her destiny demanded that it remain inside of her. Both were strong possibilities.

"I think I'm finally getting the picture here," she said at last, understanding that the mitres information in her mind was a far more serious matter than she'd yet realized.

"What does it mean that I'm the . . . 'Beloved of Refaria'?" Kelsey asked Jared, still sitting comfortably with him by the fire.

"Ah, love. That will take some time to explain. It ties

into our prophecies and mythology, but the shorthand version"—he paused, lifting a hand to touch her cheek—"is that you will bring healing and peace to my people. You will lead them."

"But you're their king," she whispered, feeling an eerie chill pass over her skin.

"And you are their queen—not just any queen, but one who has been foretold by our mystics."

"Could I read this prophecy?" she asked, a sudden hunger to understand her role burning within her.

"I will give you the book later tonight."

She smiled wickedly. "I'm not sure we'll be doing any reading later tonight, Jared."

He lifted a hand to her cheek, rubbing his knuckles against her jaw. She'd made no effort to contain her natural disarray of heavy auburn curls; this was Kelsey at her most beautiful, flushed by the fire, her hair unkempt and loose. Mating season or not, he felt a strong flash of desire for his soulmate. "Jared?" she prompted, glancing up at him. "Are you even listening to me?"

"I'm highly distracted by my wife and her"—he paused, just staring into her azure eyes—"exotic beauty."

Her large smile spread wider, and she squeezed his hand, still held in hers. "Maybe later I can distract you down in our bedroom," she practically purred. "I am the queen of distractions."

"Ah, my human queen, you are a wicked, dangerous woman to have on hand."

"Don't tell me you're still thinking of sending me back to Laramie?" she gasped, her lovely eyes ringed with instant panic. How had she interpreted his comment that way?

He slipped his other hand onto her shoulder, wanting to reassure her that his earlier decision to send her away had only been a momentary lapse of judgment. "No, no! I can't live apart from you—and you're truly safest here, where I can guard you myself." He gestured toward the letter in her hand. "The letter is a warning and a wake-up call. Our enemies are closing in upon us, and I won't have you anywhere but near me, right here in my camp." He gave her a seductive half smile. "*And* in my bed, love."

"Whew! That's a relief." She laughed joyously, tugging him down to the floor where she sat. She looped both arms about his neck, drawing his mouth toward hers for a kiss. "We have a lot of serious work to do—speaking of your bed."

A low, rumbling sound escaped his chest, but the supernatural fire he'd felt last night—the telltale physical signs that his mating heat had begun—still felt cool. He cupped her face in both hands, crushing his mouth against hers, a fierce display of his anger and passion. He desired her as much as ever, yet he knew his own D'Aravnian body better than she ever could. Something had shifted cold in him last night after finding the letter—and after the arrival of the visitors. Something that he couldn't seem to click back into gear.

Oh, gods in heaven, how will I tell her? he lamented, all the while plunging his tongue deep into the liquid warmth of her mouth. *Love, love*, he reflected, *I don't want to hurt you!*

Groping at his face with both hands, Kelsey pushed his mouth off of hers. "Hurt me how?" she demanded, all color draining from her face. "What aren't you telling me, Jared?"

"You weren't meant to hear that," he panted, still aroused from her kiss.

"Of course I heard it."

"No, those were my thoughts." He shook his head in disbelief; he'd never intended for her to hear what was in his mind. "Our bond must have . . . opened. Even though I never felt it engage."

"We're probably connected half the time now, Jared," she told him evenly, the scientist in her emerging. "I mean, our bond keeps intensifying and growing, keeps becoming a more natural part of us all the time."

He reached for her again, drawing her face closer toward his until he could feel her warm breath against his cheek.

"Tell me what you're hiding," she persisted. "I need to know." There was anguish in her voice that almost leveled him to his knees.

He drew in a shaky breath. "My . . . cycle." He couldn't bear to tell her the rest.

She began to laugh, a nervous, explosive sound. "Is that what this is about? Again? We've already talked about this, a bunch of times. I know it started for you when we bonded—"

"It's over," he told her bluntly. "My mating season has ended before it even began."

"That can't be true!" she insisted, shaking her head in stunned disbelief. "Last night—"

"Was probably the best I'm capable of," he explained hoarsely, gathering both of her hands into his own. "I've not cycled in all my thirty years, Kelse. I told you so, you know it. Something sparked in me after our mating and marriage, yes, but . . . with the turmoil of last night's events, it seems to have snuffed out the urges altogether."

"But you want me!" She clutched at his arms in desperation. "Just now, I felt how much you want me. This is insane."

He dropped his head, feeling his eyes sting with emotion. "I wish I were different, Kelse. I wish I were wrong."

"I refuse to accept this." She flung herself into his arms, burrowing against him. "Not without a fight. I felt what happened in you last night—I know what was starting."

"Perhaps I've given you a child already," he half whispered against the top of her head, but his voice sounded as dull as the words did to his heart.

She clung to him hard. "I won't give up, not like this."

He fought the urge to cry. If there was any single thing he ached for in all the universe, it was to make this woman happy. To give her a full life, children, family. A home. Gods, he wanted her to have it all; and he wanted to have it all with her. "Then, love, I shan't give up either," he lied. His heart pounded a dull, lifeless beat inside his chest.

She pulled apart from him, her eyes bright and alert. "You can talk to Thea," she suggested, full of excited enthusiasm. "That's it, she can totally advise you. I mean, you've told me she cycles—and a lot, right? Then you need to ask her for help and advice."

He grimaced. Kelsey was so intent on solving their

crisis that she wasn't thinking through the situation properly. "I couldn't hurt Thea that way."

Kelsey shook her head, over and over, as if she could deny their destiny—could prevent it from happening. "But she could help."

"I'll think about it. Right now we have other issues to address," he reminded her, reaching for the letter. "Like whether I can truly trust this Marco. According to his letter, he betrayed us a first time, and I need to make my decision about his presence in this camp."

Chapter Eight

Language Specialist Hope Harper stared at her computer screen, luminous in the dungeonlike darkness of her work cubicle, and blinked. Retrieving her eyeglasses from atop her head, she leaned in closer, needing to verify that her eyes hadn't misled her once again. Granted, she'd been translating intercepts for the past few days with hardly a break except to catch a few hours of sleep, but this latest batch seemed highly irregular. Working in linguistics for the FBI, she was accustomed to unusual data, to unrecognizable dialects or obscure languages. But these new intercepts were far more disturbing than any they'd had her transcribe before.

For months they'd had her working with the counterterrorism unit, code-breaking the same unknown language, running it through filters and programs and all sorts of data interpretation. Security had briefed her in so that she had the clearance for what she was doing, but she wondered why, despite that fact, they were keeping her on a need-to-know basis, telling her almost nothing about the language itself. Then, in the past weeks, her superiors had urged her to go deeper, further and further into her analysis until she could practically speak the strange language in her sleep—and until she'd finally become convinced as to the truth of what she was actually dealing with. *Lost dialect my ass,* she thought, adjusting her Bose headphones, listening for perhaps the thousandth time to the man known sometimes as Jared, other times as J'Areshkadau, rattle off instructions and other directives in his native tongue.

The language was totally alien, not any undiscovered

eastern European dialect as they had suggested to her—classic cover story. Her higher-ups didn't say it and they didn't have to. She was no idiot, and listening to the latest cassette tape—an aerial transmission intercepted by the Air Force—only confirmed one fact: The people they were tailing were into some serious, heavy stuff. But it wasn't her job to question or interpret, at least not in this case, only to analyze data. She had wondered, too, why they hadn't simply sent the tapes off to headquarters; after all, they had an entire language team there in DC. Surely someone would have been better equipped to handle the case. But they'd chosen her. For whatever bizarre, inexplicable reason, she was the one with the job.

In the past ten days the heat surrounding the case had been turned up considerably. More military intercepts had been sent in to the Denver office where she worked, and although she wasn't certain, she believed there had been some kind of crash over in the Yellowstone area of Wyoming. She'd heard rumblings to that effect within the counterterrorism unit, though she was being kept in the dark by her superiors. She couldn't shake the sense that there was a connection.

But at least she had an inside track on information. Her twin brother, Chris, was the lone special agent manning the Jackson, Wyoming, office, in charge of more than twenty-five thousand square miles of backwoods territory. Usually he focused on bank robberies, the occasional Al Qaeda suspect, violent crimes—but if there'd been a crash in Yellowstone he'd be right in the thick of things. That's why she'd been pestering him for days trying to get more details. So far, he'd kept quiet except to indicate through slight voice inflections that she was onto something with the link between the crash and her case. But that was the way with them; as children, they'd shared their own private language, often not even needing to exchange a word aloud. They still possessed their intuitive understanding, even now, well into adulthood. Her family had laughed at their "twintuition," as they called it; as adults it sometimes still served them well.

Leaning forward in her chair, she began typing an e-mail to Chris.

Special Agent Harper:
Am thinking of ski trip to Jackson Hole. Want to do some boarding?
Your loving sis

That ought to get a response, she thought with a mischievous grin. Chris smothered her like a doting father, and it always ticked him off that she continued to snowboard despite her illness and, now, the ever-increasing problems with her eyesight. But she needed to hear his take on recent events, and the only way to get that out of him was in person over a few beers.

Almost immediately a reply appeared in her in-box, Chris practically shouting at her across cyberspace that she was insane and going to get herself killed one of these days. Then after his cyber-rant he added much more pleasantly that he'd love to see her. She picked up the phone and dialed his number at the Jackson FBI office.

Marco pulled his Chevy truck up to the main cabin, his lungs barely able to fill with oxygen. It seemed he'd begun to hold his breath eight miles back down the road. He hadn't seen Thea again since she'd left his room last night, but it hardly meant he hadn't thought of her. She crowded his brain with images and memories and feelings, all of them as alien as they were familiar.

Sabrina, riding at his side in silence, had been right that his need to follow Jared, to serve at his side, wasn't the only thing luring him back to the compound. Thea Haven possessed a mystic's power. She had lain with him, in his bed—he, a ridiculously underexperienced virgin—tantalizing him to the far edge of his self-control. In that moment, he'd known what it would be to make love to Thea, over and over, tumbling in her arms, inhaling her wildflower scent, pushing her lithe, petite body beneath his own massive one.

Did he remember making love to her in some other lifetime? Not exactly, but the memory-thoughts were so fresh, so powerful, that he had no way of determining what they'd actually experienced together and what might be glimpses of their future. His hands tightened around the steering wheel, trembling against his will.

Beside him Sabrina sat up tall in her seat. "So this is it," she said, watching as three soldiers filed out of the cabin and toward their vehicle. She turned to him curiously as the men raised their weapons, gesturing for them to remain in the Chevy.

"I didn't say he trusted me yet." Marco held up both hands as the soldiers approached the vehicle. "But he will."

Their doors were opened simultaneously, and Marco was wrangled outside roughly, then pressed face-first against the side of the Suburban. Hands frisked him, confirming that he was unarmed, and he endured the entire process patiently. Jared would come to trust him—all of the Madjin—soon enough.

"The main compound is connected to Base Ten via an elevator-shaft system," Thea explained to Marco as they stepped into the corridor that led to the transport loft. She was keenly aware of his body near to hers, just behind her, and rued once again that she had somehow been tapped to give him a tour of their base facility. "We chose this location because of its position atop an old mining shaft. We installed a state-of-the-art elevator system, easily converting the former structure to suit our needs."

Arriving at the elevator, she pressed the panel. Beside her Marco listened, nodding dutifully, but she had the distinct impression he wasn't hearing a word she said. When the lift arrived, the doors slid open noiselessly and they stepped inside. Staring up at the lit panel that indicated the ten levels they had to descend, she struggled to keep her body in check. Being so near to Marco—and now in such confined quarters—was almost more than she could bear.

Reaching around her, he slammed his hand against the panel, causing the elevator to stop middescent.

"What are you doing?" she demanded hotly.

"This." He cupped her shoulders in his large hands, backing her against the elevator wall. His massive body pushed against hers; his hot breath fanned her cheek.

"And this," he murmured, reaching for both of her hands. Their fingers threaded together as if they were one. Slowly, he lifted her hands over her head, pinning them against the wall. The position caused her full breasts to strain within her uniform top. With his knee, he spread her thighs apart. From top to bottom, he'd laid her bare.

She could hardly breathe and he just stood there, sliding his gaze up and down her very exposed body. "I like you like this," he whispered huskily, licking his lips. "You belong this way."

"Looking like you're about to take me?" she gasped, and he spread her hands a bit wider over her head, tightening his grip on her.

"Yes," he agreed thickly, leaning his dark head closer until she noticed the damp, curling hairs along his nape. From the snow, she thought, but then she noticed his heavy breathing and a thin sheen of perspiration on his forehead. "I want to take you," he said. He worked his knee between her thighs, up and down, massaging her until she felt her panties grow damp.

"Last night you said we couldn't be together," she ground out, gasping. "Now?"

"Now?" He released her hands, letting them fall to her side, and began unbuttoning her uniform top. "I want *this* now." He growled as her shirt fell open.

"But you told me it's forbidden."

"It is—in the worst possible way."

With his fingertips, he slowly stroked both of her nipples, watching as they puckered beneath the silken material of her bra. Thea snapped her head toward the elevator panel. "Someone will notice—they might send an engineer, thinking we're stuck."

He tracked with her, looking at the panel, then turned back and, in one smooth gesture, covered her mouth with his own. She opened to him, unable to resist, and his rough tongue darted inside her mouth, seeking her out. His breathing became heavier, layered atop a low, keening growl—the sound of a Refarian male at his most aroused. She closed her arms around his neck, threading her hands through his silky black hair, then rubbing them lower down his back, feeling every line of his powerfully muscled shoulders and back. He had the body of a god—sleek, massive, seductive.

She thrust her hips against him, and in turn he wedged his hard thigh firmly between her legs. They began to rock together, he steadying her hips beneath his palms, working the motion of their two bodies; she edgier, perhaps more eager. So eager that she seemed to rush ahead of the motion he created, unable to hold back. She heard a rumble of his laughter, and he stilled her hips—forcing them back against the elevator wall. "Slow down, baby. Slow."

She gasped, sucked in air, tried to still her heart. He stroked a lock of loose hair back from her eyes, slipping it between his fingers like a caress. "You have such beautiful hair." He sighed. "So rare and gold—I'd never even seen this color before I got to this planet." He lifted the lock to his lips and, closing his eyes, kissed the ends ever so slowly. Thea felt the dampness between her legs grow hotter.

"I-I'm from the border lands—you probably never went there as a boy."

"I never left Thearnsk," he agreed, still stroking her hair, working her ponytail loose until the curling, thick locks fell to shoulder length.

He sucked in a breath. "I love you with your hair down," he said, his black eyes widening.

She felt her face flush hot and stared at the far wall of the elevator. "I wear it back because of work."

"You shouldn't." He gathered handfuls of it, kneading it, then leaned in close and began to sniff. Her hair, her neck, her chest—gods help her, her breasts! Heatedly, he growled his pleasure, slipping her bra off of her shoulders until at last his lips made contact with one bare, exposed nipple. Drawing it into his mouth, he cupped the rest of her breast within his rough palm. The feel of his skin against hers, his warm mouth over her cool nipple, caused Thea to arch her back, her own body quaking with hot, wet tremors. She slapped her open palm against the wall, tamping down her overpowering desire to scream Marco's name at the top of her voice.

Curling heat began to roll from the center of her being, unfurling over her body, touching her toes, the top of her head. *My Change! I'm going to Change!*

But she couldn't stop. Marco urged her downward, dropping to his knees, slowly sliding her along the elevator wall until she was on the floor, legs open wide to him. He knelt between her thighs, working them even farther apart. His jeans bulged in front, and kneeling there—right between her legs—she couldn't believe how large and prominent his shaft obviously was.

"What . . . are . . . we"—Thea gasped, sucking in a hot breath—"doing? Please . . . someone will come. Someone will know. . . ."

He hesitated, and she reached with both hands and stroked his thighs. Just barely, she slipped her fingertips over his erection, caressing him. His eyes drifted shut and he growled again, louder than before, so she stroked him again—back and forth beneath the material of his blue jeans. Throwing his head back, he voiced a cry of pleasure, but then shocked her by stilling her hand. For a long moment, their gazes locked and it seemed she felt him inside of her mind. Intimate, within her, whispering. *You're damned beautiful, baby. I could love you . . .*

Was it a past memory? She couldn't be sure, but it made her shiver with an eerie sense of being invaded by another time.

Marco seemed to sense it too, his dark face—flushed by the heat of their tussling—seemed to pale slightly. He dropped back onto the floor from his kneeling position. "We've gotta stop," he announced heavily, burying his face in both hands.

"Someone might come," she agreed flatly. Still, she didn't want to stop—not for a moment. She made up her mind. "But I don't care!" she announced, reaching for him, gathering his dark hands within her own much paler ones.

"I'm sorry, Thea. I can't control myself with you. It's absurd"—he dropped his hands away, staring her hard in the eyes—"but I swear to All that I can't."

She smiled, leaning forward until her lips met his. She cupped his face in both of her hands. "I didn't say I minded," she teased him, giggling. "Just that I didn't want the Refarian army to bust me in the elevator shaft. *Your* shaft in the shaft, know what I mean?"

He stroked her face with his fingertips. "This is all wrong, Thea. I shouldn't have . . ."

Her smile turned downward into a frown. "You're not still insisting that you're not allowed—"

"I'm *not* allowed, Thea."

She wrestled past him, leaping to her feet. "Your vows are ridiculous! Stupid!" she spat angrily, launching toward the control panel and hitting the button. "And wholly unfair." The elevator lurched, resuming its descent, and still Marco knelt on the floor, gazing up at her. His black hair was disheveled, his dark eyes wide and filled with emotion, and his jutting erection was still prominent in the front of his pants. He looked for all the world as if she'd been about to take his virginity. Only his hard-on proved that she hadn't.

She knocked her head against the panel. "Please—don't do this to me again unless you mean to finish it."

Chapter Nine

Sabrina knelt before Jared, her familiar blond head lowered in a subservient pose. She looked no different than she had on that last day he'd seen her so many years ago. It was almost as if time itself were playing a trick on him. Of course he knew she was a shape-shifter and could assume any form that pleased her. He himself could appear eternally youthful if he wanted to, but apparently, unlike Sabrina, he had no desire to appear younger than his natural age—gray hairs and all. Or maybe she'd simply chosen a form that would be most familiar to him, rather than that of a nearly sixty-year-old woman.

Her chest rose and fell with anxious breaths, her sweater visibly vibrating with the obvious thundering of her heart. She was nervous as hell; of course she was. His own stomach roiled with anxiety since he had no idea what he would say to the woman he had always regarded as the true mother of his heart. The one who had sat with him for hours as a boy, coaching and training him to be king, answering his endless, thoughtful questions. The night of his parents' murder Sabrina had held him close in her arms for hours, just rocking him as he cried. And when the next day dawned, his whole life had utterly changed. His people had crowned him as king when he was only ten years old.

After his coronation, Sabrina had never spoken to him the same way again, becoming much more formal and distant in their relations. He was no longer a prince—overnight he'd become not only a ruler of an entire kingdom, but the official military leader of a widespread warfare campaign. It would have been too much for any young man's shoulders, but was nearly unbearable for a child. No wonder he had needed Sabrina, had relied on her so completely.

In the months that followed, Sabrina still stayed close to him, but her tutelage morphed and became more intense. Even now Jared attributed much of his leadership acumen to Sabrina Y'lansk, the very woman who knelt before him now.

Staring down at her, he knew he should be angry; he should feel betrayed that she'd never returned to him that last night in the palace. And he *certainly* had every right to feel abandoned. But most of all he should be furious that during all his time on Earth, she'd been secretly running the Madjin in circles around him. *Why didn't she come to me?* he reflected, staring down at her mutely.

Yes, he should feel betrayed, furious, bitter; the list of appropriate emotions was multifold. But what he wanted—desperately wanted more than anything else—was simply to cry. To fall to his knees and weep like a little boy in the presence of his long-lost mother. His heart ached so hard in his chest, he could hardly breathe. His throat tightened convulsively. What could he possibly say to this woman who had raised him for the first years of his life? It was like she'd come back from the dead, and he was at an utter loss for words in any language.

With a trembling hand, he reached to touch the top of her head, noticing for some reason the contrast between her fair hair and his own very dark skin. They'd always been different, she Madjin and he a born king; their physical differences only underscored their class distinctions. Slowly he settled his palm over the crown of her head, blowing out a weary, emotion-filled sigh.

She shook visibly at his touch. "My lord, I-I wish . . ."

She never finished her sentence. For a long moment Jared waited, hoping she would speak her heart. He ached to hear her say more, anything at all. *I wish we'd never been parted. I wish you hadn't been exiled. I wish that I'd protected you from a host of things I couldn't protect you from.* Was that what his near-mother wished? He longed to hear those things from her like a child yearns for his parents' approval and praise.

"Rise, Sabrina Y'lansk. Rise and speak freely."

She nodded, slowly lifting her gaze toward him. Tears shone in her brown eyes, and it was a visible struggle for her to compose herself. "I tried to come back to you," she whispered in a choked voice. "That night. I would have moved the heavens to reach you. To have spared you so much pain."

Averting his eyes, he pushed past her toward the far side of the room. He stared out the large glass windows, bracing both hands on the window frame over his head. Outside the snow showers continued, swirling white in every direction, blinding the valley below with sheets of hoary precipitation.

Finally, she continued: "I've thought so many times how I might have reached you that night."

"But you didn't," he told her flatly. "I was left alone, and the Antousians came. . . ." He shook his head, unable to finish; the memories were too powerful and engulfing.

He heard a soft sob from behind him, then silence for long moments while he simply stood and stared at the pure whiteness of the world beyond the windowpanes. His own planet was polluted, dirty. Ruined. Sometimes he was thankful to be gone—seeing Sabrina amplified every heartbroken memory he'd brought along with him of his lost home.

"I-I was afraid that if I came to the palace, they would find you," she explained in a strangled voice. "I never wanted to leave you like that."

He whirled toward her, furious. "And yet you've lived here on Earth—knowing I was near—and never came to reveal yourself. You've hidden from me, your king. Your lord." Bitterness tinged his every word. "That is not the behavior of a mother or a protector," he insisted, shaking his head indignantly. "You were my Madjin, Sabrina. The only one I had in my life who could have stood between me and harm, but you left me to th-those—" He broke off, unable to voice his emotions without stammering. For a few seconds he gathered his composure, turning back to face her. "You left me to those *vledjasks* like meat thrown to the wolves."

She folded both arms over her chest and began to cry. Tears of anguish seeped down both her cheeks, her mouth twisted into an expression of such heart-rending pain that Jared's own eyes stung. The room all around him, and Sabrina, grew blurry. "I was only a boy," he continued hoarsely as his own tears began to fall, hot on his face. "I wasn't ready for the Antousians. I wasn't ready to lead, not really. I was a child and you were my mother. You were the only real mother I ever had." His own mother, distant and aristocratic, had never opened her heart to her son.

Sabrina was across the room, opening her arms to him before he could say another word, making a pained sound like the cry of a small bird. "Jareshk." She tugged at both his shoulders, pulling him down and into her motherly embrace. She began to shush him in their shared language like a little boy, and that only made him cry harder. He was half a foot taller than her now, and pressed his face against her hair, breathing in her scent. Gods, he'd lost everything since the day he'd last seen this woman. His innocence. So much—too much. The war had extracted a higher price than even she might imagine.

But he'd found important parts of himself over the years too, like his soulmate.

"I've a wife," he murmured against the top of her head. "A mate."

Sabrina began to laugh, and pulled apart to stare up into his eyes. An expression of such joy lit her tear-filled eyes, he wasn't sure he had ever seen her so happy when he was a boy. "Yes, I know," she said, still laughing. "Kelsey Wells Bennett. We know all about our new queen. And I'm so happy for you, dear Jareshk. So very, very happy that you've found love." Then she did something that took him back at least twenty years: She lifted her fingertips to his cheek and slowly stroked his face as if he were still a little boy.

"How do you know about Kelsey?" He thought back to last night, how Marco and Riley had seemingly known all about their new queen.

Sabrina's smile slipped a bit. "Marco told me you know about Anika."

He closed his eyes. He'd yet to delve into that particular perfidy. "Why didn't she tell me she was a protector?" he demanded, anger and hurt twining hotly together. "Why did you instruct her to stay silent about her true calling?"

Sabrina stepped apart from him, once again inclining her head respectfully. "She asked me—many times—for permission to tell you everything. I thought she could protect you better without your knowing."

Jared nodded but he didn't understand, nor did he forgive Anika for her deception. Hers was the ultimate betrayal. They'd been friends—very close friends—for all their time serving together, and now he knew that she'd never once given up her secrets. The woman was Madjin, mated when he'd believed her single . . . How had he ever thought her one of his dearest, best friends?

"How many of you are there?" he asked. "Anika and Anna here in my camp—anyone else that I should know about?"

"There are only the five of us. We're all that remains of the Madjin."

"That makes five more Madjin than I'd have said still existed."

"It's not the powerful numbers that once completed our Circle," she observed. "But it's a start at rebuilding."

He nodded, stepping apart; he needed distance again. Needed time to gather all of his thoughts. And, most of all, he needed Sabrina's guidance, after so many years. "Kelsey has the mitres data inside her mind," he told her bluntly. "I'm sure you already know that from Anika."

Sabrina gave a brisk nod, running her hand thoughtfully down the length of her braid. It was a gesture he had observed many times in his childhood.

"We have to retrieve it—and soon." He wouldn't tell her why the retrieval was so urgent since Marco's letter was going to stay a secret between Kelsey and him.

"You placed it within her, correct?"

"I had no other choice at the time," he lamented, still painfully sorry that he'd been forced to rely on Kelsey to safeguard that kind of powerful intelligence. "But we have to get it out."

"If you placed it within her, then you're the right person to extricate it from her mind."

"I don't think so." He stared into the roaring fire. "I'm too clumsy with my gifts. After my crash, I was empowered by my rushing adrenaline, my desperate state . . . otherwise I probably would've been unsuccessful in linking up with Kelsey to begin with."

"I doubt that, my lord. She is your true soulmate. You'd connected with her years earlier—it was the power of that connection that enabled you to leave the data inside of her."

He glanced over his shoulder and couldn't help smiling. "You really do know everything, don't you?"

"I've followed your movements and your life very closely. I've watched over you faithfully."

He closed his eyes. "I put her in a lot of danger. It was a reckless thing to do to someone I love."

"You didn't know—"

"No, a part of me always knew. I've loved Kelsey since I was almost sixteen years old—I just spent years unable to remember that fact."

"What makes you think you're too unskilled with intuition to help her? You're her bondmate. That carries a lot of power."

"I'm awkward and untrained—Thea's the one to do it."

"Then why have you waited to ask for her help?"

Oh, such a pointed, difficult question. "She's very angry about my marriage." That was the simple answer, when in fact his feelings on the matter were much more complex—he didn't want to hurt Thea, but it was more than that too. He felt guilty that he'd never loved his cousin in the way that she'd wanted.

"That doesn't matter. This is a serious security and military issue." Sabrina gave a brisk, serious nod. "If you believe Thea's the one to undertake the effort, then Thea should work with her queen."

"Something keeps holding me back," he admitted honestly. "Maybe because I'm scared of putting Kelsey in danger."

Sabrina gave him a sage smile. "But she knew the risks going into your marriage."

That much was true. But the thing he most feared was what he hadn't yet voiced—they didn't just need to retrieve the data. They needed to upload it into the mitres itself, which meant putting his lifemate in the direct path of danger because he felt certain that US officials had been watching Mirror Lake since the night of his accident. It was the one crucial fact he'd been dodging for days, even though putting the thought into the atmosphere made him shiver with palpable apprehension.

"For this to work," he finally said, "really work, Kelsey has to enter the chamber."

Chapter Ten

Thea's commander had required many sacrifices from her over the years, some of them difficult to grant, others almost impossible to bear. But Jared couldn't be serious about this latest assignment. And she told him so in a whisper, both hands clenched and trembling at her sides. "Please tell me you understand how difficult this would be for me."

Jared gazed out over the flight hangar from their position in the ready room above, solemn in his demeanor, but did not reply. His dark eyes swept across the deck below them, taking in every plane, every engineer, every possibility. At last, he cleared his throat but never turned to face her. "You must do it," he insisted simply, bracing both hands on the instrument console. "I have no other course of action."

"You have plenty of other choices, cousin!" she shouted at his back. The situation infuriated her as much as it terrified her.

Slowly he turned to face her, a gentle smile on his face. "So I am your *cousin* again, not just your commander? Does this signal your forgiveness?"

Thea closed her eyes. "I can't stay angry with you, Jared—not about your marriage, you know that. I told you I wanted you to be happy."

His smile faded. "But that didn't mean you weren't upset."

"I cannot enter the human's mind." She shook her head emphatically. "It's too personal, too intimate—"

He took a step toward her. "Too intimate for

Kelsey?" His voice softened. "Or too intimate for *you*, dear cousin?"

"For me!" She flung both hands in the air. "Of course for me!"

"She won't be able to know your thoughts," he told her quietly. "She's human."

"She's mated to you," Thea replied, working to keep her voice calm and even. She felt anything but calm on the inside. "A link between you both would be the best way to accomplish this transfer."

"No, it needs to be with a true intuitive like you."

Suddenly, Thea had a realization—something she should have thought of before this moment. "What makes you so sure that your gifts haven't passed on to her? If they have, then—"

Jared lifted a regal hand, silencing her. "Because she is human," he repeated, his voice edged with audible tension.

From his tone, Thea realized Jared actually worried that he *had* passed his Refarian gifts on to his new wife; naturally he would wonder what such transference might mean to her weaker human anatomy.

"For all we know, when humans and Refarians mate, they do receive our gifts," she persisted. "We know little of her species, especially in these . . . intimate matters." Thea's faced burned suddenly and she noticed that her cousin's did too.

He stared at the floor between them, avoiding her gaze. "I know my wife extremely well, cousin. Extremely. For many years now I have known her—"

"What does that mean? I thought you met her at Mirror Lake a few weeks ago."

"Years ago, Thea. I met her at Mirror Lake years ago." He lifted his gaze, staring meaningfully into her eyes. "The elders wiped our memories of each other—and so I must protect her, don't you see? They allowed this marriage, but it was not easy convincing them."

"That can't be true. The elders would never betray you that way."

"But they did." He leveled his most serious gaze at her and she knew he was telling her the truth. "They recognized our connection even as mere children. I was fifteen that summer, coming of age. They knew I-I . . ." His voice trailed off, the blush in his dark face deepening.

"You were entering your first season," she finished simply.

He gave a solemn nod, but said nothing more. Suddenly Jared's bond with his wife came into sharp, obvious relief. He had experienced his awakening with her. No wonder their reconnection, all these years later, had proved so powerful and the bond so overwhelmingly easy to engage. She had captured his heart at the most crucial moment for any Refarian male—the moment of his sexual and spiritual stirring. To have found someone he loved at that precise moment—well, Thea could hardly blame her king for having chased that kind of love across the galaxies, never fully forgetting.

She closed her eyes, trying to process his revelations. "They wiped your memories—both of yours?" she asked. "But somehow you remembered?"

"When we met again and I made the temporary bond with her in order to leave the data—our connection from those many years ago was reopened. They couldn't keep us from one another."

"Apparently not." Despite herself, bitterness tinged her words, but Jared either refused to acknowledge it or did not notice.

He clasped her shoulder, his dark gaze locking with her own. "If they catch wind of the mitres data inside her mind . . ." Jared wrapped both dark arms around himself in a protective gesture, his voice growing intense and quiet. "I need your help, Thea. Please don't deny what I beg of you. Please don't refuse Kelsey, either. She needs you even more than I."

Suddenly all her excuses seemed pale and flimsy in the face of Jared's earnest plea. "Are you certain I'm the right one?" she asked. "You're as intuitive as I am."

"Hardly." He snorted in self-derision. "I'm completely awkward and unskilled. You know how weak my abilities are."

"And whose fault is that?" She couldn't help smiling. Jared had always been self-deprecating when it came to his gods-given gifts.

"I'm a leader, a rebel, a soldier—"

"And a natural-born intuitive who has always denied his giftings," she urged him, reaching out to touch his arm. "Why wouldn't you try to reach into her mind? You left the data there."

"Because I love her, Thea. And right now, she's in tremendous danger. You are the only one I trust to do this—and to do it right."

Thea was out of arguments. She bristled at the thought of a temporary link with the woman who had stolen her intended, but she still served her king with all her heart and her mind, and this was what he now required.

"When? Tell me when."

"Tonight. But the more important question, cousin, is where."

Thea's eyebrows shot up toward her hairline. It had never once occurred to her that the location would be important. "I just assumed—"

"You and a team must take her to the mitres," he answered evenly. "That, Lieutenant, is why this mission is so critical. It's about Kelsey, yes, but it's about the future of our resistance as well. You must take my wife into the chamber this night. And help download the codes from within her . . . into the mitres weapon."

All at once Thea swore the future opened before her eyes—and what she saw ahead of them, the entire army of their rebellion, was only murky, concealed danger.

The transport lifted smoothly off the ground, a fluid motion enabled by the craft's soundless motor and advanced propulsion. Unlike the Refarians' stealth fighter planes, which were launched via a catapult system from within the mountain, the transports were somewhat like the humans' helicopters—only sleeker, stealthy, and undetectable. Thea knew that heading to Mirror Lake wasn't a safe move, not after Jared's recent crash nearby. By all rights they should stay clear of the location for a few months, but despite her aversion to linking with the human, she had to agree with Jared about the mission's priority.

She'd given it a great deal of thought, all afternoon

and into the evening hours leading up to this moment. Now, despite her earlier complaints, she felt edgy. Ready. Determined. She had trained for moments precisely like this one. Besides, she hadn't spent so many months studying Prince Arienn's journals about the mitres and its significance not to feel a sense of hushed expectation about entering the chamber. It would be an almost holy moment for her. It was the seat of their power, their one true weapon that could turn the tide in this godsforsaken war that had gone on too long.

And Kelsey Wells Bennett contained the power to unlock it all, a fact that both galled her and awed her at the exact same time.

Thea buckled in on the transport's side bench, avoiding Kelsey, who faced her across the aisle. For a brief moment, however, their gazes locked. Her new queen wore a determined, almost proud expression on her freckled face, her wild hair drawn back into a tight braid for the occasion. Thea gave her a curt nod of acknowledgment; the woman was beautiful, to a degree. But Thea had no doubt that it was far more than Kelsey's looks that had snared her cousin. The human possessed a strong intelligence, visible even in her simplest glances. It was something that, despite all her inner complaints, attracted Thea to the human. Made her want to know Kelsey. But she quickly dismissed the thought, glancing away from her and about the transport.

Four of them were going on the mission: Scott, Kelsey, Thea, and—gods help her—Marco. When Jared had flagged Marco for such an important mission, she'd been surprised. Why would her commander trust his new bride with someone he hardly knew at all, and just because he said he was a protector? She pegged his reasoning on whatever had transpired during her king's long meeting with Sabrina, after which Jared had emerged from his upstairs study and begun firing off orders.

Marco was buckled in two seats down from her, an empty space between them. Thank the gods! Every part of her body and mind was aware of his close physical proximity. She'd managed to give him the full tour of the base without another "encounter," but only barely. There'd been another odd moment inside the dark elders' chambers when she'd sworn he was going to kiss her all over again. The man needed to decide what was and wasn't possible for a Madjin; he couldn't keep leading her to the edge, tempting her, then backing away.

He'd entered the transport after her, and for a brief moment their gazes had locked. Impossible, but he seemed even more beautiful than before, his face half shadowed by a late-day beard, his skin appearing darker and his eyes even richer than the night before. His bloodline was so purely Refarian that she marveled that he walked around Jackson without shifting. Not that he didn't appear fully human, but the dangerous darkness that seemed to emanate from his very soul felt distinctly Refarian to her. It was the same kind of dark grace that Jared possessed. Natural, exotic, gorgeous.

The transport headed smoothly off the mountain and into the inky darkness surrounding the Tetons. It was well past one a.m., a time they had pegged as the safest for entering the mitres chamber undetected. Suddenly from beside her she heard the clattering sound of a harness unbuckling. Marco was sliding one seat over to sit directly beside her!

Panicked, she faced forward, training her eyes on Kelsey. The woman smiled at her, a warm and open look on her face that only made Thea feel even more trapped. Marco settled next to her, his muscular thigh pushing into hers as he began refastening his harness. *Why the hell did you move?* she wanted to demand. It had been so much easier without feeling his firm body pushing against hers, which only reminded her of what it had been like to lie in his arms last night.

It was all she could do not to groan out loud. Against her cheek she felt sudden hot breath. "You seemed lonely over here," he whispered in her ear—so low only she would hear.

She cut her eyes sideways at him in annoyance. He knew what they'd agreed upon last night and then again today—after all, he'd been the one who insisted they couldn't get together. He returned her gaze with a sexy half smile—and once again his single dimple appeared. Every look he gave her, every time he smiled, it seemed he was intentionally seducing her.

"So, are you?" he asked a little more loudly.

"No, *Mr. McKinley*, I am preparing myself mentally for our mission," she shot back at him. "I thought, as a Madjin, you would be all about that."

He gave her a serious nod. "Already done. Of course I'll continue honing my perceptions," he said, "but it's a good twenty minutes to Mirror Lake."

Just enough time for you to taunt me, she thought, again closing her eyes. She rubbed both her palms over her thighs, working to still her thoughts. To center herself. But then she felt the electric heat of Marco's knuckles barely graze her hand. Such a subtle touch, it was meant only for her. She kept her eyes closed, aching to feel him again. He shifted slightly in his seat, pushing his hip firmly against hers.

She didn't move. She kept perfectly still, ablaze with fire. Here it was again! She craved her Change so suddenly, so unexpectedly, all because he had touched her hand. No man had ever elicited such natural desires in her. Briefly, she lingered on an image of revealing herself to Marco. Of standing before him, naked, and then in the power of a moment, transforming to her most natural form.

Would he be shocked? Horrified? Last night he'd claimed to know all about her dual nature.

She licked her lips in heated anticipation, feeling her hands tremble against her thighs. She'd never been more physically aware of anyone than she was of Marco. The man was a terrible seducer of women. How could he possibly claim to be a virgin, with these kinds of deliberate maneuvers?

"I don't have enough room," she finally managed to choke out, her voice sounding like that of a panting schoolgirl.

"Hmm," was all he said, but he didn't budge. She turned sideways in her seat and found him smiling at her again, a faint blush having crept into his dark face.

"Could you move over a bit?"

"I *could*," he teased—again intentionally keeping his voice so low that it wouldn't be heard by Kelsey or Scott from where they were seated across the aisle.

"You're impossible," she muttered under her breath.

He leaned his head close beside hers, breathing against her cheek. "Why, Lieutenant Haven, am I bothering you?"

She said nothing, only gave him a scathing glance, feeling her face burn as if she were in heat. He laughed softly, and at last shifted in his seat, giving her a bit more room.

Strange, but as badly as she'd wanted him to move, now that he had, she wanted nothing so much as to have him near again.

They touched down at the base of the rocky incline where the mitres chamber was located. She had made the climb before, in the daylight, and while it wasn't easy, it was traversable enough. Now she wore her night-vision goggles, as did all the others, and worked to regulate her breathing. She knew the human authorities were nearby, the FBI from what they had been told, but positioned on the far side of the lake. Their transport's stealth was leagues ahead of anything the humans possessed, so they had easily flown under the humans' noses without detection. A quick drop, and the transport had jetted away soundlessly, leaving their team of four here on the ground.

It was time to move quickly, they all knew that, and Scott began the climb, assuming the lead. Kelsey followed after, then Marco, and now Thea had the rear.

There were a few scrawny lodgepole pines, but mostly scratchy little saplings, the kind that grew from crevices. Parts of the trail grew more thickly wooded, and at those times Thea increased her pace, not wanting to fall behind the others—all of whom had longer strides than she did. Yet again, as at so many other critical military junctures, she cursed her petite size.

Arriving at the top of the trail, a large outcropping of rocks jutted toward the lake below. They stepped into the cleft that dipped back into the side of the cliff. Now was the moment they had spent so many years waiting and hoping for. Thea prayed that the data truly was secure within Kelsey's mind.

The group of them crouched low, Marco taking a security position, studying the trail and the sweeping landscape below for enemies of either the Antousian or human variety. Scott urged Kelsey against the side of a large boulder, wordlessly indicating the most secure position. His pulse rifle in hand, he too assumed a protective position. Even with his night-vision goggles on, Thea could read the message in Scott's eyes: *Get on with it, and let's get out of here. Fast.*

Kelsey gave a nod, extending both of her hands—a receptive gesture that surprised Thea. None of their own species was so open, not after so many years of warfare. Wordlessly, Thea drew both of Kelsey's hands within her own, focusing all of her intuitive abilities on a mind-link. With a shiver, she immediately felt the woman's consciousness. Thea bristled, wanting to retreat, but Kelsey was so forceful, so open, so focused, that it was almost as if she chased after Thea. After her initial recoil, Thea pushed forward again, this time meeting Kelsey in the center of the tentative link.

Can you hear me? came the human's familiar voice within her own mind.

Yes. I can hear you. Unlike Kelsey, her own voice sounded belligerent.

How do we . . . do this? Kelsey replied, her voice soft but confident.

You don't do anything. I do it.

Of course. I'm ready.

There is a portal here; the mitres will only open if I first link with you, Thea explained tersely, *which we are doing—and then access the data to connect with the portal.*

Go ahead. I'm ready.

Thea marveled that Kelsey never seemed to know fear or apprehension; she always propelled herself right into things.

Thea worked into her human mind, felt, sensed memories and experiences, all manner of intimate impressions. She acknowledged none of them, dwelled on none of them. She would honor Kelsey's vulnerability by preserving as much of her privacy as possible. The only time she hesitated was over a memory that held particular power—the death of Kelsey's mother. Thea paused then, closing her eyes, remembering her own mother's death.

They had something in common, a strange thought for Thea—something else in common besides a love for Jared. But then she pressed onward, at last locating the data, lodged hard within Kelsey's subconscious, but it was there—and intact—nonetheless.

I have it! Thea proclaimed excitedly. Across their link she felt Kelsey's own thrilled reaction.

What now? the human asked, sounding almost breathless.

We create the portal and the four of us—Thea glanced at Marco and Scott where they squatted on the edge of the cliff, guarding the two of them—*move inside the chamber.*

Chapter Eleven

Marco found himself face-first on a cold, smooth floor. Somewhere. Nowhere. He had no idea how he'd landed where he was, and it almost seemed as if his arms and legs were made of thick rubber. His stomach rolled with nausea, and as he worked to move his fingers, the air around him thickened.

Last he remembered Thea and Kelsey had been mind-linked outside the mitres chamber, working to upload the codes. He recalled the twin expressions of intense concentration on both their faces—each with her eyes closed, each seemingly reaching beyond the moment. After that, there'd been a bright blue ring that formed around the four of them, swirling and undulating as it tightened like a lasso about their group.

Then only free-falling through memories, impressions, images. He saw the ranch he'd lived on in Idaho. The palace hill in Thearnsk. A lifetime of memories and half-remembered places, all lost to him now. Then . . . nothing. This dark, dank place with the cold floor, and a body that refused to bend to his will.

"Thea?" he mumbled, his mouth thick as gauze.

He felt someone nudge his booted foot. No answer. Soft groaning. Then, "Dimensional . . . sickness." That was Thea. "Arienn . . . wrote . . . about it."

Pressing his forehead against the cold floor, he gasped for air. So they'd been successful—they had managed to create a portal and enter the chamber.

Someone else stirred, off to his right. With a painful movement he managed to turn his head sideways. Scott Dillon was sitting upright, his face buried in both hands.

He appeared in better shape than the rest of them. Farther away from them he heard a soft, feminine moan that he was pretty sure came from his queen. *Must . . . recover. Kelsey. Queen*, he thought foggily. Struggling past every unholy physical sensation, he managed to lift onto his knees at last.

Thea lay on her side, near to him. She had been the one to touch him. Had she been reaching for him? Slowly, he slid toward her, placing his palm in the center of her back. *Strength. Can give her my strength*, he thought, studying Kelsey where she lay about six feet away from the group of them. He had to crawl to her somehow and make sure she was all right. *But first,* he thought, *I can help Thea*. Beneath his hand, she stirred, groaning. "Thea, here," he urged, "let me help you up."

"I'm . . . all right." Her voice was hardly recognizable. Slowly she struggled to a sitting position, her face ashen.

Again, he looked toward Kelsey, and finally sure he wouldn't pass out, began to crawl toward her, every movement demanding a supreme amount of strength.

She lay on her side, curled into a ball, and seemed to be totally unconscious. It concerned him; what if her human anatomy had been ill-equipped for dimensional travel? The mitres did not open by a door or a hatch or any basic method: it could only be entered via a dimensional portal. That was what ensured its safekeeping from all their enemies. But as far as he knew, no human had ever made such a dimensional journey.

When he reached Kelsey, he saw that she was breathing—a slow, deep rhythm as if she'd been asleep a long time. He was pleased to see a peaceful expression on her face.

Thea worked her way toward him, sliding on her knees. "Gods, that was awful!" she cried, sounding again like herself.

"It still is awful," Scott groaned, continuing to sit cross-legged, his face buried in both hands.

"Arienn wrote all about this. The first time he traversed the portal, he was sick for days."

"Thanks for the warning." Dillon grunted.

Thea stared in his direction, an irritable expression on

her face, then, catching Marco staring at her, she rolled her eyes. They both laughed softly.

Hearing them, Scott barked, "Shut up."

"Did I say a word?" Thea shot back at him as he stared down at Kelsey where she lay on the floor. Looking up at Marco, she asked, "Do you think she's all right? I mean, she's out cold."

"I'm not sure," he said, reaching for her wrist to take her pulse. "She looks well enough, but—she's certainly different from the rest of us. This obviously took a huge toll on her."

"It wasn't the dimensional jump—it was the data removal." Thea shook her head, reaching to touch Kelsey's shoulder with surprising gentleness. "She's tough. It wasn't easy on her at all. But we have it now." She reached to her hip and indicated a data collector, a slim, portable device no bigger than a cigarette lighter; it was what they used to house and transport all their critical data and intelligence. "I linked with her, found the data, exported it . . . and then uploaded it into the collector. In the process, I was obviously successful in creating the time portal. Damn!" she suddenly cried, her beautiful face spreading into a huge smile. "We'll chalk this one up to our side!"

"Good work, Haven," Scott Dillon said, sounding less than enthusiastic. He was slowly regaining his composure, and was looking in their direction. Marco was about to ask the lieutenant if he needed help when he noticed Dillon's gaze track past them all, fixing solidly on the far side of the room. "What in All's name is *that*?" he asked.

It was the coiling unit, Thea thought. It was what the large, glowing cylinder had to be. Jared had seen it the night he dismantled the codes and managed to enter the chamber. Arienn had detailed it in his journals, describing how he had seeded his own energy inside the large tube. Still, knowing what it was did nothing to spoil the powerful magnificence of the object. Thea rose unsteadily, walking toward where the unit stood in the center of the room. The device was transparent, revealing only the cool, last embers of the prince's long-ago-seeded energy.

Reverently, she reached her palms toward the cylinder's smooth surface. Would it scald her? Change her? She hardly cared, so drawn was she to connect with her ancestor's energy still glowing cool green within.

"Thea, watch out," Scott cautioned her brusquely. "You have no idea what the hell that thing is!"

"It's the core of this chamber," she said. "We should be quiet, respectful."

"Because of a device?" Scott pressed, taking the place beside her. His black eyebrows corkscrewed into a scowl.

Thea turned to him, smiling at her longtime friend. "Because it's my ancestor's energy inside. A part of him is still alive"—she pointed toward the tube—"in there."

"There's a difference between the prince's energy and his essence," Scott countered.

"No," she disagreed quietly, "it is part of who he was, and it continues in there. He left that in order to protect all of us. It was the ultimate sacrifice to give up part of his core self."

Scott turned to her, his familiar black eyes troubled. He had never fully understood what she and Jared were, that they were dual beings. It had disturbed him, confounded him, but he never could seem to wrap his mind around it. Glancing between her and the coiling unit, she could see how fast his mind worked. "Does he know we're here?" he asked at last, and Thea couldn't help laughing a little.

"Lieutenant, no. It's his power. His raw energy. Not his spirit." She turned back toward the coiling unit, lowering her voice. "But we should still be respectful."

Suddenly the hairs on the nape of her neck prickled, standing on end. Marco spoke from just behind her, giving voice to her deepest emotions at the moment. "You feel a strong connection with the prince," he said, his voice barely more than a whisper.

She nodded, saying nothing, feeling tears sting her eyes.

"Because you're like him," he continued.

This time the tears burst forth, beginning to stream down her cheeks, and again she nodded. All her life, she'd felt alone. Different. And all her life she had craved the company of someone like herself.

"You have always felt alone," Marco continued, slipping one large palm onto her shoulder. Her entire body erupted in flame at his touch—perhaps because of the intimacy, perhaps because he understood her to the depths of her fiery soul. She wasn't sure; all she knew was that suddenly she found herself sobbing, staring at the long-dead prince's lingering energy shadow.

You are not alone, my sweet lady. She stiffened instantly. Marco had whispered within her mind, she was certain of it! Behind her, he took another step closer, until hardly any distance separated them at all. He moved his hand from her shoulder, slowly roaming his fingers to her neck, caressing her. *I wouldn't let you be alone.*

They weren't bonded, but it had to be Marco. She trembled beneath his touch, unable to stop the tears.

How are you doing this? she asked, but no reply came. There was only Marco—towering, proud, beautiful Marco—standing behind her like her very own Madjin. Which he was. He was her protector in every way.

With both palms extended, she reached toward the unit again, ready to feel its surface. Scott moved to stop her, but much to her surprise Marco caught his arm. "Let her, Lieutenant," he urged. "She needs to do this."

"We have no way of knowing if it's safe or not," Scott argued, his voice rising.

"It is safe," Marco told them evenly. "I sense it."

Thea spun to face him, but still he kept his hand firmly on her shoulder. "You're intuitive?" She thought of the night before, the way he'd wooed and calmed her. Such a strange gift the man possessed!

"Something like." He gave her a cocky, proud grin.

"Something like . . . what?" Scott pressed. "We need to know."

Marco dropped his hand from her shoulder, and seemed to think for a long moment. "The best way to explain my gift—in a way that will make sense to you—is that, yes, I'm intuitive."

"So you're sure the coiling unit is safe to touch?" Thea pressed, feeling her entire body burn.

Marco nodded toward it. "Go on."

She swallowed hard, felt Dillon tense at her side, but reached with both hands as she might have reached toward a treasured doll as a little girl. Gently—ever so gently—she closed both hands around its surface.

And felt nothing. No spark, no awareness. Just . . . nothing. Her earlier tears turned to genuine sobs and she sank to the floor, still holding on, desperate for the slightest quiver of energy inside her soul. She was aware of the others around her, but she didn't care. She pressed her face flat against the glass and cried. For her lost ancestor; for her dead parents; for everyone who had died in this damnable, bloody war. And shc cried for Jared; that she had managed to lose the one person on the entire face of the planet who was anything like her.

A strong arm slipped about her shoulder. "Thea," Scott whispered. "Come on. It's okay."

She shook her head. What had she really expected? She was a military leader, she had to pull it together. "I-I don't know what's wrong with me," she said, leaning her forehead against the tube, but letting her arms fall to her sides.

"The journey through the portal exhausted you," Marco volunteered. "Look at our queen. She's still asleep." Our queen. *Why does he have to call her that?* Thea thought. While linked with the human her antipathy toward the woman had faded; she'd felt compassion, understanding. Even kinship. Staring at her from across the room now, it was still surprisingly easy to resent her once again. Thea doubted she would ever accept Kelsey as her true queen.

Thea rocked back on her heels, wiped her eyes, and said, "We need to wake her up. We have work to do." All soldier once again, she rose to her feet and brushed her knees off.

From across the room Kelsey suddenly stirred, bolting upright, wild-eyed. "I'm awake," she declared, and at that precise moment—not one second sooner, not a millisecond later—a powerful hum began in the center of the chamber.

Beside her, Marco's entire body tensed as he spun first one way, then another.

"What in All's namc is that?" Scott hissed.

But the hum—that eerie, otherworldly sound—grew louder until it seemed the entire chamber shuddered and lurched. It was at that precise moment that Prince Arienn's energy began to brighten.

Thea raced to the giant cylinder. "My gods," she whispered, feeling her heart thunder so hard it seemed she'd never breathe. "His energy!"

"Whose energy?" Kelsey asked, staggering unsteadily toward the mitres center.

Thea reached once again to touch the cool surface of the tube; this time it had grown warm. But it was only when Kelsey reached her side, just in front of the tube, that the energy turned a warm, glowing orange.

"It's responding to the queen," Marco said, taking position between them all. "Here, my lady, reach toward it, just as Thea is doing."

Thea shook her head dazedly. It couldn't be! If the prince's energy was reacting at all, it had to be to her own core nature as a D'Ashani. Not to the human.

Kelsey took a bold step closer and spread both palms against the surface, trembling as she did so. Again, the cauldron of luminance reacted, turning a blazing reddish gold. "Wh-what's happening?" Kelsey asked in awe. "Tell me, please." She cut her eyes sideways, never dropping her hands. "Thea, please explain this to me. I'm lost here."

Thea closed her eyes, almost unable to bear the reality of the situation. "My ancestor's energy is contained inside the cylinder," she explained numbly. "It's . . . reacting to you, Kelsey. It somehow—he—his essence—recognizes you, I think."

"Recognizes me?" Kelsey repeated, shivering visibly. "Recognizes me as what?"

It was Marco who spoke next, his dusky features glowing in the light of the powerful energy. Dropping to both knees he said, "Recognizes you as our true queen."

"That's energy inside there," Kelsey told them, never releasing her grip on the large coiling unit. "How could it know who I am?"

Marco rose to his feet again. "Because you bear the

mark of the D'Aravni. You are the true queen. That has to be significant in some way."

"No, that's not it." Thea walked briskly to the other side of the circular room. Marco watched as she moved, aware as always of the lieutenant's sleek grace and erotic beauty. Every motion of her body, every simple gesture electrified him, even at high-tension moments such as this one. He shook his head, struggling to center his thoughts.

Beside him Kelsey stood, eyes trained on the glowing cauldron of power. It seemed she was riveted to the spot, unable to break contact. The thought concerned him for her safety on one level, but on the other hand he knew this moment was crucial. Reaching with his intuition he sensed no danger to his queen, so he didn't try to pull her away.

Across the room Thea worked with the data collector, her blond eyebrows drawn into a tight frown of concentration. "It's not possible," she announced. "Damn it all! This is *not* possible!"

"What's happening here, Haven?" Scott demanded. "You lost me a while ago."

Thea cursed rapidly in low Refarian, studying the data collector within her hands. "Outside"—she paused, shaking her head in disbelief—"I had it. I had the mitres data downloaded into this collector. Now, it's . . . gone. As if I never captured it at all."

"Let me see that damnable thing," Scott said, yanking it from her hands. After a few moments of fiddling with buttons and staring at it, he slowly raised his eyes to meet Thea's. "Empty. Completely empty."

"And the data was *in* there!" Thea shouted, seizing the instrument from Scott once again. "I don't understand. How could it have been in here while we were exterior to the chamber and then just—"

"It's still inside me," Kelsey announced calmly, sweeping her gaze around the room. "The data never left my mind."

"What makes you so sure of that?" Thea demanded.

Kelsey slowly dropped her hands to her sides and immediately the luminance cooled, turning a softer dull orange. "Because that's why the energy reacted to me.

Not because I'm the queen. It's the data inside of me. Somehow this device reacted to those codes in my head."

"Kelsey, do you understand how serious this is?" Thea asked her, obviously trying to soften her tone. "It means that . . . I wasn't able to remove the data from your mind."

"You made a temporary upload," Kelsey explained evenly. "In order for us to traverse the portal. That's all."

"But how do you *know* that?" Thea insisted.

Kelsey glanced about the group of them. "It's nuts, but I have absolutely no idea." She laughed, tugging thoughtfully at the end of her braid. "But I know I'm right."

"Let's try again," Thea suggested. "Let me link with you again—"

"Thea, I'm telling you that it won't work," Kelsey said. "I know that it won't, just like I know the data is still inside me. I never had any kind of feeling about this whole situation before. It was just an abstract idea, knowing the data was inside my mind. I never would have had a clue about it if Jared hadn't told me. But now"—she swept her arm in a circular arc, indicating the chamber—"now that I'm in here? I feel it. I feel it deep, in my bones. It's like it's burning inside of me, same as that energy is glowing."

Marco thought for a long moment, trying to figure out what his queen really meant. It seemed that somehow, by the simple act of entering the mitres, she had activated the codes inside of herself. That deep within her core self the data had come . . . alive. And that meant only one thing: It had fused with her mind and consciousness.

Kelsey and the mitres data had become one.

Chapter Twelve

Scott paced the circular perimeter of the mitres chamber. All his life he'd lived in awe of this place, wondered if it even truly existed. His scientist parents had been leaders in the movement to unseal the chambers. From the time the mitres were installed here on Earth, no one had ever entered again; only as the war had escalated—a war with his own traitorous people—had his parents begun to lobby for the chambers to be opened. The balance of energy and weaponry within the mitres had always been viewed as a delicate thing. But they'd also been placed on Earth as a protection for the Refarian people, for times of hardship or warfare. Scott just couldn't believe that it had turned out to be his own race that had made that war on a people he loved so dearly. On a king he served so wholeheartedly.

If Kelsey was right about the mitres data being locked inside of her, they would have to find a way to resolve the issue. None of them could afford to have the data at such risk—nor could their queen become that priceless a commodity. Being the keeper of such technology would put a price on her head—one so high that she could never take a step without worrying about assassination. Jared would never be able to live with himself for that.

At the moment Kelsey stood in front of the central cylinder—the coiling unit, as he knew it was called because he'd studied the schematics with his parents as a boy. When she drew close to the thing, the energy inside grew brighter and hotter. When she stepped back, it seemed to calm back down again. It was spooky as hell, all that stuff Thea had told them about Prince Arienn.

He was almost beginning to wonder if she was wrong, if maybe the prince didn't somehow *know* they were inside the chamber.

Again he took a turn about the large circular room, studying all the machinery and technology. He wasn't sure what he hoped to see, or what he was looking for precisely, but he couldn't shake the feeling that his parents were trying to tell him something from beyond the grave. Not literally, but just this itchy sort of feeling that if he gazed long enough and hard enough, then he would see the one element in this room that would help them download the data from Kelsey and into the data collector. Permanently.

He swept his glance in a wide arc. He was a gazer—it was what he'd always been. It was the one special gift All had given him at birth. Sometimes he gazed people, other times objects or rooms. Right now, he was gazing for the truth. For revelation. It had to be here somewhere.

"Okay, so we're going to try again," Thea pronounced calmly, gazing up into Kelsey's blue eyes. "Maybe it had to be done from inside the chamber. Maybe the first time was just for the opening of the portal. This is where the data needs to upload anyway." She tapped on the large central console that stood beside the coiling unit. "We want to store it in here where it belongs."

"What about the codes that created the portal to begin with?" Kelsey asked. "That's how we got in this place, right?"

"I was going to keep a copy on the collector while uploading it into the main console, but"—Thea stared down at the empty data unit in her hand—"it just didn't work that way. The first time. So let's try again." Thea sat down on the floor, right in front of the coiling unit, still awed by the way Arienn's energy reacted to Kelsey. Or the data. Or whatever it was that was happening. She couldn't figure out which theory she fully believed, but Kelsey clearly seemed convinced that it wasn't Arienn's energy reacting to her, but the mitres itself.

Kelsey took the position facing her, each of them sitting cross-legged. Just past Kelsey stood Marco, his keen black eyes trained on her. Thea tried to forget he was there, tried to dismiss him from her mind, but it was an impossible task. She reached for Kelsey's left hand, her right hand grasping the data collector. She would link into Kelsey's brain, locate their technology, and then create a psychic connection with the collector. Essentially, Thea would act as a conductor between Kelsey and the unit.

Closing her eyes, she tried to focus anew, but instead all she saw, like an afterimage from staring at the sun, was Marco McKinley watching her. She allowed her eyes to flutter open and met his intense, penetrating gaze. "I'm sorry, but"—she waved toward the right, making a shooing motion—"could you move in that direction?"

He appeared surprised, then a slow, languid smile formed on his lips, and he ambled out of her line of vision. And that just annoyed her to pieces. He was the biggest flirt she'd ever met, and the last thing she needed these days—and right now, in particular—was a distraction.

Sighing, she closed her eyes again and was surprised when Kelsey gave her hand a light squeeze. The second time around it was even easier to link up with Kelsey and within a moment she heard her voice, warm and friendly inside her head. *He's a nice-looking guy.*

Kelsey, please, she sidestepped, *I've got a job to do in here.*

Here? This would be my brain.

Inside of you, Thea huffed. *Okay? I've got work to do inside of you—which is mostly about helping you, don't forget.*

I know you don't like me, Kelsey told her matter-of-factly.

That's not—

Thea, don't try and deny it. I know you don't like me, Kelsey pressed. *And that's okay.*

I'm sorry you feel—

But I hope someday, some time, the human persisted, *you'll consider being my friend. We are cousins now, you know.*

Thea was speechless. Dumbfounded. Angry. Here she'd dreaded forming a link with the woman—for this very reason, the profound intimacy of it—and somehow Kelsey had slid right past all her natural protective barriers by declaring her interest in friendship. There was nothing to say at all. Thea grunted and proceeded in her quest.

Marco squatted off to the side watching Thea work. She had an intense, adorable scowl knitting her blond eyebrows together. He smiled to himself, thinking of how she'd made him move to the side. Intuitives were aware of the people around them at any time; Thea was highly aware of him, he knew it. He felt it every single time they were in a room together. Something electric and important always seemed to attract them. Something beyond the moment that was the source of all the memories.

He stared into the powerful coiling unit, watching the undulating energy. The sight was breathtakingly beautiful—the shimmering colors, the knowledge that Thea was a similar being of pure energy when in her most natural state. He shivered, lost in the swirling power, just drawn to it. Unable to look away. He stood, stepping closer. Maybe he could touch it . . . because he had to. All of a sudden there was nothing nearly so important as getting closer. And closer.

I'm possessed, Marco thought foggily, laughing. With a quick glance across the room he noticed that Scott Dillon had been drawn toward the unit and bore a trancelike expression on his face. Marco shook his head, wanting to step back, but it was as if an iron hand had riveted him to that precise spot on the floor. "Dillon," he called out, but the name came out elongated, distorted, and strange. As if Marco had a terrible fever that made everything slow down inside his brain.

"Diiiilllllonnnn," he tried again, his mouth feeling like rubber. But Dillon was laughing, a strange doubled-over kind of thing as if he were blind drunk.

Must be a gas, Marco thought dimly. *The unit is leaking gas. Gasssssssssssss.*

He sank to his knees, groping at the floor. *The queen! Must save queen!*

Struggling to turn, he reached a long, distended arm

awkwardly behind him. *Get queen out! Theaaaaaaaaaa-aaaa!*

But at that precise moment, the floor opened up beneath them all, a rush of wind and light knocking him face-first onto the chamber floor again, suspended over the roaring abyss. Marco was spread-eagle facedown, but it wasn't the hard floor that met him. It was wind and air and light, as if he were hurtling through time and space. A glowing oval the color of cobalt encircled him. Seemed to circle time itself as he was catapulted across the expanse of his memories. Like earlier, he saw Thearnsk again, only this time he was in the palace courtyard, playing. He wasn't allowed to be there, the prince might see. And the young crown prince *did* see him that day, the one and only time Marco ever met the man who would be his king. Marco was five then, Jared seven. Sabrina had scolded him.

He saw Sabrina scolding him now, same as if she were in the room. Then he and Riley were getting drunk back in their apartment in Santa Fe. That image dissolved, slingshotting across the glowing blue oval and he landed in a bar somewhere, a real dive of a place. His forehead hurt like hell, and when he lifted his fingers to touch the eyebrow, he felt warm, sticky blood. *Where the fuck am I?* Marco wondered, glancing around. There were picnic tables scattered around the dingy bar, ringed by the glowing sapphire energy of the mitres chamber.

It was some kind of memory—only he'd never lived this one. And then in walked Thea, coquettish and raw, her blond curls loose down her back. Something dead in her eyes, though. Something off. He got a killer erection suddenly, just from watching her stroll across that damn bar. Then, with the elastic, audible *snap* of time he found himself tumbling in her arms, making love in some low-rent motel room.

You're a virgin, she panted.

This wasn't his Thea. This was the darker one—the one from his memories. And he was much darker too. Ugly, wrong, black-hearted. He'd betrayed someone he loved dearly. Who was it? He could almost remember.

Thea straddled him, tossed her head back with laughter and he plunged through the wind and light, finding himself kneeling. Begging. It was Jared! Marco was begging in front of his king, begging for mercy and forgiveness.

You kissed my wife! Jared shouted. *Did I* misunderstand *that?*

Oh, in All's name *no!* Not that, not his king. Not his beloved queen. Marco began to shake all over, grasping at the floor, flailing through time and space as he catapulted from dimension to dimension.

It's the mitres, he thought weakly. *We've opened the mitres.*

I'm a traitor. I'm a traitor.

I betrayed my king and queen.

"Okay, I don't even want to think about how much power is locked inside your head," Thea said, eyeing Kelsey warily. The human seemed pretty nonchalant given Thea's resounding failure at data retrieval. Jared was going to be quite displeased. She clearly didn't understand the ramifications of the data's apparent *fusion* with her mind.

Kelsey stared down at Marco and Scott, each of whom had passed out cold on the floor. "You guess it's that dimensional illness again?" she asked, and resumed pacing to and fro; for the past few minutes she'd practically been doing laps around the coiling unit.

"It has to be," Thea agreed, thinking of the mystic experience she herself had just undergone.

"What did you feel? While the portal opened?" Kelsey asked curiously. Unlike the rest of them, her body was coursing with energy, alive and electric. She bounced excitedly on the balls of her feet, and even her face glowed.

Thea wiped a rivulet of sweat from her forehead. The whole chamber had heated up by multiple degrees since their entry. "Thea?" Kelsey prompted her when she didn't answer. "What did you see?"

"I'm not sure," Thea said, dodging the question. She had no intention of telling Kelsey Bennett what she'd just glimpsed in the cross-dimensions. "But one thing we do know—that data in your head refuses to be removed."

Kelsey's expression grew slightly troubled, but then she smiled again. "Maybe so, but I feel fan-freaking-*tastic!*" She snaked her hands up and down her body to demonstrate. "It's like my skin is alive. It's like this whole *room* is alive." She strode toward the cylinder, staring into it. "And it's like just being here is where I belong."

"Kelsey," Thea told her softly, "you're frightening me a bit. The mitres seems to be having some kind of . . . effect on you."

"It is! It's setting me on *fire!*" Kelsey did a little spin, sort of like she was in the midst of a *walsak* dance, throwing both hands into the air. It was extremely uncharacteristic behavior, at least from what Thea already knew of the smart, stable-tempered human. Kelsey always seemed so intelligent and determined. At this particular moment she was unbalanced and giddy.

Thea's heart began to hammer. She didn't like Kelsey's reaction, not at all. It wasn't the pure joy on her queen's face, or the thrilled reaction in her body—it was that her exhilaration stemmed solely from her proximity to the mitres. The same weaponry that was controlled by the data codes stuck inside her brain.

"I'm going to get these guys up," Thea pronounced, gesturing toward Marco and Scott, "and get you out of here, Kelsey. Fast."

What she didn't say was that after what she'd seen and felt in the slipstream, the unfolding spiral of memories and images from their past—and shared future—she felt suddenly very protective of Kelsey Wells Bennett.

Nothing could happen to her queen.

Chapter Thirteen

The mission was taking far too long. Jared glanced at his watch, perhaps for the hundredth time since the transport had left bearing his wife and trusted lieutenants. They should have returned hours ago; in retrospect, he wished he had chosen to accompany them, risks be damned. This waiting was as endless as a trek across the *Maerhtka* lands: Time seemed to stretch on and on and on, without a word about their safety. Perhaps Lieutenant Dillon didn't realize that his party had been away for almost five hours now, or perhaps it was the only way to accomplish the job, with this extra time. But with daybreak imminent, he needed his wife and the others back now.

He stood in the control room that serviced the hangar and launch deck, staring out at the ready fighters and the engineers going through checks. The flight controllers kept him apprised of the transport's trajectory. He probably should have called the aircraft back on deck—would have done so, if he'd realized the team would be gone for more than four hours. It was never a good idea to keep any of their craft on a flight for longer than necessary, but the transport was stealthy, and especially at night there was no way the US military would detect it.

"No word from Dillon?" he asked the main controller.

The man stared at his computer screen and verified what Jared already knew. "No, sir. Still no contact."

"How do the fuel levels look?" Jared stared over the man's shoulder at the display monitor.

"Getting low, but we're okay so far," the man advised him, then spun in his chair to face him, awaiting further instructions.

Jared sighed. "Keep me posted, then." He strode toward the door, but was unable to shake a growing sense that something in this mission was going very wrong. Turning back toward the controller, he hesitated.

"Sir?" the man inquired.

Jared rubbed his jaw thoughtfully. "How long would it take to get a second transport out there, just in case we need it?"

"We can launch in five." Again, Jared felt a dark wave of precognition roll over his senses. He wasn't sure why—or if they'd need the craft at all—but he issued the launch command anyway.

Scott Dillon sputtered curses under his breath, unable to believe that the chamber had created some kind of time warp. His watch didn't say six A.M.—none of the others' watches did either—but here, on the exterior of the chamber, daylight had begun to crack the morning sky. They were running out of time for the transport to meet them at the lift point.

On the path behind him, the other three hiked in his wake, and Scott surveyed the surrounding landscape through his night-vision goggles circumspectly. With Jared's recent crash in the same vicinity, the US military activity had been high, making this mission risky to begin with, but now? They were losing the advantage of darkness, and he wasn't at all pleased with the jeopardy it placed them all in.

He'd signaled the transport moments before, but they were nearing the trailhead without any sign of the craft's approach. Again, not good. That would mean exposure at the open area along the lake. Mentally he scrolled through strategy; where to fall back, where to wait. How to protect the queen, first and foremost.

Ahead, he located a giant boulder and pegged it as the safest area of coverage where they could await the craft. Dropping low onto his haunches, he demonstrated for the others the best way to proceed. At that precise moment, an ear-splitting noise rent the early morning light. "Get down!" Scott called, waving his team to the ground. "Down, down!"

Another crack of gunfire came then, followed immediately by the answering whir of a bullet right over his shoulder; at that precise moment it seemed as if holy hell broke loose.

"The first transport seems to be having a malfunction, sir," the controller advised Jared. He wished he could claim surprise. "According to their instrumentation, they have a fuel line leak and have to turn back now—or they won't make it back."

Only moments before had the transport's captain finally heard from Scott Dillon; the team was ready for pickup—and now, the craft couldn't reach them. "How long ago did we launch the other transport?"

"It's within ten minutes of the drop site, sir."

"Ten minutes. Good." Jared just prayed there weren't any issues on the ground. Ten minutes was like an eternity in hell if you needed immediate pickup.

They were never going to make it out alive, not a one of them, if Scott didn't come up with some sort of strategy in the next thirty seconds. Marco had Kelsey prone on the ground, beneath his body, firing off rounds at the exact same time. Thea crouched at Scott's right side, pulse rifle gripped in both hands, letting loose quick, sputtering rounds without hesitation.

But it didn't take a military genius to realize they were cornered and outflanked by a far superior force. They were only a small band of four; the guns turned on them had to belong to a force of ten or more soldiers.

Scott's mind whirled, grasping at possibilities, and at last he arrived at the only workable strategy that just might save the others. "Thea," he said, reloading as he talked, "you're going to lead the others back up the trail, toward the other side of the chamber. I'll cover you down here. There's a flat area around the ledge. It'll be tricky, but the transport can get you there."

Thea peppered the landscape with a shower of pulse fire, breathless, and then announced that she wasn't about to leave him behind.

"It's the only way, Thea," he insisted, sensing their attackers moving in closer. "They're advancing on us. Do it now. That's an order."

For a brief moment she stared at him, pain reflected in her familiar eyes, and then she nodded, crawling toward the others and issuing orders. Scott never looked at them again; he worked his way farther down the trail, intermittently firing rounds and crouching low for protection. He would either die or be captured, and deep in his heart, he'd always known it would come to this—there was no other way this scenario could end. But at least he would have protected his queen and his second in command and Marco in the process.

Stopping to reload, it seemed that the gunfire died down some. He wished he believed that was a good sign, he thought with a bitter laugh, but a lifetime of warfare had taught him better. Suddenly, from behind him, the long barrel of a machine gun jabbed him hard in the center of his back.

"You. Drop the weapon," shouted a deep, human voice. "Now! Now! Now!"

He knew the tactic—subdue the enemy by being assertive and intimidating; hell, it was the same tactics *they* used when cornering an enemy. But he wasn't intimidated, not for a moment; humans were easy compared to the Antousians' genocidal ways. If he was indeed going to die at the hands of his captors, at least he had a prayer that it would be carried out decently.

Scott let his pulse rifle fall to the ground and shoved both hands into the air.

"*Identify* yourself, soldier!"

He said nothing.

"Identify!"

Scott remained silent.

A pair of rough hands gripped him from behind, shoving him face-first onto the frozen ground; someone else's boot shoved between his shoulders; yet another soldier let loose a sneering laugh. Others joined in. "Fucking Nank," someone muttered from behind him.

Nank. That's what the human soldiers called any alien; why, he'd never known. But it wasn't a compliment.

His mind drifted to the images he'd seen inside the

mitres, of some other life he would supposedly live—or had lived, only he didn't remember it. There was a woman with long golden hair and haunting gray eyes. But she'd been beautiful—and his. Wrestling for breath, he tried to hold onto that woman like he would a lifeline or a rare, fading sunset. The thought of her stilled his hammering heart just a little, made him breathe a bit easier. At least for a few seconds.

Another soldier dropped down to the ground, pushing his face close to Scott's, his putrid breath overpowering Scott's Antousian senses until for a moment he thought he might be sick. "Nank," the foul-breathed soldier whispered against his face, almost like it was some kind of seduction, "you're gonna fucking die tonight."

Thea sat in Jared's chambers, whiskey in hand—he'd insisted that she drink some of his favored human liquid—and trembled from head to toe. Kelsey sat beside her on the floor, staring into the fire, silent, but somehow oddly . . . comforting. Marco braced both hands on the mantel, clearly upset. He felt as if he'd failed them all, she sensed it. Jared had led them to his chambers rather than into the meeting room because Scott Dillon's capture was going to rock the very foundations of the resistance. The men and women within Jared's army were unfailingly loyal and devoted to the Antousian lieutenant, and followed him with almost mythical dedication.

Tears burned Thea's eyes. If she'd done something different, if she'd not listened to him, if she had chosen to stay and fight . . .

They would all be in enemy hands at the moment.

She took another swig of the burning whiskey, her hands trembling so badly that the ice cubes rattled in the glass.

Kelsey turned to look at her and said, "Thank you. You saved my life out there."

"No, I didn't." Thea shook her head. "Scott did."

"You carried out his order," Kelsey answered softly. "I owe you my life."

"Just . . . don't," she countered bitterly. "Please, just don't."

Jared crouched low to the ground—he'd been pacing

the room, questioning them about the mission—and took Thea by the shoulder. "Lieutenant, it wasn't your fault."

Marco cleared his throat and slowly turned to face them all. "No," he said in a strangely hushed voice. "It was mine."

Jared rose to his full height and swept his gaze among them all. "Stop it. Now," he fairly roared. "The assignments of blame get us nowhere. It happened. It was a risk, and Dillon knew it—we all knew it—going in. You came under enemy fire and were outflanked and outmanned. If we're assigning blame, then let it be with me. I sent you in without sufficient backup."

"No, sir—" Thea began, but Jared lifted an authoritative and silencing hand.

"Enough." He glanced around the room, his eyes shining with power. "Enough. What we need now is to focus on getting the lieutenant back. That, and removing this data from Kelsey's mind since—apparently—it's proving a hell of a lot more difficult than we'd hoped. Those are the top priorities right now. If either of you'd been captured out there tonight, Kelsey would have fallen into our enemy's hands—right along with the data. This is not acceptable that it simply . . . fused with her. We must find a way to dislodge it from her mind."

"Jared, you weren't there," Kelsey whispered, staring into the fire with an almost trancelike stare. "You have no idea. The mitres reacted to me."

"She's right, sir," Marco agreed. "And when it began to power up, what we experienced . . ." Marco's deep voice trailed to nothing. Thea gazed up at him, wondering what he was thinking. There was a deeply troubled expression on his face; his black eyes narrowed to catlike slits. She knew what she had seen tonight, but now she wondered what had confronted Marco in the slipstream.

"Tell me more," Jared urged, taking a position by the hearth near Marco. "Marco, tell me everything that you experienced."

"My lord, I can't."

"You can't?" Jared turned on him, surprised and a bit angry.

Marco inclined his head respectfully. "It . . . is impossible to describe, sir."

Thea had the definite sense that Marco was holding back. Had it been images of their other life together? That other timeline where they'd been the worst kind of lovers?

Her commander turned to face her. "What of you, Lieutenant Haven? What did you see? Or can't you describe it either?"

Briefly, almost imperceptibly, her eyes and Marco's locked. She swore she heard him speak within her mind: *I saw my true, dangerous nature.*

She quickly shifted her gaze to meet Jared's. "Sir, I experienced my own memories," she explained, speaking formally with her cousin as she always did when they were not in private. "Some of them from the past, but some of them . . . were not known to me. They seemed like memories that belonged to someone else."

Jared turned to Marco again. "Madjin, tell me," he questioned, "is this what happened to you?"

Marco nodded slowly, but said nothing.

"What is your hesitation, Madjin?"

Marco's black eyebrows drew together in a scowl. At first it seemed to Thea that he would never answer, but after a long, thoughtful moment he replied, "I didn't like what I saw, my lord. Of myself. It was disturbing."

"Disturbing how?" Jared pressed, slipping a hand onto Marco's shoulder. "Tell us."

Thea interjected, "Commander, Prince Arienn wrote about this same experience in his journals. He told how powering up the mitres seemed to initiate some sort of parallel universe to the one he lived in. After his experience in the chamber, he was forever haunted by images from another life—one he did not live."

"And you believe you saw that, Lieutenant? Images and memories that belonged to another version of yourself."

"Yes, my lord."

Once again—unrelenting—Jared turned back to face Marco. She knew her cousin well, and there was something he was after from the man. Something he was determined to learn. "Again, Protector, I ask what you saw in the mitres. I command you to tell me."

Marco nodded his head, his naturally dark face growing pale in the firelight. "I saw that in that other universe," he admitted quietly, "I was your enemy."

Kelsey lay on the far side of the room, fast asleep. The queen had only gotten a few hours' rest, and the experience in the mitres had clearly exhausted her. Jared stood beside the bed, gazing down at his new wife, a look of such unabashed love and adoration on his face that Marco experienced a pang of jealousy. Not because he felt sensual love for his queen—as his other self apparently had, or did—but rather because he longed to tuck Thea into his own bed. To stare down at her beautiful, peaceful face and know that she belonged to only one man in all the universe. Himself.

Quietly, Jared crossed the room to where Marco sat on giant throw pillows in front of the fire. It was the custom with their people, to sit on the floor rather than on sofas or chairs. Marco, of course, had been raised for most of his life on Earth and preferred a slouchy easy chair over the floor, but his king had no such furniture in his chambers.

Jared poured himself a straight whiskey; no ice or water, just a few shots of the liquid. It was the breakfast hour, but for the past day time had assumed an endless, suspended quality that had worked a dark spell over all of them. Jared extended a glass toward Marco, but he shook his head. He had no doubt that his king had kept him here in his chambers after dismissing Thea and urging Kelsey into bed for one purpose, and one purpose only—to interrogate him. But if that were the case, Marco planned to have his full wits about himself during the process.

Jared slowly dropped to the floor, spreading his socked feet before the fire. It was an intimate moment, just the two of them quietly sitting together—Jared with his whiskey, Marco cross-legged beside him. All his life Marco had anticipated a moment with his king just like this one; it was a disconcerting experience to live it as his current reality.

They were silent together for a while, the crackling fire and Kelsey's soft breathing the only noises between them. Occasionally Jared would sip from the whiskey and comment on its taste, but otherwise neither man spoke for quite some time. That silence began to make Marco nervous; he feared the questions that would soon come—if indeed they would come at all, although he felt certain they would. His presence in the king's chamber seemed far too pointed and deliberate otherwise.

"Tell me of your life here on Earth," Jared said at last, draining the remains of his Scotch.

Marco drew in a breath, staring at the flames. "There's not much to talk about, sir. I've been here since I was eight, always training and preparing for this day."

"I'm told you saved Kelsey's life tonight—that you covered her body with your own."

Marco turned to him in surprise. "How did you—"

"Thea told me when you first arrived."

"I didn't have any other alternative, my lord."

"A brave choice, nonetheless."

"I'm her Madjin," he replied matter-of-factly. "It wasn't a choice—it was my only option."

Jared nodded, growing thoughtful. "Why wouldn't you tell me what you saw there in the mitres? Did you fear my judgment?"

Marco swallowed hard. He hadn't expected such a direct question—and had been fairly sure his earlier answer had proved satisfactory. But Jared's question hit the truth like a poison arrow to a bull's-eye. "Yes, my lord," he answered simply.

"How was it that you were not good?" Jared asked, turning to face him. "I must know this for you to serve me here, in close proximity to my wife. It is only fair that you reveal the facts to me."

Marco raked a desperate hand through his hair, feeling cornered. All the years he'd imagined serving his king, never once had he dreamed that their first interaction alone would come to this. But he needed to confess the truth, as much for his own conscience as for the man who asked it of him. "I . . . betrayed you. In that other life."

"I see," Jared answered simply, but asked nothing more, almost as if he weren't surprised by the revelation. Marco waited, poised on the brink, anticipating his next question, the one that would bring everything crashing down: *How did you betray me?* But, strangely, it never came. Jared had to be curious, but there was a certain respect conveyed in his leaving the question unasked. A kind of trust extended. After several long moments, Marco began to breathe easier.

"My whole life I've waited for this—serving you, and now my queen," Marco said. "I never pictured anything else. Whatever happened in that other world, the one I saw . . . it's not me."

"I believe that."

Marco turned to him, shocked. "How can you be so sure?"

"Because Sabrina raised me as her son, and even with everything that has happened over the years, I still trust her with my life," he explained somberly. "And she trusts you. Therefore, so do I. It's fairly simple, really."

Marco inclined his head, releasing a sigh. "Thank you, my lord."

"I wouldn't have sent you tonight if I didn't trust you—you do realize that?"

Marco nodded; he'd already considered that point. But he'd also viewed it as a sort of test. It appeared that, the mitres visions be damned, he had passed this first trial. That was a very good thing because Marco had an idea in mind, something that would help both Jared and Kelsey—but especially his queen.

"Sir, I'm glad to know that you trust me," he began, sounding far more tentative than he would have liked. He cleared his throat, continuing, "Because I have an idea that could really resolve the issue with the mitres data."

Jared nodded. "Go on—I'm listening."

"I can help you develop your intuition. Help you extract the information from Kelsey's mind—and upload it into the mitres."

"What makes you so certain?"

"Because my gift is unique—and because my duty is to guide you in your *own* gifts. It's part of why I'm here. You know the role of the Madjin throughout history. We train and teach—not just protect." Marco lifted his chin proudly, but despite his outer calm, he was shaking inside. It took a serious set of balls to tell Jared—his king and a man two years older than he was—that he was here to train him.

And yet Jared didn't flinch; he turned to him seriously. "What are you suggesting?"

"That I work with you both—begin a series of training sessions—and help you master your own intuition, my lord. You've got the ability, you've just resisted it."

Jared stared at him, mouth open, and then, much to Marco's surprise, he began to laugh. "How do you know that? Thea I'm used to knowing my mind, but she's fought beside me for years—"

"Because *I'm* intuitive—same as you. And I can teach you how to know things the exact same way. But only if you're willing."

Jared rose suddenly, pacing the room with the tightly constrained energy of a wildcat—first in one direction, then another—until at last he spun to face Marco. "Yes," he said. "Yes, this is what is needed. I am willing indeed. I'm willing to do whatever is necessary to protect my people . . . and to save my wife."

Chapter Fourteen

Scott Dillon's mouth was dry and his body sore; he was relatively sure they broken some of his ribs when they worked him over upon his capture. He'd been airlifted to an unknown location, camouflaged in an Air Force uniform before armed military escorts had driven him into an underground facility. After that, he'd passed out cold. Drugs had been administered to him, no doubt. And he'd been manacled and bound ever since. Was it daytime? Night? He couldn't be certain at all. Stirring on the concrete floor of a small, dark room, he tried to lift his head, only to discover that they had him trussed up like a prize bird. Hands bound behind his back, feet chained to a small desk.

With a groan, he pressed his cheek against the floor and prayed that All, who had always watched his back and kept him safe, might get him out of this mess alive.

They just want to question me, he tried to assure himself, *and they have no evidence or reason to hold me. These Americans have civil liberties. Without any direct link or evidence, they can't keep me here.*

At that precise moment he heard a buzzer sound, a door open, and there was the sound of footsteps, then the scrape of a chair. "So you're awake now," a human male said. Scott sniffed at the air, revolted by the odor of sweat mixed with tobacco, but did not reply. The room was completely dark, so he could see nothing.

"Lieutenant Dillon, we have a lot to discuss—and I suggest you plan to talk."

Shit. They knew his name, and his rank, which meant he had only one option: to refuse to speak English.

A pair of hands jerked him onto his knees and he cried out; his ribs were bruised and swollen. The overhead light came on, and he winced at the startling brightness. As his eyes adjusted he saw that two Air Force officers stood over him. They would be his interrogators, which was hardly a surprise since they'd been his captors too. No doubt he was currently in Cheyenne, at Warren Air Force Base.

"Will you cooperate?" the beefy, second man asked. He wore a colonel's insignia on his shoulder.

Scott gave a brief nod, but said nothing, and they hauled him onto his feet, unfastening his hands from behind his back. His feet remained manacled together, attached to a chain on the table leg. The other man, the sweaty one Scott presumed would be his interrogator, smiled at him and indicated the chair across the table.

"Good. Then let's begin by discussing Refaria."

Thea scrambled down the path that led from the cabin to the security perimeter along the main road. Snow and glazed rocks caused her feet to slide, but she had to get away, had to breathe. The sun had set and they still had no idea where Scott had been taken, more than twelve hours after his capture. She loved her commanding officer like a brother, and now their enemies had him. Those horrid, despicable humans who didn't have a clue that Jared and Scott—all of them—were risking their lives to protect this planet.

Tears burned her eyes, and still she stumbled headlong into the darkness. The emotions were too familiar, reminding her of all the people she'd lost back on Refaria. All the bloodshed. She couldn't add Scott to that list, not him of all people.

Ahead of her she heard a noise and stopped stockstill for a moment. There was someone just below her on the trail, probably one of the patrols. But then she caught the familiar, earthy scent of Marco McKinley, even before she made out his shadow in the snowy, moonlit path below her.

She took several more steps in his direction, slipping and sliding. She'd never needed another person so badly in all her life; her heartbreak over Scott's capture had clearly left her too emotional. *I have to pull it together.* But sharp flashes of images flipped through her mind: Marek holding her, wrestling her body beneath his own angrily. Bad love, possessive fury, brutal passion. Had it ever been good for them in that other life?

Tears immediately burned her eyes, and all their mutual protests fell to pieces in her heart. *I don't care if it can only lead to pain,* she thought, stepping over a fallen limb. *I don't care about duty or obligation. I only want to be with him!*

Marco stood near the security gate, all his senses on alert. He kept inhaling deeply, trying to detect the scent of their enemy, the frigid air burning his lungs. It was almost night and other patrols were on duty, but as Madjin to those back up the mountainside, he couldn't rationalize being anywhere else but on this security detail. With Scott Dillon taken, all his fears for his king and queen had intensified multifold. He was thankful for the full moon and that it lit the path clearly, taking some of the edge off the darkness.

He ran a shaky hand through his hair, brushing it off of his forehead, as he turned back along the path that tracked beside the main road. He raised his night-vision binoculars to study the terrain, but was alarmed when he heard a soft rustling behind him. He spun on his heel, inhaling quickly, as he raised a hand to throw up his shield. But the scent that quickly filled his senses wasn't that of the enemy; it was the heady perfume of wildflowers touched by sunlight.

Thea stood just above him on the path. The moonlight shimmered over her long blond hair, which fell loose and wild over her shoulders. Shadows played across her features, obscuring her face.

"Thea," he whispered, his heart pounding frantically. "Why the hell are you out here?" She'd scared the living shit out of him, appearing from nowhere. It wasn't safe for her to be here, either, and not just because of their enemies.

"I'm sorry." Her voice sounded broken. "I was . . ." Then he got it—of course, she was devastated by Scott Dillon's capture. The two of them were obviously very close, and he had hardly seen her since their return to base camp.

"You were what?" he asked much more gently, taking several steps closer. She stared down at the ground between them, then turned as if to walk away. He caught her arm, spinning her back toward him. "Tell me, Thea. Tell me why you came down here."

She shook her head, taking a step back. "I had a dream—about the ambush last night, and I felt so trapped," she whispered. "Scott . . ." He could see her so clearly now, the moon illuminating her water blue eyes perfectly. "And I was worried about you; I knew you were out here on patrol . . . It was stupid. I'll go."

She tried to wriggle out of his grasp, but he tightened his grip on her small wrist. "I'm okay," he stated simply after a long moment.

"I see that now," she breathed, and he realized he'd been stepping slowly closer toward her so that only the smallest distance separated them.

"You shouldn't have come out here," he chided her, stroking her hair. "It's far too dangerous."

"I see that now too."

And her simple words were too much for him—he had no choice but to kiss her. He cupped her face within his hands, and bent down toward her. Gods in heaven, she was so small, much more delicate even than he'd realized in his bed the other night. But finally their lips did meet as she tilted her face up toward him. Her breath was incredibly warm, and her mouth even softer than he remembered. They kissed slowly, their lips just lingering together for a long moment, and he felt her tongue dart within his mouth.

Then the most unexpected thing happened . . . something absolutely exploded between them. All the tantalizing desire they'd been toying with just ripped wide open, and Marco felt energy roil all through his body. In his stomach, his chest, all along his skin. Nothing had prepared him for it; nothing possibly could have.

Her sure hands threaded through his hair as she trailed kisses across his jaw, down onto his neck. He nipped at her ear, kneading her thick hair within his hands, as he worked her backward against a nearby tree, pinning her there with his body. He already strained painfully within his uniform pants, and now he knew she could feel it. But this time he didn't care . . . he *wanted* her to know just how strongly she affected him. He was dizzy with it, desperate as the heat just kept cresting within his body.

She touched him below his parka, rubbing her flat palms across his chest, and he slipped his hands beneath her sweater, right up against her warm, smooth skin.

Unable to stop himself, he growled his need for her—loudly. But he couldn't control his Refarian nature, not with her. Not like this. At the sound of his mating cry, Thea threw her head back, arching against the tree where he had pinned her. She made her own, much softer, answering growl of kittenish pleasure. He dipped his head lower, nibbling at her collarbone, licking, tasting. And, ah, so beautiful, taking her scent into his lungs. For a long moment the overpowering sweetness of her aroma dizzied him—so much so, he had to still for a moment.

"Thea," he panted, burying his face against the top of her head, "I have never . . ." *Never what? Never ached like this? Longed like this? Never made love to anyone in my life?*

She took hold of both his hips, pulling his groin tight against her. His hardened cock pushed into the softer flesh of her belly, making his face burn. She smiled up at him, holding onto his waist with both hands. "Never what?" she asked seriously.

"Never needed a woman like this," he barely managed to whisper. "I'm sorry."

She frowned at him. "Why would you be sorry?"

"You're upset—I can't give you . . . anything."

"I was upset when I came out here," she explained patiently, staring up into his eyes. "But the minute I saw you, Marco? The moment you spoke and I felt your protection . . . there was only one hope for me. Just like the other night. That you'd make love to me."

He sucked in a breath of air, pressing his eyes shut. "I told you that I can't."

"That was before," she whispered huskily, slipping one hand between their two bodies, then gently between his legs. Slowly, arousingly, she took hold of his erection through the material of his uniform pants, which did nothing to protect him from the erotic touch of his lieutenant. He wrestled with her, grasping her wrist, trying to stop her.

"Please, Thea—" he choked, trembling with his intense need for her. "I beg you, please."

She stilled—but did not remove her hand. "Am I doing it wrong?" she asked earnestly, searching his face.

He couldn't help laughing. "Hell no!" He released her wrist, clasping her shoulders. Slowly he pushed away, leaving her breathless and with lips parted, still backed up against the tree. "That was perfect."

"Then why did you stop me?"

He smiled at her, adjusting his pants so that his jutting hard-on wouldn't be so apparent by the bright moonlight. "Because otherwise, Thea Haven, I'd have dropped you to this frozen ground and fucked you senseless. That's why. Not terribly romantic, but there you have it."

"What if I wanted that?" she asked, pushing off from the tree. He began to walk along the trail, hoping she would let him leave her. Praying to All to give him enough strength to walk away.

"Doesn't matter," he told her, trying to sound cold and unfeeling. Behind him, he heard the crunch of leaves and frozen ground as she matched him pace for pace.

"It does to me."

"I'm Madjin," he reminded her again. "We don't take lovers."

"I'm a soldier. We don't abstain."

He spun on her, hot jealousy bursting forth within him. Unexpected, but absolutely suffocating. "Who the hell's had you, Thea? You tell me now or—" He clenched his hands at both sides, ready to storm any of Jared's military compounds. Whoever had slept with his Thea would know his wrath.

"Or what? You'll make love to me, right here, right now?" She snorted. "Now that's a threat."

He took hold of her by the shoulders, wrestling to still his frantic heartbeat. "Just because I can't have you doesn't mean I'm not jealous," he confessed in a hushed voice. "Doesn't mean I don't want you, more than you'll ever understand."

"Your Madjin rules are insane. It's asking too much, that you remain alone." She shook her head, staring at the ground between them. For long moments neither of them spoke, with only the nighttime wood noises filling the void. Then, at last, she raised her clear blue eyes and leveled him with her gaze. "I wouldn't tell anyone," she whispered. "It could just be our secret."

"Who has had you?" he countered in as even a voice as he could muster. "Many? Few? Hundreds? At least tell me that."

She closed her eyes and shook her head. "You don't deserve to know." She put her back to him, slowly hiking away.

Suddenly all the sacrifices, all the Madjin ways, shattered into nothing. He caught up with her easily and, clasping her arm, spun her to face him. "I'm a virgin," he told her softly. "I wasn't lying about that."

"You're telling me that now because . . . ?" She made a rolling motion with her hand, urging him to fill in the blank. It was hard to believe how jealous Marco had become. Was he grappling for her trust, was that it? Or did he feel genuinely repentant for his unearned possessive streak?

"Because I do want you, Thea Haven. So damn bad it's killing me." He raked both hands through his black, thick hair until it stood on end, disheveled and sexy. "The feelings—these emotions—gods help me! It's an avalanche and I'm getting buried here."

She planted a hand on her hip. "Then why don't you *do* something about it?"

Clouds of breath formed between them as he struggled to breathe. Watching her—thick blond curls shimmering in the moonlight, tight little figure outlined by her uniform pants—actually led him to one thought: He would drop her right here on the trail and possess her, just like he'd told her. And he would allow her to possess him, his vows be damned to hell—and their class differences be damned to hell too. He took a step closer toward her, touching his abdomen with his open hand.

He knew all about her core self, the one made of fiery, golden energy—that had to be the explanation for the inferno building within his body. It was beyond desire; it was palpable heat.

He took another step closer, ready to take her completely, when there was the sound of a car on the highway along the perimeter. Instantly, he stopped, turning from her as he grabbed his binoculars.

He stood watching the eerie glow of the fading headlights, and guilt engulfed him—terrible, agonizing self-blame because this little indiscretion might easily have cost them all their lives. He'd just compromised a security patrol because he'd been unable to control his mating urges. He stood, his back toward her, drawing in uneven, burning breaths. Slowly, he turned to face her, and knew exactly what he had to say.

He stepped toward her quickly, pushing her until she stood with her back still against a tree, panting raggedly. The way they affected one another was unbelievable . . . *insane.*

"Thea," he began quietly. "This cannot happen." His voice was firm, his words final. "It will only lead to danger for all of us, don't you see?"

She shook her head in silent disagreement, and he swore tears pooled within her large eyes. He didn't want to hurt her. Gods, it was the last thing he wanted. "In the chamber, Thea? I saw things. New things, not just the memories of you and me. I'm dangerous. You're right about that. I've done bad things . . . or could do bad things, I guess," he blurted, reaching to touch her hair. "You make me half crazy, and I'm not sure that's good. Not with what I'm capable of."

Her lips parted as if she were going to say something, but then she hesitated, simply regarding him for a long moment. Then, at last, she whispered, "What are you capable of, Marco—other than breaking my heart?"

He winced, dropping his head for a moment. He longed to tell her of his betrayal. That he had—in this parallel universe or time—kissed their queen. Had apparently been in love with her. But he knew that to explain that, he would have to hurt Thea. "A bonding between us can only bring heartache in the end," he explained, his voice incredibly thick with emotion. "Don't you see that?"

Her head jerked upward in obvious surprise, and only then did he realize what he'd let slip. "Who said anything about bonding?" Thea asked quietly, not mocking him, just genuinely taken aback. "Why can't this just be something . . . casual?"

Because nothing with you could ever be casual for me . . . if I take even one step with you, there's no turning back. Never.

That was what he wanted to say, but he could only stare at her, his heart hammering like a freight train. He had no idea how to answer her at all, and was grappling with some kind of explanation when his communicator beeped, piercing the silence abruptly.

He punched the button on his forearm. "Marco, you need to get back right now," came Sabrina's voice over his mobile unit. "We've tracked Lieutenant Dillon. We know where they've taken him."

He reached for Thea's hand and began sprinting with her up the path. They'd just been spared a very painful moment, but he also felt they'd lost something precious in the process. They'd been at a crossroads, where the balance might still have swung either way—but this interruption had changed that irrevocably. Because he had no doubt that either of them would ever let things explode so heatedly ever again.

Chapter Fifteen

Hope Harper was jarred awake by the sound of her bedside phone ringing. Reaching for it, she managed to knock a bottle of water on the floor and send her alarm clock flying halfway across her bedroom. "Damn it!" she muttered, cursing her bad eyesight as she pulled the receiver to her ear. Even in the dark, she should have been able to make out shadowy details because of her alarm clock light. Not anymore.

"Harper." She put on her professional voice; it was probably somebody from work.

Her supervisor said, "Morning, Harper." Her first thought: She'd have to leave her very warm bed to deal with whatever was going on.

She heard him draw a breath, then hesitate. She sat up; she knew Robbie Chambers extremely well, and something big had gone down. "You need to get dressed and come on in," he said quietly. "There's a subject we may need your help with. Pull up everything you have on those intercepts once you get here."

Hope's heartbeat sped up. "The subject's Refarian?" she asked, her thoughts racing wildly, but her boss made no answer.

The receiver simply went dead.

The main cafeteria at Base Eight buzzed with soldiers and activity; Thea took her seat at a long table, choosing to dine alone. Usually she ate lunch in the main cabin, but she'd hoped to avoid Marco this way. The last thing she wanted was to spend a whole meal staring into the man's beautiful, sexy eyes. But her dining choice wasn't proving to be as peaceful as she'd hoped: Too many of her soldiers kept glancing her way, questions reflected in their Refarian eyes.

The rumors had been flying since Scott Dillon's capture—this despite Jared addressing the troops last night. But since then they'd learned who had Scott, the US Air Force, and although they'd suspected as much, their latest intel hadn't been put out to the troops just yet. So speculations were running rampant, which meant the ranks were looking to her for answers. She buried her nose in a strategy plan and refused to look up.

"Why would a beautiful soldier like you be dining alone?" Marco asked from behind her.

Marco, you're the last person I need right now, she thought with a groan as he swung one long, lean leg over the bench to take a seat beside her. He slid his tray onto the table, assuming a very close seat on her right side.

"I thought we reached an agreement last night." She didn't turn to face him, but instead focused on the strategy manual in her left hand.

When he spoke again, his voice was less cocky and flirtatious, gentle even. "I wanted to apologize," he said softly. "If you'd let me."

"No need to dine by my side to do that."

"Would you please look at me?" he implored, reaching beneath the table to touch her hand. "Thea, please."

Slowly, she turned on the bench until she found herself staring into those arresting, languid eyes of his. Eyes that spoke of sex and fantasy and thousands of other things he always made her desire. Things he'd made it clear she could never have.

He was beneath her, bed frame creaking with their thrusts and gyrations. His large, dark hands gripping her by the waist; those same sultry eyes drifting to half-mast . . .

She closed her eyes, gave her head a slight shake, and forced herself to focus. ". . . whatever this is," he was saying, "it seems to be a force beyond us both."

Training her eyes on him again, she gave a half nod. For the first time she noticed what silky, thick eyebrows he had. Not like he was some sort of wild *gnantsa* from the jungles—that kind of bushy eyebrows never turned her on in a man—but his were dramatic eyebrows, arcing with a wide grace. She had the unshakeable urge to lift her fingertip and slowly outline the left one, just tracing it from side to side.

"It's a force all right," she agreed, *forcing* herself to look into his eyes, not at his elemental beauty.

"And I'm not sure it was a particularly good thing, what happened in the mitres, Thea," he continued, reaching for a bottle of water and tilting it back for a chug. A rivulet of the liquid spilled onto his chin, and he wiped it away with the back of his hand. She had a flashing desire to reach up and lick it away with the tip of her tongue, tasting him as he had already tasted her skin. With a quick sniff, she stole a bit of his scent. The earthy, tangy smell of it caused gooseflesh to form all over her body.

He leaned back a bit, his eyes narrowing and that damnable sideways smile spread across his face, forcing his single dimple to pop into view. He knew! He'd caught her scenting him, which only proved what a farce this whole "controlling the force of nature that's compelling us together" thing was all about!

"Was it nice?" he teased her, the smile widening.

"My lunch?" she deflected, facing forward again to avoid him altogether. "Delicious. Commander Bennett always feeds us well."

"My scent, Thea."

Her face flushed violently, her jaw tensed, but she made no reply. For his part, Marco bent close, pretending to examine the strategy journal she held before her; he lifted it from her hand—any observer would have interpreted the maneuver that way—but managed to dip his face much closer to hers. Close enough to catch her own scent.

"Yours certainly is," he pronounced, releasing a slow, powerful exhalation of breath against her cheek. "Wildflowers." He sighed again. "You've given me a massive hard-on."

She slammed both hands on the table. "You are being totally unfair," she said, thankful for the din of Refarian voices filling the cafeteria. "You sat down, claiming you wanted to apologize—and then, next thing I know, you're talking about your ever-loving *strka*!

"You're the one who scented me," he reminded her with a light laugh.

"That doesn't matter," she protested, though admittedly he had her there. She had gotten this particular session rolling herself. She swung one leg over the bench so that she faced him fully. "Look, I'm onto your game, Marco. You're all about 'Come close, I'll push you away'," she said. "Or it's 'Stay away and I'll keep coming after you until you *let* me get close.' "

A deep scowl furrowed his eyebrows. "Am I really that bad?"

"You are! And I can't live this way, so please"—she extended her hands in a pleading gesture—"just stay away. Keep your distance, and leave out the part where you keep trying to get closer. That's the only way I can handle being near you—since I'm stuck with you. Unless you can send another hellishly handsome Madjin to take your place."

"No," he said with a grudging smile, "I'm it. You're stuck, like you say."

"Then just keep away from me—and take all your damnable memories with you too. I don't want them plaguing my mind another minute."

"Thea, I have nothing to do with what you keep seeing," he told her as she rose to walk away. His eyes tracked with her, locked on her intently. "I may be intuitive, but I can't make anyone see things."

She shook her head, reaching for her tray. "I'm not an imbecile," she told him hotly. "I do realize you're not causing them, but I wish they'd stop. They're making my heart hurt and my body fevered while you—apparently—have no intention of acting upon them."

"Sit down, Thea," Marco half begged, staring up into her eyes. He'd waited hours for this chance, had followed her down from the main cabin in hopes of just a moment of time alone with her. And he had intended to apologize, that much was true, but his motives had also been far more complex: He'd needed to be with her. Ever since their kiss on the trail, it seemed that things inside his heart had intensified multifold, always leading back to her innocent question: *Why can't this just be something . . . casual?*

Thea's jaw tensed as she clearly deliberated about sitting down again. He reached for her forearm, urging her downward onto the bench. He had to tell her the truth. If she didn't know now, he might never find the courage again. "Only for a moment," he promised. "You won't have to tolerate me for longer than that."

Her shoulders slumped in frustrated surrender and she dropped her tray back onto the table, slowly sinking onto the seat. "All right," she told him, her jaw flexing angrily. "I'm listening, McKinley."

Gathering his thoughts, he tried to center the swirling emotions battling for dominance inside of him. The memories of her were coming so fast and hard now, it was becoming increasingly difficult not to simply fall in love with her. For he had loved her, in that other time. Maybe he'd never fully admitted it to himself, but it had at least come close to love. Carefully, he reached for her hand where she braced it on the wooden bench frame, covering it with his—his movements as circumspect and cautious as if he were approaching a skittish mare.

"I need to tell you something, Thea. Something I wanted to tell you the other night on the trail—and didn't."

She nodded, her blond eyebrows knitting together seriously.

"You asked why we couldn't just get together and have something"—he hesitated over her word choice because it still hurt him—"*casual*. That was the word you used."

"It was a good question." She wriggled her hand out from underneath his. "You seem so convinced that we're doomed, that all the bad images from the other time are true—and equally convinced that we'd go so far as to bond."

"Thea, don't you understand?" He bent down until his nose was within an inch of hers. His whole body burned, wildfire darting over his skin, across his senses. He gulped for air, attempting vainly to steady his heart. "Don't you get it? Nothing with you could ever be . . . casual for me. Casual?" He shook his head, laughing bitterly. "Every time I hold you, every time I taste of you—or catch your scent—you have the power of the universe over me. And that's not casual, Thea," he hissed. "Not for someone like me."

She gaped at him, her clear, mysterious blue eyes widening. Slowly, she lifted her fingertips to her lips, touching them as if he'd just brushed a kiss across them.

He continued, "So you see, that's why I keep pushing you away. 'Cause it's the only thing I know to do. My vows exist—they're the only real thing I've ever known—and I'm here to serve our king and queen. Could we have a secret affair? Maybe. Maybe if I were capable of holding back with you." He stood, gazing down at her for one long, naked moment. "But I can't hold back, and if we so much as contemplate truly making love, I'll be utterly soulbound to you in a heartbeat. And I can't do that to either one of us."

Then, he did the hardest thing—but the only thing—he could possibly do. He turned and walked away.

Hope Harper walked across the tarmac of Warren Air Force Base. The forceful wind of fighter jets taking off caused her scarf to fly up into her face, which only made seeing all the more difficult. In bright daylight such as this morning, she could make out blurry images overlain by dark floaters. Spots basically, all the way around, but usually better if it were a bright, sunny day such as this one. That was how she still managed to snowboard on the baby slopes. So she was thankful that arriving on base today she could rely on the morning light to orient her somewhat; it took some of the edge off of stepping into such an unknown situation.

Her supervisor, Robbie Chambers, took hold of her arm, urging her along toward what looked to be an entrance. The thing with the fully sighted was that they never realized you didn't want to be tugged—you simply wanted to *hold on*. Thank God she wasn't completely blind yet, just legally so, and she let him pull her inside the building.

With a series of turns and welcomes from shadowed military personnel (the greenish overhead light made it much tougher for her to make out their forms), she quickly found herself filing down a long hallway, hearing the distant sounds of shoes clicking on concrete flooring. "Harper, we're counting on you to make some headway here."

She'd been briefed about the details by the special agent in charge back in Denver, and now her months of work on the Refarian language would finally be put to the test. In the two days since capturing the man they knew as Scott Dillon, they'd been unable to get a single answer out of him. She knew he spoke English; she'd heard him on the intercepts. And the other thing she now knew—since she'd been briefed into this higher clearance, even higher than her regular top secret clearance—was that in all likelihood her suspicions had been correct.

They continued to rely on their flimsy cover story about Dillon belonging to an obscure political cell in eastern Europe: That's how compartmentalized information worked. Very few people had the full picture, and they would only put small pieces in various individuals' hands. For her part, they needed her language expertise, nothing more. But that didn't alter what her training and common sense told her: Scott Dillon belonged to an alien race, one that directly threatened the security and safety of the United States. Possibly Planet Earth.

"Any word on Lieutenant Dillon's release?" Jared asked his chief security officer, Lieutenant Nevin Daniels, who was sitting with him on the other side of the meeting room table. The man shook his head, his expression grave.

For three days they'd been stumped; they now knew where Scott was being held—at Warren Air Force Base—where the US military had kept him for the past almost seventy-two hours. Jared felt nauseated at the thought of his best friend being interrogated, possibly tortured. Humans, he thought with a weary sigh, a people with such capacity for beauty, but also capable of such hateful vengeance.

"Keep the base under surveillance—but be careful.

We want to track any movement they might make with the lieutenant, but we don't want to risk losing anyone else."

"They might try to transfer him to another facility," the other man suggested. "What then?"

Jared leaned back in his chair and thought about the many engagements they'd had with the Air Force over the years—most recently, he himself had been shot down by a pilot from Warren. Of course the humans believed them their enemies; after all, the USAF pilots came under constant fire from the Antousians, and how could they possibly discern the difference between Refarians and Antousians? Aliens were all perceived as security threats, no matter which species they belonged to. Never mind how many of Jared's people had been killed by the Antousians since their arrival here on Earth six years ago. And never mind that he and the Refarians were here to protect Earth. None of the human governments ever seemed to understand such subtleties.

"I wonder what Dillon has told them," Jared reflected aloud. "Perhaps he could arrange a summit; they might be willing to meet with us to discuss military matters and practical solutions."

Nevin leaned forward in his chair, his demeanor intense and serious. "My lord, I think the time for talking is long past—surely you'd agree."

Jared stared at the wintry landscape beyond the window. "Perhaps," he said thoughtfully. "Or perhaps the time has come at last."

"What of our other matter?" the man asked him. "Your wife?"

Jared's gaze shifted back to focus on his lieutenant. "I assume you're speaking of the mitres data?" He didn't like his officer calling Kelsey "our other matter." It indicated the overall suspicion that he sensed among so many of his soldiers toward his new wife.

"Sir, we've obviously been ineffective so far in retrieving the codes. Surely even you must be concerned by now."

"Concerned? Surely even *I* must be *concerned*?" Jared felt hot anger boil within himself—even, for a moment, felt the compulsion to Change. It was always there, and provocations such as this one only baited it. "Yes, Lieutenant, I am concerned about my wife and about the safety of my people!" he roared, the furnace of his core self stoking hotter. "You should be concerned about your *queen*."

His officer clearly caught his tone and, visibly chastened, bowed his head. "I mean no disrespect, sir. I'm merely registering my extreme concern about this security matter."

"We have tried numerous methods, so far none successful, in retrieving the mitres data."

"What I'm suggesting, sir, is that it's time for new measures. Time to think of what we haven't tried."

Jared recalled Marco's offer the night before, his suggestion that he could train them both to use their intuition. He'd acquiesced at the time because he believed Marco was correct; he himself had planted the data within Kelsey, and despite all his previous objections, he was now the one to finally extract it.

Without another word, Jared rose from the table, determined to find his Madjin.

Chapter Sixteen

Kelsey and Jared sat on their living room floor facing one another. Marco knelt beside them both, his large hands resting on their shoulders.

"Close your eyes and take deep breaths," he coached in his sure voice. "It will begin with your establishing a connection between the two of you."

Kelsey glanced at Jared, who smiled at her almost a bit shyly. She knew exactly what he was thinking at that moment, because it was her own thought—did Marco have any idea how powerful their connection could be at times? During the short time of their bonding, it had been magnifying exponentially. Last night, she'd felt him enter her dreams.

"Okay," Jared answered, and Kelsey felt him open their bond; wild heat began welling within her. Quickly, she connected with him, without any of their usual seductive dancing. This was all about accomplishing something via their connection.

Kelsey, sweetheart, Jared said softly, the minute the flow opened. *Don't be scared,* he soothed her.

I'm not.

Yes, you are . . . I can feel it. Don't be. I'm right here, he promised.

I want all of you, Jared . . . all of myself, too. And if this helps you get the data back, I'm willing. I'm willing to do anything for you—you know that.

I love you, he whispered softly.

Their bonding was interrupted by the sound of Marco clearing his throat with a rumbling cough. Kelsey glanced sideways at him, and was surprised to find him staring at her strangely, his mouth slightly open. She sensed that he knew they'd been communicating silently between themselves. But she could also tell he was studying them, trying to decipher something about how their relationship worked.

"Are you connected?" he asked, raising his dark brows in amazement. "Just like that?"

Kelsey nodded vigorously. "Yeah, we're ready, Marco."

"You can do that?" Marco pressed, his voice full of undisguised wonder. "Without even touching?"

"Well, yeah. Can't everybody?" she asked in surprise, but then quickly rushed to elaborate. "I mean can't all . . . bonded mates . . . do that?" She felt her face flush very deeply, remembering that bonding for the Refarians was a very sexual experience.

"No, Kelsey, everybody *can't* do that," Marco answered with a faint smile, shaking his head. "Most need to touch, or make a more determined physical connection. Riley and Anika are the only two I've ever known capable of it otherwise."

Her bond with Jared had become so second nature to her already, it was easy to forget how intimate a connection was for their kind. She noticed Jared's own face glowing with obvious embarrassment. She smiled; Jared was so shy and ashamed of certain things about his nature, it almost amused her. Like his mating cycles.

Please, love, he said seriously, *let's not focus on our problem.*

It's not a problem! she snapped, unable to resist feeling frustrated.

He dropped his head, frowning, and she was immediately sorry. *You know what I mean.* She felt deep pain radiate from him—and only when he glanced up at her did she realize it was a mirror of her own pain.

Why are we feeling all of this? she reflected, unsure why such raw emotions were cresting so fast between them.

As if reading her thoughts, Marco announced, "Practicing your gift of intuition is a vulnerable experience."

He glanced between them, something strange in his eyes—something sad. "*Intensely* vulnerable. Don't be surprised by what surfaces."

Jared nodded seriously. "Thank you, Marco. We are ready."

"So we'll begin." Marco's black eyes darted between them, and they both nodded their readiness.

Jared covered her hands gently with his own. She hadn't even realized that she'd been wringing her hands slightly for the past few moments, and now he stilled them beneath his. He hadn't missed her jittery gestures.

"I'm going to start you on a kind of exercise," Marco began, placing his hands lightly on both their shoulders.

"Okay," Kelsey answered, her heartbeat quickening as she felt a warmth begin to pervade her shoulder right where Marco was touching it. Jared tightened his grip on her hand, and she knew he'd felt it too. Was Marco releasing some of his power to them?

"I want the two of you to open your minds . . . clear them first, okay?" he began. "Remember, just keep taking deep breaths. Close your eyes . . . allow your connection to build."

Kelsey shut her eyes and felt Jared's warmth surround her, envelop her. She wondered if Marco had any idea what their bond was really like, because if they just sat here like this, drinking one another in, their energy would begin to escalate like crazy. Jared might not even be able to hold back his Change.

Especially with the particular cycle they had recently touched. And lost. Again, the overwhelming sadness overtook her, smothering her.

Deep breaths, baby, Jared coached softly.

I know, I just . . .

Don't worry about our mating cycles. We will deal with the problem, he assured her. *Right now, we have to focus.*

I'm afraid, Jared.

I won't let anything happen to you.

No, about your fertility. I want to have your baby.

He rubbed a palm over the top of his head, staring hard into her eyes. *Why are we talking about it now?*

I don't know, she told him, feeling anguish well anew.

Maybe because I've hardly seen you since you told me you'd stopped cycling.

His black eyes narrowed, filled with pain and concern. *Have I neglected you?*

No, Jared. That's not it . . . I just want you to help me. I can't make it happen alone.

You're never alone now that you've married me, he reminded her, and she felt warm joy begin inside of her anew.

Glancing up at Marco, she said, "We'll focus now—sorry." But something in his expression, a certain way his face had blanched, made her wonder if he'd sensed their thoughts. He cleared his throat, nodded, and drew in several steadying breaths. Kelsey noticed that his hands trembled softly.

"Marco, what's wrong?" she asked, but he stepped quickly apart from them, backing away.

"I'm—not feeling well suddenly," he told them. "Mind if I use your bathroom?"

"Of course," Jared said. "We'll wait for you."

Marco bent over their bathroom sink, splashing cold water onto his face repeatedly. He couldn't stop gasping, drawing heated breaths into his lungs.

He stared into the mirror at his wet face, trying to get his breathing under control. *Gods above,* he thought, panicking. *What the hell just happened?*

For a full ten seconds he'd dropped into the middle of Jared and Kelsey's connection, and it had been as if the floor had literally been yanked from underneath him, catapulting him right inside their bond.

The emotions had been unbelievable and overpowering, and it was terrain where he'd never been meant to go because it was far too intimate. He'd felt heat rush all through his own body as their mutual energy spiraled within him.

And he'd experienced so much love that it had literally knocked the air from his lungs.

He'd never believed that two people could love one another like that—the way he'd just sensed between them—and it left him feeling horribly lonely. It was as if in the wake of intercepting their connection, his solitude had stood in stark relief. As much as he cared for Thea already—as deep as it was—he would be forever denied what he'd just glimpsed.

He blotted his face with a towel, his body calming somewhat, recovering from the unexpected shock. He could never have anticipated the physical reaction to what he'd just experienced; he'd been hit with a huge blast of Refarian energy so strong it had nearly driven him to his knees.

Jared and Kelsey Bennett were far more powerful than anyone suspected, and it had nothing to do with the mitres data. The key lay in the way they joined. They could do it without even touching; he shook his head in disbelief because the power he'd felt was unlike anything he'd ever even heard of. And being suspended right within their bond for those few moments had changed his understanding of their relationship permanently. Of what a relationship could be. More than that, the pain and heartbreak he'd sensed between them over Jared's infertility had almost destroyed him.

He stared at his eyes in the mirror, and couldn't shake the eerie sensation that somehow, even more significantly, this event had just altered his own relationship with the two of them . . . irrevocably. And he prayed with all his protector's heart that the change was a good thing.

Marco rushed headlong down the hallway, frantic and wrestling to still his thoughts. He should never have been able to intercept such tender emotions between his king and queen—much less have known their deepest pain. He felt as if he'd violated them without ever intending to. His head hammered with a violent headache, the likes of which he hadn't had in years—not a good sign at all, not for him. What would be a casual annoyance to anyone else was a deep signal that his darkest self had been awakened.

He was contemplating that fact and how he would explain it to Sabrina—for, after all, any violations between a Madjin and his protected had to be reported to his unit leader immediately—when he rounded a corner in the hallway and slammed into Thea.

"You all right?" she asked quizzically as he steadied her by the shoulders.

"Sorry," he grumbled, pushing past her.

"Just like that, huh?" she called after him, but he hurried on to his room. When he reached it, he yanked open the door and, feeling his legs grow unsteady beneath him, sank onto the edge of his bed. The room was spinning; his emotions were careening. Nothing in his universe felt sane or still. For a brief moment he thought he'd actually be sick, his stomach was knotting and protesting so heavily from what had just opened in him.

"Gods," he whispered, then, "All! Help me. Help."

Almost as if on cue, his door flung open without even a knock. Thea stood in the brightly lit doorway staring at him in irritated concern. "What was that about?" she demanded. "Just brushing past me."

He groaned, burying his face in his hands. The contrast between the bright light in the hallway and the dark, womblike shadows of his bedroom only caused his headache to ratchet tighter behind his eyes. "Thea, I'm sick," he managed, wishing everything would stop spinning.

He heard the door close softly, and then the sound of her quiet footsteps on the hardwood. Then her cool hand pressed against his forehead. "You're fevered," she said quietly. "When did this happen? Jared told me you were working with them this morning on training."

"I was," he said with a gasp. "Was. Feeling unwell. Please, Thea . . . go."

She settled on the bed beside him and slowly rubbed a hand across his tight shoulders. "I'm not leaving you like this," she said plainly. "I've got a simple healing gift, not much of a gift really, but I can probably help you."

Jerking his head sideways, he stared hard into her eyes. "No." His voice sounded like cold-edged steel, so he worked to soften his tone; none of this was her fault. "Please, no. I need time alone."

"Something happened," she observed, suddenly sensing it within his heart. Something so troubling and upsetting, he had shut down like a wounded animal—run to protect himself in the privacy of his room. "I feel it, Marco. You need to talk to me."

"I was working with them," he breathed, burying his head deeper in his hands. "And it was wrong. Dead wrong. I have no right to know these things—the intimate feelings they have for one another."

"Was it your intuition?" She wasn't entirely following him; in fact, he was talking somewhat nonsensically. She wasn't sure if it was how ill he felt or whatever had happened in Jared's chambers that was upsetting him so much.

"I sensed things, Thea. Felt things. I . . . slipped into their bond. Was right in the middle of it, suspended, couldn't leave." He gave a pained, wounded cry, pressing both hands to his temples. "In All's name, this headache!" he moaned. "It's been so damned long. So long."

"So long since *what*?" she urged. "Please, Marco, tell me more."

"This has to have been how it happened in that other life," Marco whispered, dropping his hands away from his face. "Don't you see, Thea? It's *me*. It's this darkness in me. That's the reason our memories of one another are all poison—because I'm capable of betrayal. Ruin. Because of this thing, this damned, cursed *thing* inside of me!"

She pressed her hand against his forehead, using her secondary gift of healing to alleviate his pain. Instantly, she saw relief wash over his features. He closed his eyes, the curling black lashes fanning against his cheeks. "Thank you," he whispered.

"You shouldn't have to hurt."

"Maybe that's the best someone like me deserves," he spat bitterly.

"Marco, you're not cursed." Thea reached for his hand where it rested on his thigh, covering it with hers. "You're good. Beautiful. Don't you understand? I could love you, Marco. I could totally, completely love you . . . and I wouldn't feel that way if you were the corrupt man you claim to be."

He turned haunted, narrowed eyes upon her. "But you don't know me, Thea." His voice was so raw it chilled her. "Not really—or what's inside of me. In the mitres, I saw what I did. I know exactly what sort of man I am."

She tossed up her hands in exasperation. "What are

you even *talking* about? You had a vision in the mitres . . . you slipped into Jared and Kelsey's bond. That's not enough basis for—"

"Listen to me, Thea." He rose and walked away from her, pacing the cramped length of his room. She waited for him to speak, and was surprised to realize her chest was heaving with urgent gasps; he was frightening her to the marrow of her bones. After several long moments he stilled, standing by the small window that looked out onto a bank of snow outside. A tiny aperture of morning sky was visible, revealing gray cloud-covering. He braced his hand on the ledge, and stared upward, somber, and at last he spoke. "What I am, Thea, is the worst kind of curse."

"That's not possible." She laughed nervously. "It doesn't even make sense."

"You asked about Marek—that first night." He gazed back at her meaningfully, as if the mention of that name would put his ranting into some sort of logical context. "You knew the name, from the beginning."

"I heard it from across the bar the first night," she agreed quietly. "What does he have to do with all this? You told me he was a dead man." She met his blazing stare. It reminded her of Jared, that deeply burning nature of a D'Aravnian, such power and intensity showed within his Madjin's eyes.

"He is a dead man."

"Then why did you just mention him?"

Marco shook his head, saying nothing. "They can't . . . cycle," he finally whispered, deep melancholy overcoming his expression. "Jared and Kelsey can't—I heard that. I have no right to know about their problems with fertility and mating. They're in such pain and I felt it all, particularly from Kelsey." He raked a hand through his hair. "It was too much, what I sensed. What I heard between them. Their feelings for one another, the love, it's beyond anything I could even imagine between two people. Except—" Abruptly he stopped speaking, the olive-gold of his face flushing deeply.

"Except between us," Thea finished for him, instinctively knowing his thoughts. He dropped his head, the blush intensifying in his face.

"I wanted it. In that moment, what I felt between them . . . I craved what they have. I craved to be Jared."

Thea jerked back in horror. "You wanted . . . her?" she asked, her throat going dry.

"No, I didn't want Kelsey." He shook his head, pressing the back of his hand against his flushed cheek. "I wanted to *cycle*," he admitted softly, lifting his eyes until their gazes locked. "With you, Thea. You experience mating heat like Jared should, right? I know you do, I sense it."

Now it was Thea's turn to feel her face flame hot. She began to tremble and her core self bucked upward, desperate to be known. Every instinct that had driven her through her past seven mating cycles squirmed inside of her, edging forward, screaming Marco's name. "Please don't," she barely managed through gritted teeth. "You don't mean that. So don't."

What Marco couldn't know was that if he didn't stop, he'd either incite her Change before she could stop herself, or, even worse, he'd spark her mating season into action. She'd had little control of her cycles in the past year; they'd been coming faster and with more velocity than she'd been able to handle. Even speaking of her season with an unmated Refarian male such as Marco—especially a man she desired to such dangerous proportions anyway—could well ignite her parched needs. Seven cycles she'd passed, each time remaining a virgin; it had become almost unbearable.

"What does it feel like to go through your mating season?" he continued, running his tongue across his lips with a motion that caused her entire body to quiver with lust. "It's important—I've got to know."

"Why?"

"Because of what I felt between our king and queen earlier—I know things now, about you and your nature, Thea. It's . . . driven me to the edge. I can't control this need anymore, and by the gods, I *need* you—so damned bad it's tearing me apart inside."

"Then forget your vows!" she suddenly shouted, bolting to her feet. "Forget everything that you claim to be, and—and"—she sputtered—"make *love* to me! Finally, just do it!"

Without meaning to, without even a breath, she Changed and appeared before him in all her golden, whirling power and beauty. She hadn't been able to control it, the compulsion had been that intense and leveling. More than any thing in the universe, she wanted Marco McKinley to see her most natural self.

Need him, she thought, shimmying in a spiral.

Need mate.

Need cycle!

Oh, trouble, she thought darkly and gave another gyrating whirl. *He trouble!*

Marco was utterly breathless. Never in all his twenty-eight years had he seen a more erotic, gorgeous being. *My Thea. Mine!* She had to be; he couldn't ever let another man gaze upon her this way, naked and glorious. His cock grew rock-hard in an instant, straining within his uniform pants. She spun, pirouetted before him, pure alluring power, then suddenly withdrew to the far side of the room. He could hardly restrain himself as she awakened such primal, driving need in his loins and heart.

"Don't." He gulped hard, yanking his sweater over his head so that he stood before her bare-chested. "Baby, don't back away," he begged in a voice so thick that even he hardly recognized it. "Show me what you are. Everything, baby. I need you . . . just like this."

With a pulsating gyration, her energy expanded, growing from its compact size into something like streaks of golden-red light. *Why in hell should Thea's natural form turn me on like this?* he wondered, reaching a hand to touch his bare chest. It burned with her heat. He took a step closer to her; then another.

No! she sang in his mind, half shrill, half whisper. *Stay. Away!*

"I've gotta touch you, baby. Please," he begged. "I can't stop."

I'll Change! No touch.

Her speech had become far simpler, primitive, which he could only assume was part of her natural self. Basic, primal, and sexy as hell!

He couldn't breathe for how badly he wanted her; he swore he was going to come right inside his pants if he wasn't careful, she had aroused him that completely in a matter of moments. Standing before her, he slipped a hand between his own legs and, just gazing upon her, began to rub his thick erection.

He groaned, gasped, and then, with fumbling fingers, unzipped his pants and they slipped to the floor, pooling around his ankles. *Yes!* she whispered in the depth of his soul. *Oh, love, love!*

"Wh-why this . . . effect?" he barely managed to groan, throwing his head back. The rigid warmth of his hardness filled his hand; back and forth he stroked, just gazing upon the woman he now realized he loved. He loved her. All that she was. He had no more arguments left—protection, duty, vows, honor, restraint—none of it meant a damn thing anymore. It didn't even matter, at least for this moment, the horrible *thing* that he was. *I can win*, he thought hungrily. *For her, I'd control it. It doesn't have to . . .*

Love! she trilled inside of his heart. *Love accepts!*

"No, no," he argued with a guttural yelp, the kind common only to highly aroused Refarian males. "This is a hell of a lot more than acceptance, Thea." He could hardly keep his eyes open, her overwhelming energy shimmered so starkly between them. Again, he growled and groaned, nearly coming in the palm of his hand. He felt light dampness form between his fingertips.

Then, in the same whirl of a heartbeat in which she'd made her Change, she stood before him completely naked, her clothes obviously consumed by the fire of her transformation. Her untamed, curling blond hair fell across her shoulders; her full lips were swollen as if he'd been kissing her all along; her pert breasts jutted outward with undeniable arousal.

And he was upon her before either of them could argue. "You said to make love to you," he breathed, taking her into his arms. "You showed me everything about who you are . . . now feel this!" With every ounce of his own soul he reached toward her, allowing his energy to spiral around her, through her, around her.

Feel me inside of you, he breathed, stroking her soul with the tendrils of his massive power.

"Wh-what . . ." she gasped, dropping to her knees.

It's what I am, Thea. He placed his palm atop her head, allowing his heat to enter her body that way as well.

Again, he rolled his energy across her essence, caressed her, touched her until, just barely, he allowed their souls to touch. Risky, so damned risky, but he had to feel her.

She stared up at him, her clear blue eyes watering, and he stroked his knuckles over her cheek. *This is all that I am, baby.*

Beautiful. Gods, I've never . . .

He pushed his soul right against hers, closing his eyes so he could see the trailing red and purple of her own soul. Inhaling her scent, he stood like that, unable to move, knowing they were a mere heartbeat away from bonding. Their mating would have to be sealed by the lovemaking, of course—finished that way. But this was the first step.

Boldly, he pushed his soul atop hers, forcefully. Brave. All his arguments against a bonding evaporating from his mind and heart. He was ready to take her, vows and honor be damned. *Mine,* he thought, *I'm making her all mine!*

And then he recalled every word that had ever been spoken about his kind back on Refaria. Dark. Ruined. Evil. Devil's spawn.

Abruptly he withdrew, releasing his soul-hold upon her, dropping his hand away from the top of her head.

"Why did you stop?" Thea demanded, gaping at him. "What I saw inside of you was amazing! Please, show me more!"

"Thea, we nearly soul-bonded just then—didn't you feel it?"

She smiled up at him. "What I felt was your gift—your soul—I can't even tell the difference. But it was beautiful."

"No, Thea, it's not beautiful," he told her coldly. "It's the worst curse, the ugliest blight. It's completely me!" Holding his hands up he worked to separate them physically, backing away from her. He had to save her from himself; he'd nearly soul-bonded with her! What would he do next time—when he lost full control?

"But it's so beautiful! Your gift is so beautiful," she

whispered in return, reaching toward him with both arms. "How can you call it a curse?"

"Because haven't you figured out what I am?" he thundered, intentionally making himself sound threatening. "Don't you *get* it, baby?"

She shook her head, still reaching toward him, and he closed the distance between them, dropping to his own knees until they knelt together, slowly stroking one another's faces. "I'm an empath," he said at last, bending low to kiss her cheek. There, he'd said it. Maybe now she would understand why, more than any other reason he'd named, they couldn't mate.

She pulled back, shaking her head. "No. No, that can't be true," she said intensely, blinking at him in shock.

He pulled her into his arms, cradling her head against his bare shoulder. He felt the warm wetness of her tears, and wrestled for words. "It's what I really am, baby."

"But . . . empaths never live," she argued. "They're insane. They always go insane. Or die before they come of age."

It was the absolute truth about his kind. On their home planet, empaths were considered a scourge, benighted by the devil himself—not endowed by All. It was a twisted, dark version of the Refarian gift of intuition.

She held onto him tightly, wrapping both her small, strong arms around his broad back and refusing to let go. "You are *not* an empath!" she finally insisted, squeezing him with determined strength.

He closed his eyes and told her the one thing he wished he could protect her from. The one aspect of his core nature that he'd endured since he was a small boy back on Refaria. "Thea, I almost did go insane—before coming here when I was eight. That's what saved me . . . on Earth, for whatever reason, I'm balanced." He gave a bitter laugh. "Most of the time, at least. On Refaria, I was blinded by headaches, sick almost every day; if not for Sabrina, I would have died."

She pulled apart and stared up into his eyes. "What are you saying to me?" she asked, reaching a palm to his heated face.

He hesitated, thinking of how the Refarian mating rites meant the sharing of gifts; Thea's natural affinity for healing and intuition would blend with his own empathy. And his empathy would overtake her so rapidly that without his lifelong skills with tempering his dark gift, she would be destroyed in a matter of days.

He pressed his forehead against hers, stroking her hair. "Thea, my vows are real, but now? Even they aren't enough to keep me apart from you—not after this. Not the way we just shared with each other."

"Then make love to me," she insisted, clasping his face within both her palms. The smell of sweat creased into her hands sent a jolt of desire down his spine. As always, it was her scent that most seemed to drive him to the edge. "Right here, right now," she begged, "let's become lovers. We'll hold back from soul-bonding; it doesn't have to be that way!" Her lovely blue gaze searched his face hungrily, desperately, and it was almost more than he could bear.

"Empaths don't make love without mating, at least not most of the time. It takes too much control," he whispered at last, staring into her eyes meaningfully. "We aren't capable of it. We're too wide open to stop ourselves. *That's* the real reason I'm a virgin—not because I'm a saint or a master of self-discipline. Not even because of my vows, though they certainly matter. But because I can't hold back my core nature, especially not while joining with you! It was like I said in the cafeteria, Thea, that if I so much as take you into my bed, I'll be soulbound to you in a moment."

"Then we'll mate! Yes, yes," she rushed excitedly, showering his jaw with hot kisses. "Oh, Marco, I want to mate. You saw me . . . you know. I accept you and you accept me—we can bond! Why not, I'm willing . . ."

He broke away, pouncing to his feet; he hardly realized he stood before her naked, aroused, angry. With a rough gesture, he threw her his T-shirt so she could cover herself, and it slapped her in the face. "We are finished." He growled furiously.

She shook her head. "We're not even close to being finished. I won't let us be!" She leaped to her own feet, facing him down like the seasoned soldier that she was. She flung his T-shirt back at him and it careened off his bare shoulder. "You don't make these rules!"

The time had come to lay it all out between them, no more half-truths. He clasped her by both shoulders, leveled her with his empath's gaze and in a calm voice shattered all of her remaining illusions. "Thea, if we mate," he told her, "it will destroy you within days."

She laughed, clearly disbelieving him. "That's ridiculous, Marco," she said. "I'll be fine."

"No, Thea, if we mate, you will become an empath just like me—and I've spent a lifetime learning to control my gift. I killed it, drove it into the recesses of my being. But you? You'd go insane—or worse. And there's no way I could do that to you. Not when I've fallen in love with you."

With a furious gesture, he reached for his pants where they lay on the floor, putting his back to her. Then he found his T-shirt and yanked it over his head; he had to get away from her, or he'd never be strong enough to end things between them.

"I don't believe you," she persisted. "Tell me who Marek Shaekai is. How does he figure in here?"

Slowly, he turned to face her one final time. "I was born Marek Shaekai, empath, son of Laliea Shaekai, also an empath . . . also a protector. But I killed Marek so that I could live. That man—the one I was before—died long ago. It was the only way. And if I mate, Thea, with anyone . . . Marek will awaken. Dangerously, horribly, he will awaken. I can't take that risk."

"It's worth the chance," she half begged as he dressed hurriedly. "We're worth the chance."

"Nothing's worth destroying you, Thea," he said, lowering his lips to brush one last kiss across her forehead. "Gods help me, I can't do it—not to you."

"Marco, all I'm asking . . ."

But he never heard the rest of what she said. He left the room and put Thea Haven, a princess and lady of the first order, out of his life forever. He was a servant, an empath, a tainted mongrel the likes of which should *never* have even touched her—much less have contemplated soul-bonding. Even though he felt her shattered tears in his wake, he knew that one day, somehow, she would thank him.

Chapter Seventeen

The room in the underground holding facility where they'd placed Scott Dillon was only ten by ten feet, small enough that the alien could be wrestled into a corner if control became necessary, but large enough that they were giving him at least a little breathing room. Either way, Hope felt surprisingly sorry for the alien. He sat compliantly at the small desk in the center of the room, despite the fact that they'd worked him over good—she heard him groan and exhale whenever he shifted in his seat, indicating a high level of pain. He smelled of nervousness and something else that Hope couldn't quite place, a kind of musky smell.

Seated across the table from him, she worked to make "eye contact": a skill that she knew made people less nervous about her eyesight problems. Part of her job as a translator was putting subjects at ease; it got them talking more freely. She never wanted to spook anybody by not quite looking them in the eye because that could render her less effective. And if there was anything Hope Harper wanted it was to be the best at what she did, not ordinary, and certainly not perceived as disabled. Still, despite her efforts to meet Dillon's gaze dead-on, all she could make out were a blur of black hair and the slash of black eyebrows against a fair face. If he had beard stubble, she couldn't see it. If he smiled, she only had a sense of it.

The lead investigator had described the room to her in detail while security officers had biometrically scanned her palm and retinas. After that, they'd performed a DNA test by swabbing the inside of her mouth. Within ten minutes they were able to verify her identity based on those tests, confirming that she was, in fact, Hope Harper. The door had been unbolted, a series of locks and codes releasing the latch, and she'd been briefed that they were working the subject hard—going the uncomfortable, less pleasant route with him since he hadn't been talking.

Apart from the small table, the only other accoutrements were a pull-down rack bed—currently unmade and against the wall—and a small toilet on the far side of the room. The alien had no privacy for his ablutions, even as it was becoming equally apparent to Hope that he had no civil liberties. It went without saying that the Geneva Convention was meaningless for extraterrestrials, and now that she'd spent hours translating the interrogators' questions, she'd begun to feel even sorrier for Scott Dillon.

He seemed so weary—had they even fed him since his arrival? Another linguist had led out with him for the first day or so; they were rotating her and unknown others. They had split up the duty, which explained why they hadn't just relied on the language lab at headquarters. While she'd been working the intercepts all these months, other translators had been hammering out their own Refarian-English translations. None of them would ever be given the entire picture. Total compartmentalization—each of them on a need-to-know basis.

Hope had spent the entire morning translating for the alien, the interrogators' questions focusing on the role of the Refarian military presence. What was the aliens' interest in Earth? Why this particular quadrant of the planet? Why did the Refarian fighter jet they'd impounded at Mirror Lake appear different from the other jets they'd sighted in the past?

The questions went on and on, and all the while Scott Dillon refused to answer except for occasional phrases in Refarian. She knew he spoke English from the intercepts, but he wasn't about to crack. She wished these guys running the show would let her free-form him for a while with a few questions of her own. Maybe, given her emerging facility with Dillon's native tongue, she could make more headway than she had simply translating the interrogators' questions.

"Ask him why we spotted a squadron of their craft near the Canadian border yesterday," the colonel instructed her. The three of them were seated at the table as if they were about to have coffee and doughnuts. "Ask him what his people are planning."

Hope drew in a breath, spreading her palms in front of her. She began her translation—it was too difficult to do so simultaneously, so each time she waited for the colonel to finish, then began speaking in Refarian.

Dillon sighed, then replied in his native language: "Not willing to answer."

It was a risk, but she decided to buck authority and shot back, "You speak English. You should talk to them."

She sensed him stiffen as a ripple of energy seemed to snake between them.

"What did you just add, Ms. Harper?" Colonel Stevens demanded, his chair creaking as he turned to face her.

"I forgot the part about what they're planning," she lied, covering her tracks. "Just tagging that on."

"You lie," Dillon observed in Refarian, laughing softly. "Amusing."

Not for me, you alien jerk, she thought.

"What's wrong with your eyes?" he continued, and she lowered her gaze to her lap.

"Harper," the colonel insisted, "what is the man *saying* to you?"

She pushed back from the table. "He's starting to bait me. You better bring in one of the other linguists."

"I like that—taking charge," Dillon snickered, but she ignored him, rising from her seat.

Still, something about this alien—a man she could hardly see—felt painfully familiar. Knocked the breath from her lungs, now that he'd addressed her personally. That was the real reason she'd stepped away: so he wouldn't see how badly she'd begun to shake when he asked what was wrong with her eyes. *It's just the tapes,* she told herself. *You've been listening to his voice for months*. He had a scratchy, husky voice and, when he spoke her own language, it had such a deep resonance to it that she'd often felt the hairs on her neck prickle while transcribing intercepts. *I know this man, somehow, somewhere . . .*

The colonel pulled her aside, speaking in tones low enough that only she would hear. "Are you sure, Harper? You've made more headway with the subject than the others."

She glanced back at Dillon's blurry form, trying to discern whether he'd desist from his provoking behavior. "If you'd give me more freedom, sir—the ability to question him less rigidly, get more of a conversation going—"

"That's not protocol," he reminded her simply, jangling the keys in his pocket. Then he made a kind of whistling noise between his teeth—he probably had a slight gap in front. "Not even close to protocol."

"I realize that, Colonel, but I might be able to hit him with the same questions, just get better results."

"Harper, you've used unconventional methods before." She'd gotten in trouble for them, too—and won the highest award for a linguist within the FBI: Language Specialist of the Year. "I like those kinds of methods, and that's why I tapped you for this project."

"You tapped me?" She couldn't hide her surprise. How did a colonel within the Air Force tap an FBI linguist for something like this?

"This is a joint project, Harper," he explained, jangling the keys again. "We've picked our team going in. Carefully."

"I understand, sir."

The jangling sound stopped. "Give it a go," he said. "We're getting it all on tape, audio and video. Why not?"

It was odd, but for the first time since she'd entered the holding facility, Hope breathed a bit easier.

Scott watched the translator as she spoke in hushed tones with the colonel who'd been questioning him for the past days. Heightening his hearing, he knew what she was suggesting: that she take charge of the interview even though she was just the linguist, not an officer or special agent. The woman had a good mastery of his language, and it had startled him when she'd first begun in that soft, feminine voice of hers to form the language of his home. To see a human mouth speaking the words of his youth and his adopted people.

For a second, he had even imagined the human woman an ally—and it was at that same moment that the strange, disconcerting images had washed through his mind. She was the woman from the visions he'd had in the mitres! It was the image of *her* that had given him comfort during his capture and his brutal beating at the hands of the Air Force soldiers. She, the same woman seated across from him now, with her gray eyes that wouldn't quite look at him—yet that seemed to slice through him somehow. Was she some sort of gazer, like he was? Did humans possess gifts of seeing that his people didn't yet understand?

"I'm Hope Harper," she began quietly, the full, sensual mouth hesitating briefly. She ran her tongue over her lower lip thoughtfully, then continued: "I work for the FBI and I have some questions for you, Lieutenant."

"I already asked you my own," he said softly, leaning forward toward her. He was fascinated with her haunting eyes, it was true—but he'd asked the question to disconcert her; the same reason he brought it up again now.

"We aren't here to talk about me," she countered matter-of-factly, setting her jaw. She was a tiny woman, just a wisp of a thing—barely five feet tall, if that. The human was delicate and lovely; maybe that's why her presence made some of his gnawing terror dissipate. She gave him comfort; he felt stronger and healed sitting near her. As if somewhere, somehow, this woman had . . . loved him. Deeply. With all her life force, until . . .

Until what? He had a dark, cloudy sense, something terribly foreboding that he couldn't quite understand. So he stared at her and began to gaze; she would never even know—that is, if his hunch about her eyesight were correct, she wouldn't realize he was soul-gazing her.

Show me who you really are. At first he saw dim fog; murky, blurry vision with dark spots covering pieces of the images. Then darker still. She was running through the woods, and reached back with her hand, taking his. *"Come! Now!"* she urged him in English. *"They're on the way. We have to go, Scott!"*

". . . listening to me?" came *this* Hope's hard-edged question. "If you won't cooperate, we have ways of making things less pleasant."

He blinked, painfully aware that his eyes were probably about to glow, and that wasn't something the humans needed on tape. Closing them he replied, "I am ready. Ask all you want."

"Why won't you speak English? We know you're fluent in our language."

He tapped his fingers on the table, but said nothing for a moment. Finally he arrived at the best and most honest answer possible: "Because it feels safer to me not to."

"I might feel the same way if I were in your shoes," Hope replied, smiling faintly. She had a lovely smile, with a full mouth he'd already noticed could assume a sulky expression or a beautiful one, depending on what he said. Her pale blond hair and light freckles finished out her appearance with a warm, innocent look that naturally made him want to confess far more than he should. *Human women,* he thought ruefully. *Why in hell did I ever develop that taste?*

Watch yourself, man! Stay focused! But then it hit him how perfectly these humans had orchestrated their interrogation, and he had to suppress a hysterical laugh. Whether intentional or not, they'd now pitted him against the one temptation he could never seem to resist: a blond, beautiful *human* woman.

He hadn't a hope in hell of survival.

Hope watched as they shoved Scott into the far corner, wrestling him to the ground. Two medical staff worked at his arm, and seemed to be injecting some unknown substance into it. Hope cringed as Scott shouted, writhed, and resisted, and she heard the sickening thud of what was probably a rifle butt hitting him hard in the face. There was the unmistakable bright color of blood, and he yelped in obvious pain, crumpling into a heap on the floor. Then all his noises ceased, the room falling quiet except for the rapid breathing of the soldiers and medical personnel who had worked him over.

"He'll cooperate better now," the colonel told her, nodding in satisfaction. "He can sleep on it." He took her arm, urging her toward the door.

With a backward glance, she thought she saw blood pooling on the concrete floor. "He's injured," she objected quietly.

The colonel snorted. "Good. Those *creatures* took out ten of our aircraft in the past three months. Killed eight of our pilots. Let him bleed!"

"Yes, sir," she said dutifully, pausing by the door for a new DNA test and biometric scan: In or out, they had to undergo the same procedure to verify their identity. Going in she understood, but it was odd to her that they had to take the same tests just to exit the holding room.

Probably because some of these aliens can change form, she thought with a backward glance and a shiver. She'd felt an odd connection with Dillon all afternoon, but it was easy to forget his kind were cold-blooded killers. Invaders. And that he could probably perpetrate countless deceptions; otherwise, there was no explaining the tests upon *exiting* the lockdown area.

"Sir?" one of the security officers on the other side of the door buzzed through the speaker by the door. "We're having trouble with Ms. Harper's retinal scan."

The colonel hit the intercom and called back, "What sort of trouble?"

"Well, sir"—the soldier hesitated, sounding confused—"it's saying she isn't who she claims to be."

Beside her, she sensed the officer stiffen, stare at her, then turn back to the intercom. "I've been watching Ms. Harper the entire time," he argued, but there was a trace of apprehension in his voice. As if he weren't entirely certain she might not be an alien herself.

"It's the retinal scan, sir. It doesn't match the pattern from four hours ago—or the one on record."

There was the sound of the colonel's weapon being drawn and instantly Hope's heart went into her throat. There was the loud flow of blood in her ears; she turned first one way, then another. "It's a mistake!" she cried, hearing the door buzz open and the rushing entry of footsteps. "Please!" she insisted, "There's a mistake. I'm FBI language specialist Hope Harper! I'm not an enemy! I'm one of us!"

Suddenly, there was the sting of a bee in her arm . . . or a needle . . . and then just nothing at all.

Such a swimmy sensation in her body, tingling down to her fingertips and her toes; Hope tried to stir in the bed, but her stomach was huge and awkward. Tighter than a drum, the skin itching, and she kept scratching at the swollen melon in her twilight-sleep. But then she remembered: They'd only stopped to rest. Their enemies were all around them, surrounding their army like a pack of wild wolves. She struggled to sit up, always hard these days, and Scott's worried face appeared in her line of vision.

"You need to rest," he scolded, his black eyebrows drawing into sharp creases. His familiar, handsome face. So clear, so easy to see.

I haven't seen this well in a year, Hope thought, trying to blink back the hazy, drug-induced sleep. *Where am I, really?*

Even now, in the midst of so much bloodshed and ruin, Scott was breathtakingly beautiful to her. "Come here," she whispered, waving him closer as she settled back onto the makeshift pallet he'd created for her in the tent. He crawled forward on his knees until he bent low to kiss her. She cupped his scratchy face between her palms—he had a three-day growth of beard going, a look she always loved on him. Too bad it was because they were being pursued to extinction. Slowly their lips met, brushing together; there was the familiar heat of his mouth, the sweet, salty alien taste of him.

He was the alien! The one she'd spent the morning interviewing. *Only, he's no enemy of ours . . . somehow, in this world, he's my husband.*

He cupped her belly with his palm, the large roundness hard and unyielding beneath his hand, even though the tiny, precious girl no longer had room to kick and squirm inside Hope's belly. Still, they felt her warm presence there, her occasional flutters and thrusts.

I'm not able to have children! Only recently, the doctors had told her that the worsening state of her diabetes meant she would never carry a child.

Scott slowly lifted her sweater until the frigid night air met her warm human skin, and bent his dark head low, slowly kissing her belly. Kissing her—and kissing Leisa at the same time. That's what they'd named her already. Leisa Dillon.

He leaned his cheek against her stomach, breathing out against her warm skin. "Stay there a while," she said, twining her fingers through his thick black hair. He'd grown it longer in the past few months, while they'd been on the run; where once he'd kept it short and trimmed, now it fell loose about his collar. He'd never looked more handsome to her than he did in these, their final days. Their very last days.

Hope's heart spasmed with grief. So unfair, to lose everything right when it had been handed to her.

But . . . I don't know him, Hope's heart whispered back. *He's a stranger to me, not my husband. Not the father of my child.*

Bolting upright, he met her gaze blindingly, his eyes glowing as they only ever did when he soul-gazed someone. She averted her own eyes, glancing away. "Hope, you have got to make them to listen to me," he hissed. "If they don't, then the Antousians will bring it all to this. What you see right now."

Hope's contractions wrenched about her waistline like a cinch, causing her to tremble with pain once again. "There, there," her husband cooed at her gently, rubbing her tummy, "you know this baby can't come now."

"H-how did we get pregnant?" she stammered, rubbing her eyes. She felt so heavy, droopy, like she was melting onto the ground beneath them. "I-I'm confused."

"This isn't our world, Hope," he explained patiently, stroking her cheek. "It was *their* world. Another Hope and Scott's world. Not yours and mine. We're just seeing it together."

"How? How can we see it?"

He pressed another kiss against her belly, flicking his tongue against her skin playfully. "I'm a soul-gazer. I've always been able to see things I shouldn't."

"But you're in my *dream*, Scott," she insisted, running her hands through his hair again. She couldn't help herself, couldn't keep from touching him, and despite being almost nine months pregnant, she wanted him fiercely.

He sat up, both palms spread against her belly. "I love you. I'm warning you—that's why I'm here with you now. Listen, you have to get through to me tomorrow. And to your people. Get them to listen, Hope. They *will* listen to you."

"What do you mean, get through to you? You're the one warning me."

He laughed. "Well, baby, it's because my waking self doesn't know about that other world. Only my subconscious mind does. And in time, you're going to remember bits of it too."

"They think I'm an alien. They pumped me full of some kind of sedative."

"Same stuff they hit me with, but they'll figure it out. You'll be back on the case when you wake up," he said, rising to his feet. "Listen to me—if the Antousians are massing at the Canadian border, and that's what it sounds like, well, your government needs to understand they're mounting a big attack. Bigger than any of the shorter, terrorist-style runs they've orchestrated before. They're out for blood."

"And your people aren't?"

Scott flashed a pensive smile at her. "No, Hope, we're not," he said. "We're here to save you."

Chapter Eighteen

Jared took the steps down to his chambers two at a time. Since their failed training session with Marco, he'd been working all morning, analyzing surveillance information intended to help them free Scott. So far, they'd not made any real headway; his best friend was in a locked-down security area so highly secured they didn't have a hope in hell of getting him out. At least not yet. He was determined they would figure a way to free his second in command.

At his door he hesitated, neatening his uniform and running his fingertips over his disheveled hair before entering. He'd promised to meet Kelsey here after lunch once she returned from his private library. She'd been immersing herself in Refarian culture, studying copies of ancient and modern texts with the aid of a handheld translator. A few of their books were already in English thanks to their longstanding tie with her world. She soaked everything up with wonderful fervor. Her endeavors typified everything he loved about his sweet human—her keen intelligence, curiosity, and determination. Her need to find purpose and understanding in the universe . . . and in him.

So he wasn't surprised when he opened the door and found her lying back on their large bed, three books cocked open beside her and one balanced on her knees. He smiled, dropping his uniform jacket onto the bed. "What are you reading, love?" He popped open his body armor vest, breathing easier that way.

"Well, mostly I'm trying to become proficient with your language," she told him pragmatically, stacking the books neatly together. "I figure that way, I can start to learn more about the mitres and how it works. The more I know, the more I can help, Jared. I've spent a lot of time studying physics."

He nodded his approval. "That's fabulous, Kelse. Whenever you're ready, I'd like to introduce you to our science team. Given your"—he hesitated, searching for words that wouldn't frighten her—"special relationship with the mitres, your scientific background means all the more."

She snorted. "Special relationship. That's one way of putting it."

He settled on the side of the bed, searching her face. "Does it upset you? That we've been unsuccessful in removing the codes?"

"Not at all." She shook her head adamantly, leaning closer toward him. "In fact, Jared—when I was in the mitres the other night, it felt right. I was energized. Electrified. I'm not sure the codes are supposed to be removed. Think about what the letter said—"

"The damned codes are coming out! There's no discussion on this matter," he shouted, bolting to his feet.

Kelsey's fair face infused with color. "So says the king," she hissed sarcastically, a resentful furrow creasing her brows.

He rolled his eyes. "Let's not tread this territory again."

"We obviously have to—so long as you keep issuing unilateral ultimatums, at least."

"I *am* the king, Kelse! I've been king since I was ten years old—mark that! That's the past twenty years of my life I've ruled the Refarian people."

"But I'm not your people, Jareshk. I'm your wife. Your queen. This has to be an equal partnership."

Ah, this business of marriage was harder than ruling any kingdom. His spirited wife had a way of burrowing through all his defenses and usual habits. He drew in a breath. "I've never thought of you as anything less than equal."

"You're way too protective of me."

"Can you blame me? I'm in a war against the most brutal of species. They've killed countless numbers of my people—many of whom I loved dearly. And you, precious wife, I love most of all. How can you fault me for wanting to protect you?" Unexpected tears prickled at his eyes. "I won't have them harm you—not ever. And not least because I took you as my mate. I refuse it! So, yes, if I've my way about it, the mitres codes will be extracted from within you. I put them there—it's my fault!"

Kelsey climbed off the bed, opening her arms to him. "Come here, you big silly king," she whispered, all traces of anger vanishing from her face. "You beautiful man, come here."

He wrapped his arms about her, willing the war to stay far from their world. Willing her to stay safe and protected, if not always in his arms, at least always in his camp. "I won't let them harm you, love."

"What makes you so sure they would?"

He gritted his teeth together. "So long as you carry the mitres codes, you are the most vulnerable part of my entire rebellion."

Kelsey shivered in his arms. "We need to try again with Marco."

"Agreed," he said, slipping his fingers beneath her chin and tilting her face upward so he could kiss her.

In a slow, erotic dance, their tongues twined together, thrusting, tasting. Kelsey's hands skimmed over his back, then lower and even lower still, caressing him playfully. Then she took her palm and gave him a forceful swat on the behind.

"Hey!" He laughed, stepping backward.

"Oh, come on. The king needs a good spanking every once in a while." She giggled.

"That's it!" he cried and lunged for her, sending her scurrying toward the bed where he tackled her, pinning her beneath his body.

"See, human, it is unwise to challenge a Refarian male in his chambers," he said, tracing his tongue along her collarbone. He pushed back the opening of her shirt, finding more warm skin to lick and nibble.

Adjusting his elbows, he felt something hard beneath his arm. Absently, he withdrew what turned out to be a book, a Refarian one. "What's this?" he asked, giving it a quick glance.

She plucked it from his hand, pinning him with one of her most seductive looks. "It's called a love rites advisory," she told him silkily. "There's some really good stuff in here. Steamy, erotic, alien stuff."

Jared rolled off of her and onto his side so that they lay together on the bed. "Let me see." He took the book from her, opening it to the page she had marked: He was surprised to find specific details about the mating rituals of Refarian royals.

He gulped, feeling his groin tighten as he read a particularly vivid passage about the D'Aravnian natural self—an erotic description that totally fit his own sexuality. The way his fire was stoked by touch and bed play; his need to share his core self with his mate. He pressed a hand to his temple, feeling a thin sheen of sweat form on his brow. All of a sudden he battled the profound urge to Change, to run his fire up and down Kelsey's body, teasing her. Tantalizing her with all that he was. She'd only seen him a few times; perhaps that truly was the answer to their problem.

"What are you thinking?" she asked in a rough voice, rolling onto her side so that they faced one another.

He stared at the book, blushing. "That perhaps we have yet more to learn about each other."

"So the book's right? About your natural self being linked to your cycles?"

"I-I honestly don't know." He swallowed hard, realizing that he'd begun to tremble slightly. His hands tightened around the book, snapping it shut. "The advisory seems to have"—he paused, daring to look at her through his lashes—"much information. This is good."

She leaned on her elbow, watching him. "Does it still embarrass you to talk about it? After everything we've shared?"

He smiled faintly. "It is still odd, Kelsey, being so vulnerable with you about . . . my nature. What I am. I've never shared it with another being before you, not like this."

"But I *love* all that you are! I love you, Jared. You know how much I love you, don't you?"

"You've barely seen my fire. Barely at all," he told

her softly, staring at the ceiling. "You think you know, but . . . you have seen little of it."

"Then show me again," she urged, staring at him seriously. "Maybe it's what we need—maybe it's why we can't seem to—"

He cut her off, unable to discuss the terrible topic of his infertility yet again. "Please, Kelse," he begged. "I can't talk about this now."

But she would not be stopped, would not back down. "I won't stop trying, Jareshk," she told him seriously, falling back on the use of the name she'd first known him by, something she often did when they were intimate. "I have to believe you're able—you came so close already!"

He took both of her pale, freckled hands within his much darker ones. "We will always keep trying," he promised her. He hadn't forgotten the deep pain she'd expressed earlier in the day while working with Marco, her feelings about his cycles. Perhaps it had taken such deep bonding to bring the emotions out; no matter what, he had determined to cooperate and work to induce his cycles in whatever way he could. "For you, love, I would give you the universe. You know that."

She broke into one of her loveliest, widest smiles, and he felt his heart turn over in his chest. To make this woman happy, well, it was worth any risk—and conquering any fear about his very core nature.

"We can make it happen," she continued. "You just have to keep faith."

He smiled at her, but although he put on a brave face, inside his heart ached. What if he disappointed her? What if he were simply unable? It wasn't a thought he could entertain. He would keep trying forever, until he was completely silver-headed and beyond his fertile season. Until then, until that outward sign of his maturity had overtaken him, there was always a possibility.

Jared hiked the path toward Base Ten, preferring to walk rather than taking the indoor network of tunnels and elevators that would lead him there much more easily. He needed to breathe; he and Kelsey had made love again—gods, he was still filled with lust just thinking about her fair-skinned body atop his, so aggressive and eager to have him. Still, despite how sated she'd left him, he was haunted by their earlier conversation and the thought of her poring over love rites advisories. He would do whatever she asked of him if it meant giving her a baby—and his people an heir to the throne. But she had wanted to see his core self and he hadn't shown her. *What's holding me back?* he wondered, increasing his pace. *She wants all of me—why do I hesitate?*

He shoved both hands into his jacket pockets, and quickened his pace. There'd been sightings of Antousian stealth fighters along the Canadian border earlier in the morning; he'd need to launch his own ready fighters if their enemies were doing more than a simple recon mission. His advisors could reach him by comm at any point, but still, he wanted to be at the base, ready to talk tactics.

"You're walking, I see," came his cousin's voice from the woods beside him. He jerked his head in her direction, startled by her sudden appearance.

"Ah, cousin, I did not see you."

"It's not such a great idea, you hiking to the base without an escort, you know," she said, joining him on the path. "I should chastise you, actually. We've talked about always bringing a guard with you." She dropped her voice lower. "Or Marco, for that matter. Or Sabrina. Your Madjin have returned to you, my lord. It's time you began to call upon them."

"Marco was unwell this morning," he told her, adjusting his jacket, "but you make a valid point, cousin."

She inclined her head respectfully with a soft smile. It seemed she was no longer angry about his marriage; he was thankful because he relied on her too completely to be at odds with her for any length of time.

"So what are you doing here on the trail?" he asked.

Her expression grew troubled. "I needed some air."

"Interesting," he observed, "so did I. Perhaps we should walk together."

She nodded formally, placing both hands behind her back. "Yes, cousin, I would like that very much."

They began the descent down the mountainside, and at times Jared had to smile at their easy formality with one another. It was a lifelong habit between the two of them, to fall into the speech patterns that harkened back to their royal youth—so different from the way he spoke with Kelsey or Scott or even Anika, whom he was slowly forgiving for her deceit about being part of the Madjin Circle.

He made a mental note to summon Anika that evening, so that they might meet in private; he'd yet to speak to her alone since the revelations, preferring to keep a polite distance. But he hadn't missed the troubled pain in her usually warm eyes. For years she had been one of his dearest friends; forgiving her for such long-term deception felt difficult, yet he understood that she had made her choices out of a desire to protect him.

"Have you spoken with Anika today?" he inquired.

Thea took the lead on the path. "Yes, sir. She and Anna are working on recon over at Warren. So far, nothing to report about Lieutenant Dillon."

Thea paused at a turn in the path, one that gave a sudden sweeping view of the valley below. Sunlight pierced the clouds, creating a panorama of color and light. "Jared, I'm worried about Scott."

When Thea addressed him by his first name he always knew their roles had shifted into something much more personal. "I am as well," he admitted. "Extremely concerned and anxious. What does your intuition tell you?"

She chewed on her lip thoughtfully, not speaking at first. Her gaze flitted to the valley and her eyes narrowed—was she using her gift even now?

"I see nothing. It's odd, cousin. Just darkness and fog."

The tempo of Jared's heartbeat increased rapidly. "Could it mean death?" he asked in alarm.

She shook her head. "No, I don't think so. I think it means . . . that events are undetermined."

"You never come up with that kind of reading."

"Unless the gods don't mean for me to know," she answered matter-of-factly. "It's a gift that comes from them, don't forget. Sometimes there are too many choices that still hang in the balance, too many possibilities and directions for destiny to take us. I think Scott is at a crossroads right now."

"I see." Jared tried to ignore the hammering sound of fear that roared in his ears.

"The Antousians have been flying back and forth across the Canadian border for several days, sir," Thea informed him, changing her demeanor and tone once again. "What do you think it means?"

"They're planning something. They've always been circumspect with crossing international boundaries—too much chance for unwanted attention." Jared had a thought. "I wonder if the Air Force knows about their activities. They might have drawn Dillon's attention to it."

"Perhaps the lieutenant might open a door for communication," she reflected, just as his security advisor had pondered yesterday. "Do you think some sort of conversation between our side and the US government might be a viable possibility?"

"I wouldn't have thought so before," he said, "but we must see how the situation with Scott plays out."

"Agreed." They began to hike again, Thea taking the lead on a narrow, slippery section of trail, and they fell silent until once again they could hike side by side.

"So, then," she resumed, "tell me what else is on your mind besides your concern for Lieutenant Dillon."

He stopped in his tracks. "Blasted!" He laughed. "It gets damned uncomfortable living among intuitives."

She gave him a grudging, playful smile. "We keep you on your toes, sir, so that you won't carry the weight of this entire rebellion on your own."

He nodded, studying his boots. "This isn't about the rebellion," he admitted quietly. Thinking of Kelsey's hope that maybe Thea would have some advice for him, he added, "I wish it were. Hell, it might be easier that way."

"It's about the queen, isn't it?"

He glanced up, surprised to hear Thea refer to her by her title. He gave an abrupt, awkward nod.

"Perhaps I can help," she encouraged, reaching to touch his arm, and he thought he might weep in sheer relief at her offer.

"Yes," he breathed. "That . . . would be much appreciated, dear cousin. I fear I need advice on"—he paused, sucking in an emboldening breath—"the business of mating."

"Sex?" she blurted with a shocked expression. "You're far more experienced than I, cousin!"

"Not sex, no," he rushed to amend, and coughed into his hand, blushing painfully. He'd made it sound like he needed help with the act itself—and that's clearly how she'd interpreted his request. With another cough, and staring at the snowy ground between them, he elaborated, "I mean, advice on mating cycles. If I'm ever to produce an heir, I require some very generous advice on the matter of—well, uh, mating heat."

"Now *that*," she answered with a confident nod, "I might be able to help you with!"

Hope stirred groggily, feeling as if her entire body had been submersed in rubber glue. Even her eyelashes stuck together as she struggled to open her eyes. Finally, she blinked back sleep, staring up into a bright corona of light. A medical lab, that's where they'd taken her.

"You're awake." It was the colonel's voice, from somewhere beside her. With great effort, she rotated her head sideways. He sat beside her bed, and though his form was little more than a blurry apparition, she did think he seemed sorry.

"Why'd you knock me out?" she asked, her tongue sticking to the roof of her mouth as she worked to talk. "Water?" she added hopefully, and immediately the colonel pressed a cup with a straw into her hands.

"You have our deepest apologies, Ms. Harper. Our very deepest apologies."

"It was a mistake," she agreed flatly.

"Of course it was—we overlooked the issue of your eyes . . ."

"It's called retinopathy," she volunteered angrily. "It's an eye disease that affects my retinal patterns—I told your security team about this going in! That a retinal scan was unreliable because of my diabetic condition."

"But the pattern changed from the time you entered the holding facility and the time you prepared to exit."

"Because I was nervous. My blood pressure probably went up, and that affected the vessels in my eyes."

"Again, Ms. Harper, our most sincere apologies. It won't happen again."

"Why'd you think I wasn't myself—I mean, how could that be, anyway?"

She was met by silence. *Need-to-know basis, here we go again,* she thought. But for once, that kind of pissed her off, them having injected her with sedative and all. "Look"—she worked to sit up in bed—"we both know that Refarians don't live on Earth. Okay? I'm not stupid; I went to William and Mary, I work for the FBI, and I'm just not an idiot. So, Colonel, tell me why you'd think a girl who looks exactly like me could somehow *not* be me?"

Again, nothing but silence. She sighed. "I'm making headway with this guy. If you'd just *need* me to *know* a bit more, I could probably get somewhere."

"Some of his kind are capable of changing form. Into anything. We know that about them."

It was exactly what she'd surmised earlier, before they sedated her, but for some reason she'd still wanted the colonel to admit it. "So you thought I wasn't Hope Harper."

"Our mandate is to DNA-test anyone who comes in or out of that room. Period."

Hope sipped from the straw, thinking. The interrogation team owed her now, so this just might be her chance for a breakthrough with the alien. She was about to voice her request, when a strange thought intruded upon her psyche: Scott Dillon meant something to her. It was as if she'd been dreaming about him, something she couldn't quite recall, but she suddenly felt a strong attachment to the man. The same sort of feelings that had been niggling at her all day during the questioning: the overpowering sense that she'd known him before. That he could be trusted.

And that he needed her help, desperately.

"Colonel, before our problem"—she indicated the infirmary bed with a wave of her hand, an intentional reminder of his miscalculated maneuver—"you and I were discussing the possibility that I might question Dillon on my own. I'd basically be rehashing some of your earlier questions, but doing it in my own way."

"Yes, I recall that, Ms. Harper."

"Well, have you thought about it any further? Because I think I could gain some ground with him."

"Right now, I think we're open to anything that might work."

She swung her feet over the side of the bed—she was still in her clothes from earlier—and dropped them to the floor. This would make an excellent opportunity to prove to headquarters that her increasing eyesight problems hadn't slowed her down any. "Good. I'm ready, sir."

"But you're barely awake—"

She cut him off, smoothing a hand over her disheveled hair. "I am always ready to roll, Colonel. Just give me a chance."

"So, um, this matter of cycling," Jared began tentatively. "I find it eludes me for some reason." He and Thea were seated together on a log along the path; their uniforms were waterproof, so the light dusting of snow that covered the thick branch hardly mattered.

"Hmm, that's surprising—I can't seem to help myself!" Thea laughed. "Rather ironic, don't you think? I have no mate, but cycle like mad—whereas you've taken a wife, and can't seem to figure it out."

He growled slightly in dismay, unable to contain his sheer embarrassment at the discussion topic. Thea laughed softly. "Cousin, don't look so mortified. It's natural. It doesn't get more natural for the two of us."

"Then why is it such a problem for me?" he cried in despair, burying his face in his hands. "I-I shouldn't need this talk or coaching. It should be as easy as my Change!"

"You mentioned something the other day," she answered, softly touching his shoulder. "About how you met Kelsey the summer of your awakening—and then she was taken from you."

"The elders," he despaired. "They were behind the

separation. I wanted to come back for her, but . . . they wiped the memories. I never knew, never remembered until I found her again."

"Exactly, Jared, exactly!" Thea said, clapping her hands.

"You find that significant?"

"You were beginning your first cycle—that's what our awakening means. I remember my own awakening was almost unbearable, and I was kept entirely in seclusion. If I'd found someone I cared about, well . . . I can only imagine the intensity of it."

"I wanted her desperately—I don't remember that much about our time together, just shadows and half thoughts—but I know how much I wanted her. We were barely more than children, but it was intense and strong."

"So what I believe, Jared, is that you stifled those feelings. Fought them. Battled them away out of desperation after you left Earth." She paused significantly, reaching a hand to touch his cheek. "And you've never allowed them since."

He gasped, staring at her. It was so incredibly obvious, yet it had never even crossed his mind in the past weeks. "I-I almost," he stammered, "almost managed it . . . a few nights ago. Our marriage night, but then . . ." His voice trailed off.

"It stopped?"

He nodded, rubbing his throat.

Beside him, he felt a quiver of energy; Thea watched him. "Jared, it's not that hard." She laughed gently. "Well, it *is* that hard, at least for the male of our kind. But getting there shouldn't be. Not for a strapping warrior like you."

He growled at her, saying nothing more, and never looking in her direction. "Cousin!" she exclaimed, clasping his arm. "You love her. She *loves* you. From all the evidence that I can see, you two have a stunning sex life."

What did his cousin know about their lovemaking? Nothing. "Ah, and what have you seen?" he asked with a laugh intended to dismiss her words of encouragement.

She faced him. "That you glow. Sometimes, after you've made love with each other. Did you know that?"

He turned to her, mouth agape. "Certainly not!" Well, the night they'd first mated, of course, but not after that.

She waved off his embarrassment. "Oh, nobody else sees it, cousin," she said dismissively. "Well, maybe some of the other intuitives, they might have. But you shouldn't feel awkward—it's beautiful, Jared. The two of you really do glow. It radiates off you, the way you've made one another feel." Thea's face had assumed a look of wonder—and was completely devoid of any jealousy.

"I worry sometimes, Thea," he nearly whispered, finally meeting her gaze full-on.

"About what?"

"Perhaps I suppressed it for too long," he admitted. "Perhaps I avoided my cycles for so many years—did anything I could *not* to have them—well, maybe I'm beyond achieving them now. Maybe I'm ruined that way."

"Then it's gone dormant, but it's not dead, Jared," she said. "You are still what you are. Your people have always experienced the heat to the greatest degree—much more than my kin. You just have to let the urges overtake you."

"Is that how it works?" he asked, feeling oddly inexperienced and innocent. "It just . . . comes upon me?"

"Jared!"

He clutched at his head in frustration. "Thea, I *don't* know!" There, he'd said it. He felt his face burn, and averted his eyes from his cousin's pointed stare. "I know nothing about how this works."

"How could you not? Hasn't anyone ever talked to you about these things?"

He sprang to his feet, pacing in agitation. "Who would have spoken of it? Who would dare school the king about his sexual urges, dear cousin? No one. No one has ever taught me anything!" he exclaimed. "I've no idea what to expect or what it takes. I am an utter virgin in this regard."

She stared up at him sympathetically. "Oh, cousin, do sit down, please." She patted the place beside her.

"Please help me understand it." He dropped heavily

beside her. They'd discussed many uncomfortable topics during their years of fighting together, but nothing that had ever approached this level of intimacy. Jared trained his entire focus on his boots and the snow. "Tell me more, cousin," he begged. "Please."

"Yes, it does just come upon you, absolutely."

"Tell me what it feels like," he urged, glancing at her shyly. "What to expect, when it begins." He thought of that night when she'd brought the fever upon herself, the way it had stirred him slightly—and of the night of his sealing to Kelsey. They'd come so close then; he'd been certain he was entering his season—until the letter from Marco had disrupted what was beginning, pulling him apart from Kelsey.

"Jared, it's like this," she said, staring at the sky overhead. "Remember the way the *dulisthrama* sounded? The way a musician would pluck a string—just barely, so that the tiniest little note would ring out? Then the sound would grow like a wave, and expand, and overtake you, and then this one single little note gained momentum, getting louder until it had become a whole symphony?"

"Yes, Thea," he said wistfully, "of course I remember the sound of *dulisthrama*."

"Well, that is what it's like to enter your season!" She gave an enthusiastic nod. "Just like that. And then the symphony kind of rings through your whole body, enfolding you until it's like warm, lapping water—" Her words, hushed and full of wonder, suddenly ceased. She sighed, closing her eyes, but offered nothing more.

"What else, Thea?" he encouraged. "Tell me what you were going to say." He ached to hear the rest, burned for it—not for her, but for this alien *thing* that she described. He was alien, this season was alien, even among their people. How he longed and lusted for it!

"That is what you can expect," she said, her voice much more subdued. "That is all. Beyond that, I do not know. I've never made love to anyone, never mated . . . so I usually endure it, each cycle more intense than the last. Surely you, who are mated and in love, will find your way there, Jared." She gave him a slight smile, but her eyes spoke of intense melancholy.

"Thea, I'm sorry that I disappointed you." He meant it even if he had no regrets that they'd not mated. "And I'm sorry that things haven't gone the way you always hoped. Perhaps we should talk about it," he suggested gently. "Perhaps it is time?"

"Oh!" She gave a light snort of laughter. "I wasn't thinking about *you*, actually."

"Then who?"

She began to laugh. "Some things a lady must keep to herself, my lord."

He was wildly curious. "Is it Lieutenant Dillon?" he pressed. "I've noticed the two of you have become quite close."

"Gods, no!" she blurted. "I adore him, but he's closer than a brother. No, not Scott, but I won't say who, Jared. You may ask all you like, but there will be no answers forthcoming from me."

"And after I've made myself naked to you."

"No, that's Kelsey you're making yourself naked to." She giggled.

"I think you're coming to like her," he observed, assessing her carefully. "Despite your inclinations otherwise in the beginning."

She tugged at the zipper on her uniform jacket, staring into the woods thoughtfully, but for long moments didn't speak. When at last she did, her voice was filled with emotion. "You never asked what I saw in the mitres."

It was true—he'd been so certain that Marco was holding back something important that he'd never questioned Thea.

"So what did you see? Tell me."

She hugged herself protectively. "By all rights, I should despise Kelsey. She stole you from me; she's taken the throne as our queen. I have many reasons to dislike the *human*." She said the last word with her usual amount of distaste for the alien species.

"I suppose that's fair," he agreed, eager to hear where Thea was leading.

"It's more than fair, based on everything I should feel, Jared—but when I was in the mitres, I saw something that altered those feelings permanently."

He leaned closer, unable to disguise his curiosity. "What did you see?"

Thea's clear blue eyes twinkled with surprising warmth and mischief. "You'll never believe it, but what I saw while in the slipstream . . ." She shook her head as if she hardly believed it herself. "I saw that Kelsey Wells Bennett—my new queen—would be my best friend."

Once again Hope sat across from the man known as Scott Dillon. *S'Skautsa* she'd heard him called by an unidentified female on one of the tapes. They never had identified that woman via voice recognition, but she'd gathered it was someone who knew the lieutenant quite well if they were on a first-name basis. That thought led her to a strategy.

"S'Skautsa, my name is Hope Harper," she stated in his language.

He jerked backward, scraping his chair against the concrete floor. Yes, she'd surprised him by using his given name; the Refarians rarely went by their real names, preferring instead their assumed human aliases. So she supposed that calling him by his given name was sort of like outing him.

"I have some questions for you," she continued.

"You never answered my own question."

"Which was?" Pushing her thick-lensed glasses up the bridge of her nose, she leaned across the table, determined to get a good look at him. All she could make out was what appeared to be a bruise across his jaw and another dark shadow beneath his right eye. It also seemed that he was staring at her . . . hard.

"Then I'll ask it again," he said sharply. "What's *wrong* with your *eyes*?"

"Why does it matter?" she fired back at him. Almost as if on cue, her eyes watered and she had to close them.

"Eyes are important," he told her with surprising gentleness. "Always, to any race."

"Or species?"

She thought he shrugged. "Even more important to some."

Hesitating, she deliberated. All her training indicated

not to reveal any personal details or to let a subject into her head. But something from her drugged sleep, something she couldn't quite touch, urged her to answer. "I have an eye problem."

"Obviously."

"You asked what was wrong."

"You told me nothing."

Blowing out a heavy breath, she stared upward, then finally said, "I have retinopathy, a degenerative eye disease."

"You're blind?"

"No." *Not yet.*

"I'm sorry."

She ignored his absurd attempt at forming a bridge with her, and spread her hands on the table before him. "We have some simple questions that shouldn't be hard to answer," she began in Refarian. "Starting with the fighter jets that have been spotted along the US and Canadian border. Tell us why you're venturing into that territory. Why it matters."

He shifted in his chair, tapping his fingers on the table; she had the sense that he was deliberating with something. "I can help you, Hope. But you have to help me too."

"We might be able to arrange that—if you're cooperative."

"What if I told you those fighters don't belong to us? What would you say to that?"

I don't know enough about this situation to even answer, she thought in panic. She pushed all doubt aside, tunneling forward. "You'll have to tell me more."

"Do your people even know about the Antousians?" he asked seriously. It wasn't a name she'd ever heard on any of the intercepts, which immediately made her doubt him.

She shoved back from the table. "If you're not going to tell the truth, then I don't have anything to say to you."

"Hope," he half begged, "you've obviously familiarized yourself with our language. Surely you know of our enemies—our mutual enemies—by now."

Scrolling through her recollections, she couldn't remember ever hearing that word—and yet Scott seemed deadly serious. "Is there another term you might use?" she heard herself ask.

Scott leaned forward toward her. "*Vlksai.* We often call them *vlksai.*"

Yes! She knew that word because, despite hearing it repeatedly in the intercepts, she'd never been able to successfully translate it. But she played it cool. "I might recognize that word. Tell me more."

"It means destroyers. That's what we always call them because of the genocide they perpetrated on our people. That's why it's so important that you believe me, Hope. Because now that these *vlksai* have ruined our world, they've come here . . . to destroy you."

Hope let his chilling words settle into her mind. Something about the moment felt strangely familiar—as familiar as Scott had from their very first meeting. "What is their race?" she asked. He'd called them Antoulians? Ansousians?

"Antousians. They have a very special interest in humanity—we've been protecting Earth from them for years."

"You expect me to believe that?" she snapped. Yet what he was saying, all of it, hit a chord within her memory.

"You need to believe it if you want to survive."

Hope shut both eyes, delving within her subconscious. Why did his words feel so familiar? Wait . . . it was her dream! Right before she woke up from that drug-induced slumber. "You've already warned me," she whispered in disbelief. "You told me about the Antousians."

She felt him visually assessing her, the heat of his gaze; the chair creaked as he leaned back in it. "Human, you make little sense."

Hope sorted through the tide of half memories from her dream. "While I was knocked out I had a dream, and you came to me. You said to convince you—*this* you—to believe me. To get through to you, that's what you said."

* * *

Scott glanced about the interview room. The camera was rolling; the tape was rolling. He wouldn't have long to speak freely with Hope, not once the other linguists began to translate their conversations. None of the others were nearly as fluent as Hope, though, so perhaps that gave them some more time.

The woman was *stlaitka* anyway, with her talk about dreams and warnings. Of course she'd dreamed about him: She'd spent the whole morning interrogating him. Still, something about her unshakable insistence that he'd visited her in a dream gave him pause because, after all, he had seen her in the mitres slipstream. Somehow, he did know her, though he was uncertain how that could be.

Heightening his vision, he began to gaze her, staring hard into her pale gray eyes, half-hidden behind the thick lenses of her glasses. Focusing, he stared into her soul, her essence, her energy.

He knelt beside her, his palms flat on her very pregnant belly; beneath his hands he sensed their baby daughter's life force—strong, determined. Just the sort of child the two of them would have made together.

Pressing his lips to her warm skin, he kissed her stomach, licking and teasing her. With all his heart, he wished that Leisa could feel his kisses too. Such a difficult pregnancy; so much heartbreak and fear. It didn't seem fair that Hope of all people should suffer so badly. They had to make it through the pass. Somehow he would get her to safety—her and their baby girl.

And then he was warning Hope. Telling her that if she didn't get her people to believe—get him *to believe—that the Antousians would bring it all to what they saw in the vision. To ruin and death.*

Scott gave his head a shake, focusing on Hope's face in order to hone in on the present. She'd been telling the truth! He had warned her within their collective dreamscape—and never even known it. His subconscious mind clearly knew a great deal about another world, one where they'd been mated. He recalled the mitres, and the visions they'd all experienced as some parallel reality had been revealed to them. Was this all because of powering up the coiling unit the night of his capture? Had it ruptured some dividing wall between himself and that other time?

Hope was his wife in that realm. He offered up a quick prayer to All, feeling the emotion of the vision overwhelm him. With every fiber of his being, his other self had loved the woman who sat before him; it was impossible not to submerse himself in that cascade of feeling. For a tenuous moment, he found himself feeling love for the human linguist sitting across from him. As if the emotions weren't mirror images of an alternate reality, but a true, desperate feeling within his own rapidly beating heart.

Struggling for words, he wasn't sure what to say. Then, never a man to hold back, he finally opted for the truth. "I believe you, Hope. Now what do we do about it?"

Chapter Nineteen

Marco entered the munitions bunker in the lowest level of the cabin. It was a lockdown facility for emergencies—where they would shelter Jared should a security breach occur without warning, leaving them without time to get him to one of the outlying bases. But the bunker also stored an arsenal full of firepower and weaponry; it was the armaments storehouse for the main compound. Anika had told him it was where he'd find Sabrina.

As expected, the door was ajar and so he pushed it open, calling out to his unit leader. He found her staring up at a ceiling-high shelving unit, entering data into her electronic handheld. "They are thin on K-12 ammo," she observed, never looking in his direction. "Generally, this compound needs to be better armed. They're operating under the assumption that Jared would move out before any real threat penetrated. But we don't know that for sure."

"Want me to look over the inventory?" he volunteered, shutting the heavy door behind him. Four-foot-thick walls separated them from the exterior hallway so any conversation between them was guaranteed to be private, which made this a good setting for what he'd come to tell her.

"We'll study it together once I've compiled the information." She entered more data with the click of her stylus, then finally turned to face him for the first time since he'd entered. Her face bore its usual intense expression, her brown eyes flickering with energy. "Something's on your mind," she stated knowingly.

She'd raised him from infancy and it was impossible

for him to conceal his thoughts, even though she wasn't an intuitive. She simply had the instincts of a mother.

"How do you do that?" He smiled, but knew the expression didn't reach his eyes. Sabrina slipped her handheld onto one of the shelves beside her and took several steps closer toward him.

"Talk to me, Marco," she encouraged, folding both arms across her chest. Her full attention was trained on him, and he knew she would never let him go without his confessing everything.

"Something happened this morning, Sabrina, and I'm . . . not sure what to do about it. Or if I should do anything. But you're my unit leader, and that means I have to report it."

Surprise registered in her eyes. She'd assumed the issues were personal, not related to the Circle. "Go on," she urged with a brisk nod.

Turning toward the munitions shelving, he pulled out a K-12, examining it thoughtfully. Anything was better than staring into Sabrina's probing gaze. "I was working with Jared and Kelsey," he began, "training them in the use of their intuition. Assuming that Kelsey has inherited his gifts," he quickly added. "Jared and I were both operating under that hypothesis."

"She's human, but she's also his mate—it's a workable assumption. This was toward helping retrieve the mitres data, correct?"

He nodded, replacing the K-12 on the shelf where he'd found it, and then turned to face her again. "That was our plan, yes."

"That's good. I spoke with Jared about utilizing his natural abilities to extract the data," she volunteered with a brisk nod. "I think you chose a wise course of action."

"One would think so," he agreed miserably, hanging his head.

"You no longer do? What happened?"

He released an anguished sigh and began to explain the entire scenario to her. How he'd slipped into their bond, the feelings it had elicited. His fears about his empathy. He held nothing back from his unit leader—

in fact, quite the opposite, agonizing at length over what he'd inadvertently heard after he'd slipped into their bond, the ensuing headache. He left nothing to supposition—except the part about Thea following him to his quarters. That part he kept entirely to himself. Only he and Thea would ever know how close they'd come to bonding for life.

"You know how dangerous this is to you," she told him when he'd finished. "You certainly don't need me to tell you that."

"This is the last thing I wanted—I didn't bring it on!" He realized how defensive he sounded, but he couldn't seem to help himself, his anxiety was too intense.

"That's not what I said," she told him carefully. "You know better than that."

"I'm sorry," he grumbled, turning to face the rack of weaponry once again. He traced his fingertips over luminators and pulse rifles and rounds of ammunition; anything felt more comfortable than staring into the eyes of the woman who had raised him. The woman who knew and understood, more than anyone else, how bitter his struggle had been to tamp down his terrible gift.

"I know you're upset, but let's talk about this rationally."

A tight headache had begun to pulse insistently behind his eyes again; he pressed the heels of his palms against his forehead, working to suppress the nauseating pain.

Closing his eyes, he confessed, "I've got the headaches too, Sabrina. Really have them. I haven't felt sick like this in years."

She clasped him by the shoulder. "You must block all of this, Marco. Do you understand?" she insisted in an urgent tone. "Do you? You cannot allow this problem an inch of ground, not with all that you've overcome."

He felt her gaze bore into him, but still refused to look at her; he was too ashamed. "Even you sound frightened."

"No." She drew his large hand within her own. "I'm not frightened. But when my adopted son suffers, I feel it too. And I don't want you to hurt, Marco. You've waited too long for this moment, trained too hard for it. I refuse to see your gift overtake you after so many years."

"Then tell me what to do," he whispered, turning to face her.

"Block their connection out. You've been blocking for years—you will do what you've always done: block."

It was a skill she'd helped him develop at a very young age; it had been the only resource that had saved his sanity and his life. "I'm supposed to work with them again tonight when Jared returns from Base Ten. Maybe someone else should do it. Anika or Riley—"

"You are their Madjin, Marco. You. Not Anika or Riley, as devoted as they both are—but you, son. You have the strongest gift, and you're the one who must train them. Too much rides on this: The retrieval of the mitres data depends on your teaching them how to utilize their bond and their gift. And we both know it's more than the mitres data at stake—it's the queen's life."

He bowed his head in shame. "My curse shouldn't be her vulnerability. Why would the council have chosen someone as dark as me to protect them?"

"Marco!" Sabrina barked, protective as always. She never let him call his empathy what it really was. She always insisted that he describe it as his "greatest gift."

With a sigh, he amended his words: "Any weakness in me should not be to the queen's detriment or peril."

Sabrina gave him a half smile, but he could see she wasn't fully satisfied. Like any mother, she urged him toward self-respect and healthy pride, not self-flagellation.

"Block. You've done it your whole life," she reminded him. "That's what you will do. You're much stronger now. You overcame this as a child and it's going to be all right."

"Yes, Sabrina," he agreed dutifully.

"And if you get into trouble, cut it off—come for me. I think it's important that you face this, not run from it."

He gave an obedient nod, but inside he prayed his leader was right this time.

* * *

Outside the windows of Jared's upstairs study, darkness cloaked the mountainside. There was a full moon causing the patchy snow to glimmer, and as Marco stared at the world below, it seemed to glow. He took deep breaths, stilling his energy and senses before he turned to face Jared and Kelsey where they sat on floor pillows by the roaring fire. It was time to train them, and he would not allow himself to repeat his previous misstep. The assignment was too critical, both to the queen's ultimate safety and to the revolution as well. She couldn't be the linchpin for operating the mitres—and more than that—without the ability to freely man the weapon, they might never defeat the Antousians. As Jared had pointed out moments earlier, perhaps the mitres could be used as leverage with the humans—perhaps even to free Lieutenant Dillon.

Drawing several deep, settling breaths he turned to face his king and queen. "Are you joined now?" he asked, though he needed no confirmation. The lustrous radiance on their faces revealed how deeply they were connected.

"We're ready, Marco," Jared told him with a brisk nod of his head.

"Good. Then we will begin, my lord." Marco closed the distance between them, kneeling beside them both. "I am going to guide you through an exercise, one meant to hone your intuition."

Keeping her eyes closed, Kelsey smiled. Clearly his queen was open and curious to this new side of herself; it seemed nothing ever daunted or frightened the human, a trait he always admired, but especially in her. He felt a swell of pride inside—Sabrina was right. This was the moment he'd spent his life training for; it caused a strange rush of love inside him toward his king and queen. On his wrist, he almost felt his protector's brand burn in answering recognition to the feeling.

Marco placed one hand on Kelsey's shoulder, allowing some of his energy to spiral across her senses. His intention was to spark her gift, but instead there was an immediate and electric answer inside his own spirit. Shuddering, he withdrew his hand, uncertain.

I can't go down this path again!

But he knew no other way to awaken Kelsey's nascent gift than by prying it open a bit—both by this exercise, and by applying some of his own energy as a kind of kindling to the fire. *I'll be careful; there's no other way. I will block. I've blocked most of my life. I can do this.*

Slowly he slipped one hand on Kelsey's shoulder again, placing his other on Jared's. Drawing in a deep breath, he plunged ahead, working to coach them into a basic skill with their capabilities.

"Go slowly and open your minds," he advised. "Open up your spirits, your essences, and then we will begin." He had several very basic movements planned, but first he had to tease them to a higher plane or the training would never work.

"Now," he began, "I've brought my backpack with me. There's something inside it—I want each of you to try and tell me what that item is." He dropped his pack between them on the floor. "I'll give you a head start: You can even touch the outside of the pack if it'll help you."

Marco watched as his king reached tentatively toward the worn pack, slowly trailing his hand over its surface; Kelsey imitated his gesture. Marco studied her features, the way her clear blue eyes narrowed seriously then widened with surprise as she seemed to discover something through her intuitive work. She had beautiful eyes, his queen, sensuously shaped, with sparks of green amidst the blue. For a moment, his thoughts wandered to Thea. Her blue eyes were not unlike Kelsey's, yet ringed with a violet color that made them totally unique.

He glanced at Kelsey again, sensing a thought of Jared's as it lightly danced on the periphery: something about the queen's eyes being gorgeous and sexy.

Hush, Jareshk, we've got to focus.

Then stop looking so damned beautiful all the time!

They smiled at one another, and Marco knew it was true—he had inadvertently slipped into their bond again.

Trembling, he formed a block; or at least he tried to. But he still quickly found himself swimming against a lusty torrent of emotion once again. Their passion. Their desire. *Their* love.

He braced for more, struggling to block, but all of a

sudden, before he even anticipated it, he was assaulted by the most intense series of sensations he'd ever experienced—even more overwhelming than what he'd felt between them earlier in the day. And, as shocking as it was, deeper emotion than he'd yet experienced with Thea.

Because she's not my bonded mate and wife. This is what should belong to us, this kind of connection.

Warm, swirling love; intense arousal; keen soul-binding. Gods, he was drowning in it! *I've gotta get out of here,* he thought murkily, yet he made no move to break away. Instead, he allowed himself to sink deeper into the experience of their bond, couldn't stop himself from tasting of what he'd never have in his own life. *This is wrong! I have no right to be here! Got to block this!*

"Is it a CD?" Jared asked hopefully.

"That's exactly what I got!" Kelsey announced joyously.

He dropped onto his haunches. Oblivious to his struggle, they were waiting for his guidance—but he had none to give. He was lost, utterly awash in their soul-bond.

The headache began to hammer again behind his eyes, driving sharp, prickling pain down the bridge of his nose and up into the crown of his head, as if someone had taken daggers and driven them into his forehead.

"Marco, we're ready," Jared prompted and he managed to gasp his assent.

Pull yourself together, man! Break it off.

Wrestling back to his knees, he prepared to physically separate himself from them. *I will confess everything—tell them exactly what a blight I am!*

But he could not make the break; the experience was too beautiful. He ached until he was raw inside, breathing in and out, longing for Thea like he'd never wanted her before. He had to mate with her!

Oh, gods, the way they need each other, love each other. So strong . . . so undeniable. Thea . . . it was everything he felt for her, only his own feelings had been stymied, corked inside. But now, let loose! His love, his beautiful Thea. Every direction he turned, it seemed he was fighting an unbeatable current and it suddenly made most sense just to swim with it. At that precise moment, he detected Thea's scent. Perhaps down the hall, he thought dazedly, or somewhere else in the cabin. His empathy was opening wider and wider like a great yawning hunger that couldn't be denied.

No! Here! Beside me. My love is here, near to me, closer than close. Ah, how I long for her.

He thought someone said something, there in the room, some question that he couldn't make out, but the headache beat harder, driving him back down to the floor. *She can be mine . . . what should stop me?* he wondered, the blinding pain making clear thought almost impossible. He tightened his hold on her shoulder, reaching for her. *Thea should only belong to me; my life mate, my love. No more fighting.*

He opened more fully, picturing Thea's gorgeous blond hair, flowing freely across her shoulders, caught briefly by the mountain wind. He kept his eyes pressed shut; someone's hand brushed across his forehead, as she whispered words to him that he couldn't quite hear.

"Marco?" Jared prompted. "Are we right about the CD?"

He nodded, though his head thrummed harder with the blinding headache as it exploded like white-hot light just behind his eyes. This was what he hadn't been able to share with Thea last night, the part he'd held back . . . how insane this all made him, how jumbled his thoughts became. After all these years, the madness had come back upon him—and never so fully as at this precise moment, as his head hummed with every emotion passing between them.

Yet it was only Thea he kept wanting, sensing . . .

And wasn't she the one right in front of him? He burned for her as the headache intensified, became unmanageable, and he knew that only one thing could end all of this.

He had to kiss his sweet, beloved Thea . . . right now.

Thea reached the top story of the cabin, heading for the library in search of more of Prince Arienn's writings. She had a hunch about something that might help Jared and Kelsey with their procreation issues, but wasn't certain. As she rounded the turn in the hallway just by

Jared's upstairs study, she heard a sound that made the hairs on the back of her neck stand on end: The sound of her commander roaring in anger. Jared rarely raised his voice, and when he did it was always with controlled intensity. Right now her leader was shouting in a state of unmitigated fury.

Something had happened! She broke into a sprint, knocking on the door frantically. From within she heard Jared thunder, "You kissed my wife! Did I *misunderstand* that?"

She knocked again, but there was no answer, only the quiet rumbling of voices competing to be heard. Without waiting for an answer, she barged in.

"What's going on?" she demanded, her gaze sweeping the dimly lit room. Marco stood by the fireplace, both hands held up in a defensive posture of denial. Jared towered upon him, stabbing the air with his forefinger. None of them seemed to even register her presence.

"My lord!" she interceded. "Tell me what has happened!"

Kelsey turned pleading eyes upon her, silently begging her for some sort of assistance. Thea crossed the room to her side as Jared roared again: "Tell me why you kissed my wife!"

Oh gods, no. Thea's heart grew sick within her. *Not this, no, no.*

"Commander, you must listen to me," she reasoned in the calmest voice she could muster. "It's not what you think."

Jared whirled upon her. "Not what I think? How could I have misunderstood him kissing Kelsey before my very eyes?"

"I repeat, cousin, it is not what you believe. There is an explanation." She spun to face Marco, urging him to confess his true nature. "Tell them," she said. "They need to understand."

Marco's black eyes were wide and he shook his head almost imperceptibly. "I should leave," he muttered, fixing her with his stare. Transmitting every fear he bore about his gift.

As he pushed past her, she caught him by the arm. "Don't let him send you away like this!"

"He *should* leave," Jared pronounced with chilling calm. "It's evident that he's not the man I believed him to be." His words were like an arrow, clearly hitting Marco's heart like a killing bull's-eye.

Marco stopped in his tracks, then slowly pivoted to face Jared one final time. Dropping to his knees, he bowed his head, thrusting his fist over his heart. "You are my lord, my king, and I serve no other but you and my queen," he swore in a low voice. "I beg you to listen—to find it in your heart to forgive me. To understand."

For a long moment there was only the crackling sound of the fire, the whining wail of wind against the windows. Thea's heart threatened to burst forth from her chest, it beat so loudly and rapidly. Yet no one spoke. She met Kelsey's eyes across Marco's bowing form and again thought her queen was pleading with her visually for some sort of intercession. That one glance propelled her into action.

"Marco, *tell* them." Thea took a step toward where he knelt before Jared.

Marco's chest heaved with quick pants. "Jared, I'm begging you," he beseeched. "Please don't do this. Let me explain."

Yes, tell them about the connection. They must know . . . he'll understand. Just tell them, she transmitted silently.

Jared shook his head, crossing his arms over his chest. "No, I want you to leave tonight," he demanded again in a tight voice. His behavior was so uncharacteristic, even at a moment like this one, that Thea couldn't help staring at him aghast.

"Won't you even hear him out?" she demanded hotly.

"Jared, think," Kelsey interjected in measured tones. "Think about what you're doing here. Think about the letter."

"What letter?" Thea asked, but the question hung suspended in the air, unanswered.

Their king stared down at Marco's prone form, his face a mask of derision. Everything hung in the balance. Thea held her breath, and prayed that Jared would tell Marco to stay. At last he blew out a disgusted sigh and shook his head, sealing Marco's fate. "I want you to leave. Tonight."

Marco nodded, rose to his feet, and left the room without another word.

"Where do you think he's going to go?" Thea stared at her cousin in disbelief. "He has nowhere else, Jared. He's your Madjin, for All's sake."

Jared stared at the empty doorway as if Marco might reappear. "He betrayed me."

"He did not!" Kelsey snapped. "You are so ridiculously stubborn. Go after him, Jared."

Jared glanced between them both, clearly seeing hot anger in both their eyes. His shoulders slumped and he rubbed a palm over the top of his head. "You saw what he did, Kelse—hell, you felt it."

Kelsey turned to face her. "We were working with our intuition," she explained, and Thea's heart plummeted to her stomach. "He was helping us learn about our gift, and then . . . he kissed me. Just like that."

"Just like that," Thea repeated dully. Why hadn't her stubborn, beautiful love not listened to her? Why had he been so hell-bent on such self-destruction? She wanted to thrash and weep and cry her anguish to the rooftops. But he needed her too much right now—if he had any hope of a future at all. Because without his protected, a Madjin had nothing. His life meant nothing. She shivered at that thought, pacing first one way, then another.

What would he want me to do? She wondered, rubbing a hand over her chest in a pointless attempt to still her thundering heart. *Wouldn't he want the truth?* Whatever Marco would want, she knew what she had to do. "There's a lot you two don't know—I wanted him to tell you, but he obviously didn't."

Kelsey waved her on. "Then you tell us—at least *I'm* listening."

There was a noise on the landing, and then Sabrina appeared in the doorway. "You said you trusted me, Commander," she announced bitterly upon entering. "You said that if I vouched for him, that was enough for you. Why would he come on to your wife, right in front of you? Think about the illogic of it, Jared."

"I will admit it does not make sense. If he desired her, then surely he wouldn't have made a move in the midst of our training session."

"Precisely!" Thea said, clapping her hands together for emphasis.

"He knew this was coming; that's why he warned us in the letter," Kelsey observed cryptically. "He said that if he ever did something that seemed totally unforgivable—"

"To try and find it in my heart to understand," Jared finished with a look of horror. "Gods in heaven."

"What letter?" Sabrina and Thea asked simultaneously. Kelsey had mentioned it earlier, and in the heat of the moment, Thea hadn't pursued it further.

Jared and Kelsey traded a look; Kelsey nodded her encouragement, then Jared strode to the small, utilitarian desk that served his needs in this upstairs study. He opened a central drawer, retrieving a plain envelope. Without a word, he extended it to Sabrina.

Marco was literally in the middle of nowhere, hunkered down in the back corner of some dive on Highway 189, the perfect geographic location for him after everything tonight. *He* was nowhere; nameless; lost. He didn't even know which bar he'd landed in, only that there were a half-dozen pool tables and a haze of cigarette smoke shrouding the place. And beer . . . racks and racks of beer, and Marco didn't give a damn about his protector's vows, not now, not tonight. He was going to get drunk and free fall into a painless state of oblivion if it was the last thing that he did.

Something about that decision felt strikingly familiar—as if he'd already lived it, as if he would always be living it for the rest of his life. Marco gave his head a slight shake, blaming the alcohol for addling his mind.

His waitress returned, her low halter top revealing a small butterfly on her right breast, and slid yet another bottle of Heineken across the scuffed wooden table toward him. "What's that mean?" he asked, pointing at her tattoo.

She gave him a blank stare, so he swung his finger closer. "That," he slurred. "The butterfly."

With a laugh, she patted the tattoo as if it might somehow fly off her chest. "Oh, hon, that's nothing but an ole drunken dare."

She was southern; practically nobody in these parts was actually from Wyoming. He was just more alien than most, he reflected, suppressing a gurgle of drunken laughter. He nodded mutely at the woman before she walked away, figuring the halter top was about right for how hot the place was. Another aspect of this frigid territory—ice-cold outside, overheated indoors. Shrugging out of his coat, he kept seeing her butterfly in his head, flapping away at his subconscious. There was something about it, something haunting. That's when it hit him—he would always bear his Madjin's mark. It couldn't be removed: Fifty years from now, if he was alive, he'd still be branded as a protector to the royal houses.

I'll always be a servant, he thought darkly. *I just have nobody to serve now.* It caused a horrible, bottomless feeling in the pit of his stomach.

Taking another heavy swig of beer, he felt the world around him grow even hazier—the dark bar was so cloaked in cigarette smoke that he could hardly tell if it was the effect of the alcohol on his system or just the cloud hanging over the place. His eyes burned, and for a moment he closed them, feeling the world swim woozily all about him.

Yes, let me forget, he thought. *In All's name, just let me forget tonight.*

Through the din of loud honky-tonk music, he could hear the phone at the bar ring, jarring him from his dazed state. The bartender—a burly guy with tattoos up and down each arm—grabbed it off the receiver. After listening a moment, he rounded the bar and stepped out back, shouting into the wintry darkness. Shortly thereafter a hippie chick with a wool knit cap tugged down over her ears entered the place, waving at someone as she picked up the receiver. As she talked, she pressed a hand against her cheek, beaming radiantly.

Even she has someone who cares about her, Marco thought miserably, sinking down into the booth. *But not me.* He was utterly alone—without his unit, without his king and queen, without his homeland—and absolutely without Thea Haven. How could he possibly explain his actions to her, not that he'd ever see her again after tonight. And yet he'd witnessed firsthand how she believed in him, felt her unshakeable faith when she'd battled with Jared on his behalf.

She loved him, of that much he was certain now. Not that he'd doubted it before, because he'd already felt her heart. And he loved her more than she'd ever know, or ever believe for that matter, because he could never explain that when he'd kissed Kelsey, in some confused way, he'd believed he was kissing her.

He lifted the bottle of Heineken to his lips and took a long drag on the bottle, and sensed a gentle movement just beside him. Slowly he raised his head to see a very familiar figure. Yet her appearance made no sense whatsoever because he couldn't imagine how she might have possibly found him.

Marco tilted his head back against the wooden booth, amazed by her angelic appearance. Maybe that's actually what she was, his own guardian angel—*his* protector—sent to watch over him tonight. She stood in front of him, and turned her head slightly sideways to match his own skewed angle.

"Marco?" she questioned gently, stepping closer, and he widened his eyes in reply. She sounded a lot like Thea, so that pretty much shot the angel theory.

"Hey, baby," he slurred and stared up at her. He suddenly felt as if it was years ago, once when he and Riley had bought a six pack for the first time and gotten drunk, and Sabrina had discovered them on the apartment floor—totally busted. Only Thea stared down at him, those full lips slightly open, her gorgeous curls tucked back in a braid, and he felt an explosion of desire. "Beauu-ti*ful*," he pronounced, dragging the word out. Yet he couldn't even seem to lift his head from where he'd rested it sideways against the back of the booth.

She smiled faintly, knitting her blond eyebrows together. "I see you didn't waste any time tonight," she observed, slipping into the booth right beside him.

"Nah . . . I'm drunk," he announced, sitting up more straight in the booth. "Best thing for me about now, don't you guess?"

"No, not really," she answered, stilling his hand as he reached for the beer bottle again. Keeping one hand atop his, she shoved the bottle out of his reach with the other. "The best thing for you is to sober up and come back with me to camp."

He shook his head vigorously, feeling morose once again. Somehow, for a brief moment when he'd first seen her, the world had become all lightness and beauty—he'd even set aside the weight of his betrayal.

Thea turned to face him in the darkened booth, her thigh brushing right against his. "Marco, you've got to come back with me."

"Jared kicked me out," he explained, uncertain if she really knew that fact.

"I know," she answered gently, threading her fingers together with his. "I was there, remember?"

Oh, yeah, she'd been there. Of course. "Yeah, well, see," he offered, squeezing her hand. "I may be drunk as hell, but I know that he kicked me out, and I can't go back, Thea. I can never go back."

He didn't miss how distressed her delicate features became, the fear that suddenly shadowed her water blue eyes. And he wanted to take that look away—had to do it. He cupped her face within his hands and drew her lips to his own. "Baby, I'm so sorry," he whispered, kissing her deeply. There was nothing tentative or gentle about the way he took her now. He wanted her to see inside his heart, and to know that at least there, he belonged to her completely.

She didn't resist him at all, and in fact threaded her fingers roughly through his hair, deepening their kiss heatedly. Her tongue danced with his, warring for position and as she melded with him like that, he felt his body gain clarity again. Thea Haven held the key to his soul, he'd known it practically from the moment they'd first met.

Slowly, he broke the kiss and just stared into her eyes. The fear was gone from her blue depths, replaced now by the specter of uncertainty. He stroked her cheek gently with his thumb, and pressed a soft kiss against her forehead.

"Leave with me now," she urged desperately. "Let's

find someplace tonight, just go there. We can make love and hold one another all night long. We can be together! And in the morning, we'll go back to camp together. *Together,* Marco, from now on."

Nuzzling her cheek he said, "What a beautiful dream, baby."

She shoved apart from him, slapping his chest for emphasis. "It's not just a dream! There's nothing to stop us but your fears."

Bedsprings creaking beneath them, Thea taking his hard cock into her mouth . . . dingy motel room, red bedspread tangled about their legs. Wrong. All wrong.

Giving his head a slight shake, he worked to clear the lurid imagery. Thea misinterpreted the gesture, her shoulders slumping. "You won't come back," she stated quietly.

Everything hung in the balance: his love for her, his knowledge about how he'd transform her if they mated. "No."

"What if I asked you to come for me?"

Pulling her close against his chest, he fell silent a long moment, just letting his lips linger against her forehead, and thought of all the many ways he wanted to answer that question. But he decided on a question of his own instead. "How can you ask that, knowing that I kissed another woman tonight? Your queen?"

He pulled back, so that he might study her expression as she answered. She glanced away a moment, casting her gaze around the smoke-filled bar, until at last she looked at him without a trace of uncertainty.

"Because I know you love me." So simple, yet so very sure.

"Don't you wonder why I kissed her?"

"You told me today," she reminded him softly. "Their connection was making you crazy, I know that. And I know something else: You thought Kelsey was me."

He sucked in a tight breath, shocked that she'd actually perceived that—that she'd seen straight into his heart.

"Don't you wonder what might be wrong with me that I could become so confused on such a simple point? Mistake Kelsey for you?"

"Nothing is wrong with you," she exclaimed. "You have a beautiful gift that—"

"Is a curse," he finished solemnly.

"You told me that already—I don't agree."

"The insanity is returning, baby," he told her plainly. "Don't you get it? How else could I think Kelsey was you? It was always only a matter of time."

"You're wrong." Her tone was emphatic, her regal jaw set and determined. But all the love in her heart couldn't drive his demons away forever. It could only buy him time.

He took hold of her hands. "Thea, this thing inside me—it will always haunt me. It won't ever go away, not really. It's in my blood and in my spirit. You know what they say about empaths back home. We're the devil's spawn."

"Old prejudice." She frowned hard. "Superstition."

"It's true, baby. You saw it firsthand tonight. How could I ever mate with you? I wouldn't wish it on you, not with how I . . ."

"Love me?" she volunteered softly, staring hard into his eyes.

He dropped his head, closing his eyes, but wouldn't answer. It would only make tonight more painful for her. "How can I serve them effectively? I was always a poor choice for the unit, for their personal protector. Now, the truth has come out."

"You have to come back with me, Marco," she insisted. "There are things you don't know—there's a letter."

He cocked his head curiously, waiting, but then she shook her head. "Now's not the time for that," she said. "But Jared sent me for you; he wants me to bring you home."

"I don't have a home—I never have, Thea."

"I'm your home," she whispered, and he bowed his head. "At least that's what I want to be."

Her words were too much for him. Reaching for her, he dragged her into his arms, crushing her against him. Her heartbeat beneath her ribs was steady against him; her scent crested across all of his senses. Reaching for her braid, he unfastened it, slowly unwinding the locks of hair.

"What are you doing?" she asked, holding onto him as tightly as he did to her.

"Letting your hair down. You have such gorgeous, beautiful hair—you should never wear it back."

She laughed, burying her face against his chest. "I'm a soldier, Marco."

With his fingers, he combed the strands; they were like silk to his touch. "You've got to go now," he told her hoarsely.

She made a sobbing sound, pushing her face into his flannel shirt. For some reason he thought back to the first night they'd met, when he'd wrangled her into the doorway outside the bar. "And what will happen to you?"

Drawing in her scent for a final time he said, "I have no idea. But whatever happens, it will be far away from here." With that he released her from his arms, feeling his eyes burn with unshed tears. "Now go. Go back to the compound before I take you with me forever."

Gaping at him, she slid out of the booth and stood. Beside the table, she turned back to him one last time. "I'll go, Marco, but only because you've asked me to. But hear this before I leave—you will return. You'll come back because it's what you're called to do, but more than that"—she leaned down over him, bringing her face within inches of his—"you'll come back for me."

It was nearly midnight, and Marco had stayed in the bar feeling numb ever since Thea walked away. But he wasn't drunk anymore, and all that remained was the sharp realization that he'd lost his soulmate forever. And not only her, but all of them, and he could hardly fathom what his place in the world might be now. *I'm a protector with no one left to protect.* For the first time in his life, he was utterly alone—without his family, his unit—and he felt so vulnerable, just sitting in the darkness, watching cigarette smoke spiral under the dim lights of the pool tables. He had less than one hundred dollars in his pocket. That, the clothes on his back, and his truck parked outside constituted all his possessions.

You could have gone back with her, you know it, a quiet voice prompted. *You could have still had her. Jared would have calmed down and listened.*

Yet how could he have faced any of them? And how could he have ever let her love him, when he'd begun transforming into this *creature*. It would have broken her to watch the madness take him—and he couldn't do that, not to Thea. He'd already hurt her enough to last several lifetimes.

Marco slid sideways in the booth, stretching his long legs out so that his rugged hiking boots dangled over the wooden seat edge. Despite all his internal arguments he still half hoped Thea would return. That thought caused a smile to play at the corners of his mouth as he closed his eyes. The last time he'd leaned his head back like this, she had appeared, after all—his angel, sent to retrieve his missing soul.

Slowly, his eyes fluttered open, and he ventured to see if the room had finally stilled—then he realized he wasn't nearly so sober as he'd thought he was. Because a figure stood studying him, just like before. But when the stranger smiled, it wasn't the gentle nurturing of his beloved. It was the wicked invitation of the very devil. And he knew there'd be no going back after tonight—not ever.

Chapter Twenty

Thea entered the main cabin feeling desolate and defeated. As she closed the door behind her, three sets of eyes immediately fixed on her: Jared, Kelsey, and Sabrina sat in the main gathering area waiting for her. Their eyes conveyed all the hope she had initially felt upon finding Marco at the bar.

Sliding out of her parka, she gave her head a firm shake—no, it hadn't gone well.

Jared rose to meet her. "Did you find him?"

"I found him all right." She passed Jared without a salute or greeting, and walked toward the fireplace. Behind her, she felt Jared's gaze on her back. Fine, she was angry and hurt with him; he didn't deserve any show of respect.

"Lieutenant, I'd like to speak with you," he called after her.

"I'm tired and want to hit the rack."

"Lieutenant."

She turned to face him, feeling her face flush with hot rage. "You could have shown me the letter, *sir*. In fact, you should have."

"I needed the information compartmentalized."

"From me? I'm your chief intelligence officer, Jared. This is me, your cousin. Your trusted. You should have shared the information!"

Jared glanced to the side, noting Kelsey and Sabrina's presence.

"I don't care who hears—if I'd known about the letter, I might have been able to prevent what happened tonight."

Jared touched her arm gently. "How, cousin? Tell me."

She wiped a hand across her eyes. She'd cried the entire drive back from the bar, surely they could all see how swollen and red her eyes were. "It doesn't matter," she muttered.

Jared took hold of her elbow, pulling her toward where the others sat. "Here, Thea, come and sit with us. Tell us what you mean."

She followed his lead, snapping, "I don't *want* to talk about it. Sir."

Taking hold of both her shoulders, Jared forced her to take a seat. "But you will. Because Marco needs you right now. We all need you. Tell us what you mean."

"He'd intercepted your connection before," she explained, casting her gaze toward Kelsey and Sabrina.

Jared squatted before her, staring seriously into her eyes. "We already know that. Sabrina explained."

"All he ever wanted was to serve you, cousin. It was everything to him—didn't you realize that?"

Her commander searched her face, then half-whispered, "You were involved with him—weren't you?"

"That doesn't matter. It's not relevant to this discussion."

"It is relevant," Sabrina piped in. "You know that it is."

"Why should it be?" Thea asked, wanting to wail her anguish to the pine ceiling beams. "He wasn't going to act on it. He told me all about his Madjin vows and how he wasn't allowed to have a relationship."

Sabrina appeared genuinely perplexed—even a bit affronted. "That wasn't really how it was, Thea. Did he tell you that?"

"It's what he believed! Completely. Whether it was true or not, it was true for him."

"I never suggested that he had to be alone—neither did the elders," Sabrina continued, leaning forward in the chair where she sat. Made completely of antlers, it gave her an imposing look, almost as if she sat on a spiky throne. "I did tell him it could be dangerous with his natural gifts, but not because of his vows."

"Then maybe he just didn't want to be with me." She buried her head in her hands. "He said that he couldn't be with me because he was an empath."

"Because he cared for you." This time it was Kelsey volunteering her opinion.

Thea dropped her hands from her eyes, feeling bitter and annoyed with the queen. "And you know this how, Kelsey? Huh? You're suddenly a true intuitive because Marco worked with you twice."

Kelsey's freckled face infused with color. "No, Thea," she replied coolly. "I know it because I know what love means. I know what it is to love someone so much, you'd do anything to protect them."

"Who said anything about love?" Thea whispered, staring at the human in shock.

Kelsey shrugged. "I guess nobody did—except you. When you went after him, flying out of here like your very life depended on it. When you stood up to your king, demanding that he give Marco a chance to explain." Kelsey paused, sighing as she stared at Thea for a long moment, then added, "I guess one of these days you'll realize it too."

Sabrina gave her a slight smile. "Maybe she already does, my lady."

Thea bounded to her feet, sidestepping Jared where he still half knelt before her on the floor. "I need some sleep," she declared. "Gods only know where Marco's gone tonight. The least I can do is warm my comfortable bed."

"Thea, please wait," Jared called after her, rising to his feet.

"What for?" she responded, not caring how abjectly bitter she sounded. They'd all seen right through her anyway.

Reaching into the front of his uniform, he retrieved the letter. "I'd like you to have this." He extended it toward her. "Please take it, read it, and give me your thoughts in the morning."

Thea stared at the white envelope extended in the space between them; she had the feeling that if she took the thing, it would change her life forever. "I may not have any insights."

"Use your gift, cousin—please." His hand seemed to tremble around the letter. "It may be critical to our future that we stop Marco from leaving. And to do that, we need to understand what happened before."

"He betrayed you and you kicked him out! That's what it says, you already told me."

Kelsey stood, walking toward her. "But you'll see more. We're counting on it."

Thea took the letter, and clasped it over her heart. "I-I don't know what else I could have done," she whispered, beginning to weep anew. "I tried everything to get him back."

"We know that," Kelsey assured her.

Thea's shoulders slumped and she felt as if her very life force poured out of her. Kelsey stepped much closer, opening her arms. "Here, Thea. Come here," she encouraged, pulling her into an embrace. The woman was so tall that Thea found her face pressed against Kelsey's chest. It was strange: She wanted to shove away from her, but instead what she felt was . . . tremendous comfort. The tears came even harder, for a long time, and then they stopped. The pain ebbed a bit, and she felt stronger. Pulling away from her queen, she whispered, "Thank you, my lady," and spun on her heel without another word.

Bright lights sliced into Scott's sleep, jarring him awake. Immediately there was the sound of the security locks and then footsteps as he turned his head sideways, spending all his energy on the simple gesture. Flanked by two military escorts and the colonel who'd been heading up this ongoing interrogation stood Hope Harper. Dark circles lined her eyes, and he suspected by looking at her that it was, in fact, the middle of the night. She had that haggard appearance humans assumed when deprived of sleep, the same look he'd seen on Kelsey's face when they'd kept her up too late.

The colonel made a gesture indicating the table, and the two soldiers headed toward him. Instinctively Scott tensed, preparing for another beating or injection, although Hope's presence promised interrogation, not torture.

"Get him up and at the table," the colonel ordered, and the men unfastened his cuffs and leg chains, wrangling him off the bed roughly.

"Come on, Nank," one of the soldiers muttered under his breath, pulling Scott by the elbow. His legs gave way beneath him. He was too weak to walk—so they dragged him across the harsh floor, scraping his knees.

Hope stared in concern, her clear gray eyes not masking the horror she felt at his treatment. She pushed her thick-lensed glasses up the bridge of her nose, watching, and for a moment it almost seemed she transmitted silent encouragement toward him. He knew she couldn't see clearly, could only guess at what was happening as he grunted and groaned while the soldiers shoved him down into the empty chair, fastening him there for a moment with their strong hands.

"Are you ready to proceed in English?" the colonel began. "If you want to eat—or have water—the time has come to cooperate, son."

He hung his head, gasping. It was the water he craved the most. In quick Refarian, Hope "translated," adding her own words: "Do it."

It took all his strength just to talk. "If . . . I . . . do?"

"We can talk about the *vlksai*," she answered. "They'll bring you water."

He nodded, struggling to lift his head to meet the colonel's expectant gaze. Licking his parched lips, he mumbled in English: "Water."

The colonel gestured toward the door, waving, and immediately a uniformed officer entered, slapping four unopened bottles of water in front of Scott. Weakly, he reached for one, but the colonel stopped him. "Not yet, Dillon. First you talk."

He shook his head, begging, "Water . . . please."

Hope turned to the interrogator, expectation in her eyes, but the man didn't look her way. "You've made this much more difficult than it had to be," he explained in a rational tone. "I'd like to hear something more from you first."

The room spun on its axis; Scott feared he'd pass out, but forced words out. The most important ones if his suspicions were true: "Antousians . . . coming."

The colonel's gray eyebrows lifted a bit, a smile playing at the corners of his mustached mouth. "Good, Dillon. Very good." With a methodical gesture the human reached for one of the water bottles, loosened the lid, and then slid it toward him. Scott grabbed it greedily with shaking hands, spilling part of it on the table as he lifted it to his parched lips. Cool, satisfying water slid down his throat as he guzzled the bottle dry. Expectantly, he reached for another bottle, but yet again the colonel stopped him.

"Not until we hear more about the Refarian collusion with the alien race known as the Antousians. We have a lot of ground to cover."

The Antousians had crossed the Canadian border yet again. Ten times in three days, and Jared now knew that some sort of massive attack was in the making. It was after three A.M., but the latest intel had him down at Base Ten awaiting further word from his security advisor. Sabrina had accompanied him, and waited silently at the large meeting table, ready to talk to him about Marco's departure once Nevin had finished briefing him.

"We've sent up the ready fighters," Nevin explained, standing at parade-rest stance by the table. In Scott's absence, Nevin was serving double duty as both military and security advisor. Like Scott and Thea, he held a military position as well as his advisory one.

"Sit down, Lieutenant, and show me the overheads."

Nevin pulled out a seat beside Jared, settling in it uneasily. The man never liked to sit in Jared's presence, preferring instead to prowl the room or to stand at respectful attention. He was true old guard, all the way. It had become clear to Jared years ago that Nevin viewed Jared as king, first and foremost, and only reluctantly did he acquiesce to the more casual forms of military respect. If Nevin had his way, Jared would be in the center of the room, high atop a dais in the ancestral throne chair wearing robes of purple and gold.

"My lord, please review the following surveillance images, taken by fighters only a few hours ago." Nevin clicked through photograph after photograph of Antousian stealth fighters, flying in full squadron formation.

After a long period of narration, his chief security advisor turned in his chair to face him. "Commander, we are preparing a battle plan for your review."

Jared studied his trusted lieutenant thoughtfully. Nevin had never let him down when planning maneuvers before. He was well seasoned in warfare, and nearing forty he bore the telltale sign of a Refarian male deep in his maturity—silver hair. He studied Jared through confident, keen black eyes.

"What now?" Jared asked, leaning back in his chair. The lighting in the meeting room was low so they could study the overhead projections—photographs taken by fighter jets, maps, and strategy charts.

"We know the targets in this region," Nevin continued stoically, changing the visual projection to an overhead shot of a missile silo, which looked to be a rather unimpressive set of square buildings. Probably sitting in plain sight, appearing like nothing so much as an industrial business.

"As you're aware sir, Warren maintains one hundred and fifty Minuteman III missiles and five launch-control centers scattered throughout Wyoming, Nebraska, and Colorado."

"They've targeted some of these silos before, Lieutenant," Jared reflected aloud, recalling the times he and his fighters had single-handedly deflected such attacks. "What makes you so sure this time is different? The border crossings?"

Nevin bent his silver head over a sheaf of papers in front of him, reviewing data as he spoke. "The Antousians seem to be mounting not a single launch against one of these targets, but preparing for a carpet sweep of sorts—at least based upon their test flights."

"Perhaps because they think we can't stop them en masse."

"That's our guess, sir. They plan to override our defensive efforts—and those of the Air Force."

"Interesting that Lieutenant Dillon is currently held at Warren."

Nevin nodded. "Likely why Dillon was taken there—they believe *we* might be targeting the silos."

"Not protecting them, as we are." Jared rubbed a

hand over his jaw. "They've never successfully distinguished our fighters from the Antousian jets."

"Without some sort of summit, Commander, there is no way the human governments will ever understand."

"What are you suggesting?" He noticed that Sabrina, although positioned on the far side of the table, was completely engaged in the conversation.

Nevin folded both arms over his chest thoughtfully. A quiet man, he had served Jared's father twenty years ago in his youth. He'd been a military prodigy despite his young age, and he had never—not once—let Jared down. "If we get Dillon back—or if we don't, Commander—it's time to broker a discussion with the US government. Straight to the top, if possible."

"How do you intend for us to accomplish that?" Jared asked, imagining a scenario where the Air Force would use such a meeting to capture more of his leaders. Perhaps himself. They had no idea what sort of torture or tests the humans might currently be conducting on Scott. He shivered, shaking off the thought.

"It's time to issue a communiqué. Something intended for the president."

The vice president was from Wyoming, still kept a home around Jackson, and they'd often pondered if his close proximity might one day translate to some sort of open meeting. They also knew it was a major reason the military had given them such a tough run for the past years; the security surrounding the vice president's ongoing presence in the region meant heightened military alerts all the way around.

Jared gave a brisk nod of agreement. "In the short run?"

Nevin met his gaze evenly. "We take out as many of those *vlksai* as we can, Commander. Before they inflict serious damage to Earth."

"How many fighters do we need?"

Nevin didn't hesitate before answering, "All that we have, Commander."

On the other side of the table Sabrina stirred, and Jared shot a look in her direction. His Madjin had something on her mind. "Yes, Protector?" he inquired.

"I believe it's time to notify the council, my lord. With

one of our unit missing, your chief military advisor captured, and the Antousians mounting this kind of attack, they should be brought into this."

Jared rumbled low in his throat. "I have no use for the council, Sabrina. This you already know."

"But, my lord, they may wish to send additional battle cruisers. Perhaps if you spoke with them, sought their advice—"

"The council does not run this military, Sabrina," he snapped angrily. "I've not forgotten their role in separating me from my wife, nor have I forgotten their subterfuge in barring the Circle from my presence."

"We can call for the cruisers if necessary," Nevin advised, "but we don't have to go through the elders."

"Leaving the council out will only complicate political matters for you in the long run, my lord," Sabrina pressed.

"Then I will deal with it in the long run."

Strange, Scott thought, but the colonel had left him alone with Hope again. He didn't understand the strategy, but after a lifetime in the military knew it was all part of somebody's plan. The colonel had never pressed him to speak more English after getting him to talk briefly about the Antousians. Maybe they thought alternating his harsh grilling with Hope's gentler discussion in Refarian would get him to cave. He didn't even care anymore: The only important thing was he was alone with Hope Harper, a presence he craved on his most basic level. He didn't question his need for her, didn't try to understand it: After so many days in containment, the elemental comfort he experienced simply sitting across from her was enough.

"We have another of your people," she said at last, speaking in easy Refarian.

His dazed state seemed to lift a bit. "Who?"

"It doesn't matter, but we do. They're bringing him in now—they will keep you in separate cells, but will probably try playing you off one another."

"Like they're using you to play me?"

She smiled, but said nothing.

"They *are* using you—right?"

"S'Skautsa, you're a military officer. You know how these things work."

"I feel a connection with you," he announced boldly. "I think you feel it too."

Her half-focused gaze shifted slightly, her eyes lowering. She removed her glasses with a deliberate gesture, setting them on the table between them. "It's almost three thirty in the morning. I'm tired and want to go to bed. Let's stay on track here."

"What did they send you in here to accomplish, Hope?" he pressed, taking a slow sip of water. They'd given him an unlimited amount and he wasn't going to waste the opportunity.

"To tell you about the capture of another of your men."

"Why else?"

She hesitated, visibly distressed. She worked for the FBI, but she was no agent, he knew that much. Her thoughts were too transparent; she didn't wear an armor of cynical protection like his interrogators did.

"When your buddy comes in here, they will start pitting you against one another—so you'd better start telling the truth, S'Skautsa."

"It is the truth. You know that it is, I sense it."

"You should probably start talking—really talking—to them in English as a sign of cooperation." She'd nailed it; he'd given only small tokens in their language, still holding back out of a need for self-protection.

He gave a nod. "You'll be off the case then."

"Probably."

"I trust you."

"I'm working for them—you remarked on that yourself."

"You don't like the way they've handled this."

Without altering her expression or tone, without even flexing a muscle she told him, "I want to believe you, S'Skautsa—and I don't like how they're treating you. Denying you food and water, acting as if you have no rights. That's not how humans are supposed to do things. You should know that."

"Then help me, Hope. I'm begging you. If what I suspect about the Antousians is true, this attack they're mounting is major. I need to be with my people, I'm their—"

He'd almost revealed his stature within Jared's rebel forces, but stopped himself.

"You're their . . . what?" she prompted. For a moment he entertained the idea that Hope was nothing but a trap: her seeming innocence; her semiblindness; her beauty—a combination that was his particular weakness, with her light-colored eyes and long blond hair. Maybe the humans were setting him up totally.

He shook his head, leaning back in his chair. He'd have to gaze her in order to feel her out. Every other time he'd soul-gazed her, she'd come up clean: She was exactly what she presented herself to be.

"What did these Antousians, the *vlksai*, do to your people?" she asked, changing her tack. Scott felt an answering avalanche of guilt. She had no idea that his race was the very ones hell-bent on destroying her world. Biologically speaking, that was. The heart that beat within his chest was Refarian, through and through. So he was telling the truth.

"Genocide." He said nothing more, waiting for her reaction.

"Your DNA is totally human—that's what we can't figure out. *Are* you human?"

He laughed bitterly. He held little love for her species, and it was the greatest irony about his genetic makeup. "I'm a descendent of your people," he admitted cryptically, unwilling to spell out the facts for her just yet. "The Antousians are murderers—they've killed millions of my people. They've killed many of yours, too, only your governments don't realize it."

She stirred in her seat. "How?"

"The missing," he explained, thinking of all the human lives taken by the Antousians already—what would happen if no one stopped them? "So many missing here on Earth, Hope. None of your people know where they go."

"You're telling me these *vlksai* took them?"

"And they will take more, but your people here, these Air Force jocks, they're never going to believe someone like me. We're all aliens to them—they don't understand that some of us are different."

"Okay, I have to think about this," Hope answered after falling silent for a long while. "They'll have the other interpreters translate as much of this as they can, but they won't catch a lot of it. From what I'm hearing, I'm far and away the best with your language."

Scott smiled. "Doesn't surprise me." She blushed slightly, which pleased him.

"I have to tell them something—what can I say?"

"That I stand by the facts: The Antousians are another race. A violent, warmongering one, and your leaders need to start taking pointers from me. Fast."

"This one speaks English. Perfect English. Our task is getting him to speak alien."

"Refarian," she corrected, keeping her voice as respectful as possible.

The colonel peered through the window of this other containment cell, where Hope had been immediately directed upon exiting Scott Dillon's holding area. She glanced through the glass, seeing nothing but blurred light and a shadowy, tall form. The colonel tapped on the glass. "This one we've been trailing for a lot longer than Dillon. Never had anything to officially link him to the others until now. If one of the local deputies hadn't called in the plate from that bar, we never would have nabbed him."

"What will my task be, sir?" She stepped back from the viewing pane. It was useless anyway—what point was there in staring at blurred shadows?

"Nothing right now. I want to debrief you about the interview with Dillon," the man explained, whistling slightly through his teeth again. He made that sound a lot while contemplating strategy, Hope had discovered. "Let's go for breakfast in the officers' club," he said, and immediately led the way, several soldiers falling in around them. Hope hadn't slept or taken a walk or even breathed without having some sort of security escort since arriving at the underground facility days ago. "Then we'll have the debriefing."

Chapter Twenty-one

Thea stared at the envelope within her hands and feared what she would discover. Had Marco's predictions been accurate? Was he as tainted as he claimed to be? Or had, in fact, his heart been pure but broken in their other life? The one where their relationship had only been bad. Dark. Wrong. Where *she* had been damaged.

Whatever would come from gazing into that other timeline, Thea knew it couldn't be good. It was an endeavor that would be fraught with danger, the outcome uncertain and possibly irreversible. Some things you weren't meant to know. That's what her mother had told her the first time she had coached her in her gift. She'd said, "Thea, darling, you are gifted by All, deeply gifted. But with that gift comes tremendous responsibility. It's a burden some are unwilling to shoulder."

But this time, no matter what her mother might have warned her, she had no choice but to find out. Stroking her fingertips across the document's surface, staring down at Marco's scrawling, nearly indecipherable handwriting, she focused. Focused, trained her intuitive sight and stepped into the abyss.

She took his hands, belted them together, feeling mischievous as she grinned up at him. But he misunderstood. Thought it was about control and dominance . . . maybe it was. Never taking his eyes off of her, he wrestled free of the loose binding, then spun her furiously, drawing her back against his chest. The scent of warm leather filled her nostrils as he strapped her hands together behind her back.

"There, you little wildcat," he breathed in her ear. "I'm in control now."

She panted, her chest heaving, struggling for words. I don't want control over you! I want you.

"How do you like it now?" he spat in her ear. She'd hurt him—badly. Whatever she'd done it had left his heart so ravaged that he sought emotional revenge upon her. Domination. The need to take her with visceral rawness. He skimmed a scintillating hand down her shoulder, then along her bare arm, lower down her thigh, then circled back, stroking her hard between the legs. Crushingly hard. She stiffened in his arms, feeling dampness form in her panties. Everything in her wanted to strike back, even as she responded to his feverish touch. I love you, don't do this, *she wanted to scream. Struggling with her hands, she found just how hard he'd bound her.*

"Just this once, you won't do the leaving," he told her coolly, forcing her legs wide apart. "I'm the one in control now."

"You can bind me, Marco—you can turn me away so you don't look into my eyes." She panted; his touch grew more aggressive. "But I will never be your precious Kelsey! Never."

"I used to want you," he hissed low in her ear. "I was a fool, but it all started with you."

"When?" she whispered. "Tell me when."

"That first night, in the bar when you came for me—the night Jared kicked me out. I thought it could be love, but I was a fool. A fool to follow you into this godsforsaken camp, a fool not to know how many men you gave your body to." They were in Veckus's camp, together; she glanced about them, knowing they were in the lair of Jared's bitter enemies.

"You loved Kelsey then," she argued, but her words sounded hollow and flat.

"True—but just that one night, I thought I could love you too."

Thea crumpled the letter against her eyes, wanting to blot out everything she'd just glimpsed. Tears streaked both of her cheeks, rolling hot without her wiping them away. Of course her mother had been right; some things weren't meant to be seen. She had betrayed her king and queen, in the most evil of ways. And she'd loved Marco; powerfully, deeply, but had been so locked up inside she hadn't known how to be different. In that other life she'd fallen so far and so abominably; how could she possibly have loved him well?

Whatever she'd done, it had been worthy of his derision, his need to punish her emotionally because in her trance, she had felt his anguish. Thea began to tremble so hard she was forced to wrap her arms about herself in an effort to still the tremors. It was the thought of Marco's empathy, of his deep, passionate nature coming in contact with that vile person she'd been that tore her apart. How had he stood that life? How had he been able to survive a world shot through with such evil, which would have confronted his empathy in every direction? And she'd been the one who'd led him by the hand right into it.

Her body was wracked with sobs, but still the tears wouldn't subside. Wiping her eyes with the back of her hand, she thought about Marco now. Her Marco, the one she loved, the one in this time whom she could still save. *I have to find out where he is*, she resolved, trying to staunch her tears with her hands. *It's not too late this time!*

She'd been the one to turn him to their enemies in that other realm; without her presence in Veckus's camp, perhaps he still had a future here where he belonged—with her.

It took every ounce of soldier's discipline she possessed, but she grasped the letter again, forcing herself to enter their world, to see what was probably never meant to be known by her. There was a dark, foggy mist swirling around a bar—the same bar from tonight—or was it smoke? She saw herself walk in, only this time . . . something was very different. Her eyes didn't have that cold, lost look in them. They were her own eyes, filled with love and concern for the drunken man in the booth. He tilted his head sideways, staring up at her. Beautiful, full-lashed eyes that almost stopped her heart.

Yes, she thought, *yes, this was only hours ago. This is the right world, yes. Thank you, All! Thank you. Help me, show me more.*

Almost as if she were taken by the hand, the vision drew her inward, sped ahead, hurtling her through hyperspace, then slowed to a slow-motion tempo. Back and forth she rocked, keeping her eyes shut, as time spread before her. Someone else had come, another. A blond-haired man, short-cropped hair. Looked like military or maybe FBI. He wore a long jacket, yes, FBI, she felt it. Special Agent Happer? No, no, *Harper.* Chris Harper. He was making a deal with Marco, telling him about Scott, saying if he cooperated then Dillon would be released. Marco had nothing left, nothing to lose—she clutched at her heart, nearly catapulted out of the vision by the pain his emotions caused her—so he went. *No choice, anyway. Had to go.*

Gasping, Thea pulled out of the vision yet again. It felt as if she were bursting forth from under water after nearly drowning. Repeatedly she dragged at air, just trying to breathe. Doubling over, she clutched at her stomach, nearly gagging.

The FBI had Marco! Her love, they had him!

One more time, she promised herself. *Just one more time, back into the vision, long enough to find out more so I can help him—and Scott.* With another gasp, she opened her psyche yet again, reaching with her intuition for the truth. It was then that she saw the critical piece, the part that had evaded her about the first timeline. Scene after scene revealed in painstaking detail Earth's destruction at the hands of the Antousians.

I can't stay here, she thought, surveying the ruined landscape. *It's too much!*

The vision changed, taking her deep inside Warren Air Force Base, through a circuitous length of tunnels and corridors. She stopped before a particular holding room, gazing through a small aperture of glass. Within the cell, Marco paced—restless and anxious—and reached toward her. Walls gave way to fire, melted into rubble, became an inferno within the hallways. Thea reached toward the room where Marco had been standing, screaming his name, sobbing. "Love! Careful! Oh, love!" she wailed and, opening her eyes, she pulled out. With a sob, she rubbed at her eyes, tried anything to blot the images of destruction and annihilation from her mind. But she couldn't wipe her mind clean; the images were too indelible. They were a cauldron of what had happened before and what might still be yet to come in this timeline.

Shaking all over, Thea leapt to her feet and grabbed her jacket. There might still be time if she acted quickly enough!

Thea banged on Jared's door, hoping against hope that she'd find her commander still within his chambers at this early hour of the morning. Five A.M. usually placed him here or at breakfast, but with security so elevated, there was no telling. No answer came at first from the other side, so she raised her fist to knock again, but the door opened. Kelsey stood before her in an oversized shirt of Jared's, all her crazy auburn curls corkscrewing in every possible direction.

"Kelsey"—she paused, correcting herself—"my lady, is he here?" The words came out breathless and desperate, and her clear urgency registered visibly in Kelsey's eyes.

"No, he's already left for Base Ten."

"Mlksa," she cursed. "You've got to get dressed and come with me." She realized she'd just issued an order to her queen, but she held a military rank and the human did not.

Kelsey nodded wordlessly, pulling open the door so Thea could enter. "I'll be dressed in twenty seconds," she told her, moving briskly across the room without a question. Her easy trust made something in Thea's chest tighten, something she didn't bother examining. All she knew was that suddenly she didn't feel nearly so alone as she had just moments before.

Thea shoved the door closed in case any officers were sitting in the media center on the exterior landing and might overhear them. For now, this was intel of the highest level, and she was taking it straight to her commander.

Kelsey disappeared into the bathroom, then reappeared a moment later fully clothed and wearing her ski jacket. "I'm ready."

Thea nodded, trying to still her heart. "Thank you—I'm so glad I'm not alone in this."

Kelsey crossed the distance that separated them, moving toward the door. "Alone in what, Thea?"

Catching her queen by the arm, she stopped her. "I know why the Antousians have been crossing the border, and if we're going to stop them, we've got to move fast."

Marco sat on an unmade pull-down cot, and considered his options. When the FBI agent had appeared in the bar, he'd known this was his chance for redemption: Allow the feds to pull him onto the base near Dillon, and hopefully he could figure some route of escape for the lieutenant. If he could help him escape—by what means he hadn't a clue—then Jared would know his loyalty without question.

Was it still tonight? They'd confiscated his watch, wallet, and other personal effects, and without windows in his cell, he really wasn't sure. They'd airlifted him onto the base, forcing him to dress in an Air Force uniform so no one would question his presence, then driven him right into the underground facility at Warren—the same lockdown area where Dillon was being held. The FBI agent, Chris Harper, as he identified himself, had explained that if he'd cooperate, it could lead to Dillon's freedom. He had no illusions about the veracity of the "promise," but still, here he was.

So far they'd drawn blood samples, offered him water, and treated him well. Still, a dark sense of foreboding clouded his senses, and every time he reached with his intuition, he felt that the lieutenant was suffering. He didn't dare engage his empathy to sense more of what his captors had planned: It was just too dangerous on the narrow line of sanity he'd already been tremulously walking. So he worked with his intuition, blocking out the dark gift that perpetually threatened to overwhelm him at every turn.

Lying back on the cot, it seemed best to try and grab a bit of sleep. No telling when he'd have the opportunity again, and often when he dreamed, All gave him visions.

Inspirations. Strategies, too, and that was what he most needed to break out Scott Dillon.

Nevin Daniels eyed Thea curiously; the thoughtful man was never given to explosive outbursts, no matter how perilous the military situation. Likewise, Sabrina sat across the table, her face a mask of calm reserve; it seemed the Circle leader rarely revealed emotion.

Jared, on the other hand, rested both hands on the meeting table, his eyes blazing in expectation. Kelsey had assumed the seat beside him, waiting with bright, curious eyes of her own. Thea noted that her queen had a remarkable gift for supporting, even as she always steered her own path. It was the perfect balance for Jared, and that thought didn't annoy or upset Thea. They needed Kelsey's wise, confident counsel in their midst.

Thea drew in a quick breath, glanced eagerly between the gathered leaders, and began. "I spent time in meditation with the letter," she stated quickly. "Commander, it is paramount that we take offensive action against the Antousians immediately."

"I have the ready fighters in place. Right now, our enemies are not on radar. Could be their stealth capacity, but we usually find our way around that."

The Antousians' fighters and craft were nowhere near as stealthy as the Refarians' were. One advantage that usually played to their benefit.

"Sir, what I saw with my intuition"—she paused, wanting to blurt everything at once, but knew she had to frame it in an orderly manner—"we've been thinking about their strategy all wrong. It's not the missiles they want to target and take out—it's gaining control of them."

"Control how?" Jared asked evenly, his black eyebrows quirking together in concern. "Those silos are buried under one hundred tons of concrete each; if they take them out, they won't be operable."

"They plan to seize control of Warren, Commander, by launching a full-grade attack on the base itself. That's how they'll get control over the missile alert facilities—the MAFs. There are a number of launch facilities near to the base—within driving distance. That's what they did in that other timeline! Seized control over three launch facilities."

"Wait, hold up, Lieutenant," Nevin interjected. "Explain what you mean by this other timeline."

"We have a letter that clearly indicates that the mitres was used to travel back from the future," Jared explained, staring at a stilled overhead projection of a set of missile silos in Nebraska. It had been taken by one of their own pilots, who had tracked the Antousians' flight pattern from earlier in the day. "We now know that there is an alternate timeline, a parallel reality if you will, where events transpired differently. That's why I asked Thea to intuit what she could about that alternate course of events."

Thea ran both hands down the length of her braid, working to still her extreme agitation. "What I saw was horrific. It's not the silos like we think, at least not in the way we're thinking about it. If not stopped, Commander, they will attack Warren, firestorm it, air bomb it, and take full control of it—including the nearby missile alert facilities. They plan to strike New York, London, and Washington, DC. Earth will be left as a decimated shadow, allowing the Antousians to harvest at will."

Kelsey gasped. "My father is in DC," she told them. "Earth? Everyone? What do they plan to harvest? I don't understand."

Thea felt compassion well up within her. She'd lost almost everything to the brutal bastards; why should Earth now pay as well? It was frighteningly easy to understand exactly what Kelsey was feeling.

But it was Jared who answered her question in a quiet, controlled way. "They need humans," he told her vaguely. "Think of them as parasites who need host bodies. That's the simplest way to put it."

"Taking control of that base and its MAFs would enable them to hold Earth hostage," Nevin added seriously, making quick notes on his handheld.

For many long moments, no one spoke, each of them stunned into silence; every officer plotting strategy, considering options. "Gods in heaven," Jared finally cried, rising to his feet, "how do we stop it? Dillon is there, surely there must be some way to reach him." No one needed to state that in the past days none of them had figured a way to get through to the lieutenant. But Thea did have a plan.

"I don't think he's the only one of ours there on base, sir," Thea admitted quietly.

"Explain." Jared waved her on, settling back into his chair.

"They have Marco too, sir," she replied.

Sabrina's brown eyes locked with hers. "You saw him only hours ago."

"*And* I saw a lot of things while in my trance state. He went with them willingly . . . after I left the bar."

Jared leaned back in his seat, scowling. "So this means we have to get through to one of them, somehow. Dillon or McKinley, those are our choices—assuming they can get the Air Force to listen at all."

"We'll obviously launch a counterstrike against them, Commander, to protect the base."

"I can reach Marco," Thea told him quietly. "At least, I think I can."

"How?" It was a group question, voiced simultaneously. All eyes were riveted on her.

Thea hesitated, but she had no time for awkwardness. "Marco and I aren't mated, at least not yet, but we've come very close. Give me a shot; I think I can contact him."

Chapter Twenty-two

Marco slept, or something approximating it, slipping in and out of a troubled dream state. There was commotion in the hallway, then quiet again, overlaid by the sound of muted voices, and that woke him briefly. Overall it was almost impossible to catch a few winks when he wondered what his captors had planned for him. He kept his eyes closed, determined to fuel his strength by getting as much rest as he could before someone came for him.

He told himself he was dreaming when Thea's wavering image appeared in his cell. She stood beside his bed dressed only in a royal gown of light blue that was gauzy and fit her scantily, revealing the ripe curves of her full bosom. Clinging to her hips in a provocative vision of a world that once was—of palaces and kings and princesses like herself—the lusty dream aroused him powerfully. Laughing at his dream-addled mind, he decided to go with the erotic fantasy.

Sitting up on the cot, he gained a better view of her luscious body. She took another step closer and he realized the gown was backless, revealing inches of bare, delicious skin. He yearned to lick her from head to toe, sniffing all that bare skin even as he tasted it. His breathing grew unsteady, his pulse skittered. "That's a helluva uniform, baby." He laughed huskily.

She glanced downward in surprise, blushing furiously, and dropped onto the edge of his bed. "Apparently it's what my subconscious came up with," she agreed with a shy laugh. "Maybe I'm tired of uniforms all the time."

He leaned back into his pillow, studying her. "I like it. No, scratch that," he amended. "I *love* it. Gods in heaven, you're gorgeous. I guess I'm dead, huh? That it? You're my vision of heaven?"

She smiled, bending over him with a slow, arduous kiss. She angled her mouth over his, lingering with her lips against his for a long moment, then traced her tongue across his lips. "You're asleep and I've come to warn you, Marco. The Antousians are planning to storm the base. You are at Warren, aren't you?"

"Yes, they came for me after you left the bar."

"You've got to get them to listen, Marco."

Her words were at total odds with the seductive way she'd appeared. But he didn't question the incongruity, and neither did she, it seemed. "So you're warning me dressed like a royal siren?" he asked roughly. "All business, aren't you, wildcat?"

There would be time for war and bloodshed another day—right now he only yearned for one thing—to mate with Thea. To pull her down atop him, strip her free from the confines of that gown, and claim her at last. Make her one with him. Tie them together for all eternity, and let duty and honor be damned. *She's mine*, an inner voice growled. *She's always been mine!*

A slow smile spread across Thea's face, and she wound her fingers through her loose, curling hair. "You wore it down for me," he observed, cocking an eyebrow suggestively.

"I want you. You know how much I want you." She slipped a shoulder strap free, allowing the dress to fall loose. He caught a glimpse of her warm flesh, begging to be stroked by his hands.

Sucking in a desperate breath, he gazed upon her. "This has nothing to do with our enemies," he said, leaning up on his elbows. "What are you really doing here, Thea? Warning me or preparing to become my lifemate?"

A gleam appeared in her azure gaze; the other shoulder strap popped free, allowing the dress to crumple low about her waist. "Both, love. We're out of time."

She leaned over him, pushing him down into the mattress with the weight of her body. Planting both hands beside his head so that she was suspended over him, she forced him beneath her lithe body. Her breath was hot, real.

"What about Scott?" she breathed, sniffing of his scent, yet keeping him pinned beneath her in an almost predatory manner.

"I-I think he's in the cell next to mine, can't be sure," Marco stammered, scenting her in return. He broke into a delirious laugh, looping his arms about her. "Baby, what's really happening?"

"I'm in a trance state," she explained, finally releasing him and sitting up. Suddenly, she grew serious, the flirtation gone. "I thought I could reach you—turns out I was right."

"Hell, yeah," he agreed with a needy growl. "More than right."

"Listen to me, Marco," she told him intently, no longer pursuing him. "We don't have much time; no telling how long I can maintain this. You have to find a way to convince those in charge there that the Antousians plan to attack the base. We're not sure when, but soon. It's got to be imminent. They intend to take charge of the missile launch controls and use them against Earth."

He stared at her seriously, assessing her—still not quite believing she wasn't simply a dream. "They've stuck me in this hole and never returned. I can't warn them this way."

She glanced toward the holding-room entry. "Then go knock on the door and demand to speak to the officer in charge. Something, Marco. Anything! But fight, damn it!"

He sat up in bed, taking hold of her shoulders. Suddenly the beautiful gown had transformed into her uniform, all trappings of seduction replaced by her full military presence. "This is real," he said, finally knowing that it wasn't a mere dream.

She gave a brisk nod. "I wish that it weren't. Well, all except the part where I'm here with you. Obviously my subconscious mind is focused on less serious things," she admitted throatily.

The vision wavered slightly, threatening to break their

temporary hold on one another. And Marco made a fateful, determined decision—the only one he could make, at least if he hoped to remain in contact with Jared and the others back at camp. "Thea, we have to take action fast," he replied abruptly. "Together. We no longer have a choice."

"About what?" She tilted her gorgeous face upward, looking into his eyes, and it caused his heart to thunder in his chest.

"We have to mate."

Hope sat cross-legged on her small bed, laptop poised on her knees. Her hot keys enabled her to feel the keypad beneath her fingertips, marked as they were in Braille, though she was still awkward with the markings. But she'd been a remarkably fast typist for years now; you couldn't make a living transcribing intercepts and interviews otherwise, and she relied on the Braille markings very little. Her laptop was outfitted with tools to help her—voice activation, audio features. She kept a journal in Word, something she once maintained in small, bound diaries until she'd begun to lose her sight.

I don't know how to get the colonel to listen, she typed. *I'm only a linguist. A woman he dismisses as half-blind and useful just to a point. How do I get him to trust Scott?*

She paused, wishing she could have just five minutes alone with her twin. She'd been told he was here on the base, too, but had yet to see him. Typical compartmentalization, at work once again, but she still wondered what his role in the whole affair was.

Shoving the laptop aside, she rose from her bed and began to pace the small quarters where she stayed between interrogation sessions. Outside in the hallway, armed guards stood, making a show of protecting her. The truth was, they were preventing her from taking any unsupervised actions.

Counting her paces across the room, she reached the small bathroom. As she bent over the sink, splashing water on her face, something rocked the barracks like a full-force earthquake. Immediately everything went black, robbing her of the remnants of her eyesight. Another explosive blast drove her to her knees; she was totally blind in the darkness. There was the instant smell of explosives, fumes. Hope felt across the floor with her hands, sweeping them in an arc around her. She knew where the bathtub was—she just had to get to it. If the barracks were under some sort of attack, as it seemed they were, the porcelain tub would be the safest place to survive any further blasts.

Her heart slammed in her chest, and with the whizzing sound of mortar fire and rockets outside, she catapulted herself into the bottom of the tub, covering her head.

"We can't mate, not in this trance state," Thea objected.

Marco gave her a wolfish grin. "You're the one who suggested it first."

"I can't be held responsible for what my subconscious wants!"

"But *you* want it, and you've told me so repeatedly."

Thea glanced around the cell in a panic. "We don't have time, Marco. There's not time for any of this!" She sprang to her feet and rushed toward the door, peering out. "I can't see anything out there."

Without moving, he was suddenly behind her, pinning her face-first against the door. "This won't take long," he promised in a low, rumbling voice, shoving his lean, hard body firmly against hers. She'd never escape him even if she wanted to; he was too big, too overpowering—not that she wished to budge from beneath his muscular body. What she wanted was to be taken by him, utterly and completely. Just not under these circumstances.

"I may not know much about mating," she argued, feeling his hands skim her hips and then trace up her spine, "but I know we can't bond in your sleep. And we can't bond with our enemies all around us!"

"Thea, what I'm talking about isn't mating, not precisely," he explained, stroking her hair away from the nape of her neck. "It's near-mating. We'll join our souls as completely as we can, here and now."

Struggling beneath his heavy form, she managed to

spin to face him. Their noses pressing together, she panted, "That's not enough. That won't ever be enough for me."

"For now. Only for now."

Her chest rose and fell, blood rushed in her ears. "We'll be able to communicate this way, is that what you're saying?"

"Across space and distance. We'll be able to link this human base with our own compound. Pass intel to our camp. Plot our attack. We'll have an open link between us when we need it."

She shook her head in disbelief. "That's not possible for most *deeply* bonded mates," she objected softly.

Slowly, he smiled at her, a strange, bittersweet expression. "But remember—I'm an empath. I'm not like other mates."

"If we survive, what then?" she asked, clutching at him in desperation. This could never be enough, to only join souls and minds. She needed all that Marco McKinley had to give her—his heart, and his body. Near-mating would never be enough: She wanted him as lifemate.

"If we make it out of this, I'll return to camp and mate with you for life, Thea. That's what I'm telling you."

She nodded, tears brimming in her eyes. "I've never wanted anything so much in my life, Marco."

"There's still the same risk to you, baby; that hasn't changed. The same threat about my gift overtaking you—"

She cut him off, burying her face against his chest. "But if we're going to stop the Antousians," she finished for him, "it's our only choice."

Marco used his energy to probe within Thea, moving quickly. Unsentimentally. Kneeling in front of one another on the hard, cold floor of his cell, this was nothing like the bonding he'd fantasized about. Still, as he entered her spirit, an explosion of heat and light threatened to choke the very breath from his lungs. Her erratic mating energy was so overpowering, he wondered how he'd keep off of her, even with such high stakes pressing in all around them.

Palm to palm they touched, their hands trembling, their gazes never leaving one another. He could feel Thea's apprehension in his gut; not that she didn't want him, but that circumstances were forcing them to bond in such an unconventional way.

I wish I could see your natural self, he purred within her mind as he pierced the veil separating their two spirits. Her soul showered a dazzling display of color across all of his senses, causing his whole body to tremble with need and yearning.

Soon, she promised softly inside of him. *Very soon.*

At that precise moment, he felt her burrow within his own essence, her soul brushing like butterfly wings against his. Tentative at first, then increasing in its demand.

Their fingers threaded together, both of their bodies wracked with tremors. He wrestled to hold back some of his dark gift, to protect her from receiving his empathy, but the need to completely mate souls with her was becoming more than he could bear. He'd hoped to control what he imparted to her, but this needy crescendo, the insistent demand to mate, had proved too much. Between his legs, his erection swelled, an insistent, impossible need at the moment. *Must mate. Must!*

"Quickly, Thea, quickly," he moaned. "Must . . . accomplish . . . quickly."

"I know, I know," she agreed breathlessly, arching her back as their souls began a tentative caress. Most natural for Refarians was to seal their bodies first, then join souls. Instead they had bypassed it all, laying themselves bare on this fiery plane of need and longing.

Marco bent his forehead against Thea's. "I-I can't hold back. I need this . . . now!" he roared, unleashing the full power of his empath's soul upon her.

"Ah! Ah!" she half cried and half moaned, over and over as their souls fused tightly together with one effortless gasp.

"One," he murmured, showering her face with kisses. "Finally . . . one!"

Panting, they clung to each other, tears streaming down Thea's face. Marco licked at her face, flicking away her tears with his warm tongue. He felt drunk off of her, off the sheer release of having her energy twined all inside him, wrapping around his heart and body and soul like loving arms.

They could have knelt that way, kissing and nuzzling and just feeling each other's souls for hours, but duty pressed hard on both their minds. Slowly they disentangled from one another's embrace, the warm hum of soul-mating buzzing through their spirits. With a barely repressed moan Marco whispered, "This is only for now, baby. Only for now. Our true mating is yet to come."

It had satisfied his alien nature, but it hadn't come close to sating his body. His swollen erection pulsed between his legs, reminding him of everything they'd yet to share. Only souls . . . not full bonding. Not true mating.

"Come on," Thea agreed, struggling unsteadily to her feet. "We both have work to do if we have a prayer of being together again. Truly together."

Thea awakened on the floor of the meeting room and discovered Kelsey bent over her in concern. "Are you all right?" her queen asked, touching her gently on the shoulder. Thea's uniform was soaked through with sweat, her entire body atremble.

"How long was I out?" she asked through chattering teeth.

"Fifteen minutes," Kelsey explained, pressing the back of her hand against her temple. "You're burning up! What happened, Thea?"

With a wordless groan Thea struggled to sit up, and Kelsey draped her own parka over Thea's shoulders. "Here, pull this around you," the human instructed. "You're shaking."

Thea nodded obediently; her throat was parched, her body ablaze . . . and the entire terrain of her soul had been permanently altered. Dimly she could make out the interior of the meeting chamber; she and Kelsey were alone.

"Where's the commander?" Thea asked, tugging the parka tightly around her body. "Lieutenant Daniels? Sabrina?" Clearly much had happened during her time in the trance—and on both sides of the veil.

Thea tried to stand, but Kelsey grasped her by the

shoulder, pushing her back down. "You need to sit a few minutes."

"I *need* to get up to speed here—what transpired while I was out?"

"Thea, rest." The woman's tone was firm. "You've been through something immense, obviously. Your body temperature has altered, and your pulse rate is off the charts. Sit still."

Thea buried her face in her hands with a groan. "What are you now, a medic?"

"I'm a scientist. And I know enough about biology, human or otherwise, that you're not going anywhere, at least not for a few minutes."

Thea nodded obediently. "Then fill me in."

"An Antousian battle cruiser has taken position over Warren."

"Have the humans fired on the ship?"

Kelsey gave a curt nod. "Without effect."

Of course not, Thea thought. Stupid humans—they had no idea what kind of force they were up against.

Kelsey continued: "The Antousians have dropped in platoons of soldiers and have begun attacking the exterior buildings."

Thea's head jerked up. "What about the underground facility?" She couldn't disguise her panic. "That's where Marco and Scott are."

"I don't know, Thea. But we're launching our own counterstrike to stop them. Without the information you brought us about that other timeline, we'd be a lot further behind the curve on this." A part of Thea wanted to bristle at her queen's newfound authority, the sheer confidence in her words, but instead she felt comforted.

"Let me . . . tell Marco," Thea told her weakly.

"I don't think you should go back into that trance again," Kelsey warned her.

Thea smiled, shaking her head wanly. "No, no . . . don't have to."

Her queen's auburn eyebrows shot upward in surprise. "Why not?" After all, Kelsey knew firsthand what a bond with a Refarian male could be.

"I-I joined with him. We're linked now—like you and Jared were at first," she explained, feeling lightheaded and dizzy. "I can warn him; maybe he can tell the Air Force what those bastards have planned."

Kelsey smiled at her briefly, her eyes sparkling despite the situation. Yes, the woman knew precisely how intimate a bond could be—her feelings about her own lifemate were quite visible on her face.

Kelsey rose to her feet. "I'll go tell Jared that we've linked with Marco, then. See if he has anything to transmit."

Thea glanced upward in panic. "Kelsey, please—don't tell him. I mean, not what I just . . . told you."

"I'll come up with a good cover story. Don't worry," she said with a conspiratorial nod. "You can share the news when you're ready."

Thea inclined her head with the full respect due her queen. "Thank you."

Hope didn't dare move from her position of safety. The blasts had continued, some in the distance, some shocking her own barracks. It would be risky enough to leave protective cover if she were fully sighted. As it was, she could only cower in the bathtub and hope that the ceiling wouldn't cave in. The acrid smell of explosives and crumbling architecture filled her nostrils; her eyes burned, though she had no idea what was causing them to tear up. Maybe some sort of noxious gas.

Covering her head, she bent face-first against the bottom of the tub, wondering if she'd make it out of this early morning attack alive. The Antousians had come, just as Scott Dillon had warned. Or *was* this the doing of the Antousians? Perhaps it was the Refarians themselves. Perhaps the lieutenant had been playing her all along.

But what about my dream? She thought, half recalling the images she'd seen of an Earth destroyed by their mutual enemies. *I can trust Dillon. I'm certain.*

She just prayed that someone, somewhere in the chain of command, had heard his warnings.

A buzzer sounded and the door to Scott Dillon's cell opened. The colonel entered, flanked by several security guards, and he gestured for the soldiers to release Scott from his manacles. They'd fed him last night, a decent meal, but Scott's belly was stone-empty once again. With expectant eyes, he searched for any sign of more food, but judging by the expression on the officer's face, he wouldn't be eating again anytime soon.

"Over here," the colonel instructed gruffly, indicating the table where he'd been repeatedly interrogated. "And bring the other one in now too."

Scott's ears pricked up. Was it the soldier Hope had mentioned?

The colonel dropped into the chair like a leaden weight and began: "I need to know everything about this attack, son. Who's behind it, how you plotted it. Everything. Otherwise you'll be executed later today."

Scott shook his head numbly. "What attack?" he asked in plain English.

"Don't take me for a fool, Lieutenant. You've known what was coming all along—it's why your people have been doing the aerial missions, testing the borders."

"Is the base under attack now?" Scott questioned directly, not skirting the issue.

"I'm asking the questions here," the other man barked.

"I've told you repeatedly who your enemies are—I've offered information and to help. If you're under attack, it's too late and there's not a damned thing I can do to help you now. *Sir.*"

"Tell me again. Tell me like I've never heard it all before. Lay it out for me," the colonel snapped impatiently.

"We're Refarian—not Antousian. We're here to protect you," Scott said. "It is our only reason for being here on Earth. We are not your aggressors. We're your protectors."

The colonel leaned back in his chair studying him. "Funny, 'cause that's exactly what the other one said." Without wavering his gaze from Scott's face, the officer hit the intercom. "I said to get the other subject in here—now!"

As if on cue, the door buzzed and several security officers wrangled Marco McKinley into the room. Scott refused to allow surprise to register in his eyes, although internally he was extremely grateful to see the Madjin.

"At the table," the colonel ordered the soldiers. "Right here."

Marco was shoved down into the seat between them. He kept his gaze trained on the scuffed wooden surface of the table.

"Look, Dillon, I want to believe you—I really do. But your DNA is different from this one's." The colonel gestured toward Marco. "His isn't human. Close, but not a match. Your DNA, however, is fully human. I need to understand why there's that kind of discrepancy. We're tending to think one of you's Refarian and the other's Antousian. So which is it?"

Scott took the lead. "I'm a Refarian sympathizer."

"I see." The colonel seemed unconvinced.

"Is the base under attack or not?" Scott blurted. "Because if so, we're wasting precious time here. Time we won't get back. I'll tell you everything about my DNA map once we mount some kind of plan."

The colonel gave him a nonplussed look. "Not buying it."

With a frustrated sigh, Scott launched into his life story—the extremely abbreviated version. "The Antousians have a vested interest in your species because humans are the key to solving a deadly virus that has killed millions of their despicable people. We've had humans on our world."

"And you're related to them, those humans?"

"A descendant." Scott wanted to shout to the ceiling in relief; he despised the gruesome details of his parentage, and was thankful not to own up to his Antousian roots. But his relief was short-lived.

"But you're related to these Antousians too?"

Scott flinched. "Not precisely, sir."

"Not precisely, huh?" the colonel mocked. "Why, *precisely*, aren't you on their side?"

"Because I revile that part of me. I'm Refarian, Colonel. In my heart, if not in my blood. I have served our exiled king, Jared Bennett, for the past fifteen years of my life. He's noble, compassionate, and has a great love for your species. A great love." Scott considered telling the man that Jared's wife was human, but his instincts told him to protect her identity.

"So if we're to believe you, your own people—"

"They are *not* my people," Scott corrected.

"These Antousians, then, are behind the launch against this base?"

It was Marco who spoke this time. "That's what we've been told, sir."

"Told how?"

Marco and Scott traded a look; Scott had no idea what had transpired in the days since his capture, so he nodded for Marco to continue.

The colonel barked at the Madjin, "You'd better tell me, son, and fast."

"We have abilities—gifts—that your own species doesn't possess," he explained in a rush. "You'd call them telepathic abilities."

"And you call them?"

"Intuitive gifts," Marco replied.

"Somebody warned you?" The colonel tapped his fingers on the table.

Marco hesitated, then answered, "Yes, a woman I'm very close to. She was able to reach into my mind."

The colonel shoved back from the table. "I don't know whether you're playing me or not. In fact, I don't know shit from shinola about what might be true here."

"Polygraph me," Scott volunteered. "I'll pass. With flying colors."

"That doesn't mean squat, son. You could use these 'special abilities' of yours to make yourself pass. Why else you think we haven't bothered with that?"

Scott leaned across the table with serious intent. "Colonel, we are both military men. We both say the word and our word is done. We also know what a threat can mean to our home world—a true, barbaric threat. I am telling you, sir, that these *vlksai* are after your blood. They will wipe out your species, taking as many hosts as they require, and burn the rest. Please, you've got to trust me here—"

Marco cut him off. "We can still align our forces and defeat them. Or you can sit back and watch them destroy this base and take hold of your missiles. That's the plan, Colonel. To seize the launch controls and strike Earth with your own weapons."

Scott gaped at Marco—was that what they'd learned since his capture? That the Antousians were that intent on destroying this planet? Briefly, he recalled the terrain of Hope's dream, how Earth seemed but a ruined shell of the world he knew.

The colonel sighed impatiently. "This underground facility is built to withstand a thermonuclear blast."

"They have weapons you haven't even thought about inventing," Marco replied calmly. "They can penetrate the base."

"Why haven't they done it before now?"

"They've been lying in wait," Scott answered. "For just the prime moment when they know they can pull it off. We don't know what's changed. More forces perhaps, bigger cruisers, it's impossible to say."

The colonel stood, paced the room, clearly wrestling with a decision. At last he turned and faced them both. "Some kind of giant starship is positioned over the base," he admitted. "They've dropped forces in and those soldiers are engaged in guerrilla attacks. They got under our radar; we can't lock in on 'em. Our soldiers are trained in every type of warfare—"

"Except with an invisible enemy," Scott said, revealing the one final piece of intel that would make the colonel understand the stakes.

"Invisible? What the hell are you talking about?"

"Shape-shifters, sir. Capable of assuming a formless condition," Scott answered plainly. "It's the same way they take hold of human hosts."

The colonel gaped at them both, and then spun away from them, striding quickly toward the door.

Scott called after him. "We're asking for your trust, sir, and if we're lying, you've lost nothing. Whatever measures you've got to take to protect the control centers, take them. Bring in more troops. Let us bring in ours."

The colonel turned on his heel to face him. "That ain't ever going to happen. We don't cooperate with extraterrestrials."

"Then you'd better explain to your generals that you've just signed Earth's death warrant."

Chapter Twenty-three

Marco! Marco, talk to me! Thea panted, watching the radar that displayed the Antousians full assault on Warren Air Force Base. They'd carpet bombed the facility by air, dropped in untold forces, and were now in the midst of a hostile takeover. The one thing they couldn't ascertain was how secure the underground facility remained at this point. So far, Thea hadn't successfully connected with Marco.

Maybe our bond isn't strong enough for this kind of distant communication, Thea worried. *Or maybe he's dead.* That thought nearly caused her to retch, but she forced her thoughts to still, focusing only on Marco.

Marco, talk to me, she attempted again. Gripping the console, she gathered all her core energy, spinning it hotter and stronger until her knuckles went white. *More power, more heat,* she thought, *then I can reach him.*

With one giant fire-burst of energy, she flung her essence across space and distance toward her near-mate, crying out to him with all her soul's passion. *Marccccccooooooo!*

Thea, I'm here, came his barely audible voice. *I'm with you. Don't be afraid. I'm here.* Even in the midst of such monumental danger, he was the one reassuring her.

Tears welled within her eyes. *You're still alive.*

I'm okay—so is Dillon, but it's going to hell here fast, baby.

You hang on! she implored. *You stay safe for me. Do you understand? You have to be safe for me—for* us, *Marco!*

I'm in my cell, but there are explosions all around, he

confided in a low voice—which was obviously instinctive, even though their communication was completely private.

They haven't listened to you at all, have they?

I think it's too late.

No, it's not! It can't be, she insisted, clutching at her head in desperation; across the console Jared glanced up at her, his face drawn tight with concern.

She put her back to him, and stepped to the far side of the control room as if she were on a private comm. She didn't want Jared and the others to see her tears. *Listen to me,* she told Marco, *you make it out of there. We're going to have a life together, a family. Please don't give up.*

She sensed his assent rather than heard any audible reply. Wiping at her eyes, she waited and didn't just rush to fill the void, even though holding silent took an extreme act of will.

At last he whispered, *How has your body handled the near-bonding? My gift, is it—*

She immediately allayed any of his fears. *I haven't felt anything. I'm fine, Marco.* She laughed, knowing it sounded forced. *See, I told you there wasn't anything to worry about.*

I guess not, he said in a voice that struck Thea as far too resigned. *I guess not.*

She sensed chaotic emotions threatening to rupture their connection, had the feeling Marco was talking to someone—and became frantic in her reaction. *What's happening there—tell me.*

Someone's coming in, Thea. I-I've got to break—

Don't break away. We might lose our link! Even if it meant staying joined with him until the bitter end, she wouldn't have him face the battle alone.

Long silence, anxiety from his side, a burst of fear and anger . . . then at last he returned. *Thea, I'll stay with you for as long as I can.*

Marco and Scott were spread prone on the cell's floor, hands behind their heads. A knot of security officers surrounded them, and there was the sound of rifles cocking. This was it; they would be executed quickly before the Antousians took over. The sounds of pulse fire and grenade explosions echoed in the distance.

"You should have cooperated," the colonel told them in a voice utterly devoid of emotion.

"Your base is falling into Antousian hands because you wouldn't listen," Scott replied just as calmly. "Because you didn't, we can't save you now."

Footsteps came closer to their heads and Marco flinched reflexively as he prepared to take his bullet. Blocking, he protected Thea from his gut-wrenching fear. The last thing she needed was to experience the gruesome reality of his death across their bond, but he also knew that duty required that he maintain their connection, no matter that cost. So he blocked—hard.

Somewhere in his heart he felt grateful; if he had to die, at least he'd been allowed to near-mate with the love of his life. For at least a few moments, he'd known what true bonding with Thea might be. The bliss of it, the driving need for her as his mate, the unshakable knowledge that they'd partially sealed themselves to one another. No, he could take any bullet now, and at least know that he'd tasted heaven before he got there.

The colonel dropped down beside Scott. "*Could* you have saved us?" the human asked in what seemed to be earnest inquiry.

Marco waited for Scott to reply, counting the silent seconds that spun out between them all. Death, decision, fate, it all hung in the balance.

"Colonel, if I could contact my own commander, there might still be a way. If we could bring our battle cruiser into position over the base—"

"How would you reach him?"

No way would Scott betray Jared's location by contacting him, but Marco had an idea. "If you give me a secure line where *he* can contact *you*, I'll relay the number . . . telepathically," he volunteered, intentionally invoking the human description that would best describe his near-bond with Thea.

"All right." The colonel scribbled on a notepad, tore the sheet off and laid it beside Marco's head. "Have him call this number. I'll be waiting." Then the officer stepped away, barking: "Get these men up. I need them ready to roll."

Jared dialed the number, not directly to Colonel Peters, but via a series of relays, rendering his call untraceable. The officer answered on the first ring. Jared identified himself as commander of the Refarian resistance.

"The situation is disintegrating rapidly, Commander," Peters said. "I understand you might be able to help."

Jared paced the length of the control room. For the past hour a thought had been gaining ground within his mind, and now that an Antousian takeover seemed unstoppable, his developing plan grew far more insistent.

"Set my men free, arm them, and I'll see what I can do."

"What assurance do I have that you'll defend the base?"

"Well, you're out of options—and Lieutenant Dillon is the best Antousian tracker I've ever seen. You need assistance, and we're ready to pour it on. But we need your cooperation. And tell Dillon he better not shapeshift, not at any cost, because we have a counterattack in mind."

On the other end of the line the colonel hesitated. "All right," he agreed, albeit reluctantly. "Done. What now?"

"You keep control of that base until we have time to put our plan in effect," Jared said, then cut the line.

Jared, Kelsey, and Thea, along with a full science team, were dropped just outside the mitres chamber within mere moments, the transport hurtling them there at maximum velocity. Without any time to spare, "proceeding cautiously" hadn't been on the commander's top list of priorities, Thea noted. Neither had entering the chamber cautiously: She and Kelsey had formed a rudimentary, hurried link, opening the portal, and they'd all been dumped unceremoniously on the cool floor of the chamber. With muddled senses and dazed reactions, they set to work on Jared's plan, and Thea noted in passing that traversing the portal seemed much easier this time around.

In order to enter the chambers, Thea had been forced to break the bond with Marco. It had taken all of her soldier's resolve to let him go, knowing she might never see him—at least not alive—again. But she'd done it, finding it surprisingly easy to form a link with her queen; much easier than last time, in fact, but then again, their relationship had already transformed drastically in only the past few days. Still, no amount of trust or developing confidence in her new queen had prepared her for what Jared declared after they'd safely entered the chamber. It was an insane strategy, yet if it worked, the ballsy move would save not only Earth, but all their lives.

"So this is all Kelsey's idea?" Thea couldn't disguise her shock. "The whole plan?"

Kelsey and Jared exchanged a look as the human strode toward the coiling unit. Just like last time, the energy inside instantly reacted, glowing hotter and brighter. "Jared's plan," Kelsey answered, "but with a bit of embellishment from me."

Thea planted a hand on her hip. "How do you already know enough about the mitres to have any plans or embellishments?"

Kelsey focused on her work at hand, palming the coiling unit so that it churned brighter and harder and faster.

"You're opening a portal," Thea gasped in understanding. "Between—"

"The base and this chamber," Jared finished. "We've long theorized how the mitres would serve as our primary weapon against the Antousians—now's our chance to test the theory. Firsthand."

"And if we fail?" Thea pressed him. "What then, sir? Earth will be gone."

Jared took her by the shoulder, leading her to the target area in the center of the chamber. "Can you name another way to fight the *vlksai*? They've infiltrated the base, and are in their ethereal form, undoubtedly. Any of our strike positions are meaningless at this point. If they succeed, Earth will be gone anyway. This is the only way."

Thea understood precisely what her commander was

proposing. Yes, they'd theorized this approach endlessly, but theories were one thing, and practical application in the middle of a deadly showdown quite another. "What will Kelsey do?"

"I'll create the portal, bridge the distance while they"—she pointed toward the two science officers who'd quietly accompanied them—"man the mitres weapon."

Hope struggled to climb through crumbling debris. The assault on the barracks had finally ended, but not before the building had caved in on top of her. Somehow she'd managed to claw her way toward an opening in the collapsed wreckage, drawn toward the smell of fresher air and the vague appearance of lights.

Feeling with her hands, which were cut and bloodied from the jagged debris, she forced the opening larger, though she proceeded with extreme caution, aware that she might send more of the structure down atop of her if she weren't careful. But she couldn't stay inside the decimated building either; there was too much possibility that it would cave in atop her. On the outside, their enemies might capture or kill her, but inside was a certain death trap.

Good thing I'm so small, she thought as she wormed her way through the aperture. With an unceremonious thud, she tumbled face-forward toward the ground, catching herself awkwardly on splayed hands, wincing as her wounded palms hit the ground. *Scott Dillon, where are you?* she wondered, trying to make out anything in the fumes and smoking carnage. Nothing. She could see absolutely nothing, nor could she determine a fucking thing.

No weapon, no eyesight, nothing; she felt her way toward what looked like a supply truck, crawling and keeping low to the ground. It was the only way she had a hope in hell of surviving.

An Antousian battle cruiser held position directly above Warren Air Force Base. So far the ship had taken out most of the barracks and other buildings across the base, but the underground facility had yet to be penetrated. Scott and Marco led a small force of Air Force soldiers in a recon mission, utilizing infrared as a means of identifying Antousian ground forces. But their best counterweapon at the moment was simply Scott's ability at tracking his own species; sniffing the air, sweeping his gaze about the landscape, he identified scattered bands of snipers and other Antousian soldiers.

So far, they'd taken out at least twelve of the *vlksai*, Marco holding the rear as they worked their way and prayed that Jared's plan would succeed.

As Scott glimpsed bombed-out buildings, torn-apart wreckage—trucks upended and jets sliced in half—he worried about Hope Harper. Without her eyesight, she would have no defense if the Antousians came after her. The colonel said she'd gone to the barracks—but all the barracks had already been leveled. During his days of captivity she had never wavered, fighting for him and believing in him; he was determined to reach her, somehow, and help her escape the clutches of his murderous enemies. The Antousians would take special pleasure with the likes of her, someone vulnerable and spirited; they thrived on breaking her kind.

Behind him, a sudden spattering of gunfire erupted, cut off by a whine and a boom. Dropping low, a quick glance over his shoulder betrayed the truth—an exploding mortar shell had just taken out most of the soldiers who'd been following him. More explosions ensued, more bullets whistled through the darkness, and there was no sign of Marco. The Madjin must have been taken out along with the human soldiers, he realized, but there wasn't time to mourn a fallen comrade, not if he planned to get out of this hell alive.

The whining whiz of a mortar round shot over his head. *Got to keep moving, I've got to get out of here!*

Hope crawled on her belly, inching her way toward what looked like an upturned truck or jeep. All she needed was good cover, then she could ride this battle out; hopefully she'd live to see the day that seemed to be dawning over the base. Pinkish light filled the sky; surely daylight would help even the playing field in this terrible skirmish.

Through the blurred darkness, a figure rushed toward her and she screamed, burying her face against asphalt, tasting blood in her mouth. Footsteps echoed off of pavement, and she cowered, unable to flee or fight.

I'm going to die. Now. This is it, she thought, wanting to vomit from sheer terror.

A hand clutched her arm roughly, and she wrestled to pull out of the firm grasp, but then a familiar voice hissed, "Let's go! Come on, come on! Go, go, go!"

She wanted to sob her relief—she staggered to her feet, lurching forward in Scott Dillon's grasp. Tears of release and terror filled her eyes while he yanked her toward the overturned truck she'd been aiming for. "Stay with me, Hope," he urged. "Stay with me. I'll get us out of here!"

At that precise moment there was the crack of rifle fire—or some other weapon, and Scott's grasp on her arm loosened. "Go on to that truck!" He gave her a shove in its direction before turning away. "Go, Hope—now! I'll cover you."

She obeyed wordlessly, making a run for it, the sound of whizzing gunfire erupting all around her. As she reached cover, she thought she heard Scott cry out, but she couldn't see a damned thing. Crawling on her belly, she managed to reach protection behind one of the truck's oversized wheels. Her heart felt like it might explode inside her chest, and she squinted, fumbling to adjust her glasses in the vain effort to see if Scott was okay.

Marco hunkered behind a pile of concrete rubble, cursing himself for getting separated from Dillon. When the mortar round had hit their band of soldiers, he'd been forced to fall back in order to cover the others. All he'd accomplished in the process was to protect the lieutenant. All the human soldiers had already been taken out. Searching for Antousians through his rifle's sights, it seemed he couldn't get a lock on anyone. His night-vision glasses, while equipped with infrared, seemed utterly useless against the formless aliens. Either that, or they just weren't in his vicinity at the moment.

It was an impotent feeling, sitting like a ready target,

barely concealed from his enemies. Something had to be done, some method had to be used to even the odds.

There was a way he could combat their enemies, but it frightened him almost as much as his current predicament—he could open up his empathy and feel for the *vlksai.* A noise off to the side sounded, and he swung his rifle in that direction, gripping the trigger tightly, ready to take out his enemies. But a leggy, disoriented antelope leaped over a bit of broken concrete, then ambled right past where he hid.

Breathing a sigh of relief, he opened himself—his empathy—and began sweeping his perception in an arc about his position. Bracing himself, he expected an onslaught of pain and nausea, the typical headaches, but, oddly, none came. What he did immediately experience were the darkest emotions he had ever felt—vile hatred, bitter vengeance, murderous jealousy. He shuddered, catching his hand against the shards of concrete in order to keep from passing out.

I have to focus, he thought, pushing himself harder. His arc of sensory perception fanned larger, opening. *They are here, and I can find them. I can save some of these humans—Dillon too.*

And I have to survive for Thea. I have to live for her, I promised.

Thea felt the floor of the mitres give way beneath her as it had the last time she was there, replaced by roaring wind and vacuum. Kelsey stood in the center point of the chamber, her hair flapping wildly, both hands extended from her sides like some powerful goddess with power over time itself. The coiling unit had vanished, dissolving around them as space and dimensions gave way to eternity. Kelsey was guiding the damn thing! Not the mitres, but the opening of the portal—apparently by sheer effort of will or desire.

"Kelsey," she tried calling out to her queen, but beside her Jared caught her hand.

"Let her do it, Thea," he shouted over the roaring noise.

She squinted at Jared, trying to understand. "Do what?"

"Kelsey . . . is . . . the key."

"To what, Jared? The key to what?"

"Maintaining the portal—she's got the codes, only she can do it" he yelled, and as the portal opened to its maximum size, Thea was thrown face-first to the floor. Only there was no floor, just memories and futures like trailing comets through her consciousness.

Somewhere in all the flotsam of impressions, she found Marco and held tight to him—knowing that doing so was vitally important. Sensing that his life, in every dimension, seemed to hang in the balance.

Baby! he called out to her.

Are you all right?

Yes—why are you shouting?

It's so loud, so crazy—we're in the mitres. Are you all right?

She felt his hesitation, then: *Yes. But I'm not sure about Dillon. We were separated. He might be dead.*

Thea cried aloud, pressing her eyes shut. *Not Scott, not him!*

I don't know for sure, Marco told her, even though she'd only thought the words, not meant to communicate them. *He could be okay still. I just don't know.*

Thea held fast to the floor, trying to lift her head to see what was happening, but extreme gravity forced it down. It was as if Kelsey, by her very presence and will inside the chamber, had unleashed a force of nature.

Wait— Thea, something's happening here, on the base. Overhead and . . . around us. I feel it with my empathy. A portal, or a dimension, I'm not sure.

We're doing that, from here! she shouted. "Marco says a portal is opening on the base!" she yelled into the thrashing wind. "It's working." She managed to tilt her head sideways, catching a partial glimpse of her queen. The human was illuminated from within, a golden hue having gilded her entire body; it was Prince Arienn's power, Thea realized wondrously, fueling the mitres and utilizing Kelsey as a sort of conductor. She held the codes; Arienn had supplied the power.

Thea began shivering uncontrollably at the monumental realization that they had finally, at long last, manned the mitres as a fully functioning weapon. And just as Jared had predicted, Kelsey was the key.

The pain was agonizing, blinding, suffocating. Scott had never been injured this badly before, not once in all his years of soldiering. His enemies had him exactly where they wanted him—prone and vulnerable—and the same snipers who had shot his legs out from underneath him would be closing in on him now. They were coming, already, to finish him off. At least Hope had gotten to safety.

He had to think. Had to breathe. Dragging at the dawn air, he couldn't seem to fill his lungs, and the pain in his legs was almost more than he could bear. Groaning, he tried to sit up, tried to stand, tried to do anything. He could only writhe in his own blood and beg for All to have mercy upon his soul.

"Gods," he groaned, clutching at the seeping wound in his right leg. The damn thing was torn half-open, and warm, sticky blood soaked his gloves. Sniffing at the air, he sensed three Antousians nearly upon him. Fumbling with his pulse rifle he cocked and reloaded, waiting for their imminent attack. Well, they might be finishing him off, but he was going to take a few of the scum along with him. Staring at the night sky, he sucked in a steadying breath. Some part of his soul wondered how all these years of fighting had boiled down to this one moment. He was going to die—maybe he was even dead already?

"Lieutenant," Hope's urgent, feminine voice called out to him from the darkness. She appeared at his side once again, crouching beside him.

"Wh-wh . . ." His mouth hardly worked, and for the first time he realized he was shaking all over—teeth-shattering tremors racking his body. *Shock, I'm going into shock*, he thought dimly. Feeling her steady hands slip beneath both of his arms, he understood she was dragging him . . . somewhere. His mouth tried to form her name, but only a gurgling sound bubbled forth. She held him beneath his arms, pulling him somewhere. His eyes searched the open lot and he remembered their objective: a large military truck parked about ten feet away. She'd never make it back there, not with him like this.

"Hope . . . get to . . . cover." He collapsed weakly in her arms. "Leave me."

She pulled harder, rougher. "Shh, we have to get you out of the open." He felt heavy and awkward in her small arms, and struggled for a moment to find purchase on the pavement, but his boots scrabbled lifelessly, his legs instantly buckling beneath him.

"Just don't struggle," she hissed in his ear. "You won't be able to walk, not like this." Something strange flashed in his head—the thought that maybe he *would* live, but that he'd never be able to use his legs again. He dismissed it, fumbling again with his rifle. His hands were weak; his body was fading.

But, somehow, they did make it to the truck. He sniffed at the air again, and detected their enemies. Close, so close, but not yet upon them. For a fraction of a second, he rested in Hope's arms, then sat upright while she positioned him against one of the truck's back wheels.

"Gotta fight those fuckers off," he slurred, collapsing against the large tire.

Her gaze shot in several directions. "We're at the truck, right?" she asked, running her fingertips along the wheels and the ground beneath them, then on up under the belly of the vehicle. *What a strange question,* he thought fuzzily. *Of course they were at the truck.*

She felt behind him, her hands outlining the vehicle's underbelly. "Here, we've got to get you under the chassis." She began her tugging and pulling again; the girl had massive strength for someone of her size and species' abilities. Before he knew it, she had him propped between two massive sets of tires that would provide at least decent coverage.

"Thank . . . y . . ." His eyes drifted shut. They were coming; he smelled them in every direction. There was no way he would survive. Blood trickled into his mouth—without realizing it, he had bitten the inside of his lip against the torturous pain in his legs. Then he remembered Hope Harper, there, right beside him. His eyes snapped open, and he rotated his head until he could look at her.

"I'm done, Hope," he rasped, wrestling for another breath. "Finished. Save yourself."

"I'm not leaving you!" She turned on him, scowling. So frightened earlier, she had now taken fearless control of the treacherous situation.

"I can't protect . . ."

She wrapped both of her arms about him from behind and began sliding him backward. "You're too exposed here. I need to get you hidden better."

"They won't go by sight," he explained, leaning heavily into her embrace as she dragged him roughly along the frozen earth. "They'll know I'm here. Won't matter if I'm hidden."

She didn't even hesitate. "But this is a better firing position."

Scott reached for his rifle, but couldn't close his fingers around thc barrel and steady it. "I ca-can't . . . not sturdy . . ." He couldn't begin to curl his finger around the trigger. His body was utterly ruined.

"I will help you," she answered purposefully, tugging him back between her legs until he rested against her chest. Her breathing was crazy and erratic—she was terrified. But strong, very strong. Strange, but he felt a certain acceptance that his death was imminent. Or at least he'd felt that way until she'd found him. As shc leaned against the inner wheel, shc wrapped her arms around his chest, and put both hands about him, steadying his rifle until it was as if he had a new pair of hands, useful, strong hands. The two of them were as one.

"I can't see, Scott—you know that—not well enough to nail those guys. But you can be my eyes, and I'll be your hands."

"Here," he grunted, putting the rifle in her hands. "You fire, I'll aim it."

"Yes," she breathed against his ear. "And we're not going to die, Lieutenant. Not this time."

He almost believed she was right. They clasped the weapon together, the mingled sounds of their breathing the only noise between them. Antousians were upon them, out in the darkness beyond. He scented them, heard them. He rolled out his sensory skills, trying to pinpoint the fuckers. Around the far end of the truck, he heard two of them, stealthily approaching. He touched two fingers to her temple, and pointed to the right. Hope nodded, and their mutual grip on the weapon tensed.

Scott couldn't bring his labored breathing under control. Too loud, too much a giveaway, he chastised himself, but he was unable to stop panting.

"Now!" he said, swinging the barrel of the pulse rifle toward the two Antousians at the end of the truck. "Fire now, Hope!" he whispered fiercely in her ear, and she did—again and again, round after round. "Keep going!" he urged, becoming more alert. He kept the rifle steady in his hand and she fired, until not one, not two, but three of their enemy dropped to the ground by the truck.

But there was another one, and suddenly, coming at them with a vicious expression on her face and with her pistol cocked toward his chest, was a black-haired Antousian soldier. It was her or them. *Her or us, her or us,* he thought as he heard the cock of her gun, and shouted, "Fire! Now!"

The blast of the weapon propelled the Antousian back against a wheel, hard, and there was the dull thud of her body before she slid to the ground. Lifeless.

"Are there more?" Hope gasped.

He shook his head. "No, thank All." He sniffed once more for good measure, feeling his head grow light and thin and dim. "Good . . . work."

Then he collapsed into Hope Harper's arms and lay there, trying his very best not to die.

In every direction Marco glanced, Antousian militants had materialized, suddenly visible, their alternative nature evaporating. Aiming, he took easy shot after easy shot—they were right in the open! Revealed! The Antousians scattered in confusion, some glancing at the massive portal that circled above them all. It spun like a giant hurricane, enveloping the base. Somehow, in creating the portal, Jared had forced the Antousians into physical form!

Several platoons of Air Force soldiers advanced, suddenly gaining the advantage. The Antousians, who while formless had been able to move freely, now found themselves in the open, fleeing for cover.

Marco wanted to whoop and holler their victory as he reloaded, then continued firing on the dispersing, frightened enemy.

Thea, he thought, *I'm coming home to you, baby!*

And that meant one thing—next time, they wouldn't hold back. They would mate for life.

Scott had lost a frightening amount of blood. More than that, his legs were torn to shreds. It was bad. Hope knew it, and so did Scott from what she could tell. Still, he was alive, breathing, and they'd just taken out four of the bad guys, and, strangely enough, that gave Hope a reason to smile. Neither of them had moved since the last of their attackers had fallen almost on top of them. Still leaning against the tire, she held him in her arms, his heavy, weary body shaking all over. Somehow she knew it was important that she continue to hold him—maybe to mute the effects of his shock with her own human warmth, or maybe because, despite his tough-guy veneer, she knew Scott Dillon was frightened. He believed he was dying, and she wouldn't let him face that alone.

"You're sure there aren't more?" she asked, sinking back against the wheel.

"No more," he replied dully.

She wrapped both arms tighter around his chest, trying to really hold the guy, despite his heavy body armor, the bulletproof vest, all the blood smeared over him. "You hang in there," she encouraged him.

He only grunted.

"Lieutenant, you've got to hold on," she repeated, and kept on whispering to him, prattling on, saying gods only knew what, urging him to live. She would not have this man's blood on her conscience—nor would she be the last woman to hold him in her arms. He had to live. "You have to live!" she whispered into his ear. "I won't let you die."

Another groan, but then . . . a faint chuckle. "Tough . . . one, you."

"Fuck, yeah," she said, stroking his thick, wavy hair to soothe him. And he chuckled again, the sound a little bit stronger.

Laughter had to be a good sign—didn't it?

Marco locked in on Scott Dillon, squarely locating him with his empathy. The battle had disintegrated into nothing more than a few lingering exchanges of gunfire now that dawn had broken over the base. Moving cautiously, he worked his way toward where the lieutenant was hiding; the man was gravely injured—Marco sensed it—but he wasn't alone. It seemed that a human was aiding him, protecting him even, but Marco still needed to get to the fallen man's side.

Rounding the side of an overturned truck, he knew he was dead-on for Dillon, and a scuffling sound beneath the chassis caused him to call out, "Don't fire! Don't fire!"

"McKinley," came Dillon's raspy, weak voice, and Marco ducked his head, crawling underneath.

There was blood everywhere, including covering the face and shirt of the human, Hope Harper, who had translated for them. She glanced toward him, blinking behind the thick lenses of her eyeglasses. "He's lost a lot of blood," she explained, undisguised fear in her eyes. Together, the two of them were propped against a wheel base, Scott crumpled backward in her arms.

"I'm gonna . . ." Scott's words trailed to nothing as he passed out cold in Hope's arms.

"It was my fault," the human told him miserably.

"No, you were just caught in the middle."

"He was trying to help me get to the truck," she continued. "If he hadn't turned back, he'd have made it to cover."

"It's war and that was his choice," Marco explained plainly. Then he took a look at the gaping wounds in both the lieutenant's legs; it wasn't pretty—even if he lived, he might never walk again.

"What's happening out there?" Hope asked him. "It sounds like something changed . . . the atmosphere even felt weird. Kind of electric."

"We created a suspended dimensional space," Marco

explained, tearing off part of his flannel shirt and using it as a tourniquet on Dillon's right leg. "It forced the Antousians out of their formless state—they had to resume their physical form. They weren't expecting it, so it left them exposed and without a position. The human soldiers pretty much conducted a clean sweep after that."

Hope nodded thoughtfully, removing her eyeglasses, which were covered in blood. They fell from her hand to the ground. "Do you think Scott's going to live?" she asked, her care for the man very obvious.

Marco stared down at Dillon's pale, bloody face. His black hair and eyebrows only made his naturally fair features appear more drawn, like a mask of death. No matter how hard he tried to be positive, he had a bad feeling about the lieutenant's chances. So he lied, "I think he'll be fine."

Good thing he wasn't dealing with an intuitive or empath; he could make the frightened human believe Scott would survive. Maybe he would, but he'd never be the same man again, not with how ruined his legs looked.

Hope voiced the same question that was on his mind. "What do we do now?"

"Stay put and wait for reinforcements." While I reach for my near-mate, he thought, and began extending his energy toward the woman he loved.

The transport touched down briefly at Warren, just long enough to pick up Marco and Scott, and any remnants of their forces who hadn't been taken into the Refarian cruiser. A few stragglers boarded, catapulting themselves from the ground onto the craft before turning to help Marco as he eased Lieutenant Dillon aboard the craft. Scott was passed out cold, tied down on a makeshift stretcher; as they lifted him onto the transport, Marco glanced about them. He was anxious that, so close to the end, they might get taken out. Minor skirmishes continued, and for all they knew, the humans would mistake them for their enemies—like so many times previously.

But one of the medics aboard explained that their commander had cleared this landing with Colonel Peters, who now swore the Refarians were most favored allies of the humans. He didn't have a clue in hell how they'd pulled off the victory, but indicated he wanted to arrange some kind of summit between Jared and the Air Force's leadership. Marco swung his right leg onto the running board, and turned back to face Hope Harper, who still stood on the ground. She ran her fingertips over the side of the craft.

"Do you really think he'll be okay?" she asked again.

One of the medics spoke up, "We'll take good care of him, of course."

From within, the craft's captain called out: "Time for liftoff—close the hatch."

Hope squinted, obviously trying to see the lieutenant one final time. It was odd, but Marco sensed that she cared for him a great deal; somehow, they'd formed a deep connection during his days of captivity.

The hatch door started to slide closed, and Hope backed away with a half wave of her hand. "Tell him I want to know—how he does, I mean."

Marco gave a nod, forgetting the woman wouldn't see, then added, "Yes, of course."

She started to turn, the hatch nearly closed, then, seeming to reach a decision, she turned back, launching herself at the craft. "Hold the door!" he shouted, reaching to pull her inside. "Hold on!"

Her legs were nearly caught in the closing hatch, but Marco helped her wriggle her small body inside, where she collapsed against the craft's floor, gasping.

"What are you doing?" Marco demanded—they'd get in a hell of a lot of trouble for bringing a human back to the compound.

"Apparently, it turns out we're in the middle of a war. My side was wrong—in all of this. And I was brought up to be on the right side of things. So since this *is* a war, I intend to be on the right side next time."

Marco grinned, admiring the small woman's tenacious, gutsy spirit. But he also smiled because, although she didn't admit it, the human didn't want to let Scott Dillon go—at least not until she knew for sure he would be all right.

* * *

Jared held Kelsey in his arms, whispered words of comfort in her ear. Together they leaned against the mitres chamber wall, every last one of them drained of energy, nauseated and somewhat disoriented.

Kelsey, however, was in the worst shape of all, and Jared was worried. She'd been drifting in and out of consciousness since they'd allowed the portal to implode on itself, dissolving about them as seamlessly as it had opened. "Love, you're all right," he reassured her, kissing the top of her head. She jerked within his arms, then settled again with a quiet moan.

"This is what happened to her last time." Thea squatted beside them both, reaching to stroke a lock of Kelsey's hair away from her face. It was a tender gesture, and his surprise must have shown on his face. Thea slowly lifted her gaze, catching him studying her.

"I'm amazed by her," his cousin offered softly. "She's very strong, Jared, and more than that—she's critical to our revolution." Thea smiled down at Kelsey's sleeping form. "Well, and more than that, she's my queen."

Jared nestled Kelsey closer against his chest. "Thank you, Thea. Your affection for her means"—his throat tightened inexplicably—"a great deal to me."

"I understand love better than I did when you first bonded with her."

Jared leaned his head against the wall, studying his cousin. "Will you mate with Marco now?"

Thea flushed visibly, making a great show of studying her data collector. "You know what this means, don't you?" she said, pointedly avoiding his question. "These codes aren't ever coming out of her, Jared."

"I realize that."

"I don't think they're supposed to come out, either. I think she's our key—*the* key—to operating the mitres."

Jared gave a thoughtful nod. He'd already reached the same conclusions that Thea had, and the weight of them was already bearing on him like a dimensional shift.

"Does that scare you?" Thea pressed.

He rubbed his palm over the top of Kelsey's head, stroking her hair as he thought. At last he put words to the idea that had slowly been forming inside his heart. "It's the way of it. She's the Beloved of Refaria, and we both know how important that makes her."

Thea's head jerked upward in surprise. "You believe that part of the letter, then?"

"Marco told us," he replied, "and that's the only proof I need."

"You trust him then? Completely?"

Jared smiled at his cousin, lifting a hand to her cheek. "You love him, and that's the only additional proof I need, dear cousin."

Thea's blue eyes shone with deep emotion, and for a long moment she said nothing. "We're already near-mated," she confessed at last. "It's how I communicated with him on the base."

Jared was hardly surprised; he'd already surmised as much, but he gave a hearty show of approval, bobbing his head up and down. "Good. Most excellent news. I can only assume the mating rites will be completed then?"

"Jared!" Thea cried, blushing furiously. "You could make this a bit easier, you know!"

"It was an honest question," he teased.

"Yes! We will complete everything!" She wagged a finger at him. "But that is all you'll know."

"Unless you display a mating glow like certain other royals did after their wedding night," he teased, and her eyes widened in mortification. "Then, surely, all the camp will know."

"There will be payback at some point, cousin. You wait!"

The radiant smile on her face, the sparkle in her eyes, told him everything he needed to know about her choice of a mate. Thea Haven had found the love of her life, and Jared for one, couldn't have been happier for her.

Chapter Twenty-four

He was on her before she had time to say his name, before she could utter so much as a word or cry her exultation. In the space of a heartbeat he had her, catching her hard against his body and half tackling her to the ground. It was graceless, unpoetic. Desperate. And Thea had never wanted Marco as badly. She could taste the lust and need pulsing between the two of them—and that before his lips had ever met hers. Their grunting sounds punctuated the silence, then soft gasps and whimpers as they fell together, rolling on the leaf-strewn earth as one.

"Baby, baby," he murmured, pushing her onto her back. She felt a rock lodge beneath her leg; she didn't care. With both hands she clutched at him, reached, tried to draw him closer against her body. Their lips met, his mouth crushing hers hard as he reached to unbuckle her belt, then her uniform slacks. She knew she smelled like smoke and battle grime, but that hardly mattered; all she wanted was Marco inside of her. Now. Forget the waiting, the endless days of torturous waiting.

Tilting her pelvis upward, she reached for him, aligning her hips against his. Against her thigh, the prominent bulge of his erection nudged her as together they began to thrust, his hand half inside her pants, she pulling at his hair.

Pressing her eyes shut she ignored the morning sunlight dappling through the trees—and she ignored the very real possibility that a patrol might discover them. There would be no stopping now, no waiting for the ideal moment for mating. They'd done a damnable amount of waiting, and she didn't want any more of it.

He could be gone by afternoon. They could both be dead. "I won't die without having you," she panted in his ear. "I won't wait another day for this."

Shoving her pants further down her hips, his large hands cupped the bare skin of her thighs. "I won't wait," he groaned against her shoulder. "Look at me, I'm shaking all over for you." His palms slid down her legs, clutching at her while she struggled with unfastening his jeans. He reached between them and unsnapped his pants, then tugged on the zipper, cursing under his breath in low Refarian until they finally came open.

"Good." She panted, sliding her palms around his hips, feeling bare skin. Like most Refarian males, he wore no underwear at all. The feel of his satiny warm flesh dusted with bristly hairs caused a jolt of desire to crest inside of her.

Their hands were everywhere, exploring, ripping apart, opening. His hair, so much wilder now, was silky thick between her fingers. "Marco," she cried, tugging his head down for another kiss. "I can't wait. Please don't make me."

He arched his back, rising off of her onto all fours, and shoved his pants all the way to his ankles, then slid atop her, levering his hips together with hers. He pressed his erection between her thighs, pushing at her opening; she was wet and hot and ready for him. She wanted him with all her heart and soul, but nothing had prepared her for the suddenness of such intimate proximity. Gasping against his face, she realized that Marco would not be stopped, nor did she want him to be. Nothing could stop her anyway.

"I thought I'd never be with you again," she whimpered, feeling tears streak down her face. "Amazing, you're amazing. Nothing will ever separate us. We're one."

But then he did stop, growing utterly still against her. Lifting his head, he stared into her eyes, his own dark ones wide with panic.

"No, Marco, keep going," she pleaded, unsure what had caused his hesitation. She pushed her hips upward, working to take him inside of her, just a bit, but he braced his hands by her shoulders and held back, shaking his head adamantly.

With a quick curse, he growled, raising his hips and slipping off of her. "All wrong," he whispered. "Baby, this—can't happen. Not now."

She dug her fingers into both of his shoulders, urging him back down onto her. "Don't you dare pull away now!" Too many times before this he had come near, only to shove her to the far side of his emotional universe. "I won't let you, not this time," she said fiercely, holding him hard and close. The tears that had already been in her eyes turned to sobbing, her chest heaving. "Now is the time, not later, not someday. Now, Marco!"

He palmed her hair, stroking it back from her eyes; his expression filled with raw anguish. "I have to talk to you first, baby," he explained. "Please."

And then they lay together, he still and drawing in huffing, urgent breaths, she sobbing softly. "Talk to me, then." She forced the words past her tightened throat. "Whatever it is, just say it."

"Not like this," he whispered, cupping her beneath the chin. "We can't breathe, neither one of us." He began to ease off of her, straddling her. "Give me a minute."

She slapped his chest furiously. "This is it, McKinley. You've done this to me for the last time."

He shook his head, sliding off of her and sitting beside her on the cool ground. He drew his knees to his chest and buried his face in his hands. "Don't hate me—not yet. Please, just hear me out."

With a jerk, she pulled her pants back up to her waist and began frantically fastening zippers and buttons. She'd be damned if this man would leave her here, not with her half-nude.

But she noticed he wasn't going anywhere; that fact had to account for her anger suddenly cooling a bit. "Go on," she told him tightly. "I'm listening."

Dropping his hands away from his face, he met her hard gaze. His hair shot in every possible direction, disheveled by her own hands. "Nothing will ever separate us again," he began softly. "You're totally right, sweet Thea."

"So what's wrong with that?"

"Think about it—think deeply. Everything that I am, you will become. Not by half measures or near-mating. You will be me and I will be you. Me. You'll have it all. Including this cursed thing that lives inside of me—my empathy."

"I already have your gift!" She gave the ground a stomp.

"It hasn't even manifested yet. You have no idea how strong it will become," he warned her.

"I don't care, Marco! I'm ready to be with you, fully, completely. Nothing will ever keep me from you again."

"Do you have any idea what those words do to me?" He laughed huskily, thinking what this bonding would mean to him; how it would change his internal landscape. More than that, of how profoundly he loved the woman beside him. "I have never wanted anything more than this, not in all my days."

She opened her arms to him, reaching, and he nuzzled her, nipping at her throat with a quiet growl of arousal. "But it's not just the empathy," he cautioned her. "It's the Madjin. It's the Circle."

"Sabrina told me that all that business about you not being able to mate is nonsense! She told me she had a husband and a son—that you can mate too."

"That's not it—it's that you'll become one with the Circle. Did she tell you that?"

Thea shook her head. "No, she didn't."

"Did you tell her about us?" he pressed, wondering what Sabrina would say about the reality of his taking a lifemate. Of his marrying a woman of a class far above his own servant status.

"I didn't, not exactly." A frown creased her forehead. "I indicated we had feelings for each other, but . . . I didn't get very specific."

"I have to ask her permission before we take this step—there's so much at stake. The curse inside me; your new link to the Madjin. She's my unit leader and I've got to talk to her first."

She groaned and fell back onto the leaves, fastening her belt. "Waiting. Always waiting. First one thing, then another. Damn it, Marco!" she shouted. "I can't keep doing this."

He sprang atop her, suspending himself over her by bracing his hands on both sides of her head. Still, their hips pushed together, their bodies felt as one. Panting heavily against her cheek, he breathed words of intent: "This won't take long. I swear it. I'll leave you now and go to talk to her. That's all the time I need."

She braced his face within her hands, cool against his fevered cheeks. "And then?"

"And then we will go wherever you want and mate. Forever. No stopping or holding back—"

"No more fears?"

He shook his head, pressing his lips against hers. "Never."

Their kiss deepened and once again they began to rock their hips together in a titillating gyration. She gripped him from behind, caressing and urging him onward as if he were a wild stud running for the finish line.

Pulling his mouth from hers, he trailed his tongue across her cheek, tasting the salty sweetness of her. With a dragging inhalation, he swilled her scent into his lungs, feeling his hard-on grow even harder.

She slipped her hands lower down between his legs, slowly caressing the sensitive place behind his erection. He buried his face in her hair, stifling his intense, yelping growl. She made him wild; she brought out the most primal side of his nature and he burned with it whenever he fell into her arms this way. His entire body blazed with her natural heat and fire.

"Help me, baby," he begged of her, unable to pull away. "We c-can't," he stammered. Somehow, in her arms, his facility with speech always faded a bit. In a way, he grew as primal as he knew her to be.

"I don't want to help you." She laughed huskily in his ear. "You know what I'm after."

"Please. Please, Thea. Please." He groaned his need as her hand tugged between his legs, tight against him where his thighs met. He arched, throwing his head back with an unsuppressed bellow of longing. "Got . . . to stop."

She stroked him harder.

"You are a vixen," he rasped in her ear.

She gave a coquettish laugh. "But I'm your vixen." And with that, at last, she shoved him off of her. "Now go!" she said in obvious frustration. "Just go! And have your big talk with Sabrina."

He studied her closely. "And then? Tonight?" The words rushed out in a breathless exhalation of need. Only this time, she was the one to put the brakes on.

"No, not until we're married," she told him, her eyes dancing with excitement. "Then we will mate—after. Not before."

He couldn't help giving her a sideways, grudging smile. "Payback, huh?"

She leaned forward, kissing him softly on the mouth. "It's just more romantic that way. We'll have a royal wedding!"

"How can I argue with that?" he laughed, feeling nervousness flutter in the pit of his stomach. A royal wedding where the groom had spent a lifetime in servitude. What would the elders say to that? Good thing his wife to be didn't seem to care.

"I plan to mate with Thea." Marco stood before the leader of his circle, the woman he had always thought of as his true mother. "I want to marry her, too. Tomorrow. I want to seal our marriage before the Circle—before everyone. I know you won't approve, I've already been over it hundreds of times in my head—"

"You can't mate with her, Marco." Sabrina blinked rapidly, staring at him—almost as if gazing right through him—and then her expression softened. "I know you love her—"

He took a step closer toward his adopted mother. "You can't begin to know how deep it is."

She smiled faintly. "And I know that you're near-mates—that you feel a deep, intense connection with her."

"Then why do you object?"

"Because you're Madjin, and she is one of your protected. You know the rules—and you remember your vows. Now that security has normalized, your bond with her will have to be broken."

He shook his head adamantly, pacing the room as if on a tight chain. "No, it won't. That won't ever happen."

Behind him he sensed Sabrina bristle. "You took vows, Marco."

"Vows you have always told me didn't include staying celibate or without a mate. I made that vow to myself!"

"And what about your empathy?" she reminded him gently. "Think of Thea—of her safety and well-being."

"So far, with our near-bond, she's fine. She hasn't even received my abilities."

"It won't happen until you're fully mated, Marco. You know this; you've always known it."

"I love her, Sabrina! I love her. I've spent my life in solitude—why would you try to stop me?"

She grasped him by the shoulder. "Because you are dangerous to her!"

Marco rubbed his jaw as if she'd just slapped him hard across the face. "I see. So now we have the truth: This is what you truly think of me."

"Marco, no." Sabrina's eyes slid shut. "What I mean is, she's from the house of D'Ashani, a royal, and you are sworn to all the royals, not just Jared. That's the vow I'm reminding you about. Not a vow of chastity or otherwise. First and foremost, a Madjin warrior places the well-being of his protected above any personal desires."

Marco implored his Circle leader with his eyes. "What better way for me to protect her than keeping her at my side? Always? We're living in different times. New times," he argued, unwilling to back down.

She set her jaw, then slowly looked at him again. "You won't let me stop you."

"No one could." He broke into a joyous, warm smile, feeling the tide turn between them.

Sabrina put her back to him, both hands on her hips; she seemed to wrestle with a great weight. Perhaps her decision to bless the union, or perhaps simply choosing what would be her next tack in trying to sway him.

At last she pivoted toward him. "Well then, there's

something you must know. Information you must have before taking the final step of mating with her completely.

"Show me your Madjin's seal—would you please?" she directed, using her unit leader's voice. He'd long ago determined that she had two voices when talking to him: One was the tone of a mother, the other that of unit commander. She was all leader right now, leaving no room for him to deny her.

"All right." He rolled up his flannel shirt sleeve, revealing his naturally olive-gold skin.

Lifting his other hand, he allowed a shiny beam of light to flow from it onto his exposed right wrist. Rarely did he reveal his Madjin's brand, and yet he always remained aware of its presence, prickling there somehow just beneath his skin—even as he was always aware of his powerful vows. *R'thasme siet falne,* he'd sworn before the council: dying to self to serve those more worthy.

The holographic marking spun into view, undulating powerfully in the air between them. "Ah, there it is," she said, her voice filled with wonder as it always did when one of her Madjin revealed their brand. They were an ancient line, and the mark had been passed from Madjin to Madjin for almost a thousand years. "It still amazes me," she observed.

Marco bowed his head reverentially. "I'm honored to bear the king's brand."

She nodded in thoughtful agreement, then asked, "Haven't you ever wondered why you were branded on your *right* wrist instead of your left, like the rest of us?"

Marco thought a moment; no, he'd never questioned the council's choice for his branding. "I assumed it was because I'm left-handed," he replied with a shrug. "Part of the Madjin sealing symbolism, or because I'm the primary protector to the king." Again, he searched within his mind, a small leaden feeling of dread beginning inside his chest. "I never really thought about it, to be honest."

She stepped toward him, reaching for his right hand. She took hold of it, gently exposing the underside of his wrist; she pressed her thumb and forefinger into the beating point of his pulse. "Right here." She smiled appreciatively. "The mark is right *here*."

Marco stared at her, confused. "What mark?"

"The mark of the D'Aravni."

"What are you talking about, Sabrina?" he blurted with an awkward laugh. "I don't have another mark."

"I know you've been intimate with Thea—maybe you haven't made love yet, but you've touched her," she said. "Haven't you felt the fire? Don't tell me that you haven't, it would be impossible."

His thoughts catapulted to the scorching compulsion he'd felt every time he was near her, the overbearing urge to touch her core self. The way he blazed inside—the way Thea seemed to brush him with her fiery nature. And he thought of how hungry he'd been for her D'Ashanian self in his room—how he'd *had* to expose himself to her, then stroke himself. He'd been compelled to mate with her beyond any urge he'd ever imagined just from seeing her naked, true form.

"You have felt it." She could see everything on his face.

"Don't . . ." he managed to choke, backing away from her.

"Illuminate it, Marco. See for yourself; even now you feel the emblem's presence, don't you?"

She was right, of course. The underside of his wrist had begun to burn and even itch slightly, as if by the very act of her telling him about the mark, some kind of chemical reaction had occurred in his body. He swallowed hard, trying to steady his thoughts. Shaking, he raised his left hand and allowed a silvery beam of light to spill onto his wrist, in the exact same manner he always illuminated his Madjin's seal. In reaction, a swelling, undulating sphere of energy materialized in the air between them, causing a quiet shudder throughout his whole body. It was Jared's mark, the emblem of the D'Aravni.

"Wh-why is this here?" he stammered, staring at the glowing mark in shock. It appeared identical to the one his king and queen bore.

The glowing light illuminated Sabrina's face with an eerie glow. "Your mother was a young protector, brought to the palace to train with the Madjin as a child. She was never strong, not like she should have been—because she was an empath, just like you, Marco. All your gifts of intuition and empathy come from her."

"I know all that," he gritted. "Tell me why this *mark* is here on my *wrist*!"

Sabrina nodded in acknowledgment. "But what I've never told you is that your mother became the king's mistress. They were in love, deeply, and had a dreadful affair that broke everyone's hearts," she explained. "When the king felt he had to end the relationship, she lost control of her empathy and went into madness. All her life she'd struggled to keep her sanity, but losing him . . ." Her voice trailed off, her eyes becoming filled with melancholy emotion. "Well, after that, we learned she was carrying the king's child. So we nursed her through the pregnancy, and when you were born, I cared for you. Your mother died three months after that day."

A sickening, blinding headache pulled at Marco's temples; he shook his head, trying to clear it, trying to hear what Sabrina was telling him. "I don't believe you," he whispered, voice thick. "You would have told me before now—someone would have told me—"

"After Jared's parents were murdered and he ascended to the throne, the elders had me bring you here, to Earth. To protect you. To protect the succession because Jared was in such terrible, life-threatening danger."

Marco gestured at her angrily. "What you're saying is that all this time I thought I was training, serving, disciplining myself as a Madjin, I wasn't really the protector. I was th-the *protected*," he sputtered.

"That's not entirely true, Marco," she argued softly. "It was never like that."

Every day that he had lived, for as long as he could remember, was a sham. They'd taken him, the bastard son of a murdered king, and hidden him. Fawned over him and prayed the day would never come when they needed to parade him in front of the people as the heir apparent. He spun to face her. "Then how, exactly, was it, Sabrina? You're telling me that the Madjin Circle brought me here for protection—"

"Just as Jared was protected."

"But you drew the Circle around *me*—not him."

"He was secure, Marco. Safe. You know it—the safest he could be during a time of war."

He jabbed at the air with his finger. "He will never know this. Never. I am his protector, his Madjin, and he will never know this, or I'll kill whoever tells him."

"You're his brother," she reminded him. "The time has come for—"

He roared, "He will never know! Nothing will change, not for him, not for me, not for the Circle." Marco barked his wishes, dimly aware that he was behaving every bit the ruler they claimed he was born to be. "From this day forward, no one mentions this to him or to me again."

"You can't pretend you're someone you aren't, Marco."

"I can't pretend I'm a prince, either."

She smiled, an annoyingly patient smile, which only stoked his rage. "You're every bit as much a D'Aravni as your brother. In time you'll come to understand that."

"What's that supposed to mean?"

"You've seen what Jared is—what Thea is, truly. The power, the gifts"—she paused significantly, tilting her head upward so that their gazes locked—"the fire."

He shook his head in flimsy denial, even as he felt a strong burning sensation catch hold in his chest. The same sensation he had felt countless times with Thea—in her arms, in his dreams, just looking at her. In that bar, the very first night. Always with Thea the growing sensation of scorching fire, when all along it hadn't just been her pure nature, as he'd believed, but his own as well. He remembered how the sight of her natural form had aroused him beyond his imagining, stoking his lust for her to outrageous proportions.

And most of all, he recalled the way that intercepting Jared and Kelsey's bond had awakened a desire to experience Thea's mating cycle with her; how palpable and real that need had been.

Because he was just like her, a being of fire and lust and power. And just like his brother. "That's why I intercepted his bond with Kelsey," he said, realization dawning.

Sabrina inclined her head, saying nothing, but she didn't have to. He saw the answer in her eyes.

Marco rubbed a hand over his eyes, trying to process

all the revelations. "Why are you telling me this now? Before my wedding?"

"Because you had to know before then," she answered opaquely.

He dropped his hands away from his eyes. "Why? You tell me."

She took several steps closer, and reached a hand to cup his cheek. Very rarely had Sabrina expressed physical affection toward him, not after he'd grown out of his headaches. But on very rare occasions she treated him as her son, except this time he recoiled from her touch.

She stared up at him, her eyes shining with heartfelt emotion. "If you mate with Thea, there's a very real possibility that you will undergo your first Change while you make love."

He shook his head, half-terrified, as much of losing his virginity as of experiencing the kind of cataclysmic transformation she was describing.

"Marco, this is your true nature. It's who you are."

"A force of nature," he muttered.

"An amazing person, a powerful being. A warrior, a prince, the king's brother . . . soon to be husband to Thea. You will likely Change the first time you lie with her."

"No," he denied, feeling vaguely excited and repulsed at the same time. "No, not then."

"You're inexperienced in these matters, but the Madjin have guided the royal houses through their Change for thousands of years. You won't be able to fight off the urge once you come together with her. It's the natural way of things for your kind. It's your natural state, far more than"—she waved her hand at the length of his body—"*this* form will ever be."

"Why haven't I experienced this Change before?" he demanded. "If this is true, tell me that."

"Because you never passed through your awakening, at least not completely, because you didn't understand it. Once, when you were fifteen, you complained to me of a terrible fever, of feeling strange and out of sorts. Do you remember that?"

He instantly knew the time she described; it had been on a ranch in Montana, a place of rest and tranquility that he'd loved almost more than any other in their nomadic lives. His body had blazed with desire for days on end; he'd felt dirty, ashamed. Certain that something dark was altering inside himself.

"I was filled with lust, my body hot and unsteady," he admitted gruffly. "I thought there was something wrong with me, Sabrina!"

"It was the first flush of your awakening. But you closed yourself off, unaware—and I prayed you'd never cycle again."

A realization hit him. "That's why you told me I had to stay apart from women. That I couldn't ever have a girlfriend, or sleep around. You knew what would happen to me!" he shouted angrily. "It wasn't because I'm an empath—it's because you knew I'd learn the truth. And it would have exposed me."

"It was a danger, yes," she agreed solemnly. "There was always the risk you might make your Change with a human during the act."

"The act?" he snarled. "The *act*, Sabrina? Call it what it is! It's having sex, making love—and for just about thirty years I've hardly been touched by anyone," he sputtered. "Because you've kept me in the dark about my identity." He shook his head, acid fury boiling over. "I'm out of here. I have nothing more to say about all of this, except that if I so much as hear a murmur that Jared knows a thing"—he jabbed the air with his finger—"I'll be out for blood."

"Marco, wait!" Sabrina reached for him, but he shrugged off her grasp.

"I've got nothing more to say to you," he told her icily. "I'm not sure I ever will."

He pushed open the meeting room door with both palms, so hard that it slammed against the exterior wall, and wondered how in the hell he'd ever face his nearmate again. Much less marry her the next day as he'd hoped.

Chapter Twenty-five

As was custom for the women of her family, Thea spent the night before her wedding alone, choosing to sleep at the stone guesthouse. The place had always been her private refuge, tonight more than ever. The outside temperature was unseasonably warm, the dark sky overhead netted with twinkling stars. It made a perfect night to sit on the outside steps and simply stare at the heavens: Somewhere far beyond what her eyes could see was her home. But after tomorrow, Marco would become her *true* home, the one central point in her universe.

The light from the windows shone brightly on the steps and surrounding ground. She withdrew a small journal from where she'd stowed it beside her. She'd come here in search of the diary, really, when she could have spent a private night in her quarters. She flipped through the pages, studying the familiar inky scrawl that belonged to Prince Arienn. In some ways—and for many years—he'd been her secret lover. She'd even fantasized about somehow traveling through time via the mitres and declaring her love for him. But based on what? Reading his innermost thoughts and ideas . . . his very dreams. It had always been an infatuation, a way to bide her time while she was waiting for Jared to simply wake up. And now everything she'd imagined for herself had been turned topsy-turvy; every fantasy, every dream remade by one gorgeous Madjin warrior. Her true soulmate.

She shivered at the thought, tracing her fingertip over Arienn's loopy handwriting; in a sense, he represented the last remnants of her childish youth, and she'd come to tell her once-cousin farewell. Reading over his journal entry, she found herself falling under the same strange spell she'd felt in the mitres chamber a few days earlier. That eerie sense that somehow the man still lived.

Arienn had been a D'Aravni, same as Jared—and the thing that still perplexed her was how drawn she always felt to the men of that line. It had always been as if something were writ into her DNA, her very soul, compelling her toward Jared—even toward her fantasy of Arienn. And then Marco had exploded into her life, altering everything, opening her eyes to what love, in all its many incarnations, truly meant. It made her lifelong compulsions fade into nothing. Still, no matter how much she loved Marco, she felt jittery and on edge; tomorrow night she would give him her body, her soul, her energy. It was an awe-inspiring, arousing thought—and it unsettled her as much as it thrilled her.

Speak to me, cousin, she whispered inside, staring at Arienn's journal. *Please help me calm my gyrating emotions.* Drawing in a deep breath, she began to read:

> *On the eve of my lifemating, I find myself embattled, grappling with my very nature. What manner of creature will Louisa find me to be when first we lie together? She claims readiness, boldness, but her frailer human temperament is surely no match for my raging, D'Aravnian blood. Ill-suited at best, disastrously paired at worst, I would as soon staunch my love for her as I would my Change. My essence. My power. But shall she flee after gazing upon me? My heart feels faint and trembles within me; what scourge shall I become should she spurn my fire?*

Oh, cousin, she thought, *I understand totally.* She'd always known Arienn had mated with a human; it had been the one secret she'd kept as her own. No one else had ever read his more intimate journals, and she'd preferred it that way. Although Marco was obviously not human, he certainly wasn't a dual being, so she shared some of Arienn's marital discomfort. The only difference was that Marco had already glimpsed her true nature, and had reacted with verve and arousal. And he loved her—*all* of her!

These fears are insane, she reassured herself. *He knows exactly what I am.*

Giving her head a slight shake, she pushed the thoughts from her mind, but then a rustling sound on the trail set her adrenaline flowing. Fumbling with her hip holster, she reached for her weapon, sniffing at the air, but Kelsey appeared from the copse of trees.

"You need to really be careful about that," Thea called out as the human approached. "I nearly pulled a weapon on you."

Kelsey appeared stricken. "Oh, man!" she blurted, hands extended. "I didn't mean to scare you."

Thea stared back at the woman strangely. "I am not a man."

"That's . . . what we'd call a language barrier." Kelsey laughed. "It's just an expression."

"I was about to fire your head off." Thea gave her a grudging smile. "I have a feeling Jared wouldn't have appreciated that."

Kelsey returned her smile. "It might have ruined your wedding day too."

"Good chance of that."

Kelsey strolled closer. "I know you're supposed to be alone tonight and all that—and I'm not going to stick around—"

"It's all right."

"No, seriously, it's part of the tradition, that's what Jared said, but I just wanted to come . . ." Her voice trailed off, a furrow forming between her auburn eyebrows.

"Come and do what?" Thea prompted, closing Ar-ienn's journal where it still rested on her knees.

Kelsey drew in a breath, then plopped down beside her on the step. "I wanted to come tell you that I'm happy for you—truly happy for you. And that you've got our blessing. Jared wanted to tell you that," she rushed, "but didn't want to make you, well, uncomfortable. Still, we know that Madjin tradition means we're supposed to bless the union, so that's . . . what I'm here to do."

Thea couldn't hide her smile of approval. "You're doing really well with this, you know."

"Well with . . . ?"

"Stepping into the role of our queen. You have a lovely manner, a way of putting people at ease."

Kelsey frowned. "You don't have to say that."

"You're right, I don't."

For a moment Kelsey's lips parted, and it was evident she wasn't sure what to make of Thea's reply—until it hit her that she genuinely meant the compliment.

Quietly bowing her head, Kelsey confessed, "I feel totally over my head. I keep going through all the appropriate motions, hoping I figure things out along the way."

"You saved all of us in the chamber—your entire world. If they only knew, they'd revere you."

"It's crazy complicated, all this knowledge in my head, and trying to figure out how to be the kind of queen Jared needs, especially with—" Kelsey clamped her mouth shut abruptly, but Thea knew exactly what she'd been about to say.

Clearing her throat, Thea took hold of Arienn's journal, and wordlessly slid it into Kelsey's hands. Her queen examined it quizzically, turning curious eyes on her.

"It's something I planned to give you—after tomorrow, but really, I don't need it anymore."

Kelsey nodded, slowly fanning through the journal's pages; it was written entirely in Refarian, and she traced a sentence with her fingertip, struggling to translate. Still, Thea was astounded at her growing mastery of their language. "You'll be able to read that in no time," she observed.

"But what is it, Thea? I don't understand—it looks really old."

"It was written about two hundred years ago."

"Is it a historic text or something?" Kelsey extended the journal back to her as if it was a hot strake stone and she didn't want to be scalded.

Gently, Thea pushed her hand away. "You need it, Kelsey—really need it, both of you. It belonged to Prince Arienn, his journal."

"The one who seeded his essence into the mitres?" Kelsey's bright, intelligent eyes lit with understanding.

"He was a D'Aravni, and he took a human mate—nobody knows that, by the way. Only me."

"And you're sharing that knowledge with me?" Kelsey whispered in appreciation.

Again, Thea cleared her throat, feeling her face flush with embarrassment. "I think there's a lot of good information in there, Kelsey—things that will help you with"—she coughed awkwardly—"well, your procreation issues."

Kelsey clutched the diary against her chest, avoiding Thea's gaze. "I see," she answered quietly.

"It's nothing to be ashamed of, what you're facing with Jared."

"No, I'm freaking mortified. You aren't going to be able to recast that."

"Arienn and his human mate struggled too—but they conceived a child."

Kelsey turned tear-filled eyes on her. "You're not serious?"

It wasn't an expression that Thea entirely understood, but she nodded vigorously. "I am *entirely* serious."

Kelsey's face crumpled and her tears fell freely. "I've been so terrified . . . that . . ." She shook her head, wiping wordlessly at her tears.

Thea turned until her knees pushed into Kelsey's. "I'm intuitive, Kelsey," she told her firmly. "He will cycle. And you will conceive a child together."

Her queen bowed her head then, saying nothing for a very long time. Thea had to smile to herself; Kelsey had come to give her blessing on the union, but what her queen had wound up bestowing was something far more precious—a moment of pure trust and friendship. It was something she'd known so little of during her life.

And it gave Thea a wondrous, expectant feeling about her wedding day.

Really, the painkillers meant shit. A crude human word, but one that Scott found to be pointedly accurate. *Meshdki,* he corrected. *The drugs meant* meshdki.

There, man, he thought, *keep yourself true to your own*

people. Gods above, he'd even begun to think like the human species.

The medics were maintaining a safe perimeter around him anyway, seeing as how every time they appeared at his bedside he cursed them in low Refarian. Oh, he would likely mend—that's what his doctors had reported, and although he believed them, the facts provided very little comfort. Not while he lay here, flat on his back, counting the ceiling tiles as the war waged on—and his best friend fought without him by his side.

He shifted uncomfortably in the bed, hitting the buttons impatiently to elevate his head as far as the doctors would allow, until he finally collapsed into the pillows again, exhausted, issuing another stream of Refarian *and* English curses.

The events of the past days still haunted him, hounded him, and the only fact he kept returning to was that he'd nearly died. And a human—a human woman, of all creatures—had saved his pitiful life. That was something to think about for many moons to come.

"I see you're up."

Startled, he swung his gaze toward the doorway. As if he'd literally summoned her into existence, there stood his fair-headed human angel, Hope Harper. He pulled his bruised and swollen mouth into something approximating a smile.

"You're recovering?" she asked, stepping into his hospital room.

"Barely."

Struggling to sit up, he finally lost that battle by the time she reached his bedside. He noticed that she didn't wear a new pair of glasses. Didn't she need them?

"You're looking good," she said, glancing toward his face, yet not really looking *at* him. "You seem to feel better."

He laughed. "I feel like crap, and am told I look even worse."

"You look fine to me." She smiled, her nose crinkling with what, he had to admit, was an adorable expression.

Suddenly, his legs began to ache worse, as if by the simple fact of Hope being near him, his body remembered the trauma he'd suffered when last by her side.

"I owe you my life." He sank back into the pillows.

Standing by his bed, she waved him off. "Oh, please." Her gaze dropped toward the floor.

"Hope, seriously. I'd be dead right now if you hadn't rescued my ass."

A faint, self-conscious smile played at her lips. "You *know* I'd do it again any day of the week."

You're my angel, sweet Hope. That's what he wanted to say, but instead he could only think to grumble about his nearly nonexistent pain meds. "They don't do much for you here," he said, fiddling with the bed controls. "I think it's some sort of endurance training."

Her eyes lit up, and she glanced upward again, not quite meeting his gaze. "Are you making the grade?"

"I don't know, ask those guys." He pointed toward the hallway, but she didn't look. An awkward silence spun between them, and he sensed there was something on her mind.

"Want to sit down?" he finally suggested, and she nodded, dropping into the chair at his bedside.

She folded both of her hands neatly in her lap, but said nothing.

"Something on your mind, Harper?"

She opened her mouth, then clamped it shut again, clearly second-guessing herself. Instead she asked: "Lieutenant, anything I can get you? Is there anything you need?"

Evasive maneuver; he recognized that one. He leaned back and studied her. She was a beautiful woman, yet nothing like the many human women he'd slept with in the past six years. Those women tended to be wild and a little bit rough, whereas she was soft all over, with golden hair that seemed to glow and fair skin that was nearly translucent. Hope Harper was ethereal, and he had a hard time reconciling that with the woman who'd helped him fire off twenty rounds against the Antousians just three nights ago.

"Why'd you come, Harper?"

Her head shot upward in surprise. "Is it a problem? Should I go?"

"Just curious, that's all." He shrugged. Yeah, he was

completely indifferent. He wondered if she'd buy that charade.

"I-I thought, well, that we . . ." Her voice trailed to nothing and, in agitation, she began spreading the edge of his sheet, smoothing it out beneath her palms. Perhaps she didn't quite realize what an intimate gesture that was, given how he was lying naked right beneath that same sheet, and the thin material was the *only* thing separating her hand from his very bare body.

"That we?" he prompted, acutely aware of her physical proximity.

She dropped her head. "I wanted to apologize."

"For what?"

"It was my fault, what happened the other night—"

"Hey, now—"

"Completely my fault," she rushed, talking over him, "and I almost got you killed. I am so sorry. I should never have been there, and if I hadn't, then you wouldn't be here, and—and . . ."

He said nothing, only watched her, and was surprised when her lovely gray eyes welled with tears. She swallowed hard, wiping at her eyes.

"Are you finished, Harper?" The only way to deal with this kind of thing was soldier to soldier, he definitely knew that.

She bowed her head, nodding silently, and returned to smoothing his covers.

"Good," he said. "Because this is war, Hope Harper. War. You've found yourself fighting on our side, and I, for one, happen to appreciate that fact. You were there with me that night because you'd chosen my side."

"I'm going blind, Lieutenant."

He shook his head dismissively. "I know about your vision problems."

"No, you don't understand. My vision is eroding . . . very quickly."

Is that why she hadn't bothered replacing the glasses?

She continued: "I should've seen those snipers, and could have shot them before they took you out."

"I scented them myself, you know." Her blond eyebrows lifted curiously, so he added, "I can track our enemies for up to a mile with my heightened senses." Understandably, he felt a swell of pride as he shared his natural abilities.

This new information seemed to register, and she rested her palms on his bedside, just thinking in silence. After a moment, she asked, "Why didn't you stop them, then?"

So much for pride, at least with this woman. "Because too much was going down."

"So," she continued, "if I'd been more help, been able to see, then I would've gotten them before they got to you. It *is* my fault, Lieutenant, and you won't convince me otherwise."

Slowly, he inched his right hand toward the edge of the bed, over the crisp sheet until he made contact with *her* hand. He moved slowly; otherwise she would have withdrawn immediately. Yes, he knew that much about Hope Harper. *Stealth attack with a blind woman. Way to go, Dillon,* he chastised himself. Then again, he wouldn't have held back, not with her. He covered her hand with his, steadying it against the mattress. Odd, but she didn't pull away, and very cautiously he closed his open palm over hers.

"You saved my life," he told her. "Get that into your head—you did it. I was dead in the water without you."

Awareness shot through his entire body; that their skin was touching, that she wasn't moving her hand. That his legs hurt like hell, and yet he didn't give a crap. All of his awareness tuned to only one fact: Hope sat at his bedside, her hand held in his . . . well, almost.

"I-I can't help blaming myself," she admitted in an anguished voice, and the tears he'd seen in her eyes began to roll down her cheeks. He could not hold back, not now; she needed to understand their shared stakes—and their collective history. There was no room for shame between their two hearts.

"I want to tell you something," he said, wrestling again to sit up in bed. "I'm not Refarian. I'm an Antousian."

Her eyes shot upward, filled with surprise and—gods forbid—wonder. She swiped at her tears, but said nothing, just waited for him to continue. And so he did.

"Yeah, that's a pretty ugly secret, isn't it?" He

laughed mirthlessly. "My genetic heritage is something I have to live with every day. We all live with things we don't really like."

She said nothing, yet she slowly rotated her hand until their fingers threaded together, palm to palm. He swallowed, continuing, "I'm human too, you see, at least in a way. And that's the truly ugly secret."

"I don't understand. You just said you're Antousian . . . and do you think it's ugly to *be* human?"

"I'm a hybrid," he whispered.

He closed his eyes, the familiar, putrid shame welling within him—but he *wanted* Hope Harper to know everything—wanted her to realize that she had nothing to blame herself for, not when it came to his life, and not when it came to dirty secrets.

He continued, "Thirty years ago a deadly virus swept Refaria. We Antousians lived there, in peace with the Refarians, at least as much as a warring species such as my own could ever live in peace with anyone. There were collectives of industry and art and science. It was a time of great development and cooperation between our two species. But the virus came, and everything ended after that. Nothing—nothing at all—could ever be the same. My kind couldn't survive in their own bodies, so they did what they had to do. All the Antousians did, in order to survive. . . . They shape-shifted rather than die of the virus."

Her hand tightened around his. Encouraging, demanding, conceding. "Shape-shifted into that transparent form? The one those soldiers assumed on the base?"

"We shifted into nothing, Hope—and it left us nowhere to go."

"I don't understand."

"Our people were shape-shifters, but they also possessed a unique gift." He paused, staring at her pointedly, and although she couldn't see, she gave an encouraging nod, so he pressed onward. "They could take many forms—and could shape into ether, the air about us, assuming a kind of formless state, just like you saw on the base. When the plague came millions of my . . . my *people* . . . were without bodies. Drifting, like ghosts. There was nothing to shift back to."

"That's horrible."

"Yes," he agreed solemnly, "it was. But not nearly as horrible as what we did to *your* people after. Genetically we were very similar, you see, and so humans were a compatible match. The Refarians had been coming here for ages, and we knew how similar your kind were to our own. And . . . so . . . our people began to seize hosts, to harvest them, using their bodies for our own salvation."

"They took them."

Ignoring the pain, he wrestled upright. "They had no *thought* for the lives they stole, Hope. They did not care!"

Here it was—all of it—laid bare to this one, frail human woman who had given him everything. Gods, she had to understand; he needed her to comprehend the depth of his sin.

Her face remained passive. "Is that what this war is really about?"

"Jareshk is protecting Earth. Fighting to prevent the harvesting of more of the humans . . . by my kind."

"You want me to hate you," she answered with surprising calm.

"No, Hope. I want you to understand that no sin could possibly outweigh my own."

"You didn't take this body . . . of yours? Did you?"

"No, never."

"I wouldn't care if you had. It wouldn't change things." Things? What things? Feelings . . . survival . . . emotion? What sort of stakes was this woman invoking?

"No, I didn't steal this body. But my parents harvested their hosts—and I am their son."

She gave his hand another encouraging squeeze. "But that wasn't your choice, it was your parents'."

Ah, she had him there. And it hadn't even been his parents' choice, not really—they'd been scientists at a time of great plague, fighting time to solve the Great Death. They had never wanted to accept harvested forms, but only because they believed they could save many lives had they ever agreed to do so. That offered Scott little comfort; he only thought of the lives his mother and father had ended.

"My parents were good people," he conceded. "But it doesn't make their crimes any less ugly."

"Why are you telling me this?"

He had no easy answer there. "You're heroic, a true soldier. You should exonerate yourself for the other night."

She wrestled her hand free from his then, rising abruptly to her feet. "I guess we each bear our own blame, don't we? I should go. Get well, Lieutenant, and please let me know if I can do anything for you."

With his left hand he fumbled with the drawer to his side table and, never taking his eyes off his angel, he retrieved her eyeglasses from where he'd kept them for her since the other night. "Here," he said, holding them out to her. "These belong to you."

She squinted in the direction of his hand so he took her hand, and placed the glasses within it. They were still streaked with his blood, but he doubted she could even see that.

"Thanks. They don't do a lot of good anymore," she admitted, still sounding upset.

"But they help some?"

"Nothing helps all that much anymore, Scott," she said, pocketing them. "Be well, Lieutenant." She turned on her heel and quickly left the room. He wondered how he could ever convince her that she hadn't caused his injuries. And he also wondered why her sudden absence made his heart ache inside his chest.

Chapter Twenty-six

By the next nightfall, Marco and Thea had been sealed to one another, married in front of only Jared, Kelsey, and Sabrina in a hushed, private ceremony. Thea proclaimed her willingness to bear Marco's Madjin seal as he professed his eagerness to serve as her husband, mate, and her Madjin. At the moment of Thea's sealing, when his brand was placed on her left wrist, he felt the jolting spasm of pain in his own wrist, as if he were the one who'd been burned.

Even now, he continued to feel the aching pain of it, the skin prickling as if it had been set on fire. The sensations were identical to what he'd felt on the day he'd taken his vows and been branded for life as personal protector to the king. He saw no regrets in his soulmate's eyes, not at the moment of sparking pain, and not now that they'd arrived at the stone guesthouse. A secluded, romantic location, it would serve as their wedding chamber.

All that remained was the joining of their souls for eternity. Marco circled Thea, literally tasting the yearning and heat between them. His uniform felt unbearably tight, the pants straining with his hardened erection. It jutted outward, creating an obvious bulge that he didn't work to hide as he had the other times with her. There were no more secrets between them anymore, not even between their bodies. Gritting his teeth together, he battled the onslaught of sexual urges that pulsed through his system. Since Sabrina's revelations about his dual nature—about his true, natural self—it was as if his body had begun the transformation process she'd predicted. He had become more primal in his unashamed lust for his near-mate. He'd become more forceful in his intent to take her. They'd spent far too long tamping down their frantic hunger.

"Let your hair fall loose," he commanded, clamping his hands at his sides. Nothing turned him on like Thea's beautiful cascade of golden curls. Well, almost nothing . . . there was her natural self. And her curving Refarian body.

She licked her lips, standing before the fire. Her bare shoulders gleamed in the golden light. With slow, determined gestures, he unbuttoned his uniform jacket, allowing it to fall open loosely about his waist. Her gaze skittered downward to his abdomen, then lower still to his groin. Her pale eyes widened slightly at his protruding arousal, then her gaze lifted upward, locking with his.

"I said to loosen your hair," he half growled, and she nodded compliantly, swallowing.

With a single flick of her wrist, the thick golden mane tumbled across her shoulders, spilling down her back.

She started toward him and he shook his head, extending his palm. "Not yet."

"Marco, this is—"

"I have a plan, wife," he said with a dangerous smile. He *felt* as wolfish as he had to appear—all Changeling and filled with unsatisfied craving. After almost thirty years of holding back his body—for all intents and purposes having saved himself—well, he had determined ideas about how his mating night would go. And most especially for the love of his life, standing before him like one of the goddesses from *Saravaitska*.

Shrugging out of his jacket, he dipped his fingers beneath his waistband, easing his undershirt loose. That white T-shirt pulled and stretched across his lean abdomen and strong back. He made a determined show of his body for his mate, reaching with his arms in a way that would cause his triceps and biceps to ripple and flex. She gasped slightly, her gaze raking over his body.

"Now," he said slowly, "unfasten the shoulder straps of your dress and allow it to slide to the floor."

She clutched at her throat, trembling visibly, so he added, "Do it, Thea. I'm begging you."

She nodded, reaching unsteady fingers to the left strap of her gown. He ached to touch her, to do the job and skim his fingers across her creamy-smooth skin. But he would spend his life stroking her and holding her: Tonight he had a very specific seduction plan in mind, and part of it revolved around being her prince. Commanding her—she who had so often been in the role of commanding others. He knew she craved his control in the bedroom, he'd sensed it mounting in her every time they came so close together.

Taking hold of his own undershirt, he drew it over his head until he stood before her in nothing more than his uniform pants and boots. "I can't get this hook unfastened," she explained in a husky voice, working at it with her hand. He nearly despaired that his entire strategy would go awry, when she cried, "I have it!" and the pearly-blue gown slipped to the floor.

She stood before him wearing only her stockings, panties, and bra; well, and her stiletto heels. It seemed that now, undressed before him, the heels caused her pelvis to thrust forward, positioning her just for him. Hot wetness formed between her legs, making her slick and ready; she stared once again at the powerful bulge between his thighs. In fact, she couldn't seem to look away, recalling how he'd masturbated in front of her during her Change.

His eyes had the black look of a predator, prowling first one way over her body, then another. She considered commanding him as he had done her, ordering him out of his pants. Insisting that he strip bare and stand before her. But for some reason, it seemed important to fall under the sway of his bedroom leadership. With a stifled giggle, she fought the urge to assume a parade rest stance as she gaped back at him.

"Now, unsnap your bra," he ordered, rubbing a palm over first one of his nipples, then the other. She noticed that they'd become as pert and puckered as her own felt, the only difference was that his were covered with downy black hairs, as silky as the curling ones atop his head.

Gods, he's beautiful. Far more beautiful than any man I've ever known.

His eyes flared with pleasure at her appraisal of his body; she dropped her gaze shyly, feeling heat flush across her cheeks.

The huffing sound of his breath filled the silence between them, but he made no move as her bra came loose in her hands. Slowly, she allowed both of her bosoms to fall free from the silken material. He'd seen her before, but never slowly and deliberately like this. For long moments, he gasped and drew in heavy breaths, just staring at her. She struggled to breathe herself, finally managing: "It's your turn, Marco."

He cocked his head, a teasing smile forming on his face so that his single dimple appeared. "Not really, Thea. I'm the one in control here."

"Don't be so sure," she whispered, lifting a hand to stroke a circular pattern around her left nipple. "I rather think I'm running this show."

With a rabid growl, he narrowed his dark eyes at her, running his hands up and down his thighs. But he made no move to unclothe himself.

"Come on, Marco," she begged, panting. "Take me in your arms. I can't stand this any longer!"

He took one step closer, then halted. "Not yet."

She threw her head back, moaning her lusty need. "Please," she complained. "I need you!"

"And you don't think I need you?" He growled, much more loudly than any time before. Louder than she'd ever heard him—that highly aroused sound that only a Refarian male made during mating rites—and the hairs on the nape of her neck stood on end.

"I think you're too controlled," she gibed.

With another step closer, he made a great show of unfastening his belt, slipping it loose from each loop, his eyes locked with hers. "And I think"—he paused, slipping the belt free—"you like control." He tossed it toward her, and with a staggering step in her stilettos, she caught it. "So have it."

"What?" she gasped.

"Control me." He nodded toward the belt in her hands. "Take me in whatever way pleases you."

She stroked the warm leather of his belt between her fingertips, wondering why a half memory seemed to beg her to take him up on his offer. "I-I don't know what you mean," she argued, though she knew exactly his intention.

"In another time, you liked to do that," he answered simply, his eyes sparkling. "It wasn't my plan tonight—and I do have one. But if you'd rather take control, I'm all right with that."

She swallowed hard, feeling the leather burn her hands, but shook her head. No, she wanted him in charge, just as he'd intended. "No, go on," she barely managed to squeeze out. With an easy toss, she sent the belt clattering to the floor.

"Good. Then we're agreed." He unsnapped his uniform pants.

"You're teasing me," she complained, knowing it was true. "You're seducing me strangely."

"It's what you want, Thea."

"How do you know that? You can't know—"

"I'm an empath. You crave to follow me; almost everyone else has to follow *you*."

She nodded, knowing in her heart that it was completely true. "Yes. Yes, Marco."

"Then tonight, I make all the rules," he said, feeling his groin tighten even harder. "And we will mate for eternity."

She panted, licking her lips, feeling a keening cry well up within her. The heat of her mating fever seemed to descend in that moment; no warning, no preparation, it simply fell over her like an instantaneous, mystic spell, causing every cell within her D'Ashanian body to quiver.

"Yes, love," she agreed with a brisk nod. "Take me completely!"

He flashed an almost wicked, possessed smile at her. "Good, baby. That's good," he soothed silkily. "Now just follow me."

Thea stood in the bedroom, literally unable to speak. Nothing could have prepared her for the sight before her eyes. The four-poster bed had been draped in lovely, diaphanous curtains, billowing softly in the roaring fire of the hearth. They floated mystically from high atop the bed, cascading downward on both sides, so that a veiled canopy shimmered in the luminous candlelight. From every direction light splashed through the sheer material, playing shadows and incandescent hues against each other. Marco had woven a spell over the room by gilding it all in golden darkness.

"Do you like it?" She could only see the side of his face, his arm, as he was partly obscured behind the lovely, glittering curtains. "I wanted it to be . . . romantic."

"You know that I do." Swallowing hard, she willed her heart to quiet its frantic tempo. It almost seemed as if it might explode from within her chest, the emotions between them were that overpowering.

His eyes glinted with seduction and something very dangerous. "Good. That was the plan."

Closing the distance between them, he dropped to his knees before her. The bedroom sparkled with dozens of twinkling candles, a chiaroscuro of dark and light shadowing her husband's face as he gently began removing her stockings, kneeling before her like she was his very own princess. After easing first one foot, then the other out of the nylon, Marco trailed his mouth across her abdomen with a hungry gesture, making raw mating sounds. Wrapping his arms about her hips, he trembled against her, quivering with a desperate, wordless desire.

Laving her belly button with his tongue, he dipped the wet tip of it lower still, trailing a path down to the edge of her panties. With a sensual gesture, he peeled the panties down her legs, then bent his dark head between her thighs. One calloused hand pushed between her legs, forcing them farther apart. With a gasp, she clutched at his head, curling her fingers in his hair. "Marco," she panted. "I'm not sure . . ."

With a mumbling groan, he pressed his lips against *her* lips, flicking his tongue like a hot, warm fiend; in and out, back and forth, she staggered with cresting desire, grasping at him, holding on as a sudden jolt shot through her entire body, electrifying every particle of her being.

Oh, my Change. She panicked, sucking in breaths. *Too soon! Too soon . . .*

"Marco," she cried out. "Marco—I-I'm going t-to—"

With a fluid gesture, he was on his feet and crushing

her against his chest before she could finish. "You will not Change yet," he told her firmly.

"You won't let me?" She tilted her face toward him helplessly, and he flashed a dark grin.

"*You* won't allow it—because you want this too much."

Her hands trembled against his chest, and she nuzzled him there, searching for her internal rhythm. If she could steady it, she would master the haywire signals urging her to transform before they could mate. She'd spent a lifetime tamping down her needs and her nature. After a moment, she eased into him a bit more, relaxing her body against his, aware that he'd teased her to an impossible precipice, then soared earthward with her in his grasp. Safe, desired. Protected above all others.

Slowly pirouetting her in a half circle, he held her from behind, his broad, powerful chest pressing hard against her body—just like the first night they'd met. She felt his hand press between their two bodies, and an answering rustle of fabric signaled what she already felt: That he'd finally shed his uniform trousers, and was completely bare. She felt the startling warmth of his rough, hair-dusted legs pushing her slightly against the mattress.

And she felt his protruding hard-on slide right between her legs, which were so slick for him she might as well have been a heated pool.

Marco knew that everything Sabrina had predicted was surely imminent. Inside his belly fire coiled like a burning serpent, wrapping its sweltering need about his loins with unrelenting force. Every single moment that he held off with Thea became one moment closer to revealing his terrible secret.

He pressed hot kisses against the top of her head, anguished momentarily by the weight of his identity. What if Thea fled him? What if she feared his own fire for some inexplicable reason? It was irrational, but he was terrified for her to see his core nature.

That is you at your most basic, most primal; of course you're afraid, a soft voice reminded him.

His trembling only intensified.

"Thea, let's lie on the bed." It was all he could do to force the words out.

With a graceful move, she slowly draped herself across the cool satin sheets, curling there like the goddess he'd imagined her to be. For a full moment, he could only gaze upon her, blinking at such a sight of pure beauty. Perfection—his perfection! His wife and soon to be mate.

"I wish to mate," he blurted with a rough growl of intent. "We must mate . . . now!" The words were a harsh roar, as fire threatened to explode even in his very fingertips.

"Yes, yes," she agreed with a breathy sigh. "I can't hold back much longer, Marco. I just can't."

He nodded, mounting her, thrusting his cock between her legs. Like yesterday, their mutual arousal was so strong, it seemed neither wanted to be gentle. "I don't want to hurt you," he lamented, bracing his hands about her head. "Gods, I'd rather die."

Lifting a fair hand to his cheek, tears shimmered in her eyes. "It won't hurt; it's too beautiful." She gave a brisk, soldierly nod, then added, "Just do it—now!"

Propelling his hips against her, he entered her as quickly as he could manage, given that it was his first time too. She flinched as he felt the warmth of her body enclose his own, and then . . . She became radiant. Literally. Her skin glowed from beneath the surface, causing the darkness to shine with luminance. Very tentatively he gave another thrust, only to feel her answer by tightening about him.

Thea lifted and begged, urged and fought, did everything in her bodily power to get Marco deeper within her. But nothing seemed enough to quench her thirst for him; nothing could ever be enough!

Baby, baby, he murmured, seizing hold of their bond, deepening it, plumbing her depths with his energy. It seemed as if tendrils of lightning shot across her flesh, even as his palms stroked and pleasured her. "Thea!" he shouted against her shoulder.

"Are you all right?" She dug her fingernails into the flesh of his shoulders, struggling to keep form. She couldn't allow her core nature to take charge, not if she didn't want to hurt him—possibly kill him, even.

"I-I'm losing control." He panted, stilling suddenly inside her. In obvious panic, he pulled back, searching her face for some sort of help.

"It's okay," she tried to soothe him. "That . . . happens." Then she began giggling crazily. "Marco! Men lose control." She gripped his buttocks, trying to work him back into a grinding rhythm atop her.

He fought her, then shook his head, his black eyes ringed with panic. "No, no, baby—you don't understand." At that precise moment, a strange sensation radiated toward her . . . from within him. A burning presence, a welling crescendo.

Terror suddenly filled Thea's heart; she was about to shape-shift! She couldn't stop herself, she was on fire!

"In All's name!" she cried, pushing at his chest with both her palms. "Get off before I-I . . . Marco, I don't want to hurt you!" Again, she pushed at his chest, but it was too late; like a fiery cauldron her Change caught hold, rolling like a tidal wave from her abdomen to her extremities and she was ablaze!

Whirling in panic, she hardly had time to process her transformation, wrestling to separate herself from his corporeal body, except . . . she met a presence. A blazing, roaring, golden being who rushed toward her, not away.

Mate! My mate! Marco thundered within their bond, spiraling toward her in a blaze of luminous glory. Every desire, every dream she'd ever held about joining with her lifemate came into pure focus at that moment. The love of her life, somehow—inexplicably—just like her!

Love mate! She trilled back, hurling herself toward his glowing form.

But something stopped her; right as she felt their souls impact one another, instantly knitting together in an explosion of light and beauty, he simply retracted, withdrawing to the far side of the bedroom.

Terror! What I?

Murmuring words of love and reassurance, she promised him that it was okay. That whatever had happened, this transformation that seemed to have overtaken him had to be a result of their mating. Her words were simple, basic as her communication always was while in her purest form.

With a static rumble, he collapsed on the floor, naked and glistening with sweat, his shoulders vibrating with every gasping breath he labored to draw. For a long moment he braced himself there, head down, struggling to regain his clarity. She shifted, returning to physical form, and knelt beside him, rubbing his back.

"It's okay, Marco," she promised. "Don't you see? It must be because of what I am. Don't be afraid—it's okay."

Very slowly he lifted his head, still slumped forward on his knees. When their gazes locked, she finally understood how feral he had become—how threatened and raw. Her own first Change had nearly sent her past the brink of sanity, it had been so at odds with her Refarian body. Obviously Marco felt exactly as she once had.

Stroking his shoulder, she pressed soft kisses against his forehead. "There's nothing to be afraid of," she reassured him, but the wild look in his dark eyes only intensified.

"Don't you get it?" he asked in a frighteningly quiet voice. "Don't you see, Thea?"

She shook her head, a hollow sensation forming in her chest. It reminded her of other conversations they'd had, all of which had begun with this same terrible prescience.

Leaning back on his knees, he reached for her, tugging her forcefully against his body. Her face met a muscled chest coated in the sheen of sex. Of Changing and mating.

"You didn't make me what you are, baby," he told her gruffly. "You know it's not possible."

She shoved his words aside. Of course it had to be possible! She'd simply never read it before anywhere, or heard it, but it had to be what had happened, because otherwise—

"Marco?" she croaked, pulling back to gaze up into his beautiful, velvet-lashed eyes. Eyes that had always reminded her of nothing so much as . . . Jared's. "What are you saying?"

His entire body blazed hot, trembling against hers, but

he remained silent. His eyes sent her a thousand words, none of which she could seem to hear. "Tell me," she begged. "Please, just tell me."

His eyes drifted shut and he whispered, "I am D'Aravni."

They hadn't finished soulmating. Odd, but that was the disconnected, shocked thought that slammed through Thea's mind. *We have to finish! We're not fully mated yet.*

"Did you hear me?" he asked her in a chilling, calm voice.

She bobbed her head up and down, blinking, trying anything to process what he'd just stated so boldly. "How?" she finally managed to gulp.

Both black eyebrows shot up, a vague look of amusement coming over his face. "I don't think *how* is really the question, baby."

"I mean, how can you possibly be D'Aravnian? Jared is the only one of his line alive—the very last of his line, Marco. But you just Changed. You touched me with your fire—you *are* D'Aravni!" She began to laugh hysterically. "By All it's true! Amazing, wonderful!" She tugged him into a fierce embrace. "I mean, it's my greatest dream come true, but . . . just tell me how!"

"I never knew," he murmured against the top of her head, showering her with kisses. "Never knew, baby, until yesterday."

"But that makes you—"

"I'm Jared's half brother," he confessed, sounding guilty and stricken—not joyous like she felt. "Sabrina never told me. I didn't keep it from you."

"Of course not," she blurted, a thousand bits of cosmic awareness piercing her mind. If Jared had a half brother, did he know? Why hadn't Marco known? Questions came at her faster than she could voice them.

Clasping her by both shoulders, he pulled back to stare at her intently. "Jared must never know, Thea, all right? He can never know. This stays between us."

"But you have to tell him, Marco—promise me you will," she beseeched. "All his life he's been alone—to learn that he has a brother—and gods, we have a prince!" She babbled on and on at him, but his face only grew more shadowed with anxiety. "Jared must learn he has a brother."

"A brother who is his servant," he amended softly, bowing his head. "A brother who is pledged to him, branded as his Madjin. A brother who is, quite simply, not of his station or class."

"That's *meshdki.*"

"It's true, Thea—you know everything that I am. Hell, you became one with me during our sealing ceremony. Your wrist still burns from the branding."

"It didn't make me someone that I'm not."

"And I'm not a prince."

"Jared's brother would be second in line to the throne."

With a quiet cry of anguish, Marco declared, "You have to promise me that he'll never know."

She shook her head, even as she heard herself agree to his terrible bargain. Relief washed over his dark-skinned face—a face that from the very first time had always reminded her of Jared's. Of course, she hadn't imagined a familial connection possible between them; there'd never been any mention of another living D'Aravni.

A D'Aravni! Her mate and husband was the one other soul she'd craved for her entire life. "I can't believe it." She touched her flushed face in wonder. "All this time, my whole life, Marco, I've thought Jared was the one for me. That he was my intended mate, that he was the man I loved when . . ."

But the words she'd spoken in an outpouring of love for Marco died on her lips; his face blanched, his mouth pulled tight, and he jerked backward from her as if she'd just scalded him.

When all along I was waiting to fall in love with you, she wanted to finish, but the wounded look on his face silenced her.

"You loved Jared? You love him? What are you really saying, Thea?"

She waved her hands between them as if she could recall the words. "No, that's not what I mean," she rushed to explain. "My whole life I thought I loved Jared—I was promised to him as an infant, you know."

His expression grew icy. "No. I didn't know."

"Of course, we were cousins, it was always meant to be."

"You love Jared," he repeated, piercing her with his hard gaze. "Love my king, my lord. You *love* him, Thea?"

"You're not listening to me!" she shouted, frustration and fear boiling over.

He pounced to his feet in the space of a moment, backing away from her. "I understand just fine, wife. You love my brother. He was the one you waited and waited for—"

"That's *not* what I'm saying."

"I understand perfectly." And he was gone from the room before she could even go after him.

Thea woke to find Marco still missing from their bed; for hours she'd lain hoping for his return, but finally drifted into a fitful sleep. A glance at the clock showed it to be almost four a.m. But where would he have gone for so long? Had he stayed down at the base on this, their wedding night? Was he really that angry and hurt with her—upset enough to stay away rather than sealing their mating rites? She couldn't understand how he'd misunderstood her to such disastrous proportions. He'd never even given her a chance to explain! Wailing, terrible pain bubbled up inside of her, and there seemed no possible way to express it.

Leaping out of bed, her bare feet met icy-cold hardwood, her naked body shivering. Glancing around the bedroom for additional clothing, her gaze fell on Marco's parka, hastily discarded on the foot of their bed.

So he is here, she thought, walking purposefully toward the main living room that adjoined their sleeping chamber. She found him there on the sofa, his jaw set in cool determination, his curling hair disheveled and wild.

"Marco?" she whispered, holding onto the door frame tremulously. "When did you come in?" He said nothing, so she took a tentative step closer. "I wish you'd come to bed with me," she pressed, but he only grunted in reply, nothing more.

He'd never before treated her so coolly, not even when he'd been telling her they couldn't be together. At least then he'd displayed something of his gentler nature; right now, he was only showing her one thing: his left profile.

"You've got a black eye."

His full mouth tensed into a hard line, and she had a strange flash of trying to soothe a *Varakeesa*, a tiny multicolored bird that had populated their home world. As a girl, she'd spent hours in her mother's garden trying to tame one. *Move slowly, Haven. Infinitesimal progress is all it takes.*

"I hit it on the door frame when I left the guesthouse. Cut my eyebrow on the fucking latch."

"I could heal it," she suggested gently.

"Don't bother."

"So you want to stay bruised and injured like this? That's smart." *Another step closer, edging there, edging.*

He cut his dusky eyes sideways at her; it was the look of a man who believed himself betrayed. For the briefest moment, she felt the physical sensation of Marco's entire body as if it were her very own. The throbbing in his jaw from the battle at Warren; the swollen pressure behind his eye; the hot pain in his left wrist. Experiencing a moment of heightened empathy with him, now of all times when he was so hurt and angry, nearly suffocated her. Oh, he was in pain all right, a great deal of pain, and not just in his body.

"Look at your face, Marco," she muttered, needing so desperately to touch him, even though she knew to keep her distance. "Please let me heal you. I *need* to heal you. I feel how it hurts."

"Like hell."

"It hurts like hell?" she asked, confused.

"No, Thea," he answered, with what was obviously very forced patience, "I mean, like *hell* am I allowing my . . . *wife*"—he speared her with his midnight gaze—"my lifemate . . . m-my . . . *cousin* to heal me!" he sputtered furiously. "Like hell you're going to touch me."

"So that's your answer?" she murmured, feeling tears sting her eyes.

"I'll see the medics later."

"Why not see your wife right now?"

"Because I'm not sure what to think about my wife," he said. "Not after last night."

She threw up her hands. "How can you say that to me? After all that we've shared, Marco? With as much as I love you, how can you possibly say such a cruel thing to me?"

"I-I thought I was your first love," he blurted, spreading one hand over his heart. "That's what I thought, Thea. I thought what we had was special. That I was the only man you'd *ever* wanted like this!" With a quiet cry of anguish, he buried his face in his hands.

"Marco!" She moved quickly, dropping to her knees in front of him. "You know what you mean to me!" She placed her palms on his knees, trying to get through to him. Trying anything to get the damned, stubborn man just to understand.

"But you loved him first." He dropped his hands away from his face, looking her in the eye. "You loved my brother before you loved me. How can I ever forget that?"

She laughed, rubbing her hands over his muscular thighs. "For an empath, Marco, you can be unbelievably dense."

"What's that supposed to mean?" His black eyebrows furrowed into a scowl.

"It means you *were* my first love."

He shook his head. "Last night, you told me that you had loved Jared, that—"

She cut him off. "Words mean everything, remember?" she reminded him. "That's part of a Madjin's training—you were the one who taught me that. 'Words have life.' " She paused, waiting for him to interrupt, to object or say something, but he did not. So, taking hold of his shoulders, she leaned up onto her knees and pressed her face close to his.

"I said I *thought* I was in love with Jared. *Thought.* Until I met you, and then I realized there was this giant hole inside of me, this place that was so hungry, just searching for a man of the D'Aravni line. It was as if I knew I was supposed to wait on you—but then you didn't come . . ." She had to swallow hard before she could continue. "When you didn't come, Marco, I mistook Jared for you. You see, you aren't my first love"—she paused, gathering both of his large, dusky hands within her own—"you're my only love."

Squeezing her hands, he leaned forward until their noses were practically touching, until she could feel his hot breath against her face and until she could inhale his familiar, woodsy scent in her nostrils. Gods, how she loved even the very smell of her mate, the way he always seemed to have just come in from the fresh air and the trails. "I love you," she whispered again. "More than I could have ever imagined it was possible to love another person."

"You make me crazy, Thea. It frightens me, what I feel for you," he admitted, releasing her hands. He slipped his muscular arms around her, rubbing his fingers along the base of her neck. "It's too much, too out of control, too . . . overpowering. And this fire in you, well, it makes me hunger for a lot more too."

"More?" She didn't dare hope that he meant awakening his D'Aravnian side; not when he'd been so frightened by it the night before.

His breathing grew heavy against her cheek as for long moments he said nothing; when he did speak, his voice was thick with unconcealed emotion. "I crave to be myself with you, Thea. Both selves. I want to understand it, what it means when I'm with you—and I want to understand the fire I feel inside whenever I gaze upon your beautiful, sexy, D'Ashanian self."

Heat infused her cheeks at his frank admission. "I would love that," she whispered huskily in his ear. "Would love to see how gorgeous you really, truly are."

He pulled back, and his black gaze shone with emotion and desire—power, too. His other nature had already begun to rouse from its lifelong slumber, she could tell. "And," he admitted, his gaze never wavering from hers, "I would love to know what lovemaking could really be for us in our other form."

Thea's lips parted, and she really did think she was going to say something. But not one word came to mind. All she could do was stare in wonder at her beautiful, strong husband. A prince! She had married a prince; and, as it happened, not just any prince. The prince of her heart. "I can show you how. To make your Change again, I mean, to learn how to control it, not just let it happen out of arousal and fear like it did last night."

A devilish gleam flashed in his tired eyes. "I'm counting on it."

"It might take time," she told him, feeling an unaccountable shyness as he cupped her warm face within his palm. "To, well, you know. Show you. Teach you . . . take you there, I mean." She shook her head, frustrated by her stammering explanations. The truth was, slipping into her natural state was the most intensely personal experience she knew. The idea of sharing it with him—and awakening it within her lover—well, it left her feeling strangely like a virgin all over again. "It's just very . . . erotic." There, she'd told him.

His long-lashed eyes drifted halfway shut, his swarthy face seemed to flush a little red, and he sighed. "Why else do you figure I'm so interested in it?"

"Because you want to know your true self?" she supplied in a helpful voice, but she knew better.

"Partly," he purred. "And partly because I know you'll be even more of a wildcat when we're having royal sex."

"Oh, please!" She swatted him on the arm. "Royal sex?"

"What else should I call it?"

"Try . . ." Well, he had her there. At least in English. She pressed her lips against his ear, murmuring sweet words of Refarian love and pleasure, and called it exactly what it was. *Llala durshk.* Translation: at least the rough, imperfect one, "the sharing of fire."

He nuzzled her cheek, pressing his full, warm lips against her face. "In other words, I'll show you my fire, if you show me yours?" He laughed huskily.

"Sort of like."

"Mmm, this will be most interesting, my lady."

And inside, right in the center of her belly, Thea felt a quaking, trembling heat begin. Closing her eyes, she knew that their mating rites had really just begun.

Chapter Twenty-seven

After breakfast, Jared finally returned to the cabin in search of his wife. She'd been sound asleep when he'd left for the day at five A.M., and now that sunlight pierced the dawn he found himself desperate to make love with her. Strange, but his compulsion to couple with her had intensified dramatically in the past day, so that it seemed the only thing he could think about. Erotic thoughts crowded his mind—images of Kelsey astride him, riding him hard, or images of them tumbling before the fire, thrusting and groaning. From the beginning, his desire for Kelsey had been nearly maddening, but . . . this rampant craving was unique.

Every new husband yearns for his mate. That's all that I'm feeling, he tried telling himself. *Of course I want to bed her as often as possible.*

But a quiet part of his heart wanted to believe that perhaps it was something far more monumental—perhaps greater than a new husband's unrelenting passion for his wife. What he wanted to believe, when he actually admitted it to himself, was that maybe the gods were smiling upon them—maybe he *wasn't* actually done with his first mating season.

He discovered Kelsey at his desk poring over a small book, glancing back and forth between her handheld translator and what he would have sworn was one of Prince Arienn's journals. With iPod headphones over her ears, and her attention focused on the pages before her, she never noticed his entry. Making his footsteps light, he crept up behind her, feeling heat sweep from the crown of his head to the tips of his toes. Flushing heat, the sort that came from nowhere and made you dizzy.

Bending over her chair, he slid his arms about her and she jolted in his embrace. "Geez, Jared!" she shouted in an overly loud voice thanks to her headphones. "You scared the living crap out of me!" He laughed, pointing at his ears, and she ripped the headset away.

Nuzzling her, he nibbled at first one ear, then the other. "I was feeling frisky."

"How frisky?" She set the iPod on his desk.

The flush in his face deepened. "I wish to bed my wife."

"That's definitely frisky."

Bending over her shoulder he asked, "What are you reading?" He gave the book a glance—it *was* one of the prince's journals, but not one he'd ever seen before. "Arienn's diary?"

This time it was his wife who blushed, and deeply. "It's something Thea gave me," was all she said, placing it atop a stack of Refarian science texts.

He plucked the book from her grasp with his most kingly manner. "I see that, but the question is why."

Kelsey averted her eyes, and he briefly scanned the journal pages, grasping the reason for her embarrassment. In painstaking detail Arienn had outlined the specifics of the first night he lay with his wife—his human wife.

"Arienn coupled with a human," he observed, shocked to the core.

Kelsey gave a nod, saying nothing.

"I've never read anywhere that he mated with a human." Jared read on, skimming until he came to one particular entry that caused the beating of his heart to increase rapidly.

Some say that humans, by temperament, are unable to partake of the mating heat. They say wrongly! Louisa has reacted with particular verve and pleasure to my cycles, often falling under the fever's sway first, inducing me, provoking me. Ah, it is a glorious mystery, this blood fever. Would the world know, I should be the envy of every non-

heated Refarian male! Every human male would declare me outrageously fortunate! So I am, so we are.

"By the gods!" Jared could hardly contain his excitement. "They experienced the heat . . . together!"

Kelsey gave him a bold smile. "So they did."

Jared gulped, feeling something powerful lodge in his chest. Was it hope? Perhaps fear? He couldn't be sure. "If they did, then you know what that means, Kelsey . . ."

Her smile, so radiant and broad, turned much more beguiling. "That things are going to get *very* interesting between us eventually."

"Are you . . . repulsed?" he asked, his lifelong shame about his mating compulsions surfacing yet again.

"Will you get over yourself, Jared? Please?" She swatted him on the hip. "I don't know how many ways to say this, so I just will: I am into this. It turns me freaking on. Okay? Do you finally get it?"

Chastened, he bowed his head, grinning from ear to ear. "The thought of you in the throes of mating frenzy turns me . . . *freaking* on."

"Don't say freaking."

He cocked his head, confused. "No? Is it somehow wrong, the manner in which I used it?"

"No, it just makes me want to giggle at you."

"Ah, so I see." He preened like the king that he was. "I do not wish to amuse you in bed. Only pleasure you."

"My point precisely." Still, she did giggle—and quite loudly.

With a final glance at the page, he realized one question still concerned him. "Tell me, love, did they . . . conceive? Have we hope from their own conception?"

For long moments she did not reply, until at last she rose from the chair, pulling herself to her full six feet of height. "Yes, there's hope."

"They conceived a child?"

Her lovely wide smile vanished. "It doesn't say—but they did cycle together, repeatedly." She indicated the journal he held in his hand. "Arienn writes about three of their cycles in there."

A jolt of heat shot straight to his groin, causing his

cock to stiffen in proud salute. "Three cycles—together." He growled possessively, jerking her against his body. "We best begin to call the fever upon ourselves immediately."

"You're not afraid of it anymore?" she asked, uncertainty darkening her freckled face.

"Damn it all, I have my pride to think about now! I won't be outdone by Arienn."

With a quick kiss on his cheek, she rumbled in his ear, mimicking his mating sounds. "If my king commands it, how can I deny him?"

"It's me who can't ever deny you, sweet queen."

Then, as the king had indeed decreed, they took to their bed for many long, lusty hours. During that time something foreign fanned across their naked bodies: subtle, barely noticeable, that thing wooed them. It lured them closer, yet remained concealed beneath the surface of their bond. In fact, they never knew it had entered the chamber, so stealthy was it.

Yes, their blood fever waited, simmered slowly, whispered their names like a creature of mischief, until the perfect moment when it would explode full-force upon their mated bodies.

Marco and Thea fell into exhausted slumber, tangled together like a serpentine *wtlsi* sculpture—arms, legs, bodies twined as one. And soon enough after that, they woke, staring at each other in wondrous silence. There were no words, just long, slow caresses their only form of communication.

Without speaking, Marco drew Thea up onto her knees so that they faced each other in the center of the bed. As they'd done during their near-mating, they placed palm against palm, allowing energy to radiate back and forth, quickly building to a pulsating climax. Thea's body tensed as she felt Marco's power encircle her, intoxicating her, arousing her. Sliding one palm down the front of her chest, he caressed first one nipple, then the other with a strange kind of innocence; as if they'd never touched each other before that very moment. As if they hadn't already lost their virginity together.

He's seeing me through new eyes, she thought in amazement. *Because we've both changed. Because we're nearly soulmated!*

That's true, came his throaty, sure voice right in her soul's marrow. *I kept thinking I was going to change you, and look what you've done to me! You're my princess.*

A princess; a royal wedding; mating rites. Thea gaped at Marco in wonder, her fingertips stilling against his bare chest. *How did I overlook something so symbolic and important on our wedding night?* With a quick glance at the sheer drapes that billowed from the canopy, she fingered a bit of the silky fabric, unfurling it between them. It wafted over her body, cool and sensual in its texture, creating a veil of separation—hiding her from her mate while also enhancing every detail of her bare body.

Thea, what are you doing? he asked gruffly, reaching to push the thin material out of the way, but she stopped his hand.

This is royal tradition, Marco. On the wedding night, the bride is covered completely, hidden from her husband like a mystery . . . until they soul-mate.

"Then what happens?" he snarled, his impatience undeniable.

Lifting up onto her knees, she pressed her lips against his, the diaphanous material brushing between both their mouths. "The prince uncovers her."

To Thea, it had always been a beautiful metaphor for the sealing of souls.

"We're not on Refaria," he argued, his voice edged with threat. "And it's not our wedding night now."

"But we aren't yet soulmated," she reminded him, her soft exhalations causing the veil to billow with each breath.

Bunching the material in his fist, Marco moaned his impatience. "I want to see you, baby!"

"Trust me."

With his fingertips he rubbed the silken material across her abdomen, sliding it downward between her legs. Back and forth he used it to pleasure her, massaging it against her most intimate place until the fabric dampened with her arousal. Glimpsed through the veil

Marco was a shadowy image of darkness and power, of ruggedness and majesty. She wrestled against her own impatience, clamping down on it almost violently.

She edged forward onto his lap, planting herself astride him, then stroked the veil against his sandpapery cheek, letting him feel its erotic coolness. Their faces pressed together again, and their heavy breaths caused the material to billow back and forth between them.

Lifting the bottom portion of the fabric, Thea took hold of Marco's erection with her free hand, sliding atop his jutting length. She was wetter than last night, burning for him, wound tight. So ready for him, so urgent.

"Take this off," he begged, clutching at the veil.

"Not yet." She panted. "Not quite yet."

"Damn it, Thea!" He groaned, wrapping his arms about her waist. "I want you now!"

"It-it's arousing us."

"I know that, b-but, I-I," he sputtered, but she cut him off by driving herself onto his rigid cock. His erection filled her completely, driving up inside of her hard. She gasped, steadying herself by clutching his shoulders, barely able to see him through the thin membrane that separated the rest of their bodies. Clasping her hips, Marco teased her into a frantic motion, up and down against his body; not like the virgin he'd been just hours ago, but as if he'd spent many nights in her arms and bed.

Within moments she felt his soul; sensed it as soon as it made explosive contact with hers. Last night they'd stopped—not this time.

Throwing her head back, she cried out her pleasure; his soul was gorgeous—a shimmering palette of more colors than she could identify. Closing her eyes, she lost herself in him, body and soul. *No stopping, no stopping,* she whispered within their bond.

Never again, he pledged, their frantic pace intensifying. Then, without hesitation, they coupled souls, fire dissolving into shards of color right between them. She felt the moment it happened, as if Marco himself lodged suddenly within her chest; as if she burrowed right into his core.

And at that precise moment, Thea ripped the veil away, crushing her mouth against his right as he came inside her, her hips thrashing wildly, a growling moan exploding from within his chest.

"I can't—breathe," she barely managed to squeeze out, and he pinned her against his muscled, heaving chest.

"Hold on," he urged thickly. "Hold me." He was trembling against her with a ferocious intensity.

"I'm here, I'm here," she promised him, feeling his heat sizzle to life. His body now sated, his D'Aravnian self was about to demand its own due. "Don't be afraid."

"I-I am . . . not." His arms tightened about her, the shaking growing more pronounced. "In . . . awe. Mates."

Thea smiled, realizing his communication was Changing first, becoming primitive and basic. *It's moments now, breaths away . . .*

Then, burrowing his face against the top of her head, a sweeping wave of electric current sizzled between them, becoming power itself as they Changed together, still clinging desperately to each other's bodies.

Marco spun, whirling in lust and maddening need. *Need mate! Need finish. Mate! Thea!*

Here! She spiraled toward him, expressing her pure, unadulterated joy. *Mate, yes!*

He sensed her more than saw her, though his Change was an explosion of sensation on every level. Nothing in his nearly thirty years had prepared him for this pure moment of oneness with his lifemate. Their souls twined together, pulsating, as her fire crested into his, joining. Sealing. Seamless. Glorious.

One. Always one. Only one.

One.

Afterward they lay flat on their backs in the middle of the floor, neither possessing the strength to so much as flex a muscle. Marco gazed at the pine-beamed ceiling, blinking occasionally, feeling radiant and reborn. They held hands, struggled to normalize their breathing and said . . . nothing. Words weren't necessary; they'd already communicated everything during the lovemaking and the Change-making. That's what Thea had called that kind of twining of their core bodies.

At last, he needed to kiss her. Such a simple thing, really, but hell, it was what he wanted. Forcing himself to roll sideways, an effort that required almost Herculean strength, he got his first look at his wife since they'd reassumed their physical bodies.

"Thea," he told her with a smug grin, "you're glowing."

A dreamy, kittenlike sound came from her lips. "I know."

"I mean, really glowing." He propped his head on one elbow, loving the outward sign his bride wore of their mating.

She rotated her head sideways, her clear blue eyes widening. "Oh, gods! You are too!"

He glanced at his chest and wasn't surprised to see that an orange-gold sheen bathed it completely. "Guess that's what happens when we make love, huh?"

"It better not be a regular phenomenon!" she exclaimed with a giggle. "The whole camp will know we're mating."

Stroking a disheveled curl away from her cheek, he laughed too. "Yeah, well I think they already know that. Your cries were loud enough to rouse the entire compound."

She gave him an indignant look. "*My* cries? Mine? Oh, that's right, Mr. Hold-on-I'm-a-raging-*shtkasa.*"

"Is that what I sounded like?" He could remember hearing the untamed *shtkasa* as a child: Their fearsome roars sounding across the palace grounds at night had been the stuff of youthful terrors.

She rolled to face him. "You sounded perfect."

"You *were* perfect."

"Were?" She cocked a flirtatious eyebrow at him.

Closing his eyes he drew in a breath, feeling her pure joy in the deepest recesses of his being. In return, he sensed that her newly gained empathy plumbed the depths of his heart. He longed for words but had none, yet, for the first time in all his days, it simply didn't matter. His wife and mate knew him from the heart that beat within his chest to the cells that comprised his newly discovered D'Aravnian self.

He was no longer alone, and instead was utterly known. For an empath and Madjin who had walked in solitude all his life, that was the most profound gift of their mating.

Known. It was a deeply powerful word, and while it was one that might require adjustment, it was also one that had changed him forever.

"I *know* that I love you," she teased him, her clear eyes twinkling.

"You heard that." He blushed, feeling shy about being so transparent with her.

She rolled onto her back, stretching her arms overhead. "I heard it and I felt it—I feel everything you're experiencing, Marco. You know that!"

In slight alarm, he sat up. "You're *that* empathic? Already?" What about the headaches, the sickness? He'd hoped—somehow—that she wouldn't inherit the full force of his nature.

"I feel settled, Marco. It's beautiful."

"But . . . what if you get sick? What if it's too much? I've spent a lifetime mastering my empathy." His panic began to mount, nearly unstoppable.

"And I inherited that same control. Our gifts are entwined, Marco, completely. I sense it—you sense it, too, if you just feel within our bond. You won't ever be ill again. And I never will be."

"But how do you know that?"

"Because in lifemating, there's completion."

Of course she was right—and he did feel it, deep in his core. "We're one," he whispered, their union suddenly vivid in his mind, its full import, the depth of it, startling and clear.

"One, yes." She rose to her knees, splaying a palm across his heart. "And I'm ready to be *one* all over again," she teased, releasing a playful mating call.

One. Perfect, fulfilled unity with his wife. Lifemated entirely. It was the ideal way for two empaths to spend the rest of eternity, he thought, scooping her into his ecstatic embrace.

* * *

Marco and Thea stood on a precipice, a particular turn in a path that revealed the valley, covered in new snow, sparkling beneath a sky so blue that Thea was convinced she'd never seen anything like it back on Refaria. These were her favorite moments on Earth. Without words, they shared the thought—that Earth, while not home, possessed moments of indescribable beauty. Marco slipped both arms about her waist, staring over the top of her head at the valley. With a glance toward the sky, its azure blueness a pristine contrast against the snow, he thought it the perfect metaphor for their love.

"I never want to leave," he murmured, leaning down to kiss the top of her head. She tensed against him.

"Earth? You don't miss home?"

"You're the one who said it—you're my home."

"Still, this place is . . ." She didn't finish, growing pensive—he sensed the mood change deep within her.

"Is what?" he prompted, squinting at the brilliant, sweeping sky overhead.

She laughed in surprise. "I was going to say this is a godsforsaken planet, the worst outpost we could have landed on—but then I realized something." Her own gaze turned skyward. "I don't hate Earth anymore. In fact, I think I've refused to see how beautiful it is for a long time."

"I've never hated Earth," he told her. "I grew up here, you know. I hardly remember Refaria. I feel this place, in my soul, my bones."

"I hated it because we were forced here."

"And now?"

"It seems different today—*I'm* different today, thanks to you. Everything feels much more important, including protecting this world."

"Maybe you don't resent Earth anymore because you don't want Jared anymore," he suggested.

She adjusted herself within his arms, turning until she stared up into his eyes, her own blue gaze nearly matching the vivid color of the sky. "Are you still upset about what I told you?"

"About Jared?" She gave a quick nod, and he threw his head back and laughed. "How could I be when I'm the one who has you?"

She brushed her fingertips over his lips, her expression growing troubled. "He does need to know, Marco. When you're ready."

"Never, baby."

"I'm just saying . . . family is so important—"

"A Madjin warrior has a unique, intimate role with those he protects. That is all Jared ever need know."

"It's your choice," she agreed, "but something tells me that it would be a mistake to keep the truth from him."

Her words called a prickle of awareness into his heart, but he brushed the feeling aside, instead focusing on their utter happiness. Their moment shouldn't be stolen by the power of secrets and past lies.

Still, even as they kissed there on the mountain, their tongues plunging into the heat of one another's mouths, their bodies flexing insatiably, something dark propelled itself onto that mountain. Something they neither heeded, nor noticed, so lost were they in their shared moment of love.

Far from the mountain, too, a stranger stepped onto the wild Wyoming land. A man who was never meant to enter their world, any more than secrets were meant not to be told. He surveyed the landscape, his eyes measuring the same clear blue sky, the same hoary terrain.

And the stranger calculated the precise distance from where he stood to their very mountain.

Read on for a sneak peek at

Parallel Seduction

by Deidre Knight

Coming from Signet Eclipse in April 2007

Hope hit the button on her bedside clock, and its mechanical voice stated, "Two fifty-three." With a weary sigh, she flopped back onto her small cot of a bed. The Refarians didn't trust her yet, at least not completely, so they'd given her lousy quarters down in the belly of their main base, right next to some enlisted guy who stayed up half the night playing what sounded like an alien version of poker.

In fact, from what she could tell, the soldiers they'd bunked her up with were basically no different from the guys she'd known growing up on half a dozen Army bases scattered around the globe. Well, with one major exception: These soldiers weren't from this planet. And most of them had golden red skin, almost Native American in appearance. A few random soldiers she'd seen seemed blond and fair-skinned, but they were the exception—and her failing eyesight might have misled her about their appearances anyway.

The soldier who had the quarters next to hers was rowdy as all getout, played his music too loud after hours, and was generally an inconsiderate slob. Like now. There was a sudden uproar of laughter, some shouting of male voices, and that did it for her. She reached around on the dark floor, feeling in the blackness for her shoe, and hurled it at the wall. "Hey! Shut up!" she yelled.

If you lived with the soldiers, you had to act like one. In response, somebody banged on the wall and shouted at her in Refarian; then there was some general whooping that she chose to ignore.

She rolled onto her side, held her pillow over both ears, and focused on sleep—something that had evaded her ever since she'd arrived at this alien compound.

She chalked it all up to the dreams. Ever since being drugged back at Warren, she'd been continuing to dream of Scott Dillon. Sometimes he was her husband; sometimes she was pregnant; often they were having dimension-shattering sex. Literally—since apparently what she kept dreaming and seeing was from some alternate reality. That was how the only other human in the compound, Kelsey Wells, had explained it to her in the most rational, logical tone. Yeah, it made total sense!

It was as if she'd chosen to step into a living *Twilight Zone* episode the minute she'd hopped on that transport with Lieutenant Dillon—a decision that had upended her world completely, and it definitely didn't help matters that her eyesight issues were taking a decided turn for the worse. The altitude up in this corner of Wyoming was even higher than in Denver, where her degenerative retinopathy had already been sliding her into darkness at an accelerated rate.

Maybe this wasn't the right thing after all, she thought, loneliness choking her thoughts. *Maybe I should have never stepped into something I knew nothing about.*

But she'd made a professional career of walking into the unknown, since that was pretty much what her daily life was like within the FBI. This situation in the alien compound was no different; it was also the right choice after witnessing the Refarians defend humanity when Warren had come under attack. No way was she consigning herself to the outside of this particular alien conspiracy now that she understood the stakes: Earth was in serious danger.

More noise erupted next door. *Enough really is enough already*, she thought. Leaping out of bed, she tugged on a borrowed pair of jeans, tossed on a military issue T-shirt, and stormed into the narrow corridor to find utter darkness. She stood there, listening to the hiss of some sort of equipment. A radiator? A weapon? With her fingertips she felt her way along the corridor wall, locating her neighbor's door.

She lifted her fist and banged hard. There was mumbling from within, then sudden light, blurred and covered with black spots—the same ones that always marred her vision. A tall figure loomed over her, which wasn't hard when you were four foot eleven.

"Listen, buddy," she said, "it's almost three in the morning."

A husky laugh was her answer, then a surly, "Look, human, you're on our base. This is *our* home on your outpost, so deal."

She tilted her chin upward, summoning a look of defiance. "Yeah? Well, get this—I work for the FBI. Want me to have your license plate called in some time?"

In half a heartbeat she heard the click of a weapon engaging. "Wanna say that again, human," Tough Guy threatened. But from behind him a softer, feminine voice called out, "Taggart, lay off of her. She just got here. And she's on our side."

The smaller figure stepped into the arc of light. "Sorry about that," the woman said and, slipping an arm about her shoulder, led her back toward her own room. "I'm Anna, and he's a nutcase. I'll see if they won't move you tomorrow so you can get some sleep."

"Not my fault humans need to rest all the time!" Taggart complained, then slammed his door behind him.

Hope could have cried from gratitude. "I shouldn't have baited him."

"Actually, you should have," Anna said with a laugh as they reached Hope's room again. "He deserves every bit of it."

"Yeah, that's what I thought."

"Listen, are you all right? Is there anything you need?" Anna asked her, following Hope into her darkened quarters.

Dropping heavily onto the side of her cot, Hope said, "Just to see someone—anyone—who can help me figure out what I'm going to do around here. I've been to visit Lieutenant Dillon a few times, but . . ."

"He's not doing very well," Anna finished, her voice clipped and formal. It seemed to be the way this alien spoke once apart from her soldier comrades next door.

"I'm worried about him," Hope admitted. "Have you heard anything more about his prognosis? The medics won't tell me a thing."

"He's going to recover, but physical therapy will be required. And time. Lots of time."

"Scott's my only friend in this place, Anna. He's the reason I came, because I knew he was on the right side of things."

And because I felt drawn to him for reasons I couldn't begin to understand, she wanted to add, but swallowed the words.

"Well, Lieutenant Dillon is nothing if not the right side of things," Anna said with a quiet laugh.

"What's that mean?"

"I'm crazy about the man, even though he rides all of us hard. He's a good leader."

Crazy about him? Crazy how? Hope wondered, slightly panicked, but shoved the emotion aside. "Is he a high-ranking officer?" she asked coolly. "I mean, he's only a lieutenant, right? I'm not sure what his position is."

"So they really haven't told you anything, have they?"

"Only about the mitres. Kelsey said there's some sort of alternate dimension created by the same device that wiped out all the Antousians back on Warren. That there were . . . side effects. But nothing about the lieutenant."

"Well, we don't have the same rankings you're accustomed to. Anyone in higher authority is called 'lieutenant.' Actual hierarchy isn't so much a part of our system, so that's the rough English translation. The equivalent, if you will."

"Then is he high up the chain?" Hope asked, her heart suddenly speeding up to a rapid tempo. At last! Some answers about the literal man of her dreams.

"He's second below Commander Bennett, over the entire Refarian military."

"Wow, didn't see that coming," Hope said, shaking her head. She'd known he must be important by the deference the night nurse showed him—either that, or she had a major case of the hots for the man. One of the two. But one of their military chiefs? That she hadn't guessed at all.

"Do you have any idea what he looks like, even?" Anna asked her seriously. "I mean, can you see much? You wear those thick glasses."

Here we go again—someone seeing me as helpless, she thought. "He has black hair and dark eyes and fair skin," she answered evenly, happy to show Anna just how capable she was despite her vision problems. "He's about six feet tall, and I gather that he's pretty darn good-looking."

"How do you know all that?"

"I still see some, it's just blurry."

"No, about the good-looking part—how can you tell that much?"

Yeah, like I want to tell you that I keep dreaming he's making love to me in about five hundred different physical positions, making me scream his name at the top of my lungs and giving me such world-shattering orgasms that I can hardly recover once I wake up.

Hope snorted. "Don't ask."

She was thinking of the dream where Scott took her home from some bar to a motel room and had her up against a wall. That one seemed to recur the most often, and always left her panties wet when she woke.

"Well, for the record, Scott Dillon is extremely handsome—every single woman in this camp has a thing for him."

An ugly shot of jealousy rang out in Hope's mind. "Oh . . . well, so then he must have plenty of women." Her voice sounded falsely peppy, too breathless.

Anna patted her shoulder and walked toward the open door. "He has plenty of women, but not around here."

"Why not?" Hope asked in surprise.

"Because, Ms. Harper, there's only one kind of woman our lieutenant likes, and that's your kind. Blond, petite, buxom, and"—Anna paused at the door—"human, Ms. Harper. Very, very human."

Deidre Knight

Parallel Attraction

Exiled alien king Jared Bennett is fighting for his people's freedom. Now his rebel force has the one weapon that can turn the tide against their enemy: the key to the secrets of time. With victory at hand, only one human, Kelsey Wells, has the power to change everything. Kelsey is unable to defend her fierce attraction to Jared Bennett, but is unaware of the truth: although Jared is exactly what he says, he hasn't told her everything. And when the future crashes into the present, Kelsey must decide if his deception will cost them the love that should have been their destiny.

"A fantastic and riveting new voice in paranormal fiction." —Karen Marie Moning, *New York Times* bestselling author of *Spell of the Highlander*

0-451-21811-6

J.R. Ward

DARK LOVER

THE DEBUT NOVEL IN THE BLACK DAGGER BROTHERHOOD SERIES

In the shadows of the night in Caldwell, New York, there's a deadly turf war going on between vampires and their slayers. There exists a secret band of brothers like no other—six vampire warriors, defenders of their race. Yet none of them relishes killing more than Wrath, the leader of The Black Dagger Brotherhood.

The only purebred vampire left on earth, Wrath has a score to settle with the slayers who murdered his parents centuries ago. But, when one of his most trusted fighters is killed—leaving his half-breed daughter unaware of his existence or her fate—Wrath must usher her into the world of the undead—a world of sensuality beyond her wildest dreams.

0-451-21695-4

"A midnight whirlwind of dangerous characters and mesmerizing erotic romance. The Black Dagger Brotherhood owns me now."
—LYNN VIEHL, AUTHOR OF *THE DARKYN* NOVELS